Home for the Heart

Home for the Heart

Copyright © 2019 by Joyce Valdois Smith

Published by Tallgrass Media
Columbia, South Carolina
books@tallgrass.media
www.tallgrass.media

Cover and interior book design by Kelly Smith.
Cover montage photograph by Erik Smith.

Printed in the United States of America
First Printing, 2019

Paperback ISBN-13: 978-0-9997626-4-6

To Bob, my husband and soulmate of fifty years, who has encouraged and supported me throughout this writing process.

To my children and their spouses: Kelly & Joice, Janna & Michael, Annette & Andrew, and Holly & Erik. You are all so special to me. Thank you for your support and help.

To all of my wonderful grandchildren: Gabby, Isaiah, Rylee, Aidan, Ridge, Sophie, April, Michaela, Sonja, Carenza, Blakeney, Dani, and Landry. You are growing up to be such beautiful people. I'm extremely proud of all of you.

"The Lord is my strength and my shield; my heart trusteth in Him, and I am helped: therefore my heart greatly rejoiceth; and with my song will I praise Him."

Psalm 28:7 KJV

In memory of my two brothers, Darrel and Marvin, and my sister-in-law, Judy. I am inspired by your testimonies of God's goodness and love. You gave me great examples of faith. I look forward to seeing you again soon in Heaven.

THE SANTA FE HOTEL
Hutchinson, Kansas

THE BISONTE HOTEL
Hutchinson, Kansas

Prologue

May 4, 1885

Four-year-old Elizabeth Tilman focused on the men who lifted the two caskets from the carriage hearses. She felt the slight breeze ruffle her golden curls. An oriole sang somewhere nearby. She noticed the neat rows around her in the well-kept cemetery and sensed the forbidding darkness of the rectangular shaped hole in the ground before her.

She felt a shiver of anxiety as she turned to her nanny and spoke softly. "Lucia, where's Mommy and Daddy?"

Lucia knelt beside her, a concerned frown furrowing her brow. "Your mommy and daddy went to Heaven, Elizabeth. They had an accident, and Jesus took them to be with Him."

"Why?" Hot tears flooded Elizabeth's eyes. She made a forlorn figure, dressed in black from her hat to the uncomfortable new shoes and socks on her normally active feet.

"I don't know why." Lucia glanced helplessly up to the minister and his wife, then gathered Elizabeth to her and wept.

CHAPTER 1

May 1, 1901

Liz Gilbertson sat on cushions in the window seat of her second-story bedroom and studied the images in her parents' wedding photograph. Her father, with blond hair and mustache, looked dapper in a three-piece suit and bow-tie. Her mother's dark hair was swept back into a chignon. She wore a stylish high-necked black dress with tucks in the bodice, accented by a diamond brooch.

The photo had sat on the fireplace mantel since Liz was a small child. Recently, she'd thought more about her parents and had asked if she could have it for her room.

She flipped the frame over and ran her finger over the names written there: "George Tilman and Mary Gilbertson, married April 20, 1880." Both had been killed in a carriage accident when she was four.

She turned toward her best friend who sat on the edge of

her bed. "You know, Anna Lisa, sometimes I wonder why God allows what he does. Why did He take my parents when I was so little? It was sixteen years ago today, according to the 'deaths' page in Mama's Bible."

Anna Lisa Stoops shook her head, a thoughtful expression on her face. "Why ask me? I don't understand things like that. My mother says God does everything for our good, but sometimes it's hard to figure it out."

Liz closed her eyes. "I've tried to remember life with my real parents. I barely recall giggling when my father threw me up in the air, then caught me in his arms. I wouldn't remember their faces at all if it weren't for this photograph."

"You've brought them up a lot lately. Why? You have a great family." Anna Lisa scooted back on the bed and crossed her legs in front of her.

"It's just a weird feeling. Maybe it's because I'm old enough now to be on my own. I'm twenty. I can't live here with Daddy and Mama forever."

"That makes two of us."

Liz surveyed her bedroom. The bedspread and canopy on her bed matched the lace curtains at the window. Green and rose patterns in the wallpaper harmonized with the roses in the carpet. She leaned against the pillow in the window seat, a pensive expression on her face. "I'm so blessed. Still, I feel restless, I want to know more about my background."

Her Uncle Daniel and Aunt Elise—Daddy and Mama—had brought her to live with them a month after they were married in July of 1886, four months after Grandma Gilbertson died. Since then, they'd lived in Topeka where Uncle Daniel was a vice president of the Atchison, Topeka and Santa Fe Railroad. They weren't extraordinarily wealthy, but lived a comfortable life.

They'd loved her and treated her as their daughter, even after their own three children were born. They were the only parents she could remember. Although they had never formally adopted her, she went by the name Gilbertson and called them her parents. When her brother, Adam—their first child—was little, he couldn't say Elizabeth, so she became Liz.

Liz glanced back at the picture. "I know about my real mother Mary's family. My Grandpa Gilbertson, her father, still lives on a ranch near Emporia, Kansas, with Daddy's younger brother, Thomas, and his family. But I'd like to find out more about my real father's family. Nobody has much information about him. I only know he came from Boston, Massachusetts, and he was a lawyer in Columbia, Missouri. That's where we lived when they died."

"Your real mother was your daddy's sister, wasn't she?" Anna Lisa giggled. "That sounds funny."

Liz smiled and nodded. "Yes, she was. She was Uncle Daniel's older sister."

"Have you talked to your mother and father about it? They may have more information."

"I've thought about it. They've been so good to me—I don't want to hurt them. They're my real family."

"I'm sure they'd understand your curiosity."

"Maybe." Liz lowered the picture, drew her knees up under her chin, and eyed the afternoon shadows lengthening across the backyard flower garden. Sunlit patterns from the lace curtains danced across her stockinged feet and a honeysuckle scent, borne on the warm breeze, drifted in through the open bay window.

Anna Lisa broke the silence. "So what will you do in the meantime? You can't just take off to Boston in search of your real father's family."

"I thought wedding plans would take up my time. Then your brother jilted me for another woman." She turned a pretend scowl at her friend, then paused, her expression becoming thoughtful. "I'm convinced now that it's best he broke off our courtship. I was devastated at first, but now I realize I'm not ready for marriage."

"I know." Anna Lisa grimaced. "He changed when he went away to college. He and his new girlfriend plan to be here for two weeks, while her parents travel abroad. They arrive Saturday. I have to share my room with her." She wrinkled her nose and chuckled softly. "Mother's about to have a nervous breakdown. She's had Lucia come in two extra days to get the house ready."

Liz raised her eyebrows. "I hope they're happy. But, don't expect me to come around while she's here."

Anna Lisa ducked her head. "I'm not excited about it, but I don't have much say in the matter."

Liz quirked her mouth and nodded. "It's not your fault." She swung her legs to the floor. "Abigail, from church, got a job as a Harvey Girl. She started to train last week. Maybe we should look into that. I hear they pay pretty well."

"Liz, Daddy's home." Rachel, Liz's seven-year-old sister, ran into the room, pigtails flying. "He brought a man to eat supper with us. His name is Michael. He just moved here today to work in Papa's office." She perched on the end of Liz's bed and tapped her feet against the carpet. "Mama says Michael's from a big city in the East."

Liz quickly slipped the picture behind the cushion in the window seat. She wrinkled her forehead and frowned at Rachel. "Don't jump on the bed. You'll mess it up. Besides, Anna Lisa doesn't want you to bounce her onto the floor."

Rachel grinned and faced Anna Lisa. "Sorry." She stood and skipped toward the door. "Anyway, Mama said get ready for supper. We're gonna eat in twenty minutes."

Liz glared at Rachel's retreating figure. "That girl! Sometimes she's more than a body can bear."

Anna Lisa scooted toward the edge of the bed. "Be glad you have a little sister. I've always wanted one."

"You're right. I love Rachel a lot. I don't tell her often enough." Liz walked to the dressing table, tucked a few errant curls into her chignon, and readjusted the hairpins. Her naturally-curly blonde hair was not easy to manage.

Elise stepped into the room. "You ready for supper, Elizabeth?"

Liz turned at the sound of her mama's voice. Elise was slim and stylish in her navy blue skirt, white blouse, and embroidered vest with a cameo brooch nestled at the neck. "I'll be right there as soon as I put my shoes on."

Elise turned to Anna Lisa. "Would you like to join us? You're always welcome."

"Oh, no. I have to go. Mother is expecting me for supper."

Elise nodded. "You ladies both look charming this evening."

Liz hugged her. "So do you, Mama."

As they descended the stairs, Liz heard her dad's familiar voice in the library to the left. "You must be tired, after your long train ride."

"Actually, I'm not. The trip was smooth and uneventful.

I had a suite in one of the Pullman cars, and the meals in the Harvey dining cars were delicious. I've wanted to travel, so the diverse scenery was fascinating."

Liz raised her eyebrows at the sound of the deep, masculine voice. It presented an immediate mental image of a tall, dark-haired male. But she was in no mood to meet another smooth-talking young man yet, not after Richard jilted her!

Anna Lisa slipped out the front door as Liz walked to the library. A giggle bubbled up inside her and nearly erupted in laughter when she peeked in the door. The young man with her father was as different from her mental image as a person could be. He was short with a full head of copper red hair. Fortunately, he faced away from her, so she could step back and regain her composure.

"Come in, Liz." Her father motioned her into the room. "I want you to meet Michael McKey, the new accountant in my office. You'll probably see each other often."

Michael turned as Liz walked toward him. She was immediately struck by his charming smile, which involved his whole face, and his remarkable hazel eyes. He appeared close to her age, maybe a year or two older. He held out his hand. "Miss Gilbertson, I'm happy to meet you."

Liz placed her hand in his. "Nice to meet you, too, Mr. McKey."

"Michael just arrived from Boston this afternoon. Maybe, when he gets settled and rested, you can show him around the city."

"Of course, Daddy, I'll be glad to." Liz felt a small jolt of excitement at the mention of Boston. Was there a possibility

Michael might know something about her father's family? Instantly, she discounted the thought. Her father had lived there over twenty years ago, and Boston was a grand, bustling city, from what she'd heard.

Elise stepped into the library. "Supper is ready." She looked back and forth between Michael and Liz. "I see you two have met."

Daniel stepped forward and offered his arm. "Yes, Sweetheart, we've completed the introductions."

Elise smiled, took his arm, and walked from the room by his side.

Michael grinned at Liz then held out his arm. "Allow me."

Liz tucked her fingers under his elbow and followed with him to the dining room. She caught a whiff of the expected meal. "I hope you like beef. We have it quite often. We are in Kansas, after all. More cattle are shipped back East from Kansas than any other state."

Michael chuckled. "I do like beef. It smells tantalizing. I'm glad to be in Kansas, and I'm eager to learn more about this state."

When they entered the spacious, sunny dining room, Adam, Liz's thirteen-year-old brother, stepped through a doorway opposite, followed by Rachel. She ran to her mother's side. "Mama, Julien is still in the sitting room reading his book. He wouldn't come when I told him it was time for dinner."

Elise stepped to the open door. "Come on, Julien. You can leave your book long enough to eat."

Daniel took his place at the head of the table. Elise motioned Michael to the chair to his left. The others took their usual places, then bowed their heads and waited, expectantly, for Daniel to pray.

Liz listened as he asked God's blessing on the food and thanked Him for the bounty of the day. She peeked at Michael across the table. His eyes were closed, a slight smile on his face. He wasn't put off by the prayer. Quickly she closed her eyes as her father said, "Amen."

When she re-opened her eyes, Michael had turned toward her dad. Liz let her gaze trail over his dinner jacket, shirt, and dark tie. They were the latest style. By contrast, his auburn hair, though stylishly cut, lay in unruly curls, which gave him a youthful appearance.

A middle-aged woman entered from the kitchen, carrying a large platter of roast beef surrounded by carrots, potatoes, and other vegetables. A young woman followed with a bowl of green beans and a lettuce salad.

Elise looked pleased, "Thank you, Catherine and Annie. This meal looks delectable as usual. Is this lettuce from the garden?"

The older woman nodded. "Yes, ma'am. The green beans are too. They've started to produce."

"That's wonderful." Elise picked up a plate from the pile beside her and began to serve the meat and vegetables, then passed it around the table.

Daniel handed a plate to Michael. "Tell us about your family. Do you have brothers and sisters?"

"Yes, my brother, David, is a year older, and my sister, Marie, is seventeen. David works at the bank with my father. He wanted me to go into the bank, too, but I'm afraid I have wanderlust."

"Does your father approve of your job in Kansas?"

"It wasn't his choice for me to leave, but he's alright with it. My mother, on the other hand, isn't thrilled at all."

"I bet she's not," Elise spoke from the other end of the table.

"What's Boston like?" Julien laid down his fork. "I've read books about it, but it's not like being there."

Michael turned to Julien. "Boston's a busy, modern city. Much larger than Topeka from my early observations. The business district is very cosmopolitan with skyscrapers and department stores. Telephones and electric lamps are state-of-the-art."

"Are there lots of automobiles?" Adam leaned forward. "I think we should get one, but Pa says we don't need it."

Michael glanced at Daniel and smiled. "Yes, they're everywhere in the city."

Julien sighed. "Why'd you come to Kansas? I'd rather go to Boston. I've read about the Boston Tea Party. Do you know where that was?"

"Yes, I do. There's a lot of history in Boston. The bank, where my father works, was started in the 1780s, over a hundred years ago. My great-great-grandfather worked in that first bank. The story is that Paul Revere, Samuel Adams, and John Hancock banked there."

"Wow!" Julien's eyes sparkled with interest.

Daniel chuckled. "I think you have a new admirer, Michael. Julien loves history." He turned his attention to Julien. "That's enough questions for now. Let Michael finish his meal."

Liz watched Michael interact with her brothers. His demeanor was relaxed and comfortable. He fit in, even though they'd just become acquainted.

As the family finished the meal, Michael spoke to Elise. "This was enjoyable, Mrs. Gilbertson. Thanks so much for the invitation."

"Most of the thanks goes to Catherine and Annie. Catherine was a cook at the Harvey House, and I stole her away. We're fortunate to have her." Elise gathered the dirty plates.

Michael faced Liz as they rose to leave. "I'd appreciate that tour around the city. Would Saturday morning work? Maybe we could eat lunch at the Harvey House?"

"Sounds like fun. I'd enjoy that."

CHAPTER 2

Liz awoke with a start. What time was it? She'd planned to show Michael around today. According to the alarm clock on her dresser, it was seven o'clock. There was plenty of time. She'd promised to meet him at ten.

She sat on the side of the bed and picked up her parents' picture once again from the bedside table. What were they like? Would her life have been much different if they'd lived? The questions burned in her chest. Her memories were so fragmented.

Liz sat up straight. It was Saturday. Lucia would be here to help with the weekly house cleaning. She'd been Liz's childhood nanny long before her parents' deaths. After the accident, they'd traveled together with Uncle Daniel—now her Daddy—to Grandpa and Grandma Gilbertson's ranch. If anyone knew about her parents, Lucia would. Why hadn't she thought to ask her sooner?

She grabbed her robe and the picture and hurried down the

hall. The room that had been the nursery for her and her siblings was now Rachel's room. Lucia usually cleaned there first.

She slowed and peeked in, then frowned. Rachel was still asleep. Noise from her parents' room caught her attention. She crept across the hall and looked in the door, then sighed with relief. Lucia was dusting the wardrobe.

"Lucia, can I talk to you?" She hugged her nanny.

"I always have time for you, sweetheart. What do you need?"

"I have questions about my mother and father." She showed Lucia the picture of her parents. "I've been beyond curious about them lately."

Lucia gently took the picture and, with almost a reverence, studied it. She sighed as tears welled up in her eyes. "What do you want to know?"

Liz sat on the small bench beside the dresser. She looked up at Lucia. "Why doesn't anyone talk about them? This picture was always displayed on the dining room mantel until I got it, but no one talks about it."

Lucia sat on the bed across from her. "When you were small, it made you sad for them to discuss your parents. You were happy with your Uncle Daniel and Aunt Elise. They wanted you to know about your past, but decided to wait until you had grown up enough to be curious and ask for information." Lucia smiled. "I see that time has come."

Liz nodded. "Can you tell me more about my father and mother?" She took the picture from Lucia. "This is all I have. I can barely recall them."

"Oh, yes. I remember them well. Your parents loved you passionately and had big plans for you. When your daddy played with you, you'd giggle and laugh. They watched your curls bounce as you danced and twirled around the house." Lucia sighed. "It was tragic when they died. I was young and didn't know what to do. Then your Uncle Daniel came and took us to the Lazy G ranch."

"Do you know anything about my father's family? Did he ever talk about them?"

Lucia shook her head. "He didn't say much about his family except that when he decided to move out West, he and his father had a falling out. He wanted to be a lawyer, and his father wanted him to stay there and do something else. I can't remember what... if I ever knew. His law practice grew even though he was young, just out of school."

Lucia looked thoughtful. "There was a trunk with your parents' belongings in it that we took to the ranch when Daniel came and got us. Why don't you ask your mama about it? I'm sure she'd be glad to help you find it. It's probably in the attic."

Surprise and excitement spiraled through Liz. "There's a trunk? Really? Why didn't anyone ever tell me?"

"You knew it was there when you were little. We looked in it when we first moved to the ranch, but you wanted to play dress-up with the clothes. Your Grandma Esther decided it was best to wait until you were older and would appreciate the contents. I guess everyone forgot about it." Lucia smiled. "Your mama will be glad to show you."

Liz watched her nanny stand and begin to dust again. "Lucia, I have another question."

Lucia stopped and faced her. "What is it, little one?"

"Why didn't Daddy and Mama adopt me? I know they love

me and feel like I'm their daughter, but they never went to the trouble to make it legal."

"Oh, baby. Have you worried about that?" Lucia gathered Liz into her arms and hugged her. "Daniel and Elise love you so much. You're their daughter as surely as Adam, Julien, and Rachel are theirs. They thought you might want to keep your parents' legal name when you grew up, but you've always been a Gilbertson." She released Liz and leaned back to look into her face. "Talk to your mama. She'll explain everything."

Liz smiled and stood. "Okay. Thank you, Lucia. I appreciate the information. I've thought a great deal about it in the last few months. I want to find out more." She gave Lucia another hug. "Now, I better move. I'm supposed to show Daddy's new assistant around town this morning."

Liz scurried back to her room. She'd have to hustle to be ready in time.

Michael left the boarding house and walked the shaded street toward Davis Livery. It was near the depot. He'd have to rent a rig until he could buy one. Transportation would be a must if he were to get around the city.

Later, he drove the rented surrey across the large trestle bridge that spanned the Kansas River. The central business district hummed with activity. People walked the narrow sidewalks. Michael drove slowly up Kansas Avenue beside the streetcar tracks. He was surprised by all the people who stood in small groups and visited. It was totally different from the streets of Boston.

He turned west off Kansas Avenue onto 6th Street. The quiet

of the morning enveloped him. How refreshing to be free of the noise and commotion of the city. He considered the two-and-three-storied homes on either side of the street. Some of them were wood frame with gabled roofs; others were stone. Most had wide front porches, quite different from the imposing brick mansion he called home in Boston. In spite of the grandeur of his house, he knew now it lacked the peace and love he'd felt at the Gilbertsons' home.

Michael thought about his new boss's prayer for God to bless their meal. His family attended one of the largest churches in Boston. His father prayed before meals, but it was more ritual than heartfelt. Somehow, they'd lost the family closeness that made for happy, satisfying relationships. Everyone was busy—scattered about, pursuing various affairs. His father was president of the largest and oldest bank in the city, and his mother was involved in the social circle required of the family's prestige. His brother and sister followed their pattern.

Michael had felt restless and overwhelmed by the expectations set by his parents. They wanted him to marry into an elitist class. He smiled to himself. They considered him somewhat of an enigma. He preferred to stay home and read rather than mingle with the pampered and coddled young people in their Boston circle.

With a start, Michael realized he was near the Gilbertson's street. Quickly, he turned left and guided the horses to the hitching post in front of their home. He jumped down, secured the horse and let himself through the gate of the white picket fence. The house was similar to the others along the street—white with a wrap-around front porch and thick columns. Beds of colorful flowers grew along the base of the porch and extended the welcome along the brick sidewalk to the entrance. As he stepped across the porch, he realized the front door stood open, with a screen door to let in the breeze. He turned the doorbell knob and stepped back to wait.

Julien dashed across the entrance hall and flung open the screen door. "Hey, Michael. Good to see you. Come in. I just read about Boston in the encyclopedia. Can you tell me more about it?"

Michael grinned. "Sorry, buddy, I'm here to see your sister. She's supposed to show me around Topeka." He stepped through the doorway into the cool foyer.

"Aww. That's no fun."

Michael tousled Julien's already disheveled hair and chuckled. "It's important for me to know how to get around since I live here, now."

He glanced toward the stairs.

Liz wore a light pink dress that floated around her as she descended. Her blonde hair was up in a chignon and shone with highlights in a shaft of light from the front window. She smiled. "I'm sorry. Have you waited long?"

Michael stepped forward and held out his hand. "No no, I just got here. You're right on time." His gaze riveted on her long eyelashes, which accentuated her bright blue eyes and slightly upturned nose. "Allow me."

She placed her hand in his and stepped down. Liz smiled at her brother. "Has Julien worn your ears out? You and Boston are all he's talked about since you came to supper."

"He's no bother." He turned to Julien. "We'll talk when we have more time. Okay?"

Julien nodded and headed toward the library.

Michael opened the door for Liz. "It's a pleasant day even if it's warm." He waved his arm. "I love this wide porch and the swing. Looks like a good place to sit and talk. More welcoming than my home in Boston."

Liz looked around. "We do like this porch. It's cool in the evening and nice to visit with neighbors who pass by."

"We rarely saw our neighbors back home." Michael guided Liz down the steps. "Everyone went their own way."

"That sounds like a lonely way to live."

"It was. I already like it better here." He helped Liz step up into the carriage and walked around to the other side. "I'll get my own rig soon. The livery owner has ordered it for me." He grinned. "I'd rather get one of those new-fangled automobiles. A lot of people have them in Boston."

Liz grimaced and wrinkled her nose. "Governor Stanley has one, but I don't like it that much. It makes so much noise, and it scares the horses."

Michael laughed. "The price of progress, I guess." He picked up the reins. "Is it okay if I use your given name?"

"Yes, of course. Please call me Liz if I can call you Michael."

"Certainly. I'm not much for formality. I had enough of that back home." He looked around. "Which way do we go?"

"Straight ahead. We'll drive by the State Capitol building."

"Oh, yes. I see it from here." They drove up to the large grassy square. The massive limestone structure with a copper dome had a prominent place in the middle with a colonnaded front entrance and a three-story wing on both the East and West sides. "That's impressive for a small city."

"We're proud of it. Have you seen the Capitol in Washington D.C.? I would love to see that."

"My father went there to a banking convention and took our family along. I was fourteen, a year older than your brother, Adam. It's incredible."

"Julien would love to see it. He's such a bookworm. He can't get enough of history and national events."

"Maybe he'll be a politician when he grows up."

Liz giggled. "I don't know about that, although he talks like one. He can be a pest."

They turned left to drive around the square. Liz pointed to the large brick building on the corner. "This is the public library if you want to check out books or just need a quiet place to read."

Michael turned right onto Jackson Street. "I'll make good use of it. Like Julien, I love to read and learn about far-off places."

Liz showed Michael the church on the left at the next corner. "This is the Baptist Church we attend. It's called Stone Church. There are churches all around the Capitol square, but we'd love for you to come with us."

Michael stared intently at the impressive limestone in the construction. He understood why they called it Stone Church. "I'll probably go with your family, for now anyway."

"There's the ATSF office buildings." Liz pointed to a large facility across the street from the church.

Michael nodded and studied it. "I'm supposed to report for work on Monday. Your dad told me where it was, but I wasn't sure." He turned and grinned at Liz. "I'll have a clear view of the Capitol."

She smiled. "It depends on the location of your office."

"I guess you're right." He glanced at the nearby houses. "I should find a room down here closer."

"Topeka boasts a lot of boarding houses. I'll show you some where the Senators and Representatives stay when they're in session." They drove past the city high school and around the Capitol Square. Liz pointed out several extravagant homes as they continued. "Up here is the new Bethany College Campus. I thought I might attend there, but I'm not sure what I want to do."

Michael guided the carriage around the campus then turned back east. Liz looked ahead. "You probably noticed that Kansas Avenue is the main street. Most stores and businesses are there."

"It was already busy when I came this morning."

"Oh, yes. Saturday is a big day for the townspeople and nearby farmers and their families. They come to sell their cream and eggs, buy their groceries for the week, and complete other business. It's also a social time when they meet up with friends. We shop on a weekday to avoid the crowds."

"I can understand that." Michael grinned.

They turned north to drive up the main street. Liz pointed to a large store on the left. A sign over the door read McDonald Mercantile. "Here's where we get our household and grocery supplies. They also have a soda fountain. Our friends from church own it. Across the street is the opera house. It'll be full this evening."

Michael smiled at her enthusiasm with the descriptions. The businesses were on a smaller scale than Boston, but he liked the small-town feel.

"Have you been to the opera? You probably went quite often when you were in Boston." Liz looked at him.

Michael shook his head. "No, I haven't. My parents went occasionally, but I haven't gone. Maybe we can go see it together?"

Liz glanced at him then down, her face a slight shade of pink. "I didn't mean to suggest that you ask me to go."

"I know, but it's a good idea. I don't care to go alone." He smiled again as he watched her facial expressions. She was so unassuming—unaware of her natural beauty. Her innocent demeanor was a change from the young women his parents wanted him to court in Boston.

Liz looked up and nodded. "I'd like to go." She turned back toward the side of the street and indicated a stone structure. "Here's the post office, and next to it is the bank where we do business. My friend's father works there. Of course, there are several banks to choose from."

"I'll need to open an account soon." Michael maneuvered the carriage between the streetcar headed toward them and another carriage which stopped beside the boardwalk. "Do you ride the streetcar often?"

Liz swung around, and her arm touched his elbow. A warm sensation raced to his fingertips. She moved quickly away. "Yes, we ride it often when we come to shop. It's hard to find a place to park the carriage, and the trolley runs close to our house."

"That might be a more suitable ride to work. I'd only have to walk a couple of blocks."

"It probably would." She watched the streetcar pass. "Do you have trolleys in Boston?"

"Yes, but my family usually takes the carriage or the automobile."

Liz turned toward him on the seat. "You have an automobile?"

"No, I don't, but my father does."

"Oh, then you know a lot about them."

"We haven't had it very long. Father has to have all the newest innovations. Mostly to make a good impression."

"It must've been difficult to leave all that behind."

"No, as a matter of fact, it was a relief." He grinned. "Although I'd like to have an automobile, I can do without the high-society life. I never did fit in." He glanced around. "I already feel at home here."

"That's good. Topeka's a friendly town." Liz wrinkled her brow. "I guess that's about all there is to see. Any questions?"

Michael waited while another horse and carriage crossed the river bridge. "Not now. I might later." He took out his pocket watch and looked at it. "It's almost eleven-thirty. Are you ready for dinner? I want to eat in the Harvey House dining room. How about you?"

Liz smiled. "I am rather hungry."

CHAPTER 3

As Michael drove into the lot at the end of the depot, Liz scanned the other carriages. The Stoops' surrey was parked at the end nearest the train track. She smiled slightly. Richard and his new girlfriend must be expected on this train. Anna Lisa said they were due to arrive today. Liz was glad she'd have Michael with her. Richard didn't need to know they were new acquaintances.

Michael pulled up to the hitching rail and jumped down to secure the horse. He grabbed his jacket from behind the seat and put it on before he walked to Liz's side and held out his hand. "Allow me."

"Thank you, kind sir." Liz took his hand and stepped down. Once on the ground, she straightened her skirt. He offered his elbow.

As they walked to the front of the depot, Liz noted that Michael was only an inch or two taller than her. Richard was a whole head taller. She and Richard had courted all through high school, and she thought they were the perfect couple. Most of their friends assumed they'd get married. So had she. When Richard left to go to the Kansas State Agricultural College in Manhattan, Kansas, he'd asked her to wait for him. He promised they'd get married when he graduated. *That hadn't happened!* She gave Michael's arm a slight squeeze of frustration.

Michael glanced at her inquisitively, and she quickly dropped her hand from his arm. The train whistle sounded down the track, and the massive steam engine came into view.

"Oh, we'd better hurry. The train passengers will be headed to the Harvey House." Liz started up the steps to the platform.

The busboy stood beside the gong with a padded stick, ready to gain the passengers' attention and direct them into the depot. "You'll want to wait until the train crowd subsides. They'll run you down in their haste to get into the dining room."

Liz nodded and faced Michael. "Maybe we should wait in the depot. They have to be done in twenty minutes to get back on the train."

"Sounds reasonable." Michael stepped forward, opened the door, and ushered her into the cool depot lobby. He guided her to two overstuffed chairs near the door. "Let's sit here out of the way."

Liz studied the other people who waited for arriving passengers as she and Michael made their way toward the chairs. Her eyes connected with her friend, Anna Lisa, across the room. Of course, she and her parents would be here to greet Richard and his new girlfriend. Anna Lisa smiled and gazed at Michael as she mouthed, *"Good move."* Liz shrugged and sat down beside Michael. They didn't need to know she was only showing him around.

The train passengers streamed in the door and up the stairs to the dining and lunchrooms.

Liz held her breath and watched the door. What would Richard's new girl be like? Anna Lisa had said her parents were on a tour of Europe. She must be high society. Would she fit with his family?

Liz let her breath out in a rush as Richard walked in with a petite brunette on his arm. Her chocolate brown traveling suit was tailored beautifully and she walked with a confident stride, her head held high.

Richard carried a large valise. Surprise flashed in his eyes when he spied Liz. Their eyes locked briefly, then he gave her a quick nod of acknowledgment.

Liz frowned. Indignation washed through her. *How dare he dump her after his promise!* She leaned closer to Michael. That girl would just have to find out about Richard's fickleness for herself. Then Liz sighed with relief. He'd proven it was best he'd dropped her, but obviously she was still dealing with the emotions. Better to learn now than after they were married. She watched as they made their way across the depot lobby toward Richard's parents.

"Do you know them?" Michael gazed at Richard, then back at her.

Liz nodded. "Yes. He's my best friend's brother and that's his new girlfriend."

"I get the impression, from your reaction when they walked in, that it was more than casual."

She smiled. "It was. We dated for four years before Richard

left for college. Honestly, I'm grateful he's found someone else. I'm better off without him. I can see it now."

Michael took her hand. "I'm grateful he found someone else, too."

"Why, thank you." She settled back and scanned the busy lobby. She'd enjoyed her time with Michael thus far. Who knew what might come of it?

They watched the passengers. A young couple with two small children, dressed in their best clothes and hats, said good-bye to their family before they boarded the waiting train. At the far end of the depot, others purchased tickets at the counter.

She turned to watch Anna Lisa's family. Mrs. Stoops embraced the new girlfriend, who looked stiff and uncomfortable as she stepped back, her arms straight at her sides. Liz raised her eyebrows. Apparently, the girl wasn't accustomed to hugs.

Michael leaned forward. "Looks like the passengers have finished their meal." He nodded toward the staircase where other people descended. "You ready to eat?" He stood and held out his hand to her.

Liz walked beside him to the ornate staircase, aware of his closeness. When they reached the top of the stairs, she surveyed the area. The entrance to the dining and lunchrooms were straight ahead on the other side of the landing. A colorful Persian rug covered the polished wood floor, and coordinated chairs sat on either side. It presented a welcome atmosphere. She'd been there numerous times with her parents, and with Richard, but felt she now saw it for the first time.

While they waited, Liz glanced into the lunchroom. Her friend, Abigail McDonald, stood behind the counter and waited for her next customers. She smiled and gave Liz a small wave when she spied them.

Several people left the dining room, Michael and Liz moved aside then stepped to the entrance. A petite young woman dressed in the Harvey Girl uniform—black dress, white apron, and Elsie collar—greeted them. Her ash blonde hair was drawn up in a chignon. "Hello. My name's Beatrice, and I'll be your hostess today. Would you like the dining room or lunchroom?"

"The dining room, please." Michael gestured for Liz to follow Beatrice across the room to a table set for eight near the window. Another couple was already seated.

Beatrice smiled as she indicated two chairs. "Will these be satisfactory?"

"Yes, they'll be fine." Liz nodded as Michael pulled out a chair for her and then sat in the chair beside her. A fresh fruit salad sat at each place.

Beatrice placed menus in front of them and stepped back.

As she walked away, another Harvey Girl approached. "Hello. My name is Alice, and I'll be your Harvey Girl today. What would you like to drink?"

Liz looked at her. "I'd like iced tea."

"Do you care for sugar?"

"Yes, please."

Alice tilted her coffee cup against the saucer and placed a sugar cube in the small plate nearby. "And you, sir?"

"Iced tea sounds good to me, too. I'll also take sugar."

The young woman repeated her actions with the cup and sugar cube. "Have a wonderful meal."

Liz smiled and nodded when a family with two small children were seated with them at their table. She scanned the list of entrees on the menu. The descriptions all sounded good. "I think I'll try an entree I've never had before; maybe the Braised Duck Cumberland. That suggests adventure." She grinned at Michael. "Did you try it when you traveled from Boston to Topeka?"

"No, to be honest, I've never eaten duck. I think I'll try it, too." He grinned mischievously. "It does sound adventurous. What do you want with it?"

She hesitated. "I think I'd like the buttered fresh asparagus and the potato souffle."

Michael frowned slightly. "I've never had asparagus. I think I'll get the cauliflower polonaise, instead."

A waitress placed two ice cubes in their glasses and filled them with tea. Alice started around their table. "May I take your orders?"

After Liz ordered, she bowed her head to pray, then took a bite of her fruit salad. She surveyed the room. "My mother was a Harvey Girl. I barely remember her in her uniform. I loved to go to the Harvey House with my grandparents."

Michael frowned and wrinkled his brow. "How could she be a Harvey Girl? I thought they couldn't be married if they worked here."

Liz turned back to him. "Oh, I forgot you didn't know." She sighed. "My real parents were killed in a carriage accident when I was four years old. I lived with my grandparents for a while. When my Uncle Daniel and Aunt Elise got married, they took me to be their daughter."

"So Mrs. Glibertson worked as a Harvey Girl before they got married?"

She nodded. "I thought she was beautiful in her uniform." She took another bite of fruit and looked back at the young women busy with their work. "Actually, it's a good job. They make good money."

Alice brought their food on a large tray and set it on a small folding table before she placed their plates in front of them. The duck was thinly sliced, served over a bed of rice and covered with cherry sauce. The food looked and smelled enticing.

"Good choice." Michael nodded as he took a bite. "This is incredible. I'm glad you decided to be adventurous."

Liz chuckled. "You don't have to remind me. But I agree. It is delicious."

Michael took a drink of tea. "So, you think you might go to Bethany College?"

Liz paused, thoughtful. "I'm not sure. I know it seems childish, but I don't know what to do. I need to make a decision soon." She gazed around the dining room again. "It might be refreshing to work as a Harvey Girl for a while. I could save some money, and I'd like to travel." She turned back to him. "Where did you get your accounting degree?"

"I graduated from Harvard. That's where my family attended."

"It's quite a prestigious university."

Michael laughed. "Well, it's handy for my family. It's right across the river from Boston. I stayed at home and commuted on the ferry. I wasn't into the fraternity life."

Liz studied his earnest expression. He was so down-to-earth. She was glad to have him for a new friend.

Michael laid his fork beside his plate and leaned forward.

"I just had an idea. My cousin, well, actually, she's quite a distant cousin. Her great-grandmother was sister to my great-grandfather, Theodore McKey, so whatever that makes us, I'm not sure." He smiled. "Anyway, she came to see me when she heard I planned to move west and wanted to know if I knew of any jobs for women. She's bold and enjoys new experiences. She also wants to get away from Boston. At the time, I didn't know of any jobs, but this might be just the answer for her."

Liz cocked her head and nodded. "It could be a good fit. There're a lot of young women from back East who come to work as Harvey Girls. She should check her local newspaper. I understand Fred Harvey advertises extensively."

"I'll write and tell her about it."

The rest of the meal was filled with pleasant conversation. Much too soon, Michael and Liz were on their way back to her home. As they drew up in front of the house, Michael faced her. "Thank you for the tour. This has been an enjoyable day. Could we have another outing soon? Maybe go to the opera house?"

She smiled. "That would be delightful."

Michael helped Liz down and walked her to her door. "I'll plan to see you at church tomorrow. May I sit with your family?"

"Of course. We'd love for you to join us. I'll wait for you."

Liz watched him return to his rig before she opened the screen door and went inside.

It had been an eventful morning. The summer looked brighter. A young man from Boston and a red-headed one at that...who would've thought?

She strolled across the front hall. Julien stuck his head out the library door. "Did Michael come back with you?"

"No, Julien, he had other business. You don't need to pester him with your questions."

"He said it was okay." He frowned and ducked back into the library.

"Do you know where Mama is?" she asked as he disappeared from sight.

"No."

Liz climbed slowly up the stairs, slipped into her bedroom, and flopped back on the bed. The picture of her parents lay where she'd placed it that morning. The desire to find out about her real father's family burned inside her, but she didn't want to hurt Daniel and Elise. Liz turned over on her stomach.

She needed a job. And now Michael was in the picture. He wanted to be with her. She realized she liked that idea...a lot!

Lucia said there was a trunk that belonged to her parents. Liz reached back and retrieved the picture. Her curiosity got the better of her. "Okay. I'll go ask." She spoke to the serious faces on the print. "I'll never know if I don't ask." She rolled off the bed and headed to the door.

When she reached the hall, Elise was walking toward her. "Who were you talking to? Is Anna Lisa here?" Elise glanced through the doorway.

Liz shook her head. "No, no one's here. I was just talking to myself."

"What do you want to ask? Did you have a good time with Michael?"

"Yes, I had an enjoyable time. He's very thoughtful. We had a wonderful meal at the Harvey House, and guess who else was there?"

"Who? Oh, Richard? He was supposed to get in today, wasn't he?" Elise put her hand on Liz's arm. "Was his new girl-friend with him?"

"Yes, they came in while we waited to eat. Richard's parents and Anna Lisa were there to meet them." She looked at her mama and shrugged. "She's a little bit of a thing. Brown hair. Pretty. But, I was actually relieved that it was her and not me."

"Oh, Liz." Elise pulled her into a hug. "I'm glad you feel that way. You'll find the right man when the time comes."

"I know. Anyway, I'm not ready to get married." She pulled back from the embrace. "Mama…?"

"What? What's bothering you?"

Liz hesitated. "Oh, nothing… I guess… I've just been think-ing." She pondered the older woman's face and blurted. "I need to get a job. What would you think if I became a Harvey Girl?"

Elise nodded thoughtfully. "I think that sounds like a great idea if you want to do it, but I thought you wanted to go to college."

"I know. I can't make up my mind."

"Well, you think about it, and we'll discuss it later. Right now, I have a Ladies Missionary Society meeting, and I'm late. That's not good when you're the president."

CHAPTER 4

When Liz awoke, the sunlight was streaming in her window. She squinted her eyes. What day was it? Could it be Sunday? The last few days were a blur. So much had happened.

She threw back the sheets and rolled over. Was it just Thursday she'd been contemplating her parents' carriage accident and deaths? Then she'd met Michael that same day. She'd felt an instant connection with him. Their excursion, yesterday, had been enjoyable, but could she hope to measure up to the socialites he'd been used to?

She sat up and stared out the window. To top it off, she'd seen Richard and his new girlfriend. How could she process all that?

Liz picked up her parents' picture from the bedside table and studied it. She wanted to see the trunk Lucia had mentioned, but yesterday wasn't the right time. Would it hold more of the information she sought?

She laid the picture on the bed and leaned forward. *"Dear God, what do You want of me? I know You love me, and You want what's best for me, but it's hard to understand sometimes. Please show me Your will."* She covered her face with her hands. *"I do need to thank You. You've taken care of me and given me a wonderful family."*

She grabbed her robe and pulled it around her shoulders. Breakfast would be ready soon. She needed to dress for church.

A short while later, Liz accompanied her family to their carriage house. She carried her Bible and a small black purse. It was a beautiful sunny day. The scent of honeysuckle permeated the air. Would Michael be at church? The prospect excited her. She was amazed at how quickly her attraction to him had blossomed.

After helping Elise in, Daniel gave Liz a hand into the middle seat of the carriage, then lifted Rachel to sit beside her. Adam and Julien were in the rear. Rachel snuggled against Liz and gave her a hug. "You look pretty. I love you."

Liz returned the hug. "Thank you, Rachel. You're pretty, too. I love you the mostest."

Rachel giggled. "No, I love you the mostest."

At the church's entrance, Liz stood aside and watched others arrive. The Stoops' carriage pulled into the parking area beside the church. Anna Lisa waved and Liz returned the greeting. Liz was aware she'd have to meet the new girlfriend. Would it be awkward?

Julien grabbed his mother's hand. "There's Uncle Arnaud and Aunt Millie. Can I sit with them?"

Elise shook her head. "You need to sit with our family. You'll be tempted to talk instead of listening to the preacher if you sit with Charles. You can spend time with him later."

Liz looked around as they entered the church vestibule.

Pastor Mitchell greeted parishioners at the vestibule door, and the elders conversed on the other side of the room. Two of her friends talked and laughed in the corner. Liz turned to her mother. "May I go talk to Abigail and Mary Jane?"

"Just for a few minutes. Services will start soon."

Liz nodded. "I know. I'll watch for Michael." She hurried to her friends. "Hey, you two. Did you have a good week?" She smiled at Abigail. "I saw you at the Harvey House yesterday. You look great in your new uniform. Do you like the job?"

"Yes, I do. There are lots of demands, but it's interesting. I needed to make my own money. This was my first week in the lunchroom." She grinned. "By the way, who was the attractive fellow you were with?"

"He's the new accountant at the ATSF office. Daddy asked me to show him around the city, and he took me there to eat."

"He's handsome. Love his red hair." Abigail giggled. "Are you sure he's just your father's employee? He kept his eyes on you."

Liz bumped her arm. "I just met him. I have to admit I was glad I was with him when Richard walked in with his new girlfriend, though."

"Yeah, I wondered if that might be a bit awkward." Abigail peered over Liz's shoulder. "By the way, they just walked in with his parents. Here comes Anna Lisa."

Liz grimaced slightly as Anna Lisa stepped up beside her.

"Hi, everyone." She laughed softly. "I bet I know what the topic of conversation is...my lunkhead brother. I'm sorry, Liz. I know it's crazy to have to see them here."

"It's difficult to know what to say. I'm sure I'll have to meet Richard's girlfriend."

Anna Lisa grabbed her arm. "Just be yourself. You'll say the right words when the time comes. She's friendly enough, in an egotistical way."

Mary Jane whispered. "Is that your new guy friend? Your father's new accountant? He just walked in." She nodded in approval. "Good looking! If you don't want him, introduce me."

"Oh, no! That's okay!" Liz whirled around and rushed to greet him. "Hi, Michael. I'll take you to sit with my family." She fell into step beside him and headed to the sanctuary door. The pastor reached out to shake his hand.

Liz spoke up. "Good morning, Pastor Mitchell, this is Michael McKey. He's a new employee at the ATSF."

The pastor nodded. "I'm glad to meet you, Michael. I hope you enjoy our service and will come again."

With Michael at her side, Liz walked to their pew near the front, ignoring the Stoops family on the other side of the aisle.

Rachel scooted over and patted the seat beside her as they slipped in and sat down. Liz sighed as she studied the stained glass windows and the ornate walnut trim around the sanctuary. She'd attended this church most of her life, and it was easy to take its beauty for granted. Would Michael approve? His family was probably prominent members of a massive cathedral in Boston.

Michael leaned toward her and brushed her shoulder with his. "This is a beautiful building." His deep, bass voice startled her.

Liz jumped and swiveled her head toward him. *Had he read her thoughts?* The pressure of his shoulder prickled the skin of her arm and sent sensations through her dress fabric. Her heart raced to have him sit so close. People near them visited quietly while they waited for the service to start. "It's probably not as grand as your church in Boston."

"Not as ostentatious. But, more friendly and intimate. Our church at home is so formal."

Michael straightened and faced the front when a young man walked to the pulpit. Liz fought the urge to touch his arm. What was this crazy attraction? Richard's touch never evoked these emotions. She took the hymn book from the rack, turned to the page the music leader announced, and handed it to Michael.

Michael held the hymnal for her to see, as the organ began to play. When the familiar chords of "Amazing Grace" rang out, they joined in the song. Liz peeked at him. His rich, bass voice harmonized with her soprano. She sang softly and listened to him as they began the next song, "At the Cross."

Pastor Mitchell's theme was the familiar story of Nicodemus, found in the third chapter of John. Liz found it difficult to concentrate on the sermon, conscious of Michael's nearness as they shared her Bible. Would he appreciate the service? What would people think? Would they assume he was her boyfriend? This is crazy! She'd only known him for a few days. They couldn't be a couple yet, could they?

The sermon ended, and she had only a scant idea of its content or the passage of time. When the congregation stood to sing the final hymn, Liz stared at the stained-glass window above the baptistry, trying to get control of her emotions. No one, not even Richard, had affected her this way.

After the benediction, Michael stepped into the aisle and waited for her to precede him. At the same time, Anna Lisa and her family were leaving across the aisle. Richard and his lady friend stepped from their pew. He still looked impressive—tall and handsome in his waistcoat and trousers, a Homburg hat in his hand. The young lady with him was elegantly dressed in a light pink gown with a small matching hat on her perfectly coiffed hair. She wore gloves and carried a stylish handbag.

Relief flowed through Liz. She realized now she didn't care that he had another companion. "Hello, Richard." She looked directly into his eyes. "I see you're back from college."

His cheeks reddened a bit. "Uh… yes, I…uh….we got here yesterday." He turned to the young lady beside him. "Uh...Sarah, I'd like you to meet my friend, Liz Gilbertson." He turned back, and his cheeks were even redder. "Liz, this is Sarah Porter. She... she's visiting with my family a couple of weeks while her parents are in Europe. She attends college in Manhattan, also."

Liz smiled. "Sarah, I'm glad to meet you. Perhaps we can get better acquainted while you're here. I'm a friend of Anna Lisa."

"I'd like that very much." Sarah smiled back.

"I hope you have a pleasant visit." Liz was conscious of Michael behind her and sensed, rather than saw, Richard glance at him, but she chose not to introduce them. She'd just let Richard stew. She placed her hand on Michael's arm as they walked toward the pastor and his wife.

Anna Lisa hurried up beside her and whispered. "You okay?"

Liz nodded and touched her friend's arm. "Yes, I'm fine. You said to be myself... I was."

Anna Lisa smiled. "Is it okay if I come over this afternoon? We need to talk."

"Sure. Come over after dinner." They'd reached the door to the foyer. They once again greeted the pastor, walked out into the bright sunshine, and stepped aside to wait for her family.

Michael touched her arm. "What did I just witness in there?"

Liz smiled at him. "I just realized, with relief, that I'm totally over my old beau. I'm truly happy for him and Sarah. Yesterday, there was still a smidgen of doubt. I wasn't sure how it would be when I saw him face-to-face. Now I know." Their conversation was cut short when the rest of her family emerged from the church.

Elise walked toward them. "Hello, Michael. I'm glad you joined us this morning."

"I am, too, Ma'am. I enjoyed the service. Sorry I was a bit late. I didn't allow myself quite enough time to get here. Next Sunday, I'll make the necessary time adjustment."

"Actually, you were right on time. Would you like to join us for dinner?"

"Oh, no, I don't want to impose. But, thanks for the invitation. I'm expected with some of the other men in the boarding house."

"Just know you're always welcome."

"Thank you, Ma'am." He shook hands with Daniel. "I'll see you first thing in the morning, sir."

Daniel nodded. "I'll plan on it."

Michael turned to Liz. "Thank you. I appreciate that you waited for me and invited me to join your family. I'll see you again, soon."

She nodded, surprised how deflated she felt that he'd declined her mother's dinner invitation. As he walked toward his carriage, she wondered, *What has happened to me?* She'd just walked away from a long-time relationship, and she'd only known Michael for a few days. Following her family to their carriage, she thought, *I need to step back, clear my head.* All she wanted was friendship.

Michael swiped his hand across his eyes as he headed toward his carriage. What was this crazy feeling that had overtaken him? The young ladies in his circle of Boston friends had never interested him. His parents had hinted at several women they thought he should pursue. But, they were empty-headed...only concerned with their appearance and what they could gain from a relationship. He was, after all, the son of a prominent bank president, a desirable target.

As he stepped up into his buggy, Michael watched the Gilbertson family as they left the church lot. Liz was unique. She was beautiful and charming. She spoke her mind. He chuckled softly at the thought of her face-to-face with Richard as she'd politely put him in his place. He wasn't even offended she hadn't introduced him.

Michael was delighted she was free from that relationship. He was also grateful he would work with her father. It should provide more opportunities to see her. He definitely wanted to become better acquainted.

He guided his horse out of the parking lot. He didn't actually have plans for dinner, but didn't want to impose on Mrs. Gilbertson's hospitality. Mrs. Barrett, the boarding house owner, was a good cook. He'd eat there with the other boarders. Maybe, when he knew the Gilbertsons better, he would accept an invitation.

His thoughts went back to Stone Church. He liked the warm, relaxed feel of the service. The pastor's sermon, about when Jesus told Nicodemus he had to be born again, or he couldn't see the kingdom of God, troubled Michael. Like Nicodemus, he wondered how could he be born again? Pastor Mitchell had explained it in the Bible story, but Michael needed to read it and study it for himself. He'd never heard that concept before. He'd see if Mrs. Barrett had a Bible when he got back to the boarding house.

As Liz watched Michael move toward his carriage, she wondered what he thought of her? And the service? Was he a Christian? She felt convicted. She'd been so concerned about Michael's nearness and what people thought that she'd missed most of the sermon. At age nine, she'd accepted Jesus as her Savior, and she loved Him, but sometimes took His love for granted. She realized that she needed to give Him the central place in her heart and thoughts, to seek His will for her life.

Catherine and Annie had dinner ready when the family arrived home, and they went directly to the dining room to eat. After the meal, Liz excused herself and hurried to her room. She changed into a light green summer dress. The temperature was climbing. The breeze, blowing in the window carried heat rather than relief. Liz sat on her bed and waited for Anna Lisa to come over. Friends since grade school, they'd been inseparable until they reached high school. Then Richard, Anna Lisa's older brother, had asked Liz to a school dance, and the two of them remained a couple through high school. After Richard left for college, she and Anna Lisa had spent more time together. Liz had prepared for marriage, and Anna Lisa had attended Bethel College to study music. Now, they were both ready to move ahead and forge their destinies.

Liz stood and slipped her feet into sandals. Maybe it would be cooler to wait for her friend on the front porch. As she stepped outside, she looked up the street toward Anna Lisa's house. There was no sign of her, so Liz perched on the porch swing, and gently rocked back and forth. It would've been nice if Michael could've come for dinner. She smiled. He had definitely brightened her outlook.

Anna Lisa stepped on the porch and sat beside her. "What's that smile about?"

"Michael. I think it'll be intriguing to know him better—it should make the summer more enjoyable."

Anna Lisa scrunched her nose and frowned. "You're so lucky. I can't get a man to look at me."

"Oh, no? Billy Walker wanted to go out with you, but you turned him down."

"I know." She sighed as she sat beside Liz. "I was so shy, and he was the class clown. I didn't think I'd know what to say. I wish, now, I'd accepted his offer."

"Maybe you can. I think Billy still likes you. Why don't you try to be his friend?"

"I don't think I'd have a chance."

"You never know until you try." Liz turned toward her. "By the way, did you see Abigail at the Harvey House yesterday?"

"Yes. She was in the lunchroom."

"I asked her about it this morning. She's just started, but she said she enjoys it. I think maybe I'd like to do that." Liz leaned back in the swing. "You have to sign a six-month contract."

Anna Lisa nodded. "That same thought occurred to me yesterday. It would be a way to make money and figure out our long-term plans. It's a decent place to work even if my folks don't think so."

"You know, my mother was a Harvey Girl. We could ask her about it." They both sat quietly for a few minutes.

CHAPTER 5

Liz sat forward. "Let's see if Mama's busy. She likes to read on Sunday afternoon."

The two girls left the porch, climbed the stairs, and walked to the far end of the hall. Liz knocked lightly on the door frame of Elise's room then stepped inside. It was tastefully furnished with two burgundy chairs and low tables. One wall was covered with a floor-to-ceiling bookcase, and a sewing machine was tucked away beside the window.

"Maybe she is on the sleeping porch. That's her favorite place to read." Liz led the way to an open door in the back of the room.

The small screened-in area overlooked the front yard and neighborhood. A chaise lounge occupied one end of the porch, and the other was a cozy seating area. A cool breeze flowed through and rustled the leaves of potted plants scattered about. Anna Lisa stepped through the doorway. "This is a neat room. I'd read out here, too."

"What can I do for you girls?" Elise sat in one of the wingbacks, her legs pulled up under her, and an open book on her lap.

"Sorry to bother you, Mama, but we wondered if you'd tell us what is required to be a Harvey Girl? We thought we might apply."

Elise lowered her legs to the floor and sat up. "So you've thought more about it? I think it's a wonderful idea. My time as a Harvey Girl is replete with fond memories. It's an excellent job for young ladies, a way to make money with some guidance toward becoming a wife and mother later. People, who think it's not a proper job for a young lady, haven't researched it enough."

She smiled at them. "Liz, I know you've thought about enrolling at Bethany College." She turned to Anna Lisa. "And you've attended there. What changed your minds?"

"Yesterday, at the Harvey House, we both saw Abigail in the lunchroom. She looked excited and happy." Liz plopped down in the chair opposite Elise, and Anna Lisa sat on a stool. "I talked to her at church this morning, and she loves the job, even with the hard work."

"Well, one favorable option is that you can sign a six-month contract now instead of the year I had to agree to. That would give you time to gain experience and determine your future. Fair warning, you may not be together after the first month. Fred Harvey sends you where you're needed after you've been trained."

"Like you and Tessa, right?" Liz grinned at her. "I've heard that story."

She turned to her friend. "She and Tessa were friends and roommates. Mama was sent to Emporia, and Tessa went to Hutchinson. Tessa quit and married a rancher with a brood of kids, and Mama met Daddy. You never know what will happen!"

"Sounds like an adventure to me." Anna Lisa clasped her hands. "Maybe I'd meet my future husband."

"It's hard work," emphasized Elise. "My first house mother, who is now my sister-in-law, said, 'If you do your work well, Fred Harvey will take care of you.' That's a proven fact."

Liz turned to Anna Lisa. "Mama and Aunt Millie worked together at the Harvey House here in Topeka. That's where Uncle Arnaud met her. He's an engineer on the Santa Fe."

"What about you and Michael? You've just met. Now might not be a good time to take off somewhere." Anna Lisa grinned at her friend.

"I like him, but I've just suffered one rejection. I'm not ready for another serious relationship. Six months wouldn't be bad. Besides, he could come see me if he wants to. He can ride the train free since he's an employee of the railroad."

"Sounds to me like you girls have made up your minds. Have you had this conversation with your parents, Anna Lisa?"

She shook her head. "Liz and I just discussed it today. Besides, my mother is busy with Richard and Sarah. I'll talk to her right away. She probably won't want me to leave, but I can't sit at home for the rest of my life. My music studies aren't practical, and I don't want to teach."

Elise set her book on the table beside her. "Think more about it, girls. If that's what you want to do, go to the Harvey House and get an application. They'll set up an interview in Kansas City."

"Thanks, Mom! I'm glad we talked about this." Liz pushed herself from the chair as Anna Lisa stood.

In the hallway, Anna Lisa grabbed Liz's arm and pulled her to a stop. "Are you sure you want to be a Harvey Girl? My parents may not want me to do it."

"Yes. I just decided. This is what I need right now, a job and some structure in my days."

"I'm just not sure about it. I'm afraid I might not do well. I've never worked like that before."

"Neither have I, but the beauty of it is that they teach you." Liz started on down the hall. "Think about it and talk to your mother. It certainly won't hurt to get an application."

"Alright, I'll let you know."

The eastern sky began to lighten when Michael awoke Monday morning. The first day at his new job. He sat on the side of the bed and surveyed the room. It was quite small and austere. A patchwork quilt and a matching curtain at the window provided the only color. A small table held a lamp and a white pitcher and basin. His clothes hung from hooks on the wall, and his trunk and travel bags were piled in the corner. Mrs. Barrett's Bible lay beside the lamp.

He chuckled. His mother would be appalled if she could see the room. Just as well, she couldn't. His bedroom in Boston had been spacious, specially decorated in blues and browns, with a four-poster bed and a large wardrobe, abundant storage space.

Michael had extra funds, but he wanted to be prudent in his spending until he had income from his job. In time, he'd find a better room closer to the ATSF building. Liz had pointed out several possibilities to him.

He struck a match, lit the lamp, then picked up the Bible. In spite of his love for books, Michael couldn't recall ever reading it.

He'd heard Bible verses quoted in church. He'd even memorized some in Sunday School years ago, but that was the extent of his biblical knowledge.

Mrs. Barrett had been glad to loan him her Bible. Yesterday afternoon, he'd found the story about Nicodemus. He was still puzzled by Jesus' demand to be born again and wanted to learn more. He'd turned back to the first chapter of John and read to the end. He was captivated by the story of Jesus and His followers. Many times, Jesus said He was the Son of God, and yet, He loved those around Him so much that He died for them.

Michael ran his finger over the gold embossed words, *Holy Bible,* on the front of the book. He wanted to read more about the man called Jesus, but there wasn't time this morning. He needed to prepare for work and allow enough time to get there on the streetcar.

～

Thursday morning, Liz drove their family carriage to Anna Lisa's house. Her friend waited on the front porch. They planned to go to the Harvey House for applications.

Anna Lisa hurried to the carriage and climbed in. "I'm ready to get out of the house. Sarah never lifts a finger to help herself. She expects us to wait on her hand and foot."

Liz raised her eyebrows. "Not all sugar and honey in paradise, huh?"

"No. Not exactly!"

As the horse cantered toward the depot, Liz gazed at the two-storied red-framed building. "Just think, we may work here soon."

They stepped from the carriage, and Liz tied the reins to the hitching post.

"I know, it's exciting, but kind of scary too."

"We have to work somewhere." The girls hurried toward the entrance, passing others leaving the depot. "Will your parents be okay if you get a job as a Harvey Girl?"

"I hope so. Right now, my mother's up to her neck with Sarah. When she leaves, my parents will probably heave a sigh of relief."

"I thought it all looked splendid at church, Sunday. Sarah seemed friendly." Liz opened the depot door.

"Oh, she's friendly enough, but I don't think she's too impressed with our lifestyle. She's an only child, and her parents are extremely wealthy. Even though my father is a banker, I'm pretty sure she thinks we're beneath her social level. I think even Richard wonders what he's gotten himself into. He shakes his head when she makes demands."

Liz pursed her lips and nodded slightly. "Serves him right."

They walked across the depot lobby and up the staircase. The Harvey Girls were busy serving patrons at the lunch counter and in the dining room.

The head waitress met them. "Hello, my name is Beatrice. Will you have breakfast with us?"

"Actually, we'd like to get Harvey Girl applications."

Beatrice looked at them and nodded. "Very well. We always need new girls."

Liz glanced around. "My mother was a Harvey Girl, here."

Beatrice swung back to her. "She was? Did she like it?"

"Yes, she said it's hard work, but worth it."

Beatrice nodded. "That's true. Let me get those applications.

Follow me." She led the way from the lunchroom to a doorway on the left. They walked through a parlor to the first door in the residence hall. Inside Beatrice's room, a small desk sat against the wall. A bed, a bureau, and wardrobe were on the other side of the room. She pulled out a drawer and took out two sets of papers. "Here are the applications. After you've filled them out and returned them, I'll arrange for an interview in Kansas City." She handed a set to each of them. "Are you girls from here in town?"

"Yes. We're friends with Abigail McDonald."

Beatrice nodded. "If you're hired, you'll be required to live in residence. The rules are listed in the application packet."

As they walked back into the parlor, Liz sighed. "This is what I want to do." She looked at Anna Lisa. "Let's eat breakfast in the lunchroom and then fill out the applications. We might as well get them turned in."

Anna Lisa nodded, hesitantly. "Alright."

Beatrice led them back to the lunchroom, showed them to seats at the horseshoe-shaped counter and handed them menus.

Abigail approached as Beatrice turned to leave. "Hi, girls." Abigail's eyes sparkled with interest. "Did you apply?"

"We got the applications. Hopefully, we'll get hired." Liz waved the papers.

"I hope you do. I'd love to have you here." Abigail smiled. "What would you like to drink?"

Liz pursed her lips. "I'll take coffee with cream and sugar. If I'm hired to be a Harvey Girl, I need to learn to drink coffee."

Abigail grinned and turned her cup over.

Anna Lisa wrinkled her nose. "I'll have hot tea with sugar and cream."

Abigail poured Liz's coffee then set a small teapot and a pitcher of cream in front of Anna Lisa. "Are you ready to order?"

Liz studied the menu. "I'd like french toast and bacon." She poured the cream and sugar in her cup and took a drink. She wrinkled her nose. "I think I need more cream and sugar."

Anna Lisa laughed. "I'm not ready to try it, yet." She poured a cup of tea. "I want two pancakes and ham."

Abigail brought their meals and suggested, "You can fill your applications out in the dormitory parlor. There's a desk in there with pen and ink. Then, bring them back to me. I'll make sure Beatrice gets them. She's extra busy today. Governor Stanley and his family will be here for dinner. She has to make sure the dining room is in top shape."

"The governor is coming for dinner? That's exciting." Liz placed her napkin in her lap. "I'm ready to start work. Hopefully, we can get an interview soon."

Thirty minutes later, they turned in their applications. As they walked across the depot lobby, they met a group of men in business suits, followed by a middle-aged woman and a young boy.

As they passed, Anna Lisa leaned toward Liz. "That was Governor Stanley with his wife, Lenora, and their son, William Jr. They do business at my father's bank. I saw them there the other day." She glanced over her shoulder. "Those other men must be congressmen."

"You never know who you'll meet in a Harvey House." Liz smiled as she pushed open the depot door. "I wonder if he drove his automobile. Adam talks about it all the time. He thinks to have a horseless carriage would be a real killer." They walked along the boardwalk toward the parking area. "Look, there it is.

It's a surrey without horses. He must use it for family outings. I think he also has a run-about."

Several men stood around the unusual carriage. Two of them ran their hands along the side and over the lights on the front.

"It would be fun to have one." Anna Lisa approached the Gilbertsons' carriage. "My father says it's run with electricity."

Liz chuckled. "Daddy says it's just a passing fancy, that electricity isn't practical. He and Adam have quite the discussions." She untied the reins and stepped up into the carriage. "Michael's dad has an automobile. and Michael said he would like to have one."

"Maybe if he gets one you'll get to ride in it." Anna Lisa climbed up beside her.

"Maybe. I don't think he'll get one anytime soon. Anyway, we're just friends. Although I do like him a lot." Liz backed the carriage and drove it out of the depot parking lot.

Anna Lisa touched her arm. "I'm not ready to go home, yet. Would you like to go to Rebecca's Millnery shop? I want to get a new hat."

"Sure, sounds good. I love to look at hats. I need to buy a few articles at the Mercantile, too."

"Liz, please don't tell my parents I turned in the application. I'll tell them, but I want to wait for the right time. I haven't had a good opportunity." Anna Lisa sighed.

"I won't mention it, but you better discuss it with your mother before you get an interview appointment." Liz guided the horse to the hitching post in front of the millinery shop. "Come on, let's look at some pretty hats. It'll get your mind off your troubles."

CHAPTER 6

Liz let Anna Lisa off at her house and headed the carriage back toward home. Adam rode his high wheeler up the street. He turned around and pedaled back toward her. "Where've you been?" He slid off the back of the cycle.

"Anna Lisa and I had a girls day out." She smiled at him. "Guess who was at the Harvey House?"

He wrinkled his brow. "Who?"

"Governor Stanley and his family. We got to see his automobile."

Adam rolled the bicycle toward the carriage. "Really? I wish I could have seen it. Which one did he have?"

"The family one."

"Cool! One of these days I'm gonna' have one."

Liz chuckled. "You better save your money." She drove the rig around the back of the house.

Henry, Lucia's husband, and the Gilbertson's gardener and handyman, met her outside the carriage house. "I'll get it from here, Miss Liz. Hope you had a good day."

"I did. Thanks, Henry." Liz gathered her purse and purchases, stepped from the carriage, then ambled back around the house to the front walk. Adam ran the bicycle up the street and jumped up on the seat. It was fun to watch him ride, although she didn't want to try it. She could just see herself crashed and sprawled all over the ground.

Julien sat on the porch step with a book. "What are you reading today?" She sat beside him.

He held up the open book for her to see. "It's a story about the Boston Tea Party. Michael said he'd come over and tell me more about it."

"When?"

"This evening. Daddy said he'd invite him for supper."

"Hmm. Why didn't I know about this?"

Julien frowned and cocked his head. "You've been off gallivanting all day. Besides, he's my guest. I invited him." He hesitated. "Well, Daddy invited him, but I asked him to."

"And you're sure he'll be here for supper?"

"I'm not sure, but I hope so."

Liz grinned. A thrill of anticipation raced through her. "I hope he does come. We haven't seen him since Sunday. Of course, he's been at work, his first week at the Santa Fe office." She pushed herself up from the step. "I better go in and let Mama know I'm home. Tell Michael 'hi' for me when he comes."

Julien had become engrossed in his book again before she even reached the door. As Liz stepped into the cool entryway, Elise walked down the stairs. "Hi, Mama. Julien said Michael may be here for supper."

"Daddy planned to invite him. Julien's been very persistent. He says Michael promised to tell him about Boston." She fell into step with Liz as they headed toward the sitting room. "How did your day go? Did you get the application?"

"Actually, we filled out the applications and submitted them. Beatrice, the head waitress, suggested it." She stopped and faced her mama. "I hope Anna Lisa's parents are alright with her as a Harvey Girl. She hasn't talked to them about it yet. Not much, anyway. Her mother's time has been totally absorbed by Sarah. Miss Sarah requires a lot of attention."

Elise nodded. "I wondered about that. I hope Anna Lisa can talk to her mother. I know some of the women in the Ladies Missionary Society think work as a Harvey Girl is below their social status. Abigail's mother was distressed by their attitude. I told her it was ridiculous—not to let it bother her. Many of the Harvey Girls are from high-class families. They just want to get away and be on their own."

"Like me?"

Elise smiled. "I suppose. I understand why you want some independence. I felt the same way at your age, although I also needed the money. Just remember you always have a home here."

"Thank you for your encouragement." Liz settled on the couch in the downstairs sitting room. She paused as Elise sat in a nearby wingback chair. "It's time I grow up and make my own decisions." She grimaced. "I thought I'd be knee-deep in wedding plans, but that didn't happen. I'm okay with it, but I feel restless. Since you were a Harvey Girl, I feel confident that will be a good fit."

"Actually, it will be good for you. I've taught you to be a

good hostess, but Fred Harvey takes it to a whole new level. What else did you do? You were gone the entire day."

"We went shopping. Anna Lisa bought a pretty new hat at Rebecca's Millinery Shop, and I got some items at the Mercantile. Oh, we saw the governor's family and some of the congressmen at the Harvey House. They arrived in his automobile and caused quite a stir. Several men admired it outside the depot." She smiled. "I told Adam I saw it."

"I'll bet he was envious."

"He was. He wants to buy one when he gets old enough."

"I know. We'll see." Elise chuckled as she stood. "I need to check with Catherine. She's making baked chicken with herb dressing for supper."

The front door slammed as she started toward the kitchen. Julien's voice rang through the hallway. "Hey, Mama, Michael's here. We'll be in the library."

"Julien William, you don't have to announce Michael's arrival to the whole neighborhood!" Elise disappeared, and Liz heard her greet Michael. Their voices grew fainter as they went their separate directions.

Liz stared at the door. The urge to go into the library and greet Michael nearly overcame her. She shook her head. There was just enough time to freshen up and change before supper. She'd see him then.

She pushed herself from the chair and walked to the stairway. As she passed the library door, she allowed herself a peek. Michael had seated himself behind the desk and faced the door. He caught her gaze and winked before he looked back at Julien. A warm glow infused Liz as she hurried to her room.

Michael was glad to see her. And she was delighted to see him. Hopefully, they'd get a chance to talk after supper.

She changed into her pink flower print, one of her favorite summer frocks, then started down the stairs. She caught snatches of Michael's deep bass voice in conversation with Julien. It wasn't proper to eavesdrop, but she couldn't resist the temptation. She sat on the top step. Hopefully, she could hear without being observed.

"Alright, buddy, what else do you want to know?" Michael focused on Julien's face. He was amused at the earnest expression in Julien' eyes. He'd been overjoyed at any excuse to revisit the Gilbertson home. When his boss invited him to dinner on Julien's behalf, he'd eagerly accepted. A few minutes earlier, he saw Liz walk past the door, and as if on cue, she'd looked in and smiled. He felt rejuvenated. She was the real reason he wanted to be here. He'd find a time to talk with her.

Julien picked up a book from the desk. "We've studied about the Boston Tea Party and the beginning of the Revolutionary War in school. Do you know where that happened?"

"It was in Boston Harbor—not far from where my family lives. There's also a museum that has two of the ships which were in the harbor that night, and two of the original tea chests that were thrown overboard. We went there on a school outing when I was in primary school."

"Oh, wow! I'd love to see that."

"The Boston Tea Party was one of the events that started the Revolutionary War. Colonists weren't happy about taxes levied by England without their representation in the British

Parliament. They wanted to govern themselves without so much control from King George."

Julien nodded. "You said, when you were here for supper, that Paul Revere, Samuel Adams, and John Hancock went to the bank where your father works. Is that true?"

"That's the traditional view. My great-great-grandpa McKey immigrated from Scotland in 1790, after the Revolutionary War. He didn't want to fight in his family's clan wars. At age eighteen, he was hired as a teller at the bank. The story handed down through our family is that he waited on the founding fathers of our country. Their pictures are displayed in the bank.

"My great-great-grandma immigrated from Ireland in 1803. She cleaned in the bank at night. That's how my grandfather met her." Michael grinned as he watched Julien's serious face.

"Wow, your ancestors go back a long way."

"Yes, they do."

"You lived right there where all those battles took place."

"Yes, there are several battlegrounds in our area. Lexington is across the river west of Boston. That's where the first shot was fired that started the Revolutionary War. I was at that battleground once." Michael watched Julien' eyes glow with interest.

"What's happening in here?"

Michael looked up as Mr. Gilbertson walked into the library. "We've discussed the Boston Tea Party and the other Revolutionary War battles near Boston. I've been to some of the battlefields."

Daniel placed his hand on Julien's shoulder. "Sounds like an interesting conversation. Right now, though, we better get ready for supper. I was detained at work, so I'm home later than usual.

I just heard your mother say supper was served." He studied Michael. "Did he talk your leg off?"

"No, actually, I did most of the talking." Michael grinned. "He just asked the questions. I think he'll be a lawyer someday."

"Quite possibly," Daniel chuckled as he led the way from the room.

Liz scrambled up from her vantage point at the top of the stairs when her dad walked down the hall. She was intrigued by what Michael had revealed about his distant grandparents. She wished she knew more about her father's background. Something was definitely missing in her history.

As Daniel led the way from the library a few minutes later, Liz glided down the stairs. She acknowledged Michael's smile as she neared the bottom. "Hello, Michael. Julien said you were invited to talk with him." She grinned. "He informed me you were his guest and not mine."

Michael held out his hand to assist her down the last few steps. "Oh, he did, did he? Well, I guess I can be your friend, too." Julien stood behind him with a scowl on his face. "Aww, come on, buddy, we can share." He offered his arm to Liz as they headed toward the dining room. "Mmm. That smells delicious. I didn't realize how hungry I was."

Elise directed them to the table, and this time Liz was seated beside Michael, with Julien, still scowling, across from him. She noticed that Michael bowed his head as her father prayed the blessing on their meal. What did Michael think of her family's habit of praying before meals? Did he mind that her mother had seated them together?

The meal progressed with lively conversation. Once when Liz passed the gravy to Michael, their hands touched. An awareness of his closeness enveloped her. She glanced at him, and he smiled as their eyes met.

As the last dishes were cleared from the table, Michael touched her hand. "Can we talk?"

She nodded. "Let's go out on the front porch."

Michael thanked Liz's parents and followed her out into the sunshine. "I was glad Julien asked me to come. I wanted to see you. " He held the swing still as she sat down, then sat beside her.

"Do you like the job? Daddy is glad you joined the office. He said you do thorough work." A warm southern breeze caused tendrils of Liz's hair to gently wave around her face.

"Did he say that?"

"He did, last evening at supper."

Michael sat forward. "I enjoy the work. I appreciate the slower pace. The lifestyle is so rush-rush in Boston." He turned toward her. "How have you occupied your time?"

"Anna Lisa and I went to the Harvey House today and submitted applications to become Harvey Girls."

"You did? Is that what you want to do?"

Liz nodded. "Yes. I need to be on my own. We applied for six months. Maybe by then, I'll know what I want to do with my life." She grinned. "It's a good place to work. Quite respectable. If my mother can do it, so can I."

Michael leaned back. "I sent a letter to my cousin and told her about the Harvey Girls. I haven't heard from her."

He set the swing in a gentle motion. "Would you go with me

to the opera house tomorrow evening? Mark Twain is lecturing. He's on tour. I read his books at college, and I've wanted to hear him speak."

Liz cocked her head. "I'd like to go. I hoped you hadn't forgotten." She felt Michael relax beside her.

"Good. It starts at seven-thirty. I'll pick you up at six-thirty, so we can get good seats."

Liz smiled. "I'll look forward to it."

When Michael arrived at his room, he opened the trunk and took out his tuxedo. Although the clothes had been folded neatly when packed, they were wrinkled nearly beyond recognition. He scrunched his face in disgust. He should have removed them sooner to have them pressed. Back home, he hadn't given such things much thought. The housekeeper always made sure his clothes were ready. He gathered the jacket, pants, and white shirt into a bundle and went in search of Mrs. Barrett.

He found her in the parlor reading a book. She looked up as he entered. "Mrs. Barrett, is there a tailor nearby who could press my clothes by tomorrow evening? I hadn't removed them from my trunk. I should have realized they wouldn't stay neatly pressed."

Mrs. Barrett laid her book aside and sat forward. "There's a laundry up the street. They wash and press clothing for the railroad and depot workers. I'll take them in the morning. They should be ready when you get off work tomorrow. Do you plan to attend a special occasion?"

"I've invited my boss's daughter to see Mark Twain at the opera house."

"Mark Twain? He'll be here? I have his books, *The Adventures of Tom Sawyer* and *Adventures of Huckleberry Finn.* I'd love to hear him speak."

"I've wanted to hear him, too. It's fortunate he can stop here on his tour." He hesitated. "Mrs. Barrett? Would you mind if I use your Bible a little longer? I read through John, now I've started to read in the book of Matthew. I'd like to complete it."

"That'd be fine. Oh, wait. I think I have another one you can keep. My daughter used to have it. She received a new Bible for graduation, so she doesn't need this one." She turned to the bookcase and removed the black book from the shelf. "She'll be glad you can use it."

"You're sure she won't want it?"

"I'm sure."

"Thank you. I'll go get yours." Michael hurried up the stairs, taking two at a time, then returned Mrs. Barrett's copy.

Back in his room, he lit the lantern and settled down to read. He was struck by the authority with which Jesus taught on the mountain about how a person should live. And there was the Lord's Prayer. He had quoted it in church many times, but why hadn't he been taught the other things in scripture? He stopped for a moment and glanced out the window. The last vestiges of daylight were fading in the sky. His family was so involved in their social circles that they'd lost track of what was important. Jesus said not to worry about what they would eat or what they would wear. If He could take care of the birds of the air and the flowers in the fields, He could supply their needs.

Michael returned his attention to the Bible in his hands. In chapter 6, verse 33, it read, *"But seek ye first the kingdom of*

God, and His righteousness; and all these things shall be added unto you." Michael closed his eyes. He wanted to seek God instead of money. "God, I don't know much about You, but I want to learn more. Help me to learn." He placed the Bible carefully on the table and prepared for bed. He glanced at the evidence he'd pulled from his trunk and baggage. Maybe he had more possessions than he needed.

The next morning, Michael got up early and dressed for work. After a hearty breakfast, he jogged up the street. He'd bought a mare from a local rancher earlier in the week, and the livery owner had said his new carriage should be delivered today. He wanted to go by and check. Hopefully, it would be there already so he could drive it to work. He was tired of riding the trolley every day. And tonight, he wanted to take Liz to the opera house in his new rig.

The sun shone brightly in the sky, and a warm breeze brushed past him as he entered the livery stable. "Hey, Will, did my rig get here?"

"Yeah, came in yesterday evening. Here it is all new and shiny. Ready to be hitched up. I'll get your mare for you. She's ready for a run."

Great. I want to drive her to work this morning. But, maybe we can get in a run tomorrow. My girl and I are going to the opera this evening."

"Wonderful. Have a good day."

"Thanks." Michael stroked the mare's neck as he harnessed her. "Dolly, girl, we're going to make a good team."

He guided the horse and rig out of the livery.

He was beyond delighted to have his own transportation.

CHAPTER 7

Liz opened her wardrobe and surveyed the array of dresses. She was indeed blessed, but she wouldn't need many of them when she started work at the Harvey House. There wouldn't be time for a lot of social activities.

She removed the powder blue evening dress. It was one of her favorites for special occasions, perfect for the lecture. She spread it on the bed then sat and picked up her parents' picture from the bedside stand. Something about the picture pulled on her when a momentous occasion was about to happen. She anticipated this date with Michael might be life-altering. Was it only a week that she'd known him? She felt a kinship, believed he understood her, at times, he seemed to read her mind.

She whispered to the picture in her hand. "Mother, I wish you could meet Michael. You'd like him. He's so different from Richard, much more caring." She laid the picture on her pillow. "If only you could be here just for a little while to talk to me." She turned, flopped down on her belly and propped herself with her elbows on the bed. "And, Father, I want to know about your family. Where did I come from?" The silence was deafening.

"Liz, do you want me to help fix your hair?" Her mama's voice came from the hallway outside her door.

She sat up and put the picture back as Elise walked in the room. "Yes, I'd appreciate that. You always have the right touch." She turned. Had Mama heard her whispers?

"Come into my sitting room, where there's more light."

Liz followed Elise down the hall to the sunny room. "You look lovely. Did Daddy get tickets for you to go tonight? I know Julien begged to go."

"Yes, we'll take the boys. Rachel wants to stay with Aunt Millie and Ruth. She'll enjoy that more." Elise pulled out a stool for Liz to sit on. "We have balcony tickets. I'm sure the opera house will be packed."

Liz balanced on the stool as Elise brushed her hair. "Mama, how long does it take to know if you love someone?"

"Why do you ask that?"

"I thought I loved Richard, but I realize now it wasn't love at all."

Elise hesitated. "It doesn't take long to like someone, but love needs to develop. Time is required to build a strong relationship, to really know someone. When the time's right, you just know." Elise brushed Liz's hair up on the sides. "Although I liked your daddy a lot from the beginning, it took us a while to figure out the love thing."

"My feelings for Michael are so different from what I felt for Richard, a connection somehow." She frowned. "I'm not sure I can compare to the ladies in his Boston social circle, though."

"Well, don't get in a hurry. If it's right, God will work it out. You're in His hands. Just be yourself. Don't try to live up to false standards."

"I know." Liz frowned. "I desire a closer relationship with God. I know I've taken Him for granted. Although He's my Savior, I don't spend time with Him as I should."

"It's easy to fall into that habit. Ask Jesus to help you. Take time to read your Bible and pray." Elise gave a final touch with the comb, then handed Liz a mirror to inspect the results.

Her mother had tamed her unruly golden curls, fastening them up in the back, with ringlets hanging down. "Beautiful! Thanks, Mama. I appreciate it."

"Now, let's get your dress on. I don't want you to tighten that corset too much. You have a nice waist. It doesn't need to be any smaller."

"But, that's the style."

"I'll help you get it on. It'll look just fine." Together, they walked arm-in-arm back to Liz's room. "Put the corset on, and I'll tie it for you." After that was accomplished, Elise lifted the dress and slipped it over Liz's head, careful not to disturb the ringlets. The fabric fell in graceful folds. Delicate hand-made lace trimmed the high neck, sleeves and the bottom of the skirt. The waist fit perfectly. Elise stepped back. "You look stunning, perfect for the opera house."

Rachel ran into the room. "Michael's here." She halted mid-stride and gasped. "Ohh. You're beautiful." She gave Liz a hug. "I'm glad you're my sister."

Liz returned the hug. "I'm glad, too."

Rachel grabbed her hand. "Come see Michael's new carriage."

"I'm coming. I'm coming." Liz laughed as she fell into step behind Rachel on the stairs.

She sucked in her breath. At the bottom of the staircase, Michael stepped toward her. He looked dashing in his tuxedo and formal dress shirt with the tall stiffened collar.

Michael stood entranced as Liz and Rachel descended the stairs. Liz's golden hair glowed in the afternoon light. The sky-blue dress fit her small figure perfectly and fell in soft, billowing folds around her feet. He'd never seen a prettier woman...even in Boston.

He stepped forward and offered his hand. "You're breathtaking." He assisted her down the last step.

Liz smiled. "Thank you. You look very handsome, as well."

"Are you ready to go?" He offered his elbow, and they walked onto the porch. "I bought a mare this week, and my new carriage arrived this morning. Now I have wheels." His face beamed with pride as he led Liz down the walk to the street. A new carriage and a lovely lady on his arm, who could ask for more?

"What's her name?" Liz walked to the mare's side and patted her neck.

"I think I'll call her Dolly."

"I like that name."

Liz ran her hand along the smooth black surface of the carriage. "Impressive! I'm excited for you. Bet you'll miss the trolley ride to work, though." She giggled.

"Or anywhere else," Michael responded as he helped her up onto the seat. He hurried around the carriage to the other side and stepped up into the driver's seat. "It handles well. It's not an automobile, but the next best thing." He looked at Liz. "Are you comfortable?"

"Yes." She ran her hand over the leather. "These are fine seats."

Michael snapped the reins, and they headed up the street. He drove into the parking area beside the Opera House and stopped at the hitching rail. As he jumped down to secure Dolly, an automobile roared in behind them. The horse became skittish and tried to pull away.

Liz grabbed the side of the seat.

Michael held tight to the reins. "Whoa, Dolly. Easy, girl." He tied her, then moved around to Liz's side of the carriage and offered his hand.

She grimaced as she stepped to the ground. "That's the problem with those automobiles."

Michael nodded. "Someday soon, though, there will be more cars than carriages."

Liz gave a disgusted shake to smooth her dress. "I don't know. Horses are much more reliable."

Michael presented their tickets at the entrance. The doorman handed them a program and motioned for an usher to direct them. He led them into the dimly lit theatre. "Here are your seats. You'll have a good view of the stage."

As they entered the row, other formally attired men and women filled the seats around them. Liz nodded to a few, while Michael took in his surroundings. They were in the middle about half-way back.

He watched Liz as she scanned the theatre, her eyes dancing

in awe of new discovery. "Ohh." She sighed. "This is incredible! I've never seen such splendor."

Michael smiled as he followed her gaze. He saw the opulence of the velvet curtains, stylish lighting, and elaborately decorated box seats, with new eyes. This was old hat to him. He'd been in elegant homes and buildings with his family since he could remember. But he'd never seen it as out of the ordinary until now.

Liz settled back into her seat. "I've been to some upscale places with my parents, but none compare to this. I love it." She turned to him. "I imagine you've seen this many times."

"Not as much as you'd think. I avoided it as much as possible."

"And now you've come for my benefit. We could've done something you'd enjoy."

"No, this is different. I'm glad we've come. I'm eager to hear Mark Twain. Actually Samuel Clemens—Mark Twain is his pen name." He handed her the program he'd received when they entered. "It's an honor for Topeka to be included in his tour. He's traveled the world."

The opera house filled, and the curtain rose. For the next two hours, they sat entranced by the friendly, funny, satirical wit of Mark Twain. Liz leaned forward, engrossed, alternately laughing at the humor and nodding agreement to his commentary, thoroughly absorbed in the presentation until the curtain went down. The applause lasted a long time.

"Oh, I'm glad we came. That was wonderfully entertaining and informational." Liz sighed as she stood to leave. "I wish it could have lasted longer."

Michael turned to her with a smile. "I've heard about Mark Twain all my life. To think, I had to come all the way to Kansas to actually see him in person."

Michael offered her his arm as they made their way out of the theatre, through the crowd, and back to the carriage.

They chatted while other conveyances left the parking lot, then Michael clucked at Dolly and turned out onto the street. "Let's take a loop up Kansas and back. I'm curious to see how this baby rides. It'll also allow us to see if anything else is going on." He gave Dolly her head as she trotted up the street. Friday night shoppers had nearly disappeared and traffic dispersed as they passed the business district and headed toward her house.

Liz sighed. "This evening was incredible. I've enjoyed it immensely."

Michael slipped his hand over hers. "Me, too."

Liz skimmed the soft cloth over the surface of the grand piano. It was Saturday morning, and Elise had asked her to dust the parlor furniture. She'd taken piano lessons for several years, but had been lazy with her practice in the last year. She'd debated whether to study music in college, but Richard had convinced her music would be unnecessary when they were married. A lot of good that did her now.

On a whim, she sat on the bench and raised the keyboard cover. Her hands came alive as she placed them on the keys. She began with musical scales up and down the keys as she'd been taught. Then, the beautiful strains of "Beethoven's Moonlight Sonata" spilled out into the room from her memory. She was lost in the music as her fingers responded to her will.

After the last notes, she dropped her hands into her lap

and sat quietly. Warmth radiated through her. Music was still a part of her.

Soft clapping caught her attention. "Oh, I'm sorry, Mama. I got sidetracked. I better get back to work. I wasn't sure I could still play that piece."

Tears glistened in Elise's eyes. "That was beautiful! Its melody drew me here. You should do that more. Are you positive you don't want to pursue your music?"

"No. I'm relieved I can still play, but I want something more productive, something practical. I want to be a Harvey Girl." Liz rose from the piano stool and picked up the polishing cloth.

"Alright. Just so you know, without a doubt, that's what you want."

"It is, for now, at least." She wiped the rag across the piano. "I'm almost through. Did you say Uncle Arnaud and Aunt Millie will be here for dinner tomorrow? I want to talk to her about her experiences as a Harvey Girl."

"She was the head Harvey Girl and house mother when I started."

"I know, that's amazing. My mama and my Aunt Millie. That's a legacy—maybe the start of a tradition." Liz dusted the lamp table. "There, I'm done, unless you want me to clean somewhere else?"

"No, Lucia has finished the other rooms. She left early today. Why don't you come into the sitting room? Tell me your impression of Mark Twain's presentation?"

Liz followed Elise from the room. "I enjoyed it immensely. What did you and Daddy think?"

"It was informative and funny. I loved his dry humor. Your

father enjoyed his travel tales and his grasp of newsworthy events."

Anna Lisa knocked on the front door, and Liz hurried to open it. She turned back toward the hallway, where her mother stood. "Do you mind if I go visit with Anna Lisa?"

"That's fine. We can talk later."

Liz followed Anna Lisa to the swing and sat beside her. "So, how are things at your house?"

"You won't believe what happened. Sarah and Richard had a horrific fight, and Sarah bought train tickets for home. Her parents weren't traveling abroad, after all. Tension is thick around our house! We're all delighted to see her go."

Liz stared at Anna Lisa in disbelief. "You're kidding! Really?"

"From the very first, it was miserable. Sarah demanded to be waited on. I don't know what Richard saw in her, maybe her parents' money. She was nice when she was the center of attention." Anna Lisa sniffed. "Richard must've given her the impression we were made of money. We're not poor, by any stretch, but we aren't what you'd call wealthy. Either her parents are well-heeled, or she's looking for someone who can elevate her financial and social status."

Liz sat in stunned silence. If it weren't for this self-centered, young woman who'd turned Richard's head, he might still be her intended bridegroom. She grimaced. Would she have realized how shallow he was before she committed herself? A shudder coursed through her. "So what will Richard do now? I hope he doesn't think he can pick up where we left off."

"I don't know. I don't think he knows." She looked miserable. "I'm positive Mother is relieved, except for the embarrassment. She bragged about this visit with her friends."

"I don't mean to be unkind, but Richard did bring it on himself."

Anna Lisa nodded. "I know."

"Have you talked to your mother about the Harvey House interview?"

Anna Lisa shook her head. "No. All this has blown up. I'll talk to her today or tomorrow."

"Don't put it off. We should hear when the interviews are scheduled in a day or two."

"I know." Anna Lisa pushed her foot against the floor of the porch and made the swing move. "What have you been up to?"

Liz relaxed against the back. "Michael and I went to see Mark Twain at the Opera House last night. He was only there for one show. He was very funny and insightful."

"I wish I could've seen him. It wouldn't be any fun to go alone. I don't know who I'd go with. " Anna Lisa smiled. "You and Michael are quite a twosome."

"We're just friends. We've only known each other for a week." Liz cocked her head and raised her eyebrows. "Although, I might like for our relationship to grow into more." She smirked. "Actually, he got a new carriage and wanted to show it off." She pulled her knee up on the swing and turned toward Anna Lisa. "Have you tried to talk to Billy Walker? You still like him, don't you? I noticed he watched you at church with obvious interest."

Anna Lisa nodded. "I've thought about it." She ducked her head. "But right now, I better get back home. I wanted to come over and tell you what had happened. Hopefully, Sarah's cab has taken her to the train station by now."

"Don't forget to talk to your mother about the interview."

"I won't. See you tomorrow." Anna Lisa stood and walked down the steps.

Relief flooded through Liz as she watched her friend trudge toward her parents' home around the corner. *Thank you, Jesus, that I found out what Richard was really like before it was too late.* The prayer of thanksgiving filled her heart.

The next morning, Abigail stepped up beside Liz as she waited in the church foyer for Michael. "I'm excited you've applied to be a Harvey Girl. It'll be fun to work together if you get hired. You'll like it. I know you will. You should probably be notified about your interview early next week. I received my notice in a few days."

"I'm eager to get the process started." Liz glanced at the door as Anna Lisa walked in with her parents. Richard wasn't with them. "I'm not sure about Anna Lisa. She hadn't talked to her mother about it when she visited me yesterday. She says she wants to be a Harvey Girl, but I'm not sure her heart's in it."

"Well, I guess it's up to her. She has to want to."

Liz nodded.

Just then, Michael entered the foyer and looked around. He smiled when he saw her.

"There's Michael." She glanced at Abigail. "I'll let you know when I hear."

"Alright."

Liz met Michael, and they walked into the sanctuary together. "I made it on time today." He touched her elbow as they strolled down the aisle.

When the last dishes were cleared away after Sunday dinner, Daniel and his brother-in-law, Arnaud Dumond, retired to the library. The boys went outside to play ball and Rachel and Ruth ran upstairs to play house in Rachel's room.

Elise turned to Aunt Millie. "I've told Liz what I remember as a Harvey Girl. But you had more experience. She's put in her application and is waiting for an interview appointment." She led the way from the dining room. "Let's take our lemonade into the sitting room where we can talk."

The three walked together up the hall into the cozy room and drew their chairs close to visit.

"I'm glad you've decided to be a Harvey Girl, Liz. It's a wonderful learning experience." Aunt Millie patted Liz's hand. "You learn social graces while you serve the most exciting people. I was eighteen when I was hired. My family lived on a small Ohio farm, and we didn't have much money. As the oldest, I needed to help with living expenses. The jobs close by couldn't provide the income we needed.

"My school teacher was considered progressive in her thoughts. She knew our family's need and showed me the ad for the Harvey Girl job in one of her magazines. At first, my father refused to consider the possibility that I could work in one of those "disreputable" eating establishments. However, our financial need outweighed his objections. I set out for Kansas City, scared to death of what I might encounter." She sat forward. "Needless to say, I was hired and worked for four years. I was extremely fortunate to work in Topeka my whole Harvey Girl career. Most girls had to move. It was difficult because I would barely get acquainted with them and they'd move to other Houses.

"A few months before your mama came to work, I was promoted to Head Waitress. We became close friends, partly because I liked her brother!" Millie laughed and turned toward Elise. "I remember when you and Tessa came to work the first day. You were both in awe of the Harvey House."

Elise nodded. "We were. Especially Tessa. She was scared of her shadow. She'd never been away from her family. We became dear friends during that month of training, and she was an excellent Harvey Girl. It was heart-wrenching when we separated."

"She lives in Hutchinson, Kansas, doesn't she?"

"Yes, her husband owns a large ranch near there. He was a widower with four children. She quit her job as a Harvey Girl and married him before her year was up. Then they had four of their own. She was from a large family, so that didn't intimidate her." Elise sighed. "I'd love to go see her and her family. I think one of her step-daughters is Head Waitress there in Hutchinson."

"You need to plan a visit." Millie relaxed and sipped her lemonade. "Did you hear that Fred Harvey passed away in March? He'd fought intestinal cancer for years. His sons have assumed leadership of the Fred Harvey Corporation. Supposedly, it will continue as it's been. His son, Ford, lives in Kansas City, and has taken over the management." She faced Liz. "He's just as tough about the rules as his dad. That's what makes the Harvey Houses so successful."

Julien and his cousin, Charles, ran into the room. "Mama, Adam and James have gone to the schoolyard to play ball. Can Charles and I go too?"

Elise glanced up. "Yes, you can go. Don't stay too long."

"Charles, you come when we call. We'll head home soon."

CHAPTER 8

It was Tuesday morning. Liz slouched in an overstuffed chair in the sitting room, engrossed in *Wuthering Heights.* A warm breeze wafted through the open window.

Adam bounded into the room and waved an envelope over his head. "Liz, you have a letter from the Fred Harvey office in Kansas City."

"Well, give it to me." Liz put down her book, sat up, and reached for the letter.

"What ya' give me for it?" Adam danced away, just out of reach.

"Adam Gilbertson, you give me that letter, right now. Or else."

"Or, else, what?"

Liz jumped up from the chair and grabbed for the envelope, while Adam avoided her reach.

"Ohh, you make me so mad sometimes. Give me that letter!"

Adam headed back out the door, just as Elise walked in.

"What's going on in here?"

"He's got my letter from the Harvey House office." Liz grabbed him and pulled it out of his hand. "Pesky brother!"

Adam laughed and ran from the room.

"You know, he wouldn't do that if he didn't love you."

Liz grimaced. "Some way to show it." She tore open the envelope, pulled out the paper, and scanned it. "They want me to come next Monday at ten o'clock for an interview. Wow, that's short notice. Do you think you could go to Kansas City with me?"

"Oh, honey, I can't go this weekend. The bazaar and auction for the Ladies Missionary Society are this Saturday. It's the largest fundraiser of the year, and since I'm the president, I have to be there. Maybe Anna Lisa's mother would want to go."

"I don't know if Anna Lisa's interview is scheduled on the same day. I'll go over and see if she got a letter." She folded the page and slid it back into the envelope.

The sun shone brightly as Liz hurried down the front porch steps. Excitement raced through her. She had an interview scheduled and hopefully, a job. She sprinted up the sidewalk to the corner and turned to the right, a route she'd walked countless times. She and Anna Lisa had grown up less than a block from each other. Liz slowed her pace and caught her breath as she approached the Stoops' red brick two-storied home. The front entrance was distinguished by imposing steps which led to an arched white door, flanked by well-trimmed greenery and white framed windows. Liz climbed the steps and twisted the knob on the doorbell.

A few seconds later, Anna Lisa's mother stood in the doorway, her arms crossed over her chest and a pinched expression on her face. "Hello, Liz." Her voice was sharp.

"Hello, Ma'am. May I talk to Anna Lisa?"

Mrs. Stoops sighed and gestured toward the stairs. "She's in her room. Go on up."

"Thanks, Ma'am." Liz gingerly stepped past her into the front hall. The room reflected tasteful elegance with hardwood floor and walnut furniture. Bright blue and green colored cushions accented the furnishings. She walked to the stairway on the right. She'd spent almost as much time in this house as her own.

Upstairs, Liz quietly knocked and slipped in the open door at the end of the hallway. Her friend lay across the bed, facing away from her. "Hey, Anna Lisa, you, okay?"

Anna Lisa sat up and faced her. Tears streaked her face. "I can't go with you, Liz. Mother nearly exploded when the letter came this morning." She looked down at her clenched hands. "With all that happened between Richard and Sarah, I didn't have a chance to talk to her. She's angry that I applied without asking her."

Liz sat beside her on the bed and sighed. "I was afraid of that."

Anna Lisa grimaced and spoke softly. "She's already upset with Richard. That whole affair was a fiasco."

Liz nodded. "Let's go for a walk, if your mother will let us."

"I'll ask her. I need to talk." She slipped her feet into her shoes.

A short while later, the two friends headed up the street toward Capitol Square. Anna Lisa heaved a huge sigh. "Mother was enamored with the fact that Richard brought home the daughter of a wealthy senator. She bragged a bit too much to the Ladies Missionary Society. Now she's embarrassed."

"She never did think I was good enough for her precious Richard."

"Oh, Liz. I don't think that's right. She wanted you two to get married."

"Huh, too late for that now." Liz glanced at her friend. "So why is she against you as a Harvey Girl?"

Anna Lisa looked down at the sidewalk. "She said it's not respectable for a young woman to work as a waitress in a railroad eating house. Then Father forbade me to go to the interview."

Liz raised her eyebrows. "So they think my mama is a low-class person? She worked as a Harvey Girl."

"I know. I don't think my parents feel that way. Maybe they don't remember that. It has more to do with their disappointment with Richard. They don't want me to be away right now." She stopped and faced Liz. "I want to be a Harvey Girl, and maybe I will someday, but I guess I better stay here. My parents want me to finish college, get my music degree."

"Is that what you want?"

Anna Lisa shrugged. "I don't have much choice."

They finished the block in silence then headed back to Anna Lisa's house. Liz slowed as they drew closer. "I'm sorry you can't go with me. I thought it'd be fun to work together. If you change your mind, let me know before Saturday."

"Okay, but I don't think I will." Anna Lisa smiled halfheart-edly and gave Liz a quick hug. "You know I'll always be your friend."

Liz nodded. Curiously, she felt a bit abandoned as her

friend turned, climbed the steps, and let herself into the house. They'd been friends since grade school and had shared so many experiences. This would have been another adventure together.

Did she want to go alone to be a Harvey Girl? As she turned homeward, heaviness settled around her shoulders and a lump of disappointment formed in her chest. The sting of eminent tears made her nose run. Why did she feel so bereft? She knew she was loved by her family, even by Anna Lisa. But she would, for the first time in her life, be going off alone.

The sense of loss sparked the yearning to know more about her true father and his family. There was an empty space in her heart. Were her grandparents alive? Did she have aunts, uncles, and cousins on that side of her family? How would she ever know?

She trudged slowly up the front walk and onto the porch, her enthusiasm dampened. Lucia had said there was a trunk that had belonged to her parents. Maybe there was some information about her father's family in it. Should she ask about it now before she set out on her own?

Her mother walked out of the dining room as Liz entered the front hall. "Was Anna Lisa excited? Is her interview close to your time?"

Liz shook her head. "Her parents have forbidden her to go. She can't go with me. She thinks it has a lot to do with Richard. Her mother's embarrassed about the situation with Sarah, and she doesn't want Anna Lisa to leave right now. They want her to finish college and pursue her music." She fell into step beside Elise."

"I'm sorry. Are you really disappointed?"

"I kind of expected it, really, but it does make me sad. It'll be strange not to have Anna Lisa with me."

"You can do this, Liz. I had to go by myself, and I survived." Elise put her arm around Liz's shoulders. "I think it'll be good for you. You'll make new friends and have new adventures."

Liz stopped and turned toward her. She felt the sting of tears again. "I know." She hesitated. "Mama, I need to ask you something. I've been wondering... Would it upset you terribly if I tried to find out about my real father's family? I know about my mother's family through Daddy, Grandpa and Uncle Thomas, but I don't know anything about my father. The questions have festered in my mind for a while."

"Oh, Sweetheart, no, that would be fine with us. We knew the time would come when you'd want to know. Your daddy and I understand your desire to know what you can about him."

"Lucia said there was a trunk with my parent's belongings in it."

Elise's face brightened. "That's right. There is a trunk. We brought it from the ranch when we moved here. It's in the attic. Let's find it."

"Lucia said I played dress-up with the clothes, and Grandma said I needed to be older so I could appreciate them."

Elise chuckled "Your grandma was a wise woman. She tried to contact your father's family when the accident happened but didn't have any luck." Elise put her arm around Liz's shoulders as they walked up the stairs and to the end of the hall. She opened the small door that led to the attic.

At the top of the narrow steps, Liz looked around. It was difficult to see in the half-light from only two small dormer windows on the front of the house. Boxes and crates sat in piles, along with assorted pieces of furniture. "How will we find the trunk? Do you know where it is?"

"It's in this corner." Elise moved some boxes and made her way across the room. "Here it is. Come, give me a hand, and we'll lift it out so we can see in it better."

Liz hurried to her side, hardly able to contain her excitement. The medium-sized steamer trunk looked like a treasure chest. Was it the key to her past?

She grabbed the handle nearest her, lifted it with Elise, and set in in the light. Dust whirled merrily in the sunbeam. "I can't believe I didn't know this was here."

"I know. I should've told you sooner. We brought it when we moved, but you were so small, and any mention of your mommy and daddy made you sad. Daniel and I didn't want to burden you with constant reminders that kept you from moving past the tragedy. We decided to wait until your curiosity spurred you to ask questions on your own. Then over time we forgot about it."

They shifted the trunk into a more open area near the windows, and Elise gave Liz a hug.

"There you are. It's all yours. You know that I love you more than I can tell you. You've been my little girl ever since I laid eyes on you in the train fifteen years ago, before I married your daddy. But I realize you want to learn more about your real parents and that's understandable. I know they were wonderful people, though I never got to meet them."

"Mama, Lucia also told me that you didn't adopt me because you thought I might want to keep my legal name."

Elise laughed. "You had quite a conversation with Lucia,

didn't you? Yes, we wanted you to make that decision. We would love to adopt you even now, but you need to decide if that's what you want. You're our daughter no matter what you decide."

"Thanks, Mama." Liz hugged her again. "Do you want to look in here with me?" She reached to open the latch. Anticipation spiraled through her as the lid creaked open.

Assorted jewelry lay in the small tray in the top of the trunk. "Oh, look! That's the diamond brooch my mother wore in the picture." She picked it up and rubbed her thumb over the diamonds in an elegant setting, then turned it over to look at the back. Her mother had worn it on her wedding dress. Just touching it, Liz felt a connection with her past that she'd never felt before.

Elise put her hand on Liz's shoulder. "Why don't we take this down to your room? You can look through it in a better light and be more comfortable. It's hot and stuffy up here."

Reluctantly, Liz laid the brooch back in the tray. "That makes sense, although it seems more like the past up here." She shut the lid, grabbed the handle on her side, and helped carry it to the stairs. "Whew, that's heavier than it looks. How will we get it down those narrow steps?"

Elise tugged it, so it was straight with the stairway. "We got it up here. It has to go down the same way. You go first; I'll hold on to this end."

Liz backed down and pulled the trunk, bump-by-bump down the steps.

They wrestled it down the hall and into the bedroom, setting it against the wall beside the bed. Elise smiled. "I'll let you go through this on your own. I'd love to see it, but you can show me the contents when you're ready."

Liz hugged her. "Thanks, Mama. This means the world to me. I love you so much."

"I know, Honey. Enjoy discovering your treasures. I'll call you for supper."

Liz sat on the side of the bed and eagerly opened the lid. She gingerly picked up the diamond brooch once more and caressed it, then picked up the picture from the bedside stand. The broach was the same. She held it to her breast. Her mother, the woman who had given birth to her, had worn that brooch. Tears sprang to her eyes. Slowly, she set it on the bed and looked further into the trunk. There were several pieces of jewelry, mostly silver: earrings, lapel bar pins, necklaces, and sleeve buttons. One accessory was a chain with a square diamond pendant. There were earrings to match. She held it up to the light. Beautiful! The diamonds sparkled in the sunlight.

There were also men's cufflinks and a black tie in the tray. Her Father's! Liz lifted a heavy object that was wrapped in cloth and unwound it carefully. Her eyes widened as a small, ornate dagger, with a distinctive crest on the handle, fell into her hand. What could that mean? She rubbed her thumb over the ornamentation, then laid it back into the tray.

Next to the jewelry were two small, flat purses; one a black leather chatelaine purse with a chain handle, the other an elegant black evening purse with beaded roses. Liz lifted the leather purse and opened the metal clasp. Surprised, she pulled out a neatly folded, lace handkerchief. There was also a small, flat, round container labeled "Lip and Cheek Color" and a cloth bag with coins in it. She dumped the money into her hand; a $5 gold piece; two $1 coins and several smaller amounts. Liz stared at the collection of items. *This was her mother's handbag. She'd carried it. She had touched these items.*

After a few moments, Liz picked up the other bag and looked in it. Disappointed, she frowned. It was empty.

The tray also held a hairbrush, comb and mirror, each with a matched, delicate, porcelain flower pattern, and several colorful hair bows. Liz lifted the wooden tray out and set it on the bed. Underneath, was a black straw hat ornamented with black ribbons and red silk flowers, a black fitted high-collared jacket with puffy sleeves, and a black skirt with ruffles on the back. Quickly, she grabbed the picture. *This was the dress Mother was wearing!* Reverently, she pulled the clothing from the trunk and laid the pieces on the bed. Tears sprang to her eyes again. This was the closest she would ever be to her mother this side of Heaven. She ran her hand over the glossy surface of the jacket as unfamiliar emotions of loss and grief swept over her. She turned back to the trunk and pulled out the next garment: a light blue silk dress with a high collar, puffy sleeves and lace down the front. It had a ridiculous amount of material pulled up into ruffles in the back. This was definitely an 1880s' gown that would have been worn only for special occasions.

In the bottom of the trunk was a man's black, double-breasted suit jacket with a high collar and pleats in the back along with matching trousers. It looked like they would fit a medium-built man. Suddenly, pent-up emotions boiled out in a torrent of grief. Liz covered her face with her hands and let the tears flow.

A few minutes later, Liz became dimly aware that Elise had moved the dresses to sit beside her on the bed. She whirled, buried her face against her mama's shoulder, and clung to her while sobs shook her body. After several moments, the sobs subsided, and she pulled back.

Elise looked into her eyes. "Oh, Honey, I heard you weeping from my sitting room. I'm so sorry. I didn't realize looking through the trunk would affect you this way."

"I...I don't know. Suddenly, it became so...so real. These were their clothes. The ones in the picture."

Elise hugged her. "Maybe we shouldn't have kept them."

Liz sat up. "Oh, no. I'm glad I got to see them. I needed to see them. It brought my parents to life for me...made them real." She wiped her tears. "I'm okay. At least I will be. Thank you and Daddy for providing such a good life for me. You're my real parents." She took the handkerchief Elise offered and blew her nose. "You know, I think I do want you and Daddy to adopt me. I want to be a Gilbertson." She hesitated. "I'd still like to find out about my father's family, but it's only curiosity, so I will know who they are."

Elise smiled. "Don't decide that right now. Wait until it's not such an emotional decision. There'll be other considerations." She gathered up the blue gown. "This looks familiar. It's like the dresses I wore when I was your age. We had to wear a bustle to support all these ruffles in the back. Glad we don't wear those anymore." She chuckled. "I think I still have a bustle up in the attic if you want to try it on."

"I'll do that. I'm curious what it looks and feels like." She dug back in the trunk and took out the men's clothing. "There are two boxes in the bottom. Let's see what's in them."

She pulled out the smaller one and set it between them

before she lifted the lid.

"These must've been my baby clothes." She unfolded a long white lace dress. "Ohh, that's beautiful. It's hard to believe I actually wore that." She held it to her cheek. "It's so soft. I'll save it for my own little girl someday."

"You probably wore that for your dedication at church." Elise laid the lace dress aside and took out other dresses and baby gowns.

"They're all so small." Liz lifted a tiny gown. "Hopefully, I'll get married and have a baby who can wear them."

They refolded the clothes and laid them in the box. Liz replaced it in the trunk and took out the other container.

"That might be their papers. Probably from their desk." Elise began folding the black skirt and jacket as Liz opened the second box.

"Oh, look. There are more pictures. Here's one of my mother and father with me when I was a baby. And another one of me on a little chair." She took them out and gazed at them. "I never saw myself as a baby."

Elise smiled. "I didn't either. You were four when I saw you the first time. You were a beautiful baby. Look at all those blonde curls. You look just like your father."

"Here's another picture of our family with some other people. I wonder if Lucia knows who they are."

"She's probably still here. Do you want me to go find her? I'm sure she'd like to see the items in the trunk. She knew your parents better than any of us."

"If you don't mind. I'd like that. Hopefully, she'll know more about my parents' clothes and jewelry."

Liz riffled through the papers while she waited for her mother to find Lucia. A few minutes later, Elise and Lucia stepped into the room. Lucia looked at the trunk, then walked to Liz's side to give her a hug. "Your mama said you'd opened the chest."

"Yes. Does this look familiar? You're probably the one who packed it."

Lucia nodded. "I did. That was a difficult day."

Liz picked up the brooch from the jewelry tray. "Do you recognize this?"

"Oh, yes. Your father got that for Mary to wear at their wedding. She wore it every time she dressed for a special occasion." Lucia picked up the dagger. "This was very important to your father. He kept it prominently displayed on a shelf in their dining room. I suppose the crest is significant, but I don't know how you'd find out what it stands for."

Liz held up the leather purse. "Look, there was money and a handkerchief in this."

Lucia smiled. "That was the handbag your mama usually carried." She ran her hand over the fabric of the black dress jacket. "Your mother wore this for her wedding." She pointed to the blue dress. "And this was her favorite gown. I'm not sure why I put that in. A whim, I guess." She sighed. "The day we left Columbia is as clear in my mind as yesterday. We had to go through everything and leave in such a hurry. I wasn't sure I'd recover. Your Uncle Daniel was determined. He insisted I go with you to the ranch." She chuckled. "I'm glad he did. If he hadn't, I'd never have met my Henry." She sat on the bed and pulled the box from the bottom of the trunk. "These are your baby clothes. You were such a sweet baby."

"Here are some pictures." Liz handed them to Lucia.

Lucia studied them and sighed again. "They bring back happy memories. I was sixteen when they hired me as their housekeeper and nanny. You were just three months old." She held up the photo with the unknown people. "These were their friends. They spent a lot of time together."

"Do you know who they were? Would they know about my father's family?"

Lucia shook her head. "Their names were William and Edna, but that's all I know about them." She handed the pictures back to Liz. "Thank you for showing these to me. I better finish cleaning the library, then I need to get home. Henry will want his supper."

Liz hugged her. "Thank you for all the information. I'm glad you could see it."

Just then, Rachel skipped into the room, skidding to a stop as she saw the trunk. "What are you doin'? What's in there?" She frowned.

Liz patted the bed beside her. "Come here, Rachel, I'll explain." She picked up the picture of her parents from the bedside stand. "See these people? They were my daddy and mommy. They were killed in an accident when I was four. My mother, this lady, was your daddy's sister. I went to live with Grandpa and Grandma Gilbertson. Then when Daddy and Mama got married, they brought me to live with them, to be their little girl, before you and Adam and Julien were born. So we are really cousins, but you are my sister, too. That's even better!"

Rachel reached to hold the photo. She puckered her forehead. "These were your mommy and daddy? They don't look happy."

Liz laughed. "No, they don't, do they?" She picked up the

other picture with her in it. "They look happier here. That's my baby picture. And, yes, they were my first parents, but Daddy and Mama have been my parents as long as I can remember!"

"Ohh, you were so cute."

"Here's some baby clothes I wore." Liz lifted out the small box and removed the lid.

"Oooh," Rachel whispered on her expelled breath. She touched the white lace dress. "That's beautiful. Look, you have it on in your baby picture."

"Here's some jewelry and a purse that was in the trunk."

Rachel fingered the brooch and other pieces. "That's a pretty necklace."

Liz picked up a red bow. "You can have this one."

"Really? Thank you. I'll take good care of it." Rachel held it to her chest. "It'll match my new dress." She threw her arms around Liz. "Thanks for showing me your treasures. I'm glad you're my big sister."

"I'm delighted, too."

Liz put the lid back on the box. "I'll go through these papers later. I've seen enough for one day."

She rewrapped the dagger and placed it in the tray then picked up the diamond necklace. "Do you think this is too fancy to wear to church Sunday?"

"No. It'll be elegant with your blue dress." Elise helped her refold the clothes and place them in the trunk. "Do you want to leave it here or move it into the spare bedroom?"

"Just leave it here. I'd like to show the contents to Anna Lisa. She'll want to see them."

"Of course she will. That's the way good friends are."

Liz nodded as she ran her hand over the trunk's surface and the leather trim. "Maybe I can take this if I become a Harvey Girl. I could put these clothes in another box."

"Wonderful idea! You'll need a nice trunk, especially if you're transferred to a different House. There's a smaller trunk upstairs for these other items." Elise moved toward the door.

The next morning, Liz carried the box of documents, pictures, and letters onto the front porch. The sun shone, and a cool breeze drifted toward her. What secrets would the papers reveal? Maybe she would find a clue to the identity of her father's family. She sat on the swing, pushing with her toe to make it rock slowly, as she opened the box. Her baby picture was on top. She took it out and studied it as a smile crossed her face. She'd been a cute baby.

"What are you studying so intently?"

Liz looked up as Anna Lisa walked onto the porch. "Oh, I'm so excited to see you. Come sit. I have treasures to show you." She pulled the box closer then handed Anna Lisa the picture as she seated herself.

"What a cute baby. Who is it?"

"Look closely. See if you can guess?"

"Is this you?" Anna Lisa studied Liz with a quizzical smile. "Where did you get this?"

Liz pointed at the box. "It was in here with a lot of other papers and documents. I told Mama I wanted to find out about my early life and my father's family and she showed me a trunk that belonged to my real parents. I can't wait to show it to you. But this was in it." She took out the other pictures. "Here's a picture of me with my parents."

Anna Lisa peered at it. "Now I can tell. In this picture, you look like your father even to the blond hair. What else is in the box?"

Liz riffled through the papers. "My parent's marriage certificate and my father's license to practice law." She handed them to Anna Lisa then picked up the next document. "And, his diploma from Harvard University." Liz sat back. "Michael graduated from Harvard. How's that for a coincidence?"

Anna Lisa raised her eyebrows. "Harvard's very prestigious, but since both men are from Boston, it's probably not too unusual. It does make your father seem more real, though, doesn't it?"

Liz nodded. "Wait until you see what's in the trunk." She removed a packet of letters and laid them beside the box. "I think these are all from my Grandpa and Grandma Gilbertson. I'll read them later." Under them were two other envelopes, both sealed. She pulled them out. "Look, Anna Lisa, this one's addressed to Mr. and Mrs. William Tilman. It has a box number in Boston." *Could that be her grandfather's name?* A thrill raced through her. Maybe this was her first lead to her father's family. The postmark was 1880, the year her parents were married.

Anna Lisa frowned. "It's stamped "Return to sender." Why do you suppose it was sent back? Maybe they'd moved."

"Maybe. Lucia said my grandfather had an argument with my father when he decided to move West and become a lawyer. Apparently, he didn't have any contact with his parents. At least, he didn't talk about them." Liz studied the address. What if it was the same after twenty years? Not likely. "Should I open it? I feel like an intruder into someone else's business."

Anna Lisa laughed. "I don't think they'll care. It's been twenty years. Besides, who else's business is it?"

Liz slipped her finger under the flap and worked it open, careful not to tear it. She unfolded the single sheet of paper it contained and read.

June 1880

Dear Father and Mother,

I wanted you to know I have married the most wonderful woman. Her name is Mary Gilbertson. She is from Emporia, Kansas, where her father owns a ranch.

I heard of a lawyer in Columbia, Missouri, who is about to retire. He wants a young lawyer to take over his practice. I've contacted him, and we'll move there within the month. I'll let you know our new address if you're interested.

I'm sorry for our misunderstanding. I hope you can forgive me.

With love,

Your son, George

Liz gazed at the letter through her tears. "He tried to make amends." She spoke in a whisper. "My grandparents didn't even open the letter. Maybe I don't want to find out any more about them."

Anna Lisa sat beside her in sympathetic silence while Liz's tears flowed. Liz pulled a handkerchief from her pocket and wiped her eyes as her shoulders slumped. "This is almost too much to take in."

Anna Lisa touched her arm. "I'm sorry, my friend, but this is all in the past. You have a wonderful family who loves you dearly."

"I know." Liz gave her friend a shaky smile. "You're right. None of this really matters."

Anna Lisa looked in the box. "Do you want to see what the other envelope is?"

"Might as well go through it all while we're at it."

"We don't have to."

"I know, but let's look, then I'll put it behind me. If I don't, I'll wonder what it is." Liz turned it over. "It just has my father's name on the front. Look, it's been opened. It's not sealed." She took out the small card.

Dear George,

I'm so proud of you for your hard work as you pursued your degree and passed your bar exam. I want you to have this Scottish sgian (dagger) which belonged to your great-grandfather. I know your father is not pleased with your decision to travel West, but I wish you good fortune. Please do not forget your family heritage. I would love to hear from you now and then

Love,

Grandmother Mabel

Liz sat back with a sigh. "Well, at least he had someone who loved him." She smiled. "That clears up the mystery of the dagger."

"Dagger?"

"Oh, right. You haven't seen it." She placed the papers back in the box and put the lid on. "Come upstairs, and I'll show you my legacy."

Later, they sat on the edge of the bed, the tray of jewelry between them. "It's kind of spooky to see the clothes your parents wore, and this dagger. What did his grandmother call it? A *sgian?* I never heard of that! It's all so interesting."

"I know. It is, isn't it?" Liz scrunched up her face. "I'll put the clothes back in the attic, but I think I'll use the trunk. It's time to move on with my life. I needed this to satisfy my curiosity about my past, though."

"You should keep this jewelry out and wear it." Anna Lisa touched the brooch. "This is beautiful."

"I will, and the papers." Liz placed the jewelry tray on the top of the trunk and turned back to her friend. "Any second thoughts about the Harvey Girl job?"

Anna Lisa lowered her head. "I'm sorry I acted so badly yesterday. I was angry with my parents, but it wasn't fair to take it out on you. I'd like to come with you, but I don't think I can now. I have to respect my parents' wishes."

She touched Liz's hand. "Please don't let it come between us. You're my best friend in the whole world, and you always will be."

"I know, Anna Lisa. That's the way I feel about you too. Forever, friends, that's us."

Chapter 9

Wednesday afternoon, Michael stood up from the desk in his office at the ATSF building and glanced out the window. A half smile crossed his face as he thought about his office overlooking someone's backyard, and not the Capitol building.

He stretched his back and rotated his stiff shoulders. He'd been staring at numbers all day. It was his job to make sure the figures in the account books balanced. He was amazed at the amount of money that changed hands in just a day on the vast railroad line. Income from the passenger's fares; freight moved from Chicago to California and to the Gulf; and salaries for the massive numbers of employees.

The account books for the Harvey Houses baffled him. They were nearly always in the red. He shook his head. He'd been told not to attempt to balance them. "Fred Harvey demands only the best for his customers. He'll not allow any of his houses to cut corners on supplies or services."

As difficult as it was to let the overages pass, Michael had to admit in the end, there was almost always a profit. The sheer number of customers the Harvey Houses brought to the rail line obviously worked well for the ATSF and the Fred Harvey Company.

He arranged the ledgers in order on his bookshelf. It was almost time for him to head to the boarding house.

As he slid the last book into place, Daniel Gilbertson stepped into the room. "You about finished for the day? Is your office satisfactory? I haven't had a chance to talk with you much this week. I've been occupied with meetings."

Michael acknowledged the greeting with a nod. "I've been busy, that's for certain." He grinned at his boss. "It's good that I enjoy figures and numbers."

"You still at the boarding house down by the depot?"

"Yes. It's not large or fancy, but it works for now. I'll probably look for a room closer, soon. At least I can drive my carriage now instead of taking the trolley."

"We've been more than pleased with your work so far. I'm glad you've settled in. Let me know if you need anything."

"Thank you, sir. I appreciate that."

"Are you ready to leave? I'll walk out with you."

Michael grabbed his valise and followed Daniel. "I enjoy the slower pace and small-town feel of Topeka."

"Good, I was afraid you'd miss the big city atmosphere of Boston."

"No, sir, I think I'll do very well here. Everyone's friendly, and I especially enjoy your church. I've made new acquaintances and heard Bible stories that I'd never known before.

"I'm glad. If you have any questions, don't hesitate to ask."

"As a matter of fact, sir, I do have a question. Mrs. Barrett gave me a Bible her daughter doesn't use anymore. I read in Matthew about the parable of the sower. If the seed falls on the stony ground or in the thorns, can that ground be changed into the good ground?"

Daniel stopped and faced Michael. "That's a good question. I'd never considered it from that perspective." He paused in thought. "I'm positive it can. Anyone who calls on Jesus and confesses his sins will be saved. You know, God's Word is powerful, like a spade or a trowel. The Bible calls it a two-edged sword. If a person, whose heart had been stony or thorny, reads and studies the Bible, God can make his heart into the good ground to accept His Word."

Michael nodded slowly. "No disrespect intended, but I think my parents are like thorny ground. They're so busy with their social life, they've ignored what they've heard in church." He frowned. "I've never heard most of the Bible stories."

"I'm thrilled you've begun to read it. I'd be honored to discuss any other questions you run across."

"Yes, sir. Thank you, sir."

They continued across the parking lot. Daniel untied his horse and stepped up into the carriage. He turned toward Michael. "Liz will be gone to Kansas City over the weekend for her interview with Fred Harvey, and Elise has a bazaar at the church. You might as well come over and spend time with the boys and me."

"Thank you. I'll plan to do that." Michael released Dolly and stepped up into his carriage. As he followed his employer out of the lot, he decided to drive past some of the boarding houses Liz had pointed out. He'd received his first paycheck the day before, so could afford to pay more rent. As Michael turned up the street away from the Capitol Square, he saw several signs advertising rooms for rent. One Victorian-style house, with large wrap-around porches on both the lower and upper floor and a bay window on the front, stood out. Well-groomed bushes flanked the front steps. The appearance enticed him to stop and check it out.

He pulled his carriage to the side of the street and studied the house. He hadn't expected to move so soon, but this caught his fancy. He jumped down from his carriage, secured Dolly, and strolled up the steps to the front door. Without hesitation, he turned the knob on the doorbell.

After a short delay, the door opened, and a middle-aged woman appeared. She wore a dark skirt and white high-necked blouse. Her hair was styled in a neat chignon. "May I help you?"

"Yes, my name's Michael McKey." He pointed to the sign in the yard. "I'm here to inquire about the room for rent. Is it still available?"

The woman studied him slowly, then smiled. "It's available. Do you have a reference?"

"I work at the ATSF headquarters. I can bring a reference tomorrow. Is that soon enough?"

She nodded her head. "My name's Mrs. Cartier. Follow me. I'll show you the room.

Michael stepped through the doorway and walked behind her through the front hall to an ornate staircase. At the top, they turned left to the room on the backside of the house. She stepped back and allowed him to enter. Michael drew in his breath. The room was twice the size of his room at Mrs. Barrett's. Sunshine streamed through a large window overlooking a backyard garden. The furnishings included a bed, dresser, desk with a chair, and a large wardrobe. Everything was spotless.

He turned toward Mrs. Cartier. "I'm interested. How much is the rent?"

"It's three dollars and fifty cents a month. This is a respectable area, after all." Then following a short pause, she added. "No women in your room unless you're married."

"I understand. I need to be closer to my work. I'll be back with a reference tomorrow. Do I need to leave a deposit?"

"A dollar will hold it for you. That'll apply to your first month's rent." As Mrs. Cartier walked with him back to the staircase, she motioned toward the shared bathroom and then pointed to the end of the hall. "That door leads to the upstairs porch. There's a nice breeze out there in the summer. Feel free to use it." They descended to the front door, and Michael handed her the bill. "I'll see you tomorrow."

Michael looked back at the house as he pulled his rig out into the street. He shook his head, amazed at all that had happened in the last hour. He'd planned to stay at Mrs. Barrett's a bit longer, but circumstances had fallen into place beautifully.

A short time later, he left his rig at the livery. After grooming and feeding Dolly, he strode the two blocks to the boarding house. He looked forward to a short pleasant walk from the new residence instead of the drive every day.

Mrs. Barrett met him at the door. "You're late today." She handed him a letter. "This came in the mail for you."

Michael took the envelope. "Thank you. Do you have a moment to talk?" He followed her into the dining room. "After work, I decided to drive past some of the rooming houses closer to the ATSF building. One that had a vacancy drew my attention, so I inquired about it and decided to rent it. I've enjoyed my stay here, but I think it would be to my advantage to be closer, and it would eliminate the drive. If I can get a reference from my boss, I'll move over the weekend."

Mrs. Barrett furrowed her brow. "I was afraid this would happen once you got established. I've appreciated you. You've been a good renter." She put her hand on his shoulder. "You remind me of my son, Oliver, who died seven years ago."

"Oh, I'm sorry to hear that."

"A body just has to keep on goin' in spite of what life throws out, but it's nice to know there are other respectable young men out there. The Lord watches over me, and He will you, too." She smiled. "I'll write a recommendation for you if that would help."

"Would you? I'd appreciate it."

"Oh, and Michael, keep the Bible I gave you." She smiled. "That is, if you promise to read it."

"Thank you, Mrs. Barrett. I've read it every day. You've been very kind to me."

He turned and headed up to his room. He opened the curtain and the window then sat on the edge of his bed. The room seemed even smaller and more crowded than before.

The letter was from his cousin, Clara Bryan. He tore open the envelope and scanned the letter quickly.

Dear Michael,

Thank you for the information about the job with the Fred Harvey Company. I received the application and will get it sent in as soon as possible. I've wanted to get away from Boston for quite some time. This position sounds ideal.

Emotions have been in an upheaval around here since my grandfather passed away several months ago. He left debts and correspondence that Grandma Grace wasn't aware of, so she's trying to sort it all out. Mother has tried to help. The other day, they went to the bank and visited with your father and brother. They said you'd arrived safely and settled in.

I hope the Harvey Girl job works out. I would like to spend time with you. Of all the family, you and I have the most in common. I'll keep you informed as I know more."

Your loving cousin,

Clara

Michael smiled. He looked forward to Clara's arrival. She was full of life, and it would be terrific to have someone from his family close.

⟳

Liz folded her new nightgown and placed it in the bag on her bed with her undergarments. She ran through the mental list of items needed for her weekend in Kansas City.

She rubbed the back of her neck, and her stomach tensed. It was the first time she had ever traveled alone. She was glad she could stay with Uncle Jule, Elise's youngest brother, and Aunt Rosanne. Uncle Jule was a banker in Kansas City.

Liz heaved a sigh. The last week had exhausted her emotionally. First, there was Anna Lisa's dispute with her parents and the decision to stay behind. Then Liz had discovered her parents' old trunk. Even though she was nervous about the upcoming interview, it would be a nice change to get away for a few days.

She walked to the dresser and picked up the hairbrush that

had belonged to her mother. She looked in the mirror. It had rained most of the day, and the dampness made her hair frizzy and wavy. How would she look attractive and in control if she had flyaway hair? She pulled out the pins, brushed it, then reassembled the chignon, but the errant ringlets would not cooperate. "Oh, piffle! It'll just have to be that way." She set down the hairbrush. Hopefully, it wouldn't rain on Monday.

As she turned away from the dresser, Adam stuck his head through her door. "Liz, you'll never guess who's at the door and wants to talk to you."

Liz frowned. "Who'd want to talk to me? In this rain?"

Adam cocked his head, a decided twinkle in his eyes. "Just take a wild guess."

"Michael?"

"Nope. Well...but someone else,"

Liz felt her eyes go wide. "Not Richard?"

"Yes, Richard." He raised his eyebrows and made a face. "He wants to speak with you."

"He can, jolly well, wait till I get good and ready." Liz placed her hands on her hips.

"Oh, and by the way, he's not the only one here."

"Adam, what do you mean?" Liz's head felt light and panic spiraled through her. "Who..? Oh, no, not Michael. Is he here? You said he wasn't."

"He wasn't who I was talking about." Adam shook his head slowly, and a smile touched his lips. "Just thought you'd want to know."

"Thanks, heaps."

"Anytime." Adam disappeared from the doorway.

Liz clenched her fists and scowled. "Ohh, that Richard. Of all the nerve for him to show up now." She stomped her foot. How could she ever have thought she loved him? What would she do with both him and Michael waiting to talk to her?

Adam reappeared in the doorway. "Julien just invited Michael in and left Richard on the porch." A huge grin split his face.

"You're kidding me. That's rude." A chuckle bubbled up and dissipated her anger. "I shouldn't laugh, but it is kind of funny after the way he's treated me." She put her hand over her mouth. "I better go down and talk to him."

She marched out of the room and down the stairs. She could hear Julien and Michael in the library as she hurried past. Thankfully, she wouldn't have to face both him and Richard at the same time in the same room. As she reached the front door, she could see Richard was headed off the porch. She opened the screen door. "Richard, I'm sorry it took me a bit to get out here. What was it you wanted?" The rain had diminished to a light mist.

He spun around and grabbed the banister as he nearly lost his balance on the wet step. "Oh, Liz. I'm glad you came out." He walked toward her. "I'm sorry I treated you the way I did. Can you please forgive me?" He reached to take her arm and headed toward the swing. "I know, now, it was you I loved all along. I should never have broken our engagement."

Liz pulled away from his hand, crossed her arms, and cocked her head. "Oh, really." She could hear the sarcasm in her voice. "It's a mite late for that, isn't it? After you brought your rich girlfriend home and introduced me as your friend? I'm sorry, Richard. It's too little, too late. In fact, I'm relieved you called it off. I'm not ready for marriage. I've got other plans." She stepped back. *How could she have ever thought she loved him?*

He moved toward her and used his supercilious voice. "I heard about the interview to be a Harvey Girl. You don't need to do that. I only have one more year in Manhattan, then we can get married. Once I get a job, I'll be able to support you."

Liz felt the heat rise up her chest into her neck. She clenched her fists. "Of all the nerve! Like I would even consider marrying you now! You can go back to your college studies and stay there for all I care. I can take care of myself very well, thank you, and I don't need you to support me. Now, go and don't come back!" She whirled around and stomped into the house.

Adam leaned against the wall beside the library door, in full earshot of the open screen door to the porch. He straightened and gave her a thumbs up as she walked toward him. "Way to go, sis." He grinned. "I'm proud of you."

"Well, I'm not proud, but I had to do it. I just wish I hadn't lost my temper."

Michael stepped from the library, and Julien peeked out around him. "What was that I heard out here?" Michael scrunched his brow. "Did he really expect you to take him back after the way he treated you? What a rapscallion."

Liz nodded. "You're right about that. Sorry you overheard. I'm afraid you saw my unpleasant side, Michael,"

He grinned. "That's no problem with me. He deserved it." He pulled Clara's letter from his pocket. "I heard from my cousin. She received her Harvey Girl application and planned to send it in. Hopefully, she'll get scheduled for an interview soon. I think you'll like her."

"I'm eager to meet her. Wouldn't it be great if she was in

is checked. You'll be in passenger car two. The train should be here before long." He glanced toward the platform. "There's the whistle now. We need to wait while the passengers disembark. Then you can board. Are you excited?"

Liz nodded as the train pulled to a stop and they watched the passengers stream up the stairs to the Harvey House. "I'm also nervous. I've never traveled alone."

"You'll be fine. I wish one of us could go with you, but there are too many demands on us this weekend."

"I know. Just pray that I do well in my interview. I've read all the rules and am confident I can abide by them without any trouble."

"We'll pray for you. Uncle Jule will meet you in the Union Depot so you won't be alone.." Elise gave her a hug.

They all walked to the platform. The train stretched out as far as Liz could see.

Daniel pointed to the second car behind the massive, puffing engine and coal car. "There's your car. Have an enjoyable weekend in the city. We'll see you Monday evening." He hugged Liz. "You'll do great. I'm proud of you."

They headed to the passenger car. Liz was elated. Finally, she'd be able to step out on her own. She turned and again hugged her parents and Rachel. She chuckled as Adam and Julien ducked out of reach.

The porter, waiting by car two, greeted Liz and assisted her up the steps and through the door. "Have a good trip," he nodded and smiled.

Liz stepped into the train car and scanned the interior. The red plush bench seats extended on both sides from back to front;

two seats faced each other to facilitate conversation. Her place was number six on the right, the side away from the depot. She wouldn't be able to see her family on the platform.

She walked along the aisle and slid into the seat closest to the window. Who would her seatmate be? Before long, a young woman with two children sat opposite her. The older child, a girl, appeared to be eleven-or twelve-years-old and the younger, a boy, maybe five or six.

Liz placed her small valise on the floor by her feet, then straightened and glanced across the space between them. The woman settled the children beside her, then looked up. "Hello. Are you traveling alone?"

Liz smiled tentatively and nodded. "I'm headed to Kansas City for an interview to become a Harvey Girl."

The other woman held out her hand. "My name's Mary Faulkner, and these are my children, Susie and Ben. We're going to visit my mother in Kansas City. Her birthday is this weekend. Would you mind if Susie sat with you? It's crowded with them both over here."

"Not at all. In fact, I'd enjoy her company." Liz patted the seat beside her. "Come on over, Susie. By the way, my name's Liz Gilbertson." She smiled. "This reminds me of my first train ride. But, I was only four and you are much more grown up than that."

Susie moved over and sat down beside her. She smiled shyly at Liz.

Mary's face lit up. "I think it's wonderful you want to be a Harvey Girl. My husband and I went to the Harvey House for our anniversary. It's the best place to eat in Topeka."

"I think so too. I hope I get the job."

"Oh, I bet you will."

"These seats are plush, aren't they? I wonder what the Pullman cars and the dining car are like? Have you ridden the train before?"

"I've gone a few times to see my mother. It's not a long trip, only takes about an hour."

Just then, a heavy-set, middle-aged man walked up the aisle and looked at the seat beside Liz. A heavy stench of whiskey and tobacco emanated from him. "I see... someone stole...my seat."

Liz tensed and felt her heart rate increase. Her mouth felt dry.

"You must be mistaken, sir." Mary's voice intruded on Liz's thoughts. "These seats are taken." She pointed to a vacant one further up in the car. "There's an empty one. Why don't you sit there?"

The man shook his head and shuffled on up the aisle. "Can't trust the railroad. Probably double-booked."

Liz released her breath with a sigh. "Thank you, Mary." She sagged against the back of the seat. "You thought that might happen, didn't you?" She put her arm around Susie. "God sent you and Susie along to protect me."

Mary nodded and laughed. "I'm glad we were here."

"Me, too."

The train whistle sounded, and she heard the rumble of the wheels as the train moved forward. The porter maneuvered down the aisle and collected tickets. Liz stared vacantly out the window as they left the depot. Did her family wave? She longed for a glimpse of them. Her shoulders slumped, and a lump rose in her throat. If only Anna Lisa could've come along. She'd wanted to work with her friend, but that wasn't to be, at least not now. What would Michael's cousin be like? He'd said her name was Clara. Maybe she'd have her interview on Monday, too. Hopefully, they would become friends.

She laid her head against the back of the seat and let her mind wander to the weekend ahead and to the last three weeks. Had it only been three weeks since Michael arrived from Boston to work for her father? She'd gone from uncertainty about her future to the decision to become a Harvey Girl, from questions about her parents to the discovery of the trunk which contained their belongings, and from the knowledge that her intended husband had jilted her for another woman to a new friendship with Michael. What did her future hold? Would she pass the interview?

She was eager to see Uncle Jule and Aunt Roseann. If she remembered right, Uncle Jule walked with a pronounced limp due to an accident when he was a teenager.

Liz surveyed the scenery out the train window. As they drew closer to Kansas City, the grassy prairie gave way to occasional farmsteads and groves of trees. Cattle grazed on the undulating hills. What a beautiful time of year! The grass and leaves on the trees were green with abundant life.

Before long, the houses were situated closer together, and the train entered the outskirts of the city. Anticipation filled her. Kansas City was much larger than Topeka.

"It looks like we're about there." Mary took a small mirror from her handbag and checked her hair. She patted a few straggling curls into place. "I'm glad it's not raining today. Yesterday was miserable."

"I agree." Liz gathered her valise and her purse. "The rain wreaks unspeakable havoc with my naturally curly hair."

Mary chuckled. "It looks charming."

A few minutes later, the train arrived at the Union Depot and pulled under the canopy beside the large stone building. "Wow, this makes our depot in Topeka look minuscule. It's at least twice as big." Liz stood to follow Mary and her children to the door of the passenger car. After they disembarked, they followed the other passengers up the walkway, under the canopy, to the highly ornamented arched doorway into the spacious lobby.

Wide-eyed, Liz looked around the large room, taking in the chandeliers suspended from the vaulted ceilings and the walnut and bronze fixtures. A sizeable ornate staircase dominated the end of the room. Men and women, some fashionably dressed, others in shabby attire, some with children in tow and some intent on their business pursuits, milled about.

"Do you have someone to meet you?" Once again, Mary's voice pulled her from her awed reverie.

"Yes, my Uncle Jule should be here, but how will I ever find him in this crush of people?"

"Did he give you instructions?"

"He said, in his letter, that he'd wait near the chairs and couches in the center of the room. Look there's some over there." Liz pointed then turned to Mary. "I don't know how I can thank you enough. You've been such a blessing to me. It would have been horrible if that man had sat with me."

"I am glad God put us together." Mary gave her a hug. "You do well in that interview, and we'll come into the Harvey House for a meal."

Liz smiled. "It's a deal."

Mary and her children walked with Liz across the room. Brocade upholstered chairs and brown and red plush loveseats were scattered cozily in small groupings. Potted plants completed the comfortable sitting area. As they approached, a tall young man rose from one of the chairs and walked toward her. She noted his pronounced limp.

"There he is." Liz rushed forward and embraced him. "It's so good to see you, Uncle Jule."

She stepped back and looked around for Mary, Susie, and Ben. They were nowhere to be seen. She frowned as she scanned the crowd. "Was she an angel?"

Jule stepped up beside her. "What?"

"I wanted to introduce you to my new friends from the train, but I guess they're gone." Liz turned slowly back to Uncle Jule. "Well, let's go. I'm anxious to see Aunt Roseann and Ellie."

"They wanted to come, but Roseann didn't want to ride on the trolley, so she decided they would stay home and wait for you there."

Liz nodded as she looked around the lobby. "I have to use the ladies room."

Uncle Jule pointed to a sign in the corner. "I'll go ahead and get your bag and wait for you in front of the depot. We need to be on our way soon. Roseann's preparing dinner, so I don't want to be too late." He started across the room as Liz headed for the bathroom. She walked through a spacious lounge and powder room to the small rooms in the back.

After she refreshed herself, Liz joined Uncle Jule outside. She studied the massive structure. "This is incredible. It looks like a French chateau or a castle with the towers and cupolas. I love the style. And look at the huge clock."

"Some people think it's too fancy, but I like it." Jule pointed toward the trolley tracks which lead up from the depot. "I came down the Ninth Street Incline from Quality Hill, which is quite a noisy ride. We'll go back on the longer trolley track. We avoid a carriage ride down here to the West Bottoms. It's less than reputable, and there's very little parking space. Most commuters ride the trolley." He led the way down the boardwalk to a ticket booth. "Here's where we board." He removed some coins from his pocket and bought their tickets.

Liz took one last look at the Union Depot as they boarded the trolley. She would have her interview here on Monday. She took a deep breath and stepped resolutely forward.

Chapter 11

"There's a tunnel ahead, but it isn't very long." Uncle Jule pointed. Lanterns situated along the sides flitted past. A few minutes later, they emerged into sunshine and traveled over a trestle bridge that spanned several streets. Liz grinned. She'd ridden the trolley at home many times, but this was more exhilarating. Shortly, they turned onto Grand Street. This appeared to be closer to the central part of town. Houses were more substantial and prominent. After six or seven blocks, they turned left onto Fifteenth Street.

"We're almost home." Uncle Jule reached up and pulled the cord which extended from the front to the back of the car and the trolley screeched to a stop. "We get off here. Our house is the third one on the right."

They trudged, bags in hand, up the dirt street. The red brick house had white trim, a brick archway that led to the backyard, and bright colored petunias in a flower bed by the steps. As they approached, the front door flew open, and Ellie darted off the porch. "I thought you'd never get here. I've waited and waited." She gave Liz a hug. "Come see my playhouse."

Just then, Roseann stepped onto the porch. "Ellie, there'll be plenty of time for that." She turned to Liz with a smile. "It's good to see you. I'll bet you're tired and hungry."

Liz climbed the steps and hugged Aunt Roseann. "I'm a bit hungry, but I'm not tired. The trip went so fast, and all the new sights kept me enthralled."

Roseann directed her into the house as Ellie ran to the backyard. "Come in. I have dinner ready. There's water in the washroom. You can freshen up, if you care to, while I get the food taken up. I fried chicken and made mashed potatoes and gravy. We've pulled some radishes and lettuce from our garden, so we'll have a fresh salad."

"Yum, that sounds wonderful." Liz washed her hands in the basin of water. "I love your house. It's so cozy."

"Thank you. We like it. It's so much nicer than the small one we had before. We moved here last fall." Aunt Roseann set the food on the table, then placed her hand on her abdomen. "I don't know if you noticed, but we're expecting another little one in September. We haven't told anyone since I've had so much trouble getting in the family way. Then with all the miscarriages, I wanted to be sure the baby progressed before I shared the news. I have a wonderful midwife, and she thinks we're fine." She smiled. "Ellie doesn't know yet."

"Oh, Aunt Roseann, I'm so happy for you." Liz gave her a quick hug. "I'll pray for a healthy pregnancy and delivery."

"Bless you." Roseann stepped to the back screen door. "Ellie, you need to come in and wash up. You can play all afternoon."

She turned toward the kitchen as Ellie dashed in.

Soon, they were all seated at the table, and Uncle Jule thanked God for the food. After the prayer, Liz looked around the table at her family. She was thankful for them. Though they weren't her blood relatives, they loved her, and she loved them. God had given them to her. She didn't know why she craved more.

Liz looked at Uncle Jule. "Mama wondered if you'd heard from Aunt Marie or Aunt Justine?" She placed a piece of chicken on her plate. "We received a letter about a month ago, from Aunt Justine. She said they were all well. Uncle Paul and their son, David, had the summer crops in and the garden was planted. The school year was nearly over for Aunt Marie and the children. Justine said Aunt Marie enjoys teaching at Pickens High School."

"We haven't heard from them in a while. I'm glad they are happy and well. " Uncle Jule took a spoonful of mashed potatoes and passed the bowl. "I wish we could get to the farm for a visit. I miss it, but it's hard to get away, with my job and all." He glanced at Roseann.

Liz's thoughts drifted to Mary and her children on the train as she enjoyed the meal. She laid her fork down. "An interesting thing occurred on my trip. I was apprehensive about traveling by myself, not sure who my seatmate would be. A young mother named Mary sat across from me with her two children. She asked if I was alone and if her young daughter could sit beside me. I readily agreed. Later, a heavy-set, rather unkempt, middle-aged man, who smelled of whiskey and tobacco, came by and said it was his seat. He made me shudder. I was afraid he'd insist on sitting there, but Mary told him the seat was taken. Thank goodness he didn't argue. And he sat farther up the aisle. I think God sent Mary to me. She stayed with me until I found Uncle Jule."

"Was that who you were looking for?" Uncle Jule studied her.

Liz nodded. "She just vanished into the crowd."

"Sounds like God used her to provide for your needs." Roseann took a bite of salad.

"I think so, too, and I'm grateful." Liz finished her dinner then faced her aunt. "Do you feel like shopping with me? I thought I'd go this afternoon, after we straighten the kitchen, if you're up to it."

"Sure, I'm fine. We can take the carriage. Main Street isn't far from here. There are some exclusive department stores; John Taylor Dry Goods Store and Emery, Bird, and Thayer."

Liz sat forward. "I'd like to find a new dress without frills for my interview."

"Perhaps you'd like one of the new walking dresses. They have a flared skirt and a stylish jacket. They're attractive but practical and businesslike."

"That sounds perfect."

Monday morning, Liz hugged Aunt Roseann and Ellie before she boarded the trolley. Uncle Jule had insisted he accompany her to the depot.

Ellie hugged her tightly. "Thank you for playing with me in my new playhouse. I'm glad you came."

"I'm glad, too. You take good care of your daddy and mommy, okay."

"I will."

Liz stepped up into the trolley and waved to Aunt Roseann and Ellie. The weekend had sped by. As she found a seat about half-way back in the car, she ran her hand down the front of her new outfit. She felt dignified and stylish in the dark green, two-piece outfit. Gussets in the skirt made it fit comfortably. The fitted jacket had a large collar and curved to fit her small waist. She looked professional. The other dress she'd bought was an elegant shade of navy blue. Ruffles decorated the bottom of the skirt and the edges of the jacket. She touched the straw hat which complemented her ensemble.

The weather had cooperated, and the curls and waves of her hair lay in a semblance of order. She'd purposefully worn no make-up to comply with the Fred Harvey rules.

On Sunday she had attended church with Uncle Jule and Aunt Roseann. The congregation was small, but the churchgoers were friendly and made her feel welcome. Liz appreciated the young pastor's message. His text was Proverbs 3:5-6. She'd had the passage underlined in her Bible. *"Trust in the Lord with all thine heart, and lean not on your own understanding. In all thy ways acknowledge Him, and He shall direct thy path."* Liz sat back in her seat. The pastor spoke about the need to trust in God and allow Him to guide your decisions and plans. The words had struck home with Liz. In her heart, she knew God would guide her. She wrinkled her forehead. The trouble was, she'd usually depended more on her own understanding than on trust in Him. She closed her eyes. *I'm sorry, dear Jesus. I haven't followed you as I should. Please have your way in this interview. I want this job, but only if it is your will. Amen.*

A few minutes later, the trolley pulled into the train station.

Liz stood and followed Uncle Jule, who carried her baggage, to the back of the car. A tremor shot through her. How would the interview turn out? Would she go home a Harvey Girl?

They entered the cool lobby. Liz looked at the clock over the ticket counter. It was nine-thirty, almost time for her interview. A few people milled about, but it wasn't as busy as it had been on Saturday.

Uncle Jule walked with her to the baggage claim area and helped her check her bag.

"Do you have your ticket?

"No, not yet. I'm supposed to get a free pass after my interview."

Uncle Jule pointed to the elegant staircase at the side of the room. "The Fred Harvey offices are on the second floor. You'll do fine. God be with you." He gave her a hug. "I need to catch the return trolley so I can get some work in today."

"Of course. Thank you for all you've done. I truly enjoyed the weekend with your family." Liz waved as Uncle Jule walked toward the door. She hurried into the lavatory for a quick freshen and checked her hair, then made her way up the stairs. At the top landing, signs indicated the locations of various offices. She found the Fred Harvey offices on the list, then headed that direction. The hallway had white tile floors with geometric patterns along the edge and electric lights situated along the walls. About halfway down she saw large double doors with frosted window panes and "Fred Harvey Corporation" painted on the glass. She paused, breathed deeply, then pushed open one of the doors, and stepped into the sizable well-lit room.

Behind a desk, in the reception area, sat a middle-aged

woman. She wore a crisp, white, high-necked blouse with pin-tucks down the front and a navy blue skirt. Her hair was neatly braided and fashioned into a coronet. Liz noticed the amiable expression in her eyes.

"May I help you?" Her voice had a soft, clear tone.

"My name is Liz Gilbertson, and I'm here for my interview."

The woman smiled and scanned the list on her desk. "Yes, here's your name. Have a seat. Miss McDowell will be with you soon." She indicated a row of wooden chairs with red leather seats on the other side of the room.

Liz walked to a chair by the open window, sat down, and placed her bag on the floor. Two skylights in the ceiling brightened the room. A warm breeze ruffled the curtains. The furnishings were immaculate, not a speck of dust on the small table beside her. She grinned slightly. That was the Fred Harvey way. Totally spotless!

She leaned back in the chair and slowly exhaled. It would've been lovely to share this experience with Anna Lisa. If only her parents hadn't refused to let her come. On the other hand, Liz wasn't sure Anna Lisa even wanted to be a Harvey Girl.

While she waited, Liz studied the room. Southwest-style pictures were on the walls, and Indian artifacts were displayed artfully on shelves and tables. Two closed doors were to her right. She leaned forward to read the words on the door farthest from her. "Fred Harvey, President" was written in black letters on the frosted window. A thrill of excitement rippled through her. She could actually be a part of this tremendous organization. She glanced at the clock on the wall. It was still five minutes before her scheduled time.

At that moment, the door from the hallway opened, and a young dark-haired man strode in. He was impeccably dressed in black pants, white shirt, black tie, and a black jacket. "Florence, have I had any messages while I was out?"

Florence sat ramrod straight with her hands clasped in front of her on the desk. "No, Mr. Harvey. It's been quiet this morning."

Liz felt her mouth fall open, then clamped it shut, and sat up straight. This was Mr. Harvey? He appeared to be about the age of her parents, much younger than she'd imagined. Then she remembered, Aunt Millie had said Fred Harvey died in March. This had to be his son.

Mr. Harvey faced her, an attentive expression on his face. "Are you here for an interview?"

"Yes, sir." Liz stood to her feet when he approached. Her breath caught in her throat, and she felt her heart beat against her ribs as he studied her face.

"Why do you want to be a Harvey Girl?"

Liz hesitated as she searched for the right answer. She spoke slowly. "I need a job. I'm confident the Harvey House is a good place to work. Both my mother and my aunt were Harvey Girls." She was relieved her voice hadn't quivered.

Mr. Harvey raised his eyebrows, pursed his lips, and nodded slowly. "You don't want it for the money or for the adventure?" There was laughter in his eyes.

Liz smiled in spite of herself. "Well, there are those reasons, too."

He chuckled. "So you're prepared to abide by the rules."

"Yes, sir."

Just then, the other door opened. A woman, who Liz surmised was Miss McDowell, and a girl about Liz's age stepped into the room.

"Mr. Harvey. I didn't expect you to be here." Miss McDowell stopped, her body tensed, and she took a small step back. "Becky, this is Mr. Ford Harvey. You'll work for him. Mr. Harvey, this is Becky Reynolds. She's just been hired."

He acknowledged the introduction with a nod. "Good to meet you, Miss Reynolds. You'll be in the next group of trainees. Later this week?" He looked at Miss McDowell and waited for affirmation.

"Yes, training will start on Wednesday."

Becky stood motionless, her eyes wide. "Thank you, sir." She looked down.

Ford Harvey gestured toward Liz. "Isabel, I've visited with this young lady. I recommend you hire her. I like her attitude."

Surprise flashed in Isabel's eyes. "Yes, sir. I was just ready to start her interview."

He nodded curtly and entered the door of his office.

Becky hurried from the room as Miss McDowell touched Liz's arm. "Come in and have a seat." Isabel motioned for Liz to precede her. The room was tastefully decorated in the same style as the reception room. A wooden desk sat opposite the door, with two red leather chairs in front. Farther into the room, a large table with additional straight-backed, wooden chairs occupied the space.

Miss McDowell walked behind the desk and sat down. "You're quite fortunate. I've heard Fred Harvey occasionally recommended that a girl be hired, but not Ford. As you may know, he and his brother Byron have taken over management of the company since their father passed away."

Liz nodded and sat down, gingerly, on the red leather seat. Her hands shook, and her knees threatened to give way. "Thank you, it's an honor, and I'm grateful. Although I think I was just in the right place at the right time. He walked in, and I happened to be there."

"That may be so, but it's good for you. I noticed on your application that your mother and aunt were both Harvey Girls. When was that?"

"It was sixteen years ago, in 1885. My Aunt Millie was the house mother in Topeka for four years, and my mother trained there."

"Is your aunt, Millie Peterson?" Isabel wrinkled her forehead quizzically.

"That was her maiden name. Did you know her?"

"She was the head waitress in Topeka when I took my training. What's your mother's name?"

"She's Elise Gilbertson. She was Elise Dumond."

Isabel sat back in her seat, surprise registering on her face. "I trained with your mother. That's astounding." She shook her head. "I was sent to Florence, and she went to Emporia, right?" Then she sat forward and looked more closely at Liz. "But how could you be old enough to be a Harvey Girl if Elise worked sixteen years ago? She wasn't married. I remember she courted a man named Daniel, and he had to leave on a survey trip."

Liz grinned. "She's not my real mother. She's my aunt. My parents were killed in a carriage accident about that time. Daniel's my uncle, and he and Aunt Elise took me to be their daughter after they married."

"Oh, I see." Isabel let out an audible breath as she relaxed. "I'd love to see them." She picked up a sheet of paper that was lying on the desk. "Here are the rules. Have you read them? Are you prepared to abide by them?"

"Yes, I've read them, and I agree to follow them." Liz took the offered paper and scanned through the regulations.

Isabel slid another paper toward her. "This contract says you have read the rules and will obey them, and that you will not marry for the six months covered by this transaction. You need to sign it." She handed Liz a fountain pen. "You will train for the first month without pay. Then you will receive $20 a month plus your room and board at the end of the second month and each month thereafter. Any tips you receive are yours to keep, and you will be given passes to travel on the ATSF, free of charge."

Liz took the pen and wrote her name at the bottom of the page. She drew a deep breath. She'd made the first step toward independence.

"Congratulations. And welcome to the Fred Harvey family." Isabel picked up the paper and placed it on a stack nearby then rose to her feet. "You need to move into the dormitory in Topeka, preferably, by Tuesday morning. You'll observe that evening, then you'll begin to train on Wednesday morning at 7:00. You'll be given your uniforms and assigned to an experienced Harvey Girl to observe the first few days. Do you have any questions?"

"None that I can think of." Liz stood and preceded Miss McDowell to the door.

When Liz stepped into the reception room, she glanced at the waiting area. Another young woman was seated on the edge of the chair, ready to rise. Her reddish, brown hair was pulled up into a chic chignon and her brown eyes, the focus of her charming face, shone with anticipation. Liz hesitated. Could this be Michael's cousin?

Miss McDowell stepped up beside her. "Peggy, are you ready for your interview?"

Liz exhaled, and her shoulders relaxed. This obviously wasn't Clara. She didn't know what she'd thought Clara would be like. Maybe she'd come with the group tomorrow.

Isabel turned to her. "Peggy, this is Liz Gilbertson. Liz, this is Peggy Baxter."

Liz grinned. "Maybe we can talk after you finish your interview."

Peggy nodded. "I'd like that."

Liz stepped back. She watched as Peggy followed Miss McDowell into the room then nodded at the receptionist and walked out into the hallway. What would the other girls be like? Would they be friendly?

Chapter 12

Liz felt giddy as she walked down the stairs and across the room to the chairs where she'd found Uncle Jule earlier. So much had happened. As she sat on a loveseat, she noticed a ladies magazine on the table beside her. She idly picked it up, thumbed through it, and looked at the fashion pages and advertisements. She had an hour and a half to wait until the train departed for Topeka.

She'd found an article about the westward expansion of the country and the importance of railroad travel when someone sat down beside her. "Hello, did Miss McDowell say your name was Liz?"

"Yes, I'm Liz Gilbertson, and you're Becky Reynolds, right?"

Becky nodded. "Did you get hired?"

"I did. Can you believe we got to meet Mr. Ford Harvey? How many girls get to do that? Not very many, I'd guess."

"I know." Becky grinned. "I about fainted when I heard who he was."

from her, so I wasn't sure if she made it to the interview this time or not."

"No, but then I wasn't sure I'd know her. There will be three more girls in our group. They have their interviews this afternoon, then come in on the morning train. We didn't meet them."

Michael took Liz's bag. "So what's the procedure here. Do you have to check in at the Harvey House?"

"Yes, I'm sure we do." Liz led the way up the stairs. She felt light and exhilarated. Even though Michael hadn't touched her, she'd known, the moment their eyes met, that he was glad to see her.

Beatrice stood in the doorway of the dining room to greet patrons from the train. She studied the girls as they approached. "Are you the new Harvey Girls?" She made eye contact with Liz and smiled. "I recognize you." She turned to the other girls. "You must be Peggy and Becky. They said you'd come this afternoon. Did you eat in Kansas City?" At their nods, she continued. "You can come to the lunchroom and get a drink or dessert or go on into the parlor whichever you prefer. I'll meet you there when I'm through here." She pointed toward the door that led to the dormitory. "Liz, you know where it is."

Liz motioned toward Michael. "Can he go with us?"

"Yes, that's fine. Gentlemen are welcome in the parlor but not the dormitory." Beatrice refocused her attention to the customers who waited in line.

"What do you want to do?" Liz faced Becky and Peggy.

"We might as well have a piece of pie while we wait." Becky motioned toward the lunchroom.

Liz glanced around as she and her friends walked toward

the counter. Pride filled her. The room was immaculate, and the Harvey Girls moved with practiced precision. She was excited to be a part of it. Hopefully, she'd learn the routine quickly.

A Harvey Girl stood ready to serve them. She placed menus in front of them. "Hello, my name's Emma. What would you like to drink?"

Liz spoke up. "I'd like iced tea with sugar." She watched as Emma angled her coffee cup against the saucer. She repeated the action as each of the others also asked for iced tea.

Emma stepped back. "I'll take your order when you're ready."

Abigail approached with an iced tea pitcher. She placed glasses in front of them and filled them, then placed sugar cubes on a small dish. Her eyes sparkled. "Liz, did you get hired?"

"Yes." She turned to the others. "This is Peggy Baxter and Becky Reynolds. We just got here from Kansas City."

"I'm delighted to have you all. I think there will be three more." Abigail faced Michael. "Do you feel left out?"

"Oh, no. I'll just bask in these ladies' successes."

"Well, it's good to have you all. I better get busy." As she walked away, Emma returned.

"You'll be fine. Trust me, I had my doubts when I started, but now I've almost finished my training."

"I hope so." Liz checked the menu. "I think I'll have a piece of the banana cream pie." After the others had ordered, she sighed and relaxed against the back of the seat. It had been an incredible day.

Peggy spread her napkin on her lap. "It'll be interesting to see who the other girls are. I'm so glad I got this job."

Michael turned to Liz. "So, did you all meet at the interview?"

"Yes, Becky had her interview first. And you'll never believe what happened. While I waited for my time, Mr. Harvey walked into the reception room."

"You got to meet 'the' Mr. Fred Harvey?"

"Well, actually, it was Ford Harvey, Fred Harvey's son. He and his brother have taken responsibility for the company."

Becky scooted forward on her seat. "We both got to meet him. I couldn't believe it. I was so nervous." She fanned her face in a mock swoon.

"I'm jealous. I didn't see Mr. Harvey. My interview was later." Peggy moved her glass away as Emma set her pie in front of her. The melted ice cream ran over the side of the warm cherry pie. "Oh, yum, that looks and smells wonderful!"

Emma smiled. "It's one of our specialties."

"Maybe I should have ordered that, although I love the banana cream. I guess there'll be time to try the others." Liz scooted her plate closer.

Twenty minutes later, Liz and the others walked into the parlor where Beatrice waited. "Are we late?"

"No. You're fine. It feels good to sit for a few minutes." She gestured around the well-appointed room. "Find a seat, and we'll talk a bit." She waited until they were seated. "My name's Beatrice McKenney. I'm the head waitress and house mother. Mr. Stecker is the house manager. I'll introduce you to him later. We have three more girls who will arrive in the morning." She surveyed Liz, Peggy, and Becky. "Tell me about yourselves. Liz, I met you when you came in to get your application. You're from here in town, aren't you?"

"Yes. My father works for the ATSF here. Michael works for

him as an accountant. I'll move in tomorrow if that's alright."

Beatrice nodded. "That'll be fine." She turned to Peggy. "Where are you from?"

"I'm from north Florida." She glanced at Liz and Becky. "I just needed a job."

Beatrice nodded. "And you, Becky?"

"I live in a small town south of Chicago. I'm the oldest of seven kids and need to help with family expenses, so my father gave me permission to come. I tend to be all thumbs. I hope I can learn how to serve like the Harvey Girls we saw today."

Beatrice laughed. "Oh, you'll catch on. We'll work with you until you do. The Fred Harvey men prefer that you've not had previous experience. Then you don't have to unlearn bad habits." She gestured toward the dormitory door. "We have three rooms available." She looked at Liz. "I've put you and Peggy together and Becky, you'll room with one of the girls who come tomorrow. Does that sound satisfactory?"

Liz grinned at Peggy. "Sounds good to me. What about you?"

Peggy nodded.

"Good. Liz, you go on home. We'll expect you back tomorrow before noon. Then you can all start together." Beatrice stood to her feet. "I'll show you other girls to your rooms. Get settled in and get some rest. Life will pick up its pace in the next few days. You'll find Mr. Harvey's a good employer, but he doesn't put up with nonsense."

Michael and Liz said their goodbyes to the women and hurried to his carriage. After Liz was comfortably seated, Michael went around to his own seat. He took her hand and intertwined

"You met Fred Harvey's son? How did that happen? Did he do the interview?"

"No, but it was neat. Mr. Harvey walked in while I was waiting for my interview. He asked why I wanted to be a Harvey Girl, then he recommended to Miss McDowell that I get hired. It's still hard to believe I actually talked to him! And, Miss McDowell used to work with my mother."

"That's keen. I wish I could have gone." Anna Lisa crossed her legs. "So when do you start work?"

"I move in tomorrow and start my training on Wednesday. I wanted to see you before I left."

Anna Lisa scrunched her nose. "It'd be fun if I could go with you, but it's for the best." She gave a little bounce. "Not to change the subject, but guess what happened Sunday after church."

"What?" Liz hesitated, then raised her eyebrows. "Wait! Did Billy talk to you?"

Anna Lisa leaned forward. Her voice sounded dreamy, and her eyes sparkled. "Yes, he asked to bring me home. He said he'd liked me for a long time, and would I go on a date with him. Of course, I said yes." She smiled. "You were right. I just needed to be more friendly."

Liz sighed, and her shoulders relaxed. "Good, you'll be okay then. Bring Billy into the Harvey House lunchroom. I'll work there while I train."

"I will."

"I better get back. It's about suppertime." Liz hesitated. "Did Richard tell you he came over and tried to get me back?"

"No-oo, did he really? After the way he treated you? He

never said a word." Anna Lisa shook her head. "He went back to Manhattan. Said he planned to get a job."

"Good." Liz leaned over and gave her friend a hug. "I'll be back on weekends…though you'll probably be busy with Billy."

"I'll always have time for you. You'll always be my best friend."

"You, too." Liz stood, and Anna Lisa walked her to the front door.

Michael straightened his back and rubbed his neck. He'd worked painstakingly, all afternoon, to make up for the time he'd been gone to pick up Liz. It'd taken an hour longer than planned but was worth every minute. He'd finally caught up on his books.

He sat and contemplated the columns of numbers, gratified that the sums were reconciled. All except for the Harvey House books. He'd heard Fred Harvey's last words to his sons were, "Don't cut the ham too thin." Michael grinned to himself. It wasn't easy to let them remain in the "red," but he was reasonably sure he couldn't change anything. Ford Harvey had assured the railroad management that the Harvey Houses would operate under the same regulations his father had established.

Michael closed the ledger book and replaced it on the shelf over his desk. Should he go see Liz? He couldn't believe how much he'd missed her over the weekend. Her smile, when she walked into the depot, had brightened his day.

He shoved back his desk chair and stood. He'd eat at the boarding house, then go to her home for a visit.

Mr. Gilbertson walked toward him in the hallway outside his office. "Hi, Michael. How'd it go? Did you meet our girl and escort her home?"

"Yes, sir. Two other girls came with her from Kansas City. They had to meet with the head waitress before we could leave, so I didn't get back as soon as I'd planned. I did, however, get the freight account finished."

"Good work." Daniel grinned. "I'd have given you some leeway. I knew you'd get it done. Did your cousin make it for the interview?"

"No, she didn't come with Liz. I haven't heard from her. I guess she could still come with the group tomorrow."

Daniel walked with Michael out of the building. "Come over for supper. I don't know what we'll have, but it's always good."

"I don't want to impose. Mrs. Gilbertson doesn't expect me. I need to go back to the boarding house. I'll come over later." They had reached their carriages. "Besides, I don't want to distract Liz from her packing."

"Alright, we'll look for you after supper. Liz will be glad for a break."

Michael watched his boss swing up into his carriage and drive from the parking lot. Suddenly, he wished he'd taken up Daniel's offer. Meals at the boarding house were quite adequate, but not the quality of a repast at the Gilbertson home.

When he arrived at his rooming house, Mrs. Cartier handed him two envelopes. "These came for you in the mail today."

"Thank you." Michael took the envelopes and climbed the stairs to his room. He scanned the addresses. Clara's handwriting; it was the letter he'd expected, only a few days late. He frowned as he read the return address on the other missive; Miranda Whitmeyer! Why was she contacting him?

He ran his finger under the envelope seal as he sauntered down the hall then fumbled in his pocket for his room key and unlocked the door. He walked in, pushed the door closed with his foot, and sat on the bed before he removed the sheet of paper.

May 16, 1901

Dear Michael,

I am so excited. Dad is coming to Topeka on business with the Kansas Governor. He said I could accompany him and visit you.

The social scene just hasn't been the same since you left. I've missed you terribly. Felicity and Camilla are horribly jealous that I get to come. Of course, they can console themselves with Ben and Joseph. They were a foursome at the May Day Ball. Mother and Father were the chaperones. Paul was my escort. He's such a bore.

I can't imagine what you have found to do out in the Kansas wilderness. I'm sure you're ready for some stimulating conversation. Your mother gave me your address. She was relieved we would come and visit you.

We will be there in the first week of June. Save me some time in your busy schedule. (Smile).

Love and good wishes,

Miranda

Michael groaned. The last person in the world he wanted to see was Miranda Whitmeyer. The thought of it made his stomach clench. She was one of the reasons he'd wanted to leave Boston. What a clinging vine! She thought she owned him, and he could barely stand to be around her.

He tossed the letter on the bed and hunched over with his

elbows on his knees and his hands over his eyes. Somehow, he'd have to keep Miranda away from the Harvey House. Hopefully, he wouldn't have to spend much time with her.

After a few minutes in thought, he tore open Clara's letter.

Dear Michael,

Just want to let you know I got my application for the Harvey Girl job sent in. It sounds compelling, definitely an adventure. I'm waiting for information about my interview. I'll let you know when I hear more.

Mother and Grandma Grace located Grandpa William's papers. He had several boxes of documents and letters that Grandma wasn't aware of. No telling what they'll turn up. Maybe they'll find some information about my Uncle George out west. No one's heard from him for years. Grandpa always said he was dead, but Grandma didn't want to believe him.

These last two months have been calmer since Grandpa died. He wasn't a happy man in his last years, and he made everyone else's life miserable as well. He was so controlling and angry, especially at the end when he was terribly sick. Grandma has freedom now. She and Mom went to the bank again this week and talked with your father and brother. Thankfully, my great-grandma left most of Grandma Grace's inheritance in trust. She had used very little of it. Now she can live on it.

My sister, Rebecca, is going to have a baby in about six months; near the time I finish my contract with Fred Harvey, if I get hired. They've been married for almost two years, so she's thrilled.

I'll keep you informed of my plans.

Your cousin,

Clara

Michael laid the letter on his dresser. He studied the calendar. If Clara's interview was four weeks away, she'd be here around June 17th. He sighed. This month would fly by fast. Life had suddenly gotten very complicated. How would he juggle all this? *God, if you listen to me, please give me wisdom. I don't want Liz to see Miranda. What should I do?*

Right now, he needed to eat supper and go see Liz. He wanted to take advantage of every opportunity. Once she started work, he wouldn't be able to see her nearly as often. Her training period would go by too quickly and then she'd move on to another Harvey House.

Anticipation raced through Liz as she and her mother pulled into the depot parking lot the next morning. She was officially starting a new phase of her life. It wouldn't be easy, but she was exhilarated.

"Let's go in. Maybe they will have someone who can get your trunk." Elise gathered her handbag as Liz jumped down to secure the horse.

"Sounds good." Liz held her chin high and her shoulders back as they strode across the lobby and up the stairs. She'd soon wear the black and white uniform of a Harvey Girl. She checked that her curls were fastened securely, then ran her hand down the front of her dark blue skirt.

"You look fine." Elise touched her shoulder reassuringly.

Liz's stomach tensed. Uncertainty threatened her confidence. Then Beatrice stepped from the dining room. "Hello, Liz. Is this your mother?" She reached to shake Elise's hand. "We've waited for you. The other girls are all here. When everyone's moved in, we'll meet in the parlor." She looked around. "Do you have your trunk?"

"It's still in the carriage. Can someone help us carry it? It's heavy."

"Yes. I'll get the busboy and one of the kitchen help to bring it up. You can go to your room. Peggy will show you where it is. I'll be there shortly."

"Thank you." Liz and Elise walked through the parlor. Elise stopped and scanned the room. "It hasn't changed much since I trained here. Your father and I spent a lot of time here before he went on his survey trip, and I was transferred to Emporia."

Liz smiled. "Hopefully, Michael will be a frequent visitor."

"I'm sure he will. He appears to enjoy your company."

They moved into the dormitory hall. "I wonder which room is Peggy's and mine."

"My room was the last one on the right."

Just then, Peggy stuck her head out of the doorway two rooms down. "I thought I heard voices." She gestured into the room. "This is our new home. Will Ben and David bring your trunk up? They've had their exercise the last couple days."

"Yes. Beatrice said she would be here soon, too."

Peggy stepped back and allowed them to enter. "Is this your mother? Hello, my name's Peggy Baxter."

Elise acknowledged the introduction. "So I heard. Liz said, you were to be roommates."

Liz looked around the room. The window was open, and a warm breeze wafted in. Peggy had arranged her side of the room and had a bright colored quilt on her bed. Her trunk sat at the foot of her bed on the left. Liz laid her handbag on the other bed. "I like your quilt. I brought one my grandma made."

"My grandma made mine, too."

Liz laughed lightly. "I think we'll get along. We think alike."

"Men in the dorm." Beatrice's voice reached them from the hall. A few seconds later, she appeared in their doorway. She pointed at Liz's bed. "Place it over there." She turned to Liz. "This is Ben and David. Ben's the busboy, and David works in the kitchen. You'll meet more of the workers when we do our tour. We're all a big family here."

"It's good to meet you. I appreciate your help." Liz nodded to the young men.

"Okay, now, shoo! You need to get back to work." Beatrice waved the men out the door. When they'd gone, she turned to Elise. "I think they've enjoyed the change of pace and also the opportunity to meet the new girls."

Peggy moved toward the door. "Come on. I'll introduce you to the other girls. It's a good group. They're all nice. " She motioned to Liz and Elise, then led the way across the hall. "Hey, girls. I want you to meet my roommate, Liz Gilbertson." She pointed to one of the girls who sat on her half-made bed. "This is Ethel Walters and over here is Maggie Bates." Maggie was hanging clothes on her side of the wardrobe.

Liz nodded to each in turn. "I'm glad to meet you both." She faced Ethel. "Where are you from?"

"Upstate New York. I've always wanted to travel and see the country. I hope to escape the snow we have back home. It's still on the ground in May."

Maggie smoothed wrinkles from a dress on the bed. "I'm

154

from the mountains of North Carolina. I wanted to help my folks but couldn't find decent work there. There are twelve of us, and it's hard to keep all those mouths fed." She nodded toward Liz. "Where are you-all from?" She spoke with a soft southern drawl.

"I live here in Topeka. This is my mother, Mrs. Gilbertson. She was a Harvey Girl." Liz paused. "I was supposed to get married, but my boyfriend found somebody else." She grimaced. "Actually, it was for my good. I need time to plan my future and save some money. This is an excellent job for that."

"Yes, it is." Beatrice gave her shoulder a squeeze.

Becky appeared in the doorway. "Oh, hi, Liz." She gestured to the girl beside her. "This is Mary Alice Ringwald. She's from New Orleans, Louisiana."

"Hello, Mary Alice. I'm glad to meet you." Liz smiled. Mary Alice looked like a blonde goddess, porcelain skin, diminutive, and absolutely beautiful. "What brought you here?"

"My father, a ship's captain, was lost at sea. My mother is totally absorbed in her grief. I'm not sure she knows I exist anymore. I had to get away." Tears welled up in her eyes.

"Oh, my goodness!" Beatrice moved to give her a hug. "You'll find good friends here." The other girls gathered around and alternately hugged her, murmuring words of sympathy.

Beatrice moved back. "Well, since you're all here, let's discuss the schedule. You have until twelve-thirty to get settled in. The noon train rush should be over by then. Come and eat in the lunchroom, then meet me in the laundry room downstairs. I'll distribute your uniforms and shoes." An excited murmur permeated the room. Beatrice smiled. "You must wear the uniform whenever you're on duty in either the lunchroom or dining room.

"This afternoon you're free to do as you wish, but come to the lunchroom by five o'clock, in uniform, so you can eat before the train gets here. I will assign you to one of our veterans so you can observe. The rest of this week, you will learn the basics of the Fred Harvey System. You may help with minor jobs if your trainer asks you to, but follow her directions carefully. Monday, you'll be assigned a section at the lunch counter."

Liz's stomach fluttered. By Monday—just a few days—she'd have her own section.

Beatrice surveyed the group and smiled. "You'll all do fine. Breakfast will be at six o'clock. Now, go and unpack." She turned to Elise. "You're welcome to stay as long as you wish."

Liz faced Beatrice. "May I get off to go to church on Sunday?"

"Yes, you'll have most weekends off while you're in training. Evenings are free, after your area is cleaned and prepared for the next day. "

Elise grinned. "She's in good hands. I'll be on my way." She faced Liz. "You've got this, dear girl. I'm proud of you. We'll be in touch." She gave Liz a shoulder hug and a kiss on the cheek, then turned and walked from the room.

A bit later, Liz looked around the room and sighed with satisfaction. Her trunk was empty, and her belongings were put away. She'd placed her family's pictures on the dresser, and Grandma Dumond's double wedding ring quilt complemented Peggy's bed covering, giving the room a bright touch of color.

Peggy lounged on her bed, absorbed in a book.

Liz checked her alarm clock. It was twelve-twenty. "We better go eat dinner."

"Oh, okay." Peggy laid her book aside, stood to her feet and stretched. "I lost track of time." She gazed around. "Your side of the room looks great."

Liz grinned. "That must be a good book. You were engrossed." She led the way from the room, and they joined the other girls in the hallway leading toward the lunchroom.

"It is a very good book," Peggy answered. "Have you ever read *Jane Eyre* by Charlotte Bronte?"

"I've read *Wuthering Heights* but not *Jane Eyre.*"

"You'll have to read it when I'm through. Do you know if there is a good library in town?"

"Yes, a big one by the Capitol Square."

Peggy sighed. "I love to read. Books were my sanctuary when my parents fought." She smiled. "Betty, the librarian back home, was my best friend."

After their meal, the house manager directed them to the laundry room and they traipsed down to the first floor where Beatrice waited for them. "I've laid out your uniforms in accord with the measurements in your applications. Go to your rooms and try them on for correct fit. We'll make adjustments if needed."

Liz gazed at the black skirt and blouse with the white apron and collar. Black stockings and shoes completed the ensemble. Excitement made her giddy. These were actually hers—she was a real Harvey Girl!

Beatrice continued, "Wear them this evening unless they need major changes. I'll hand out your other two in the morning. You'll need to have at least one clean and ready at all times, in case the uniform you're wearing gets soiled."

The girls gathered their clothing and shoes and trooped back up the stairs.

In her room, Liz laid the pieces out flat on her bed. "I guess we have a while to relax until it's time for supper."

Peggy danced from one foot to the other. "I'm too anxious to wait. Let's put on our uniforms to make sure they fit."

Liz grinned at her. "I'm eager to try it on, too."

In short order, she had donned the black skirt and blouse. "I think mine fits well. Does yours?" Liz turned toward Peggy. "Oh, yes. You look good." She slipped the apron over her head, tied the strings, then looked at herself in the mirror. She breathed out a sigh. "Wow! I actually look like a Harvey Girl."

"Me, too. This makes it official." Peggy held up the collar. "Can you help me get this straight? Then I'll help you."

"Okay. Beatrice said to fasten the collars so that the pins are invisible."

Soon they were dressed, complete with shoes and stockings. "Now, what shall we do? We still have two hours before time to eat." Liz sat on her bed.

"Let's wait in our parlor." Peggy grabbed her book and marched out of the room.

Liz hesitated. What would she do in the parlor for two hours?

Peggy stuck her head around the door. "Are you coming? You can read a magazine or something."

Liz rose and followed her roommate. Seconds later she stood in the parlor doorway and surveyed the room. Her fingers itched to play the piano in the corner. Peggy had already flopped on one of the overstuffed chairs and was totally engrossed in her book. Would it be too distracting if she played softly? She hesitated, then moved across the room and ran her hand over the polished wood surface. Sheet music rested in the music rack, and a hymn book lay on the top.

She sat on the stool and shuffled through the sheet music. There were some older familiar songs and newer popular tunes, "Mandy Lee" and "Ma' Blushing Rosie." She played a few chords, then ran some scales up and down the keyboard.

Peggy laid her book down. "Do you play the piano? I wish I could play, but I never had a chance to take lessons." She stood and walked over behind Liz.

Liz lowered her hands from the keys. "I'm sorry, I didn't mean to interrupt you."

"Oh, pshaw. I'd much rather hear you play." Peggy reached over and looked through the music. "Here, play "Mandy Lee." Betty played it a few times on the Victrola at the library."

Liz opened the sheet music and began to play the familiar tune. Other girls filtered into the room and gathered by the piano.

As Liz finished, Becky sighed. "I love to hear you play. Can you play another song?"

Time flew by, and soon, it was time for supper. Liz rose. "We better go. How do your uniforms fit?"

Pretty, Mary Alice laughed merrily. "Look, my skirt is too long. It'll need to be shortened. I guess they don't expect a Harvey Girl to be four-foot-eleven."

Maggie frowned and pursed her lips. "Mine's a bit snug. It's good I have the apron to wear over it. My fault, though...I eat when I'm nervous, and I've been worried about leaving my family for the last couple of months."

"We'll all have to be conscious of that with the tasty food served here, or we won't fit in our corsets!" Liz remarked with a chuckle.

"Maybe the bustling around, when we serve, will help." Becky led the way into the lunchroom.

Finding seats at the counter, the girls ordered. They laughed and made small talk, getting to know each other while they waited for their food.

As they finished their meal, Beatrice walked in. "Come with me. I'll introduce you to your trainers."

Liz and the others followed Beatrice into the dining room, where they were introduced to the more experienced girls. Beatrice motioned toward Liz. "You'll observe Alice. She's an excellent Harvey Girl. Keep your eyes and ears open. You'll learn a lot."

"Welcome, Liz. I'm glad to meet you." Alice indicated tables in the far corner of the room. "Come with me. These two tables are ours. The train will be here soon. We have a full house. I have the tables set." She pointed toward a tray. "You can help me place a salad at each place."

They'd just finished distributing the salads and returned the tray to the kitchen when the gong sounded. Alice stood to one side. "Here, stand beside me. The crowds will arrive in a few minutes. Don't try to help today. Just watch."

Liz caught her breath as she waited. Her heart palpitated. In her excitement, she tried to focus so she wouldn't miss anything.

"Don't worry. You'll learn the routine." Alice's whispered words reassured her.

Alice stepped forward and directed the patrons to the chairs around their tables. There were eight places at each square table, two to a side. As soon as they were seated, she made her way around and asked for drink preferences, then adjusted the coffee cups per their requests.

Liz watched in amazement as the meal progressed. The drinks girl appeared and poured the beverage of the patron's choice. All the Harvey Girls worked with practiced proficiency. She shook her head. Would she ever remember it all? Almost before she could believe it, the people had finished their meals and headed back to the train. Most of them thanked Alice, and many left tips.

Alice turned toward her. "You look baffled."

Liz nodded. "How do you get all that done in such a short time? What if you forget something?"

"You do it so many times, it becomes second nature. Soon, you'll be able to do it, too. I felt the same way when I started. I didn't grow up like this and I had no idea you used a different fork to eat salad from the one you used to eat a meal, and then another one for dessert. I was sure I'd never get that figured out." She chuckled. "Thankfully, you get to practice. By the time you're ready to serve, you know it like the back of your hand. Here, help me clean these tables. I have to reset them for the local crowd. They'll be here soon."

Sooner than seemed possible, Alice repeated the process, setting the tables with no wasted effort. The rest of the evening went by in a whirl of activity. After Liz helped Alice set the tables for the next morning, she strolled with the others back to their rooms.

CHAPTER 14

It was dark outside. It had cooled off during the night, and there was moisture in the air. Liz pulled her quilt up around her neck. What time was it? She squinted but couldn't see the clock.

She threw the quilt back and moved over to quietly close the open window. Almost five o'clock. The alarm would go off in a few minutes. The urge to use the bathroom propelled her out the door and down the hall. When she returned, she heard voices from the far end, where the more seasoned Harvey Girls roomed.

Peggy sat on the side of her bed. "Ugh. It's still dark. I'm not used to waking up at five." She put her hand over her heart. "That alarm nearly scared the wits out of me. It's loud."

"Oh, no! I'm sorry. I should have turned it off before I went down the hall."

"No, it's fine. We need to get moving so we'll be ready by six." Peggy stood and started toward the door.

Liz grabbed the pitcher from the dresser. "Here, would you

bring back some warm water when you come? I like that it stays warm in the holding tank over the bathtub."

Thirty minutes later, Liz had washed her face and dressed in her uniform. She gazed at her reflection in the mirror over the dresser and gave a huff of frustration. "The damp air is playing havoc with my curly hair this morning. I guess it's good we have to wear hairnets." She leaned down to tie her shoelaces.

"I wish my hair had more curl. My ma has natural curl like yours. I don't know why there can't be a happy medium."

Liz straightened and gazed at Peggy. "You have beautiful hair. It's a rich chestnut brown and so thick. I think that should make up for straight hair."

"Thank you. I guess I shouldn't complain." Peggy gave her hair a final pat. She started toward the door. "I'm starving, it won't hurt to be a little early."

Beatrice greeted them as they entered the lunchroom. "Good morning, girls." She motioned toward the lunch counter. "Eat your breakfast, then report to your trainers. I'll meet with you after breakfast."

Liz and Peggy found seats at the counter and nodded to the other workers beginning to join them. Liz inhaled deeply. "Those pancakes smell so good. I'm hungrier than I thought." She smiled at Emma. "I want coffee with sugar and cream and a plate of those delectable pancakes with bacon."

Emma turned to Peggy. "What can I get for you?"

"I'll take hot tea with sugar and the egg and ham special with hashbrowns. We need to eat a hearty breakfast so we'll have enough energy for the day."

When they'd finished their meal, Liz and Peggy, along with

Maggie and Ethel, walked into the dining room. "Well, here we go, girls, we can do this." Liz reassured the others as they separated and proceeded to their various stations.

"Hello." Alice placed a folded napkin on the table in front of her. "How are you? Did you sleep well?"

"Yes, I did. I'm fine. Ready to get started."

"Good. The first train usually arrives at about five after seven, so we have twenty minutes to get ready. We should receive the count momentarily. The conductor on the train gets a tally of how many passengers plan to eat with us, then telegraphs the number and their food preferences to the House manager. Right now, let's go to the kitchen and get our syrup and butter pats for each table, since pancakes are on the menu." She paused, then added, "We also need a tray of fruit and bowls. Each customer gets a choice of fruit or fresh-squeezed orange juice."

Liz accompanied Alice to the kitchen, a large room operating like a beehive. Three men were frying pancakes on huge grills while others were busy plating them and placing them in large warmers. Bacon was sizzling, and hash browns were browning on another large griddle. Liz stared, fascinated by all the activity and precise movements. She had to consciously close her mouth.

Alice touched her arm. "It is pretty amazing to watch, isn't it? But we've got to get these on the table." She handed the tray with a large container of fruit salad and two piles of small bowls to Liz. Then she picked up a plate of individually sliced pats of butter and two pitchers of syrup. "Thank you, David."

"You're welcome." The young man grinned. "My pleasure."

At that moment, a man in black trousers, a white shirt, and a black day jacket stepped in the door. "We'll serve ninety in the dining room: thirty-seven pancakes, forty-three eggs and ham, and ten cereal and toast. Forty-five will eat in the lunchroom."

Alice grabbed Liz's arm. "We gotta get out of their way." They hurried back to their tables. "That's almost a full house. We can hold ninety-six without setting up more tables."

Liz stood to one side as Alice finished preparations for the train passengers. A few minutes later, they heard the gong, and patrons poured in. Alice graciously welcomed them and asked them for their drink preferences. She deftly adjusted their cups on the saucers. Liz watched closely, then noted with a smile the customer's reactions when Louisa, the drinks girl, wordlessly filled their cups and glasses and offered them juice or fruit. Liz quickly picked up the code: the cup right side up on the saucer meant coffee; upside down on the saucer meant hot tea; angled on the edge of the saucer was for iced tea; and upside down and off the saucer meant milk. The handle toward the server meant white milk and the handle away from the server, chocolate milk.

Next, Alice took their orders. Liz was amazed she could remember the orders without writing them down. At the kitchen, Alice listed the items on each plate. She remembered the meat choice and how eggs were to be cooked. Eight plates were placed on each tray. David picked up one of the trays and two wooden racks and followed Alice to the tables. Other chef's helpers assisted the other Harvey Girls.

"Thank you, David. I appreciate your help."

"You're quite welcome," He responded and headed back to the kitchen as Alice distributed the plates.

Liz shook her head in astonishment as Alice finished and stepped back beside her.

"How do you remember all that? I don't think I'll ever be able to do it."

"Yes, you will. You picture each place at the table and visualize a plate there. I always do it in the same order around the table. You'll learn the technique."

Liz pursed her lips. If others had conquered it, surely, she could too.

Later, when the last of the local crowd had left the dining room, Beatrice walked in with the well-dressed man Liz had seen in the kitchen and motioned for all the girls to join her. "Okay, girls, how'd it go? Are you totally confused?"

"Not confused so much as in awe of what these girls can do." Peggy grimaced as she and the others walked with Beatrice across the room. "I hope I can learn it all."

"You will. Many Harvey Girls before you have accomplished it. You will, too."

Beatrice turned to the man who stood beside her. "This is Mr. Stecker. He's the manager of this Harvey House and the one who answers directly to Ford Harvey. You will find that he is an understanding boss and will help you if you have a problem, but he's strict with the rules." Beatrice smiled as she introduced each of them in turn. Liz extend her hand for a handshake, the other girls followed suit.

"I'm glad to meet you all." Mr. Stecker nodded acknowledgement. "Our goal is to work together as a team. You'll find the other employees very helpful, too. I'll have contact with you often."

As Mr. Stecker moved on, Beatrice continued, "Now, I'll introduce you to the kitchen staff."

When they reached the kitchen door, Liz could tell the frenetic pace had slowed considerably, but all were still busy. Some were cleaning up from the breakfast rush, and others at the stove and worktables, were preparing ingredients for dinner selections. They talked and laughed easily with each other as they worked.

"Hello, fellows, can you stop for a few minutes? I want to introduce you to our new Harvey Girls."

"Oh, we're always ready to meet the new girls." A tall man stepped forward with a grin, wiping his hands. The other men gathered around.

Beatrice laughed and pointed toward him. "This is Hank. He's our baker. He makes the best bread, cakes, and desserts in the world. If you're nice to him, he might make you a special treat."

"Sure thing, Miss Beatrice. I love to bake and make the staff happy."

The next man was short and stocky. "This is Etienne. He's the head chef. He's responsible for all the wonderful food we serve every day. We're very fortunate to have him." Beatrice pointed toward the third man who stood with his arms crossed. "Here is Fred. He's our head cook. And then the cook's helpers are John, William, David, and George." They all wore white aprons and white chef hats. "They work hard to have the food ready on time. They also have the responsibility to keep the kitchen spotless and ready for inspection, including walls and floors. We never know when a Harvey superintendent will disembark the train unannounced for an inspection." Beatrice paused to let the girls absorb that information.

"And then, there's Charles, he's the dishwasher and Ben, our bellboy."

She turned toward the girls. "These girls are Peggy, Becky, Liz, Maggie, Mary Alice, and Ethel. I know it may be hard to remember, but you'll get acquainted soon."

"Pleased to meet you, ladies." Hank gave a wave. "Check back later. I'll have some cookies for you." The men returned to their duties.

"Girls, come with me, and you can practice on table settings. You have to learn the Fred Harvey way. It'll be the same in any Harvey House, no matter where it is along the Santa Fe line."

The rest of the week sped by. The new Harvey Girls practiced, observed, and learned. Each night Liz and Peggy climbed into bed exhausted but arose the next day, ready to begin again.

Friday morning, Michael McKey awoke to a flood of sunshine through his window. He gazed around the room, thankful for this bright, spacious accommodation. If it hadn't been for the first two weeks in the cramped little room at Mrs. Barrett's, he wouldn't appreciate the extra space here. He had settled in, and his clothes were all pressed neatly and hung in the wardrobe.

On the other hand, if he hadn't spent time in the first boarding house, he might not have had a Bible or been introduced to the stories about Jesus. He rolled over and sat up on the side of the bed, then reached for the Bible on the bedside table. The short walk to work allowed him a few minutes to read every morning before he got ready. He turned to the last chapter of Mark. As he read the account of Jesus' resurrection, joy and amazement filled his heart. His thoughts went back to the brutal crucifixion in the last chapters of Matthew. Jesus, who was the Son of God, had given His life on the cross, but the beautiful truth was He'd risen from the dead. Michael frowned slightly. The two books told a lot of the same stories but in a different style. He felt compelled to read on. He wanted to learn more about Jesus.

What was it he'd read in the third chapter of John? He needed to be born again. Deep down, he desired to understand what that truly meant.

He glanced at his clock. It was time to get moving. Fifteen minutes later, he hurried down the stairs.

Mrs. Cartier sat at the table. "Good morning, Mr. McKey. Did you sleep well?"

"Yes, Ma'am, I did. I'm ready for another day's work, although, I'll admit, I'm glad it's Friday."

She laughed softly. "I am, too. Do you have big plans for the weekend?"

Michael filled his plate from the breakfast buffet. "After work, I plan to drive to the Harvey House for supper. My friend is a Harvey Girl."

"Harvey Girls," the middle-aged Mrs. Cartier sighed. "That's a good job, I hear. I considered applying there myself before I met Mr. Cartier." She added under her breath, "I'd been better off to work for Fred Harvey."

She wrinkled her nose. "But then, you can't live on regrets. I better let you eat. You don't want to be late to work."

Heading out the front door a few minutes later, Michael briskly walked the two blocks to his office. A cool breeze wafted from the north and flipped his jacket tails as he leaned into it. The prospect of a weekend with Liz heightened his awareness of his surroundings and quickened his steps. Lilacs and snowball bushes were in full bloom. The lilies were finishing and roses just beginning to bloom, providing bright splashes of color along the walk.

Hopefully, Liz had sent him an interoffice message about her time off. He walked into the office ten minutes early and headed to the communication office. "William, do I have any messages?"

William looked up with a huge grin. "You do. From the boss's daughter, no less."

"Yep, he introduced her to me," Michael replied, a bit flippantly. "Now, give me the message."

"Aww...okay." William handed him the sealed missive. Michael was glad Liz had thought to seal it. He didn't want William's nose in his business.

Michael walked slowly to his office, sat at his desk then loosened the seal on the envelope.

Thursday afternoon

Dear Michael,

This is to let you know I'll be free after seven on Friday evening. I also have Saturday and Sunday off this week, so I will go to my parents' home.

My head is about to burst with all I've learned these last few days. I need a change of pace. Tomorrow is my last day to observe. Next week I'll have a station at the lunch counter.

I'd be happy to have you visit whenever it fits your schedule.

Your friend,

Liz

Michael stared at the words, eagerness filling his heart at the opportunity to spend time with her. He was glad she had the weekend off. He'd find a way to be with her.

He refolded the message and slid it in his inside coat pocket. He had a day's work to finish before he could get over to the Harvey House for supper and a visit. Maybe he could accompany her back to the Gilbertsons' home.

Liz stared at the clock on the wall. Five-thirty. Would Michael come? She'd sent him a message but hadn't received a response.

She followed Alice to the storeroom by the kitchen. Alice chose the plates, silverware and crystal goblets for the tables and placed them on a tray. She turned to Liz, "Please carry the tablecloths, napkins, and the tray with the cups and saucers. You can set one of the tables and put what you've learned to practice."

Liz gathered her assigned items. "I appreciate the opportunity while you can observe me. Next week, I'll be on my own."

"You'll do fine. You're a quick learner."

"My mother taught me to set the table when I could barely carry the plates. We used the formal Harvey House place settings when we had company. Being here has reinforced her instruction."

"You're fortunate. When I was a newbie, I didn't know the first thing about it." She laughed.

"Well, you're an expert now." Liz set the tray on the table and the linens on a chair.

"I should be, after two years." Alice indicated the empty table. "Here, you set this one. Work as fast as you can. We don't want to run out of time.

Liz spread the tablecloth and made sure it was even on all sides, then began to place the tableware and folded napkins in their prescribed places. As she had been taught, she used her finger to measure the proper distance between the pieces of cutlery. She breathed a sigh of relief as she placed the last crystal goblet. She had ten minutes to spare before the evening train would arrive.

"Good job," Alice praised as she moved a cup and saucer a bit to the right. "Now we'll get the salads set out. We have a full house again tonight."

Liz was finishing with the salads as the gong sounded. She stepped back to stand beside Alice, and the train passengers streamed in. Once again, Liz watched Alice spring into action.

After the meal ended and the room emptied, Alice cleared the tables. "You can help now. I'll carry these dishes to the dish room. You collect the linens and tableware for the next crowd. We don't have much time. Bring the linens first, then you can put them on."

Liz hurried back to the storage room. Sooner than she could believe, they had reset the two tables

"Now you can breathe." Alice patted Liz's arm. "We're done."

Liz let out her breath, not even realizing she'd been holding it. Her hand flew to her chest, and her heartbeat quickened as Michael walked toward their tables.

"Is there a place at this table for a poor, starving man?"

Alice stepped forward. "There is. Since you're the first one here, you can choose your spot."

"I think I'll sit here." He winked at Liz as he chose the chair in front of her. "How has your week been?"

"Actually, it's been good." Liz gestured toward Alice. "I've had a good teacher. This is Alice Parker." She turned to Michael.

"This is my friend, Michael McKey. He works with my father."

Michael nodded. "I'm pleased to meet you, Alice."

Alice ushered the incoming customers to the seats at their tables and began to take orders. Liz stepped forward to observe the beverage girl fill the drink orders, gratified to realize the code came easily now. Michael's presence seemed to fill her little area in the room. Tempted to touch his shoulder, she caught herself and kept her hands firmly clasped at her waist.

Liz watched Alice serve the dessert. Relieved her observation time was almost over, she was confident she'd learned the Fred Harvey system, at least good enough that she wouldn't embarrass herself. She was eager to have her own station at the lunch counter on Monday.

When the diners finished, settled up, and began to move out, Michael scooted his chair back and gazed at her. "What's your schedule? Will you have time to visit?"

"I wondered if you could take me to my house." She gestured toward the table. "I need to help Alice clean and set the tables for the morning. Then I'll be free for the weekend." She gestured toward the door. "Go into the parlor, and I'll meet you there. I won't be long."

"Sounds good. I'd be happy to take you home."

CHAPTER 15

Fifteen minutes later, Liz, Peggy, and Mary Alice walked into the parlor. Electric lamps were lit along the wall around the room. Michael visited with another young man by the window. Michael turned as the girls approached. "Here you are. Liz, you probably know John." Michael gestured. "We just met, and I found out he attends your church."

"Of course, I know him. We grew up together...well, sort of." Liz turned toward the other girls. "This is Abigail's older brother, John McDonald."

She focused on him. "Hello, John. Are you here to see Abigail?"

John nodded. "Yes, she's finished her training and is to be transferred this week. She wants to spend the weekend at home before she leaves."

"I heard she will go to Las Vegas, New Mexico." Peggy spoke up. "She seems excited. La Castañeda is a favorite Harvey House of many of the girls."

"She is excited," he agreed. "That's what she wanted. Our mother's not very happy, but she knew it was inevitable." He peered over Liz's shoulder. "Here she comes, now."

"Hello, everyone." Abigail greeted the group. "I'm glad you all got together. John, you know Liz and Michael, but have you met Mary Alice and Peggy? Mary Alice's from New Orleans and Peggy's from Florida." She glanced at them. "Right?"

The two girls nodded.

"Mary Alice, Peggy." John held out his hand. "I'm glad to know you, both."

John's gaze remained on Mary Alice, and he held her hand for several seconds; longer than required for a casual greeting. Liz raised her eyebrows but wasn't surprised. Mary Alice was a striking beauty, with her classic features and golden hair.

Mary Alice withdrew her hand slowly and smiled. "I'm pleased to meet you."

Liz stepped away. "You all can visit. I need to get my clothes changed, and my bag packed. Michael, will you still be able to take me home?" She looked at him expectantly.

"Yes, of course. I haven't seen you since I picked you up on Tuesday. I've looked forward to this weekend."

"I'm off until Sunday evening. We begin to work in the lunchroom Monday.

Abigail followed her from the room. "I need to get ready to go home, too." She stopped in Liz's doorway. "I think John will miss the excuse to spend time with the girls here at the Harvey House."

Liz chuckled. "He seemed interested in Mary Alice."

"He's always on the lookout. He wants to get married. I

told him that this wasn't a good place to look. These girls have all signed a pledge not to get married for at least six months, and most of them will move to another House. But he's still interested." Abigail shook her head as she walked to her room.

Liz changed quickly, donning her navy skirt and white blouse. She grabbed her small valise and filled it with the items she needed for the weekend.

As she left her room. Abigail was headed toward her. They walked together into the parlor in silence. Liz realized she would miss her long-time friend.

Maggie, Ethel, and Becky had joined the others. John turned toward Liz and Abigail. "We've talked while you were gone. Would you two like to go to the park tomorrow evening? Maybe have a picnic? All of you could come." He gestured toward Abigail. "And your friends, too. We have a croquet set. We could take that."

Liz scanned the group. "Sounds like a wonderful idea to me. I haven't been on a picnic this spring and it would be a lovely way to bid farewell to Abigail."

"That'd be an excellent way to spend my last Saturday evening here." Abigail smiled. "You new girls can get better acquainted. I'll invite, Emma and Minnie, too. The River Park is the best and it's not far from here. Let's meet there at six o'clock."

"Okay, we'll plan on it." John looked at Liz. "Can you girls plan food for the picnic? Michael and I will provide transportation."

Liz turned to Abigail. "I'll bring sandwiches and a vegetable plate. Do you want to bring a dessert and drinks?"

Abigail nodded. "I'll make some cookies."

John hefted Abigail's bag then turned toward Mary Alice. "I'll be here to pick up you girls about a quarter till six."

"Sounds good." Michael nodded. "We'll see you all then." They headed out of the depot and toward the carriages.

As they settled into Michael's rig, Liz heaved a happy sigh. "I'm glad we met up with John and Abigail. The picnic will be fun."

"I am too. They both seem friendly." Michael grabbed the reins and drove from the lot. "How was your week? Are you glad you got the job?"

"Yes, I am. It'll take some practice, but I like the Harvey House, and I think I'll learn the routine."

"I'm sure you will." He reached over and grasped her hand. "I missed you this week." Michael intertwined his fingers with hers.

People had gathered along the sidewalks as they drove along Kansas Avenue. "Look at the crowd at the opera house tonight." Michael motioned toward the people who stood in line for tickets. "I saw they have a traveling minstrel group this weekend."

They turned onto Liz's street and Michael halted the carriage then jumped down and hurried around to help Liz. "I'll carry your bag in."

Liz thrilled at the warm pressure of his hands on her waist as he guided her to the ground. "Come in and chat for a while."

"Okay, I'll stay a bit. Let me get Dolly secured then I'll be right in."

The screen door flew open and Rachel dashed out to greet them. "You're home." She threw her arms around Liz's waist. "You've been gone forever!"

"It's only been a few days, you silly girl, not forever." Liz laughed and wrapped her little sister in a tight hug.

Rachel stepped back and looked at Michael. "Why'd you bring my sister home?"

Michael grabbed her in a bear hug. "Because she asked me to."

Rachel giggled as he sat her down. "Do you love my sister?"

Heat spread across Liz's face as she grasped Rachel's shoulder and spoke emphatically. "You talk too much! Mr. McKey and I are friends."

Liz refused to look at Michael as they climbed the steps to the porch. Rachel ran to open the screen door and announced their arrival. She danced around them as they moved through the front hall.

Elise greeted them, a smile illuminating her face. "Hello. I'm so glad to see you've arrived. Your daddy said you had the weekend off, but we didn't know when to expect you. He is at a church meeting." The women exchanged a quick hug.

Elise gestured up the hallway. "Come on into the sitting room where we can visit. The parlor's too warm and stuffy." She led the way. "Are you off the whole weekend?"

"Yes, I have to be back on Sunday evening. We start in the lunchroom on Monday. I'll have my own section." Liz walked beside Michael. He brushed her hand, entwined his little finger with hers, and gave her a wink. She was sure her heart would burst with happiness.

Julien stepped from the library, an open book in his hand. "Hey, Michael. You're here! I thought I heard voices."

Elise motioned them into the sitting room. "Julien, will you please take Liz's bag up to her room? We want to visit in here for a while." She rearranged a couple of pillows then turned to Liz. "So tell me all about it. How was your week?"

Liz was delighted when Michael took a position beside her on the chaise lounge.

Michael leaned forward and spoke before Liz could. "She was very professional in her uniform. I got to sit at her table."

Liz rolled her eyes. "I didn't get to serve you."

"That's alright. I was glad you were there. Soon you'll do it all yourself."

"I do feel more confident after observing all week." She turned toward her mother. "John McDonald was at the Harvey House to pick up Abigail. She's really excited because she's going to be transferred next week to the La Castañeda in Las Vegas, New Mexico. They've just built a new building, and it's like a resort. Everyone wants to go there. Anyway, John suggested we have a picnic in the park for her last weekend here. I said I'd bring sandwiches. Hopefully, Catherine will help me make them."

Elise nodded. "That'll be enjoyable. She'll probably just make them for you. She loves to spoil you.."

Liz faced Michael. "Do you think it'd be okay if I invite my friend Anna Lisa and her beau, Billy? They both know Abigail, too. "

"Sure, sure, the more, the merrier." Michael nodded as he stood. "I better be getting home. What time should I come tomorrow?"

"Why don't you come around four. You can visit with Daddy or the boys while I finish getting everything ready. We're supposed to meet Abigail and John at the park at six."

Liz accompanied Michael as he said his goodbyes and

walked to the door. As they stepped out onto the porch, Michael took her hand and looked into her eyes. "Thank you for this evening. I enjoyed the time with you."

"I've enjoyed it too. I'll look forward to tomorrow."

Michael lifted her hand and slowly, gently kissed the back of it, then he turned and walked down the steps.

Liz's knees felt weak as she watched him drive off. She touched her face with the back of her hand. He'd kissed her. Happiness flooded her. It wasn't the first kiss she'd received, or the most passionate, but it was the sweetest. What was this captivating sensation?

She'd dated Richard for five years and planned to marry him, but she'd never felt breathless around him. Suddenly she remembered Rachel's question earlier. Did Michael love her? She didn't know the answer and she wasn't sure of her own emotions. It was too soon after her betrayal from Richard. Was it possible she, a simple little Kansas girl, could measure up to the women Michael had known in Boston?

Michael couldn't stop the smile on his face as he drove his rig into the livery behind the boarding house. He jumped down and lit the lantern that hung from a post by the stable. He'd missed Liz while she was gone over the weekend, but the glad welcome in her eyes when she saw him in the Harvey House made his heart race. How could his feelings for her be so strong, so quickly? The high-toned women in Boston couldn't hold a candle to her.

Still deep in thought, he methodically unhitched Dolly,

brushed her coat, and led her into her stall. "There you go, girl." He slapped her rump as he walked out and shut the gate.

The desire to kiss Liz had nearly overpowered him, but it was too soon. He'd only known her three weeks, though it seemed longer. The kiss on her hand was a small substitute. But, what if she thought he was too forward? By the expression in her eyes, she hadn't minded. He pushed his carriage into its assigned space next to the wall, blew out the lantern and let himself out into the waning twilight. He'd see Liz again tomorrow.

He frowned and shook his head as he headed to the house. Why did Miranda Whitmeyer have to be headed this way? She better not mess up his chance to court Liz!

Liz sat with Elise in the dining room the next morning, enjoying a leisurely breakfast. As expected, Catherine had graciously agreed to prepare the food for the picnic.

Rachel ran into the room. "Anna Lisa's here. She wants to talk to you."

"Oh, good. I wanted to see her too." Liz stood and walked toward the door.

Elise rose and gathered the dishes. "I'll let you girls visit. I need to check with Catherine about tomorrow's dinner."

"Anna Lisa, I'm so pleased you came over." Liz sat down and patted a chair for her friend to sit beside her. "So what has happened? How are things with you and Billy?"

Anna Lisa's eyes gleamed. "Wonderful! He took me to see the minstrel show at the opera house last night. Can you believe it? I did get to go. I have you to thank for that."

"That's great," Liz gave her a quick hug. "By the way, we saw John and Abigail McDonald at the Harvey House last night. Abigail's to be transferred to New Mexico next week. We all thought it would be fun to have a picnic at the River Park this evening. Would you and Billy like to come? You've been friends with Abigail for a long time."

"That sounds delightful. I'll ask Billy when he comes to my house this afternoon. I'm pretty sure he'll want to come. He's always up for a good time."

"Hmm…he'll be over this afternoon?" Liz cocked her head. "This sounds serious?"

Anna Lisa laughed. "We'll see. He said he's liked me for a long time. He waited for me to show an interest. You were right."

She stood. "I better get home. I need to help my mother clean. It's Saturday, you know. I wanted to come over and say, 'Hi.' I'll let you know about tonight."

"Why don't you just meet us here at five o'clock? John and Abigail will be at the park around six. They'll pick up some girls from the Harvey House."

"Do I need to bring anything?"

"Not unless you want to bring a lawn game. John will have croquet." Liz gestured toward the kitchen. "You know Catherine, she'll fix enough food to feed an army."

"Okay, I'm sure we'll see you at five."

Liz stood and pushed in her chair, as Anna Lisa left. She'd better get around, or Michael would be here, and she'd still be at the breakfast table.

That afternoon, Liz stepped into the kitchen. She'd dressed in a light blue summer frock. "Mmm...smells good in here. Apple pies?"

Catherine nodded. "They're for dinner tomorrow." She stood at the work table and rolled out a pie crust. "I've got one in the oven, and this one will be ready in a jiffy." She paused and wiped her hands on her apron. "I thought you'd be here soon. I made two dozen beef sandwiches and two dozen chicken salad. They're in the icebox. There's also a tray of carrots and radishes, from the garden, and I made some deviled eggs. I thought that would be a good addition. They're wrapped in newspaper to keep them cool until you get ready to eat. Those boys are gonna be hungry."

She hurried into the pantry. "Here's a picnic hamper you can put it all in. There are twelve tin plates and cups in here. Is that enough?"

Liz counted in her head. "There'll be eleven of us with the girls from the Harvey House. I'm not sure how many Abigail will invite. Surely she'll bring some plates and cups too. Thanks so much." Liz gave her a hug. "I don't know what I'd do without you."

"Oh, you'd manage."

Liz laughed. "I'm not so sure. You know how Mama hates to cook. We might all go hungry."

"Then you'd just have to learn. Someday you'll want to set up housekeeping." Catherine's eyes glowed with mischief. "How're you and Michael gettin' along? In my opinion, he's more husband material than Richard ever was, more responsible and considerate, it seems to me."

"Miss Catherine, I cannot believe you'd say that! Michael and I are just friends. It's too soon to think anything else!"

"Don't be too sure. When you find the right man, things can move along pretty fast. Me and my Charles got married three months after we met. We both knew it was right, and here we are, eighteen years later, happy as two clams in a shell!"

"Well, I can't get married for six months at least. I just signed up to work as a Harvey Girl."

Catherine nodded. "So I heard. I hope you enjoy it as much as your mama and I did."

"You weren't a Harvey Girl, were you, Miss Catherine? Mama talks about stealing you away from your job as a Harvey House cook."

"I wasn't really a cook. I wanted to be a Harvey Girl, but I was already married so they wouldn't hire me. Charles was working for the railroad, and we lived right next to the Harvey House. I was lonely, and would go visit with your Aunt Millie who was the head waitress.

"One of the cook's helpers quit, and they were short-handed. The house manager had the prerogative to hire local workers for kitchen help and house cleaning. He hired me, temporarily, as a salad girl, and I also did some cleaning. I ended up working for about six months.

"When your mama and daddy got married, Millie recommended that she hire me to cook for your family. Although I wasn't an actual Harvey House cook, I gained invaluable experience, from the head cook, the chef and the baker, that has served me well over the years."

"That's incredible. I don't know why I didn't know that." Liz smiled. "You've just always been here. I guess I never thought to question how it all came about." She gave Catherine another hug. "Thank you for all you do for us."

"You're welcome. I love you like one of my own children. Now run along. Michael will think you've abandoned him."

Liz removed the food from the icebox and placed it in the picnic basket. "Thank you, again, for making these for us."

"My pleasure, sweet girl. I'm gonna miss you around here."

Liz carried the hamper into the parlor where Michael waited. He'd exchanged his more cosmopolitan clothes for Levi's, boots and a western style shirt like her dad wore. Liz couldn't stop her smile. A short, red-headed cowboy with a bass voice and from Boston, no less. She loved it. "Michael, I see you've fully embraced this new lifestyle. You look like a real Kansan."

Michael smiled mischievously. "I needed a change. Not so formal."

"I think you look fabulous." She set the hamper on the floor. "The food's all ready. Let's see, we have blankets to sit on. Catherine put in plates and cups. Can you think of anything else we need? The sun should be down enough that we won't need a parasol."

She picked up the pile of blankets. "John and Abigail said they'd provide the drinks and dessert."

"And the croquet game." Michael retrieved the picnic hamper. "Let's be on our way."

Billy and Anna Lisa drove up in Billy's carriage as Liz and Michael walked down the porch steps. "We made it." Anna Lisa waved. "I have our game of lawn darts. And my mother made some meat pies."

"That will be a nice addition to our meal." Liz waited as Michael placed the hamper and blankets in the back.

He turned to assist her up onto the seat then motioned to Billy. "We're ready to go. Follow us." He swung effortlessly into the carriage.

Liz tingled with awareness as she felt the warmth of his body next to her. As Michael took the reins in one hand, he fumbled to find her hand and laced his fingers through hers. Breathless, she relaxed against him. Could this be happening? Besides being the most handsome man she'd ever met, he was also thoughtful and kind.

Liz sighed happily as they drove down Kansas Avenue. "This is a beautiful evening for a picnic."

"It sure is. There's just enough breeze to take the edge off the heat."

They pulled up to the park a short while later. "There's John and Abigail with the other Harvey Girls. Look, they're already setting up the croquet game." Liz pointed. "That massive oak tree would be a good place to have our picnic. It's close to the game."

"Look's good to me." Michael jumped down, then turned and instead of offering a hand, lifted Liz down by her waist. He twirled her around.

Liz giggled as he set her on the ground. "Michael!"

He grinned. "I'll bring the blankets and hamper."

Liz couldn't stop her smile as she headed across the park. Abigail, Peggy, Mary Alice and Anna Lisa joined her. Liz turned toward them. "What do you think? Shall we have our picnic under that huge tree?"

"It looks like the perfect spot to me." Abigail set her basket down near the tree trunk. "It's cooler here in the shade."

Michael deposited their hamper and blankets then set off towards the other men.

Liz grabbed a blanket and gave it a shake to unfurl it under the tree.

"Here, let me help you." Peggy grabbed the other end as they spread it out. Mary Alice and Anna Lisa place the other blanket nearby.

Abigail opened her basket. "Don't you think we need to eat while the food's fresh. Then we can play games when it's cooler."

The girls agreed. They worked together to set out the sandwiches, vegetables, and eggs. Peggy lifted the plates and cups out of the hamper, and Abigail and Anna Lisa added their food contributions.

"The food's ready. Come and get it!" Abigail yelled to the men.

As everyone gathered around, Michael spoke up. "You go first, Abigail. You're our guest of honor."

After Abigail chose her food, they all quickly filled their plates and settled on the blankets. Liz was thrilled when Michael lowered himself beside her.

Anna Lisa turned to Abigail. "I hear you'll be transferred to New Mexico."

"Yes, I'll be at the La Castañeda in Las Vegas. It was built last year. I hear it's beautiful and modern, built in the Southwest mission style with Indian accents. I'm excited."

"I don't think I'd want to be so far from home." Anna Lisa grimaced.

"That's the beauty of a job along the Santa Fe. You can always hop the train and come home for a visit."

Peggy leaned forward. "I hope I get sent somewhere like that."

"There are a lot of interesting Harvey Houses." Abigail took a bite of her sandwich.

Mary Alice shifted her weight and faced John. "Let's talk about something other than work. This park is delightful. I haven't been on a picnic in years. Not since I was a little girl."

"Then I'm glad we planned it." John set down his sandwich. "Tell us about your family."

Mary Alice ducked her head, and tears sprang to her eyes. Everyone quieted while she regained her composure. When she spoke, her voice was devoid of emotion. "There's not much to tell. We lived in New Orleans, by the water. My father was a ship captain. Mama always lived for the times when he returned from sea. One voyage his ship wrecked and he didn't return. Mama forgot I existed." She turned back to John. "What about you? Where do you work?"

John looked at her wide-eyed. "Oh, my goodness! I'm sorry about your father." He hesitated. "I work at the McDonald Mercantile on Kansas Ave. Our parents own it. I'm a clerk and a soda jerk. I stock shelves, clean, and most anything else that needs to be done. I've been helping with inventory the last couple of weeks." He gestured playfully at Abigail. "My sister had to abandon me to be a Harvey Girl." He added, "You all need to stop in if you're downtown."

"We may do that next weekend," Liz replied. "I need to buy a few items." She curled her legs up under her and got up on her knees. "This was a delicious picnic meal. Thank your mother, Anna Lisa, for the tasty meat pies, and Abigail, your sour cream sugar cookies were delicious...my favorite!"

"We all need to thank Catherine, too." Abigail chuckled. "Her sandwiches and deviled eggs were, well, just heavenly." The group laughed. "I just had to say that." She rose to help Liz pack up the plates and the leftover food. "I'm so full, I'm not sure I'll be able to play games."

"That's why we need to play...to work it all off." Anna Lisa grinned as she folded one of the blankets.

John held out his hand to help Mary Alice up. "Let's go help set up the rest of the croquet game. I brought some extra balls and mallets, from another set, so we can all play."

The others set off toward the games while Michael and Billy carried the picnic baskets and blankets to the carriages. With the girls helping, all the hoops and pegs were soon in place.

"Everyone choose a ball and mallet. I'll take blue." John grabbed them out of the holder. "Mary Alice, what color do you want?"

"I'll be yellow." Mary Alice pulled out the mallet and ball.

Liz relished the pressure of Michael's hand at the small of her back as he pointed toward the game. "What color do you choose?"

"I think I'd like red."

"I'll take the green one." Michael took the mallets from the rack and handed the red one to Liz. "We'll be Christmas."

Billy gestured to Anna Lisa and Abigail. "You two take the orange and purple. The rest of us can use the ones from the other game."

"You go first, then, since you got the mismatched mallets." Abigail gestured toward the first set of hoops.

Soon everyone was involved in the game and each one took a turn to hit their ball through the hoops. The game became extremely competitive. A couple of the players were a little reckless, maneuvering to strike their opponent's balls off course. The feigned indignation played out merrily.

"John McDonald, that was mean." Liz frowned, playfully. "You didn't have to whack my ball so hard." She stood with her hands on her hips and glared at him. "Mary Alice's was close by, too. You could have bumped hers away."

He gave her a mischievous grin as he hit his ball through the hoop. "It's all in the game. You were farther ahead."

"Just you wait. I'll get you back." Liz ran across the grass and stood by her ball to wait for her next turn. She was a bit frustrated to be knocked so far off course.

"Hey, where'd that come from?" John, playfully, swung his fist through the air as his ball was struck by Billy's.

"What goes around comes around." Billy set up his shot, then smacked John's ball away in the opposite direction.

John laughed. "Well, I guess I asked for that, didn't I?"

They all continued with the game until Michael knocked his ball through the final hoops and hit the stake. He held his hand in the air. "Yea, I won!"

Becky clapped her hands. "That was exciting. I haven't played this game since I was about ten. My family used to have a croquet set. I wonder what happened to it."

Michael placed his mallet in the rack. "I was probably about that age the last time I played, too."

"Is everyone ready to play yard darts?" Anna Lisa laid two hoops in the grass. "We divide up in teams and use these badminton rackets and birdies. John and Billy, you be team leaders. Each team takes turns to hit the birdies into the circles. The team with the most inside the circles wins." Before long, they had chosen sides and were all laughing as they swatted furiously. Billy's team eventually won.

When the game was over they all plopped down on the grass. Abigail gazed around the group. "I'm thankful you all came tonight. This has been incredible. I'll remember this when I'm out in New Mexico."

Liz glanced at the setting sun. "This has been great fun, but now we better get the games picked up. It'll be dark soon."

They all lingered a bit, talking and laughing casually, as they gathered the games pieces and walked toward the carriages. Streaks of pink, purple and orange mingled with the clouds in the west as twilight lowered.

John placed the croquet game in his carriage and cleared his throat to get their attention. "Thank you, everyone, for making this evening special for Abigail. See you all at church in the morning."

"We'll be there." Michael gave Liz a hand up into the carriage. "We can take some of the young ladies back over to the Harvey House on our way home."

After Michael and Liz dropped the girls off, he drove along Kansas Avenue. People had begun to disperse from the Saturday events, and carriages were leaving as they drove by.

"Oh, look, John and Abigail stopped at the mercantile," Liz waved as they passed. "Maybe we can come downtown next Saturday. We can stroll the streets, check out the Saturday night specials and get an ice cream treat at the soda fountain."

"That sounds like a great idea." Michael guided the carriage onto the Gilbertsons' street. "I'll carry the hamper and basket in, then I better head on home. We need to be fresh for church tomorrow. May I come by and pick you up?"

"Yes, that would be wonderful. We usually leave about twenty-till-eleven."

"I'll be here." Michael stopped the carriage, helped Liz down, then gathered the hamper and blankets from the back and carried them into the house.

As Liz prepared for bed, her mind was brim full of happiness. Michael was so attentive. Except when he won at croquet, he'd been by her side all evening.

CHAPTER 16

Anxiety flooded through Liz as she stood at her station in the lunchroom on Monday morning. She nervously moved the napkin and readjusted the silverware on the counter as the train whistle sounded in the distance.

Abigail appeared beside her. "You'll do fine, Liz. Remember, I'm right here. Don't rush. Take one person at a time. The passengers don't mind a short wait." She touched Liz's arm. "I'll pour the drinks, you take the orders."

Liz nodded. "Good, I'm shaking so much, I'm afraid I'd pour coffee in someone's lap."

Abigail laughed. "I remember those fears, but I guarantee, when you get started your jitters will go away. You can do this."

Just then, Beatrice began to direct train passengers into the lunchroom. They flooded into the room and claimed the swivel stools. In minutes, all the seats in Liz's section were filled. Abigail started at one end of the eight-seat section, asked about drink preferences, then adjusted the cups.

Liz followed her and handed out the menus. After she gave them a few minutes to choose, she stepped up to the counter. "May I take your order?" One-by-one, she took orders of french toast or pancakes with eggs and ham or bacon. After the first four, she hurried back to the order window to relay the requests to George, the cook's helper assigned to the lunchroom. Amazed that she'd remembered what they'd ordered, she turned back toward the counter and repeated the process with the other four.

Before long, the orders appeared in the serving window. Abigail helped Liz distribute them, then they stepped back to allow the customers time to eat.

Abigail turned toward Liz. "You did a great job. I'll be here as back-up for you until I leave on Thursday. By then you'll have it down pat."

"I hope so. It was easier to remember the orders than I thought it would be. All the advice I've received has helped. " Liz scanned the customers in the room. There were forty seats at the horseshoe shaped counter, and nearly all of them were full. The other girls were busy in their sections. "I'll refill drinks."

Soon the train passengers had finished their meals and left to reboard the train. Liz noticed Beatrice was outside the door collecting their money on the way out.

Abigail and Liz cleared away the dishes and cleaned the counter. Liz distributed the napkins, silverware, cups, saucers, and glasses for the local patrons.

"This time, you take the drink orders and arrange the cups, before you take the orders," Abigail gestured toward the counter. "I'll fill the drinks. You'll need to be ready to do it all. You might not always have someone to assist you."

The local customers began filing into the lunchroom. Soon the stools were filled again. For a few seconds, Liz's mind went blank, and panic roiled through her. She blinked and scanned the men and women. They were people like her and her family. She turned to the woman nearest to her. "What would you like to drink?" Her mind cleared, and she moved on down the row, shifted the cups by the code then circled back around to take their breakfast orders.

To Liz's surprise, the morning routine progressed smoothly. She was gratified that after her moment of confusion, she hadn't forgotten an order or had a spill.

As the last few customers wandered out of the lunchroom, Liz gathered the used dishes while Abigail wiped the counter. "Thank you, Abigail, I appreciate your encouragement and support." She grinned. A total of thirty cents in tips was scattered over the counter. "You seemed very calm and collected. I'm sure you'll do well." Abigail paused. "Don't try to rush. When I first started, I was afraid I'd run out of time since the train passengers only had twenty minutes. But, you'll find that everyone works so efficiently, there's plenty of time to get it all done."

Liz wrinkled her nose. "I may have looked calm, but I wasn't on the inside." She held up her hand. "See, I'm still trembling."

Abigail laughed. "That's natural. It'll get better."

Liz carried the dishes to the dish room and stopped beside Mary Alice and Maggie, who stood by the door. "How was your first morning?"

Mary Alice grimaced. "I got the orders mixed up. Thank goodness, Emma was there to help get it straightened out. I hope I do better next time."

Liz shook her head. "I forgot the drink code—just for a moment!. I nearly panicked."

"I guess it's happened to almost everyone." Maggie shook her head. "That's what Minnie said. I suppose we'll survive."

"I'm sure we will." Liz carried her load into the dish room. At least she wasn't in this alone. She nodded and smiled at Charles, the dishwasher, before she headed back to her station at the lunch counter.

Wednesday evening after the last customers left the lunchroom, Liz wiped her area and turned toward Abigail. "Thank you for your help. I'm more confident in my abilities than I was on Monday. I even received fifty cents in tips today." She grinned.

"I've loved these days with you. You'll do well. I can tell you enjoy the customers."

"I do. There are a lot of fascinating people who travel the rails."

"Yes, there are. Mark Twain came in my first week of training. Everyone was excited to see him. He had a show at the Grand Opera House."

Liz beamed. "I got to attend his performance. Michael had just moved here, and he wanted to go, so he asked me to go with him. It was delightful." She straightened the salt and pepper shakers then took the cleaning supplies to the dish room. "We better hurry. Beatrice should have the going-away party set up in the parlor. Will John be here?"

"Yes, he and my parents are supposed to come."

"I sent a message to Michael, but I didn't hear back from him." Liz pouted.

Mary Alice joined them. "John's here?"

Abigail smiled. "He should be. He planned on it."

Liz's eyes sparkled. "What's this with you and John?"

"He just seems nice is all." But, Mary Alice's cheeks were rosy.

"Well, I think he's pretty special." Abigail chuckled as she led the way to the parlor. "He's a good brother, and I'll miss him."

Liz scanned the room as they entered. Had Michael come? At first, she didn't see him, then happiness filled her as they made eye contact. He stood beside John. She wanted to rush toward him but restrained her impulse as she followed Abigail and the others across the parlor. Liz noticed that his eyes followed her progress across the room.

He reached to take her hand. "Hello, Liz. I'm sorry I didn't respond to your message. I let time get away from me, but I thought I'd come anyway. I wanted to help give Abigail a send-off."

"Just think, in a few short weeks I'll be the one who leaves."

Michael squeezed her hand. "I don't look forward to that."

She gave him an impish grin. "You like to travel. That's what trains are for. You can come to see me."

Michael scrunched his face. "I guess, but it's not like you being here."

Liz pursed her lips. "I know. Let's not talk about it until that time comes." She gazed around the room. Hank and Etienne stood to the back of the room. Fred leaned against the wall in his habitual slouch, his arms across his chest—he was a talented cook, but it was hard to tell by his appearance. John, George, Charles, and Ben were scattered among the other Harvey Girls.

The beautiful refreshment table sat against one wall. Hank had been busy. An alluring chocolate cake was at one end, with a full punch bowl and cups on the other.

Beatrice and Mr. Stecker welcomed everyone and introduced the Harvey Girls who were moving to other Houses, then Beatrice motioned toward the men in the back. "Hank, Etienne and Fred will serve this delectable chocolate cake and punch."

Michael and Liz followed the others to form the short line and waited their turn for cake and punch.

While they were enjoying the refreshments, Michael turned to Liz. "Are you off work again this weekend?"

"I have to work through the noon meal on Saturday."

"Can I come and pick you up?"

"Yes, I'd like that. I thought maybe we could go downtown. Remember, I need to get some things at the Mercantile. I may invite a friend or two for the afternoon."

"That sounds good. I'll look forward to it. Right now, though, I better get back to my room. I have some reports to finish before tomorrow." He took her hand and squeezed it gently.

Liz smiled and returned the gesture as pleasure flowed through her. "I'll see you on Saturday."

Saturday morning, Liz awoke with a sense of accomplishment. She'd finished her first full week of training. This was her weekend to work the morning shift, then Michael would be here to pick her up for what promised to be a fun afternoon in downtown Topeka. She'd invited Peggy and Mary Alice to accompany them.

She squinted at the clock. The alarm would soon sound. She threw back the sheet, sat on the side of the bed, and gazed out the window. The eastern sky had begun to lighten with pink and orange streaking the blue dawn. A slight breeze rustled the leaves in the trees across the tracks. Peggy was still rolled in her blanket fast asleep.

Liz stood and walked to the bureau. She turned off the alarm then picked up the old photograph of her parents and stared at it. If only they knew how happy she was with her life. She'd be entirely satisfied, except for the nagging questions about her father's family. She set the picture back down and headed down the hall, water pitcher in hand.

After the noon rush ended, Liz gathered the dessert plates from the lunch counter and slipped two dimes into her apron pocket. It was fun to have money of her own. Once she'd finished cleaning her station, the rest of her afternoon would be free. She needed to freshen up. Michael would soon be here to pick up her and her friends. Her mother had invited all of them to their house for supper.

Liz wiped the counter and straightened the napkin holder then made sure the salt and pepper shakers were spotless, full, and in their proper place. Mary Alice appeared at her elbow. "You ready to go? I'm glad we have the afternoon off. I'm excited to go shopping."

"You go ahead. I need to finish up, then I'll come."

When Liz walked into the parlor a few minutes later,

Michael was sitting on one of the sofas with a book in his lap. He looked up as she walked in. Lightness filled her chest when she saw the sparkle in his eyes.

Michael laid the book down as she approached. "How was work? You look wonderful."

She sat beside him. "Work was fine, but it feels good to sit for a bit." She glanced at his book. "What are you reading?"

Michael picked it up. "My Bible. Mrs. Barrett gave it to me. It was one her daughter didn't use any more. She challenged me to read the New Testament. I've been so busy I haven't had time to read the last few days. I thought I'd bring it and read while I waited for you."

Guilt washed over Liz. She hadn't read her Bible, except at church, for several months, since she found out Richard was unfaithful. "What have you read?" she asked quietly.

"I've just finished the book of Luke." He frowned. "The first three books are quite a bit alike."

Liz nodded. "They all tell the story of Jesus' earthly life, just from a different viewpoint. They each told it as they saw it."

Michael cocked his head, a thoughtful look on his face. "Jesus was convinced He would die. He told his disciples several times. How did He know?"

"Jesus was just as much God as He was a man." Liz leaned forward. "Do you remember when it says that the Holy Spirit came upon Mary, in the first part of Luke, I think it was? That was when Jesus came down from Heaven. When He was with God the Father, before He came to Earth as a baby, He knew the reason He was to come. It was to die and for our sins. The book of John tells more about Him."

She shifted on the sofa. Time was slipping away. "I better go change my clothes. Peggy will wonder where I am."

Liz hurried to her room. She realized Michael had put her to shame. She'd accepted Jesus as her Savior when she was nine years old. But lately, she hadn't acknowledged Him in her life, except when she needed His help, like on her trip to Kansas City.

Peggy was sitting on the bed reading a book when Liz hurried in.

"Hey, girl, you ready to go?"

"I've been ready for the last hour. What took you so long?" Peggy smiled.

"Some of the locals sat and talked after they finished their meal. I had to be polite, but I thought they'd never leave."

"That always happens when you want to get away." Peggy laid down her book, stood up, and checked her hair in the mirror. "Who'll pick us up?"

"Michael's here. I just talked to him in the parlor."

Peggy raised her eyebrows. "It must be nice to have a boyfriend."

"He's not really my boyfriend. At least there's nothing formal." Liz paused. "I like him, but we're just friends."

Peggy cocked her head. "Are you sure? Looks to me like it's more than that. You may not have acknowledged it yet, but there's a definite spark. I've seen the sparkle in your eyes when he's around."

Liz felt her face warm as she took off her uniform. "I'd like that to be the case." She slipped on her light blue dress and sat on the bed to put on her shoes.

Becky stuck her head around the door. "Are you two ready

to go? Michael's waiting in the parlor."

"Yes, I know. I'm about ready." Liz grabbed her satchel and her handbag. They walked into the hallway as Mary Alice headed toward them.

Michael stood, his Bible tucked under his arm, as Liz, Peggy and Mary Alice approached. "You all ready? What a lovely group of young ladies I'm escorting this afternoon."

Happiness infused Liz as Michael touched her elbow and directed her to his carriage. He gave her a hand up so she could sit beside him on the seat then assisted the other girls into the second seat. They were soon on their way through town.

Liz touched Michael's arm. "Don't forget to stop at the McDonald Mercantile. We want to shop before we go home."

Michael guided Dolly up to the hitching rail. "I'm glad we're stopping here. I could use a few things myself."

Liz smiled as they entered the store. It felt cool after the afternoon heat, and varied scents assailed her senses—the aroma of weathered hardwood floors, the clean fragrance of soaps and candles, and the fruity bouquet of fresh apples. Toward the back, a soda fountain with stools, small tables and chairs was on the left by a staircase which led to the second floor. John greeted them. "Hello, friends. Come in, come in. Let us know if we can help you."

They each scattered to various areas in the store. Liz picked up a small basket and wandered up and down the aisles, checking out the new merchandise as well as the old standbys.

She moved to where the new bolts of cloth were displayed. Peggy was already examining some pretty aqua flowered fabric. She ran her hand over the length of summer-weight cotton.

"Maggie said she'd make a dress for me if I'd get the material. I need an outfit to wear to church. I have some tip money I received at work, and there's a little bit left from what my mother gave me. I think Ma would approve of me using it for a new dress."

"That color would look nice with your dark hair," Liz mused. She fingered a bolt of royal blue cotton. "There are so many pretty fabrics."

"Maggie said to get two and a half yards. I think I'll get the aqua." Peggy picked up the fabric from the table and headed to the sales counter. She stepped behind two older woman who waited ahead of her in line.

Liz ambled slowly along the aisles to the area with soaps and lotions. She needed a new bar of soap, and her hands were dry from the soapy water they used to clean the lunchroom. She chose a bar of lilac-scented soap and a pretty bottle of lotion to match. Next, she found some hair pins, then added a white silk rose and some shampoo to her basket.

As she walked toward the back of the store, she saw Mary Alice at the soda fountain with John. Liz walked over beside her. "Did you find what you needed?"

Mary Alice turned around. "Yes, and now I plan to have a cherry soda with ice cream in it. John says they're delicious."

"Oh, that does sound good. I think I'll have one, too. What about you, Michael?"

"I'll take one, only I want root beer in mine." Michael joined them. He carried a pair of socks. "The walk to work every day is hard on socks, and I don't have anyone to darn them so I need another pair."

Liz turned to find Peggy and joined her at the check-out

counter where Mrs. McDonald waited. Peggy laid the cloth on the table. "I need two and a half yards." She turned toward Liz. "I don't think I'll have enough money for a soda."

Liz spoke up, quickly, "Oh, you have to have one if the rest of us do. I'll pay for your soda, Peggy. You can return the favor when you get more tips."

"Did you young ladies find what you wanted?" Mrs. McDonald unrolled the fabric and began to measure it.

Liz nodded. "Well, we saw a lot of beautiful things we'd like, but we better limit our purchases."

Mrs. McDonald cut and folded the material. "We try to bring in the latest items for our customers." She turned to Peggy. "That will be twenty-five cents. Do you want me to wrap it for you?"

"Yes, please." Peggy dug in her purse for the coins and handed them to Mrs. McDonald.

Liz laid her items on the counter. "I'll also pay for two sodas."

John's mother added up the purchases. "Forty-five cents. I'll wrap yours, too."

"Thank you." Liz laid the coins on the counter.

They collected their packages, and joined the others at the soda fountain. John had finished making their sodas. Liz perched on a stool beside Mary Alice and took a bite of ice cream. "Yum. This tastes fabulous. It's been a while since I've had an ice cream float." Michael paid Mrs. McDonald then joined them on the stools.

John wiped the counter. "I'm glad you came in. We were just talking about how we missed Abigail."

"We miss her, too." Liz sipped her soda. They made small

talk as they finished their treats.

Liz pushed her empty glass back on the counter. "This has been fun, but I guess we bettter go on home. Mother will wonder what's kept us."

"Come again soon." John gathered their glasses. "It's always good to have friends come in."

At Liz's house, Rachel skipped out the door and down the steps as they strolled toward the porch. "Guess what we're having for supper?"

Liz gave her a hug. "How could we know?"

"Just guess. It's my favorite thing."

"Chicken and noodles?" Liz grinned at her. "I should have known since you're so excited."

Elise waited at the door. "Hello. I'm so glad you're here." She waved them toward the sitting room. "Let's sit in here. It's too hot and stuffy in the parlor."

Peggy and Mary Alice chose comfortable chairs, and Michael sat beside Liz on the sofa with Rachel snuggled up on Liz's other side. "I'm sad that you're gonna move to another town."

"I know, sweetheart. Hopefully, I won't be too far away. And we can always travel on the train to see each other."

Julien peeked his head around the door. "Michael, do you want to come into the library and play a game with Adam and me?"

Liz turned to Michael. "You can go, Michael, if you'd like. You'd probably enjoy that better than girl talk."

Elise sat on one of the side chairs. "So how are things at the Harvey House? Are you feeling more confident?"

Peggy shrugged. "It's still kind of intimidating, but I think

I'm learning the system."

"It helped to have Abigail and the other girls there to assist us." Liz leaned forward. "I'm more confident than I was at the first of the week. As long as I follow the same routine I do alright."

Elise smiled. "You will all do fine. Before long you won't even have to think about it."

Mary Alice grimaced. "I hope so. I'm not so sure."

The girls continued to share, recounting some of their experiences.

After a while, Elise smiled at Liz. "Will you please play a song on the piano before we go in to eat? I'd love to hear you. I got the music for "Mandy Lee" the other day."

"Oh yes, Liz! We want to hear you play." Peggy made piano playing motions with her fingers. "I love that song." She turned to Elise. "She played for us on our first day at the Harvey House."

Liz hesitated...why had she let Richard disparage her music?

"Okay, I'll play." She led the way into the parlor and sat on the piano bench. She flipped through the pages of the sheet music, then played a few chords.

"There, that sounds like it." Peggy scooted around behind Liz.

Liz forgot herself as she found the notes and music poured out into the room. The other girls sang along to the end of the song.

Mary Alice walked over to stand beside Peggy. "Can you play, "Let Me Call You, Sweetheart?" I heard that song on my friend's Victrola, back home."

Liz launched into the familiar tune. When she finished, she

looked at Elise. "It's probably suppertime, isn't it?"

Her mother nodded. "Please play "Amazing Grace" then we'll go into the dining room."

Michael, Adam, and Julien all stepped into the parlor as she played the beautiful hymn. When she finished, Michael clapped, and the others joined in the applause. "You're amazing! You need to do that more often."

Warmth flooded through Liz at his compliment. It was the opposite of Richard's disdain at her desire to play. "Thank you. I do enjoy it and have missed it more than I realized."

They all filed into the dining room and enjoyed a delicious meal. Liz enjoyed watching Peggy and Mary Alice interact with her family.

After the meal, the girls walked out to the front porch. Peggy rubbed her stomach. "That was delicious. Fred Harvey food is good, but there's nothing quite like home-cookin'."

Mary Alice settled on the porch swing. "Now we need to go back downtown and walk it off."

Liz sat on the porch step. "Michael, do you want to go? There's a lot I haven't shown you. We can take the trolley. Then we won't have to find a place for Dolly."

Julien burst onto the porch. "Can Adam and I go?"

Liz nodded. "Sure, that'd be fine if Mama and Daddy approve."

"Yeah." Julien pumped his fist in the air. "I've still got my birthday money to spend."

"Come along. We'll walk to the trolley track. Don't forget you need a nickel to ride."

Julien raced back into the house. "I have to get my money.

You go on, and I'll catch up."

A short while later, they all paraded up the street. Peggy and Mary Alice laughed and visited with Julien and Adam while Liz and Michael trailed behind.

"It's hard to get you alone these days." Michael took Liz's hand. "I'm afraid these next few weeks will fly by too quickly, and then who knows where you'll be assigned." He intertwined his fingers with her's. "I got another letter from Clara. Her interview date is June seventeenth. I'm anxious for you to meet her. I think you'll like her."

"I'm sure I will."

CHAPTER 17

There was a buzz of excitement throughout the Harvey House. Earlier in the week, a secretary from the Kansas governor's office had informed Mr. Stecker that the Massachusetts Senator, Mr. Henry Whitmeyer, and his daughter, Miranda, would arrive from Boston on the noon train and have dinner with Governor Stanley.

Liz paused in the task of gathering the dessert plates, glasses and cups from the lunch counter. The governor, his wife and a group of Kansas congressmen had met the senator and his daughter in the depot. Liz watched the entourage as they waited to be seated in the dining room. She had a clear view of Miss Whitmeyer through the lunchroom door. She was attractive in her teal blue traveling suit. Her dark curls were accented by a stylish teal hat. From what Liz could see she carried herself haughtily, disdainful of those around her.

It was Wednesday, the fifth of June, and the train crowd had just rushed away to continue on their way. Liz carried the dishes into the washroom and set them on the worktable. Charles stood at the sink with his arms in suds up to his elbows. "This has been a busy morning. You gonna make it?"

"Aw, sure. Just have to keep goin', or I'll get buried in dirty dishes."

"Maybe I can come back and help you after I get through with dinner." Liz turned to walk back to the counter.

"Oh, that's not necessary." Charles grinned. "John and William usually come in to help when they get through in the kitchen. But thanks anyway. I appreciate the offer."

Liz nodded and hurried back out to prepare her station for the locals. She wiped her area and replaced the napkins, silverware and cups and saucers. Then she stepped back.

Unexpected pleasure flooded through her as she recognized the little family from the train trip. Mary Faulkner, her two children, and a man walked toward her. "Mary, I'm so glad to see you! I hoped you would come in." Liz motioned toward the stools in her section. "I thought maybe you were an angel when you disappeared on me that day in the depot."

Mary laughed as she assisted little Ben up onto the seat. "An angel? You're kidding, right? I'm far from an angel. I saw that you had found your uncle, and my mother was waiting for me, so I just went on." She turned toward her husband. "This is my husband, Joe Faulkner. He'll tell you I'm not an angel."

Liz held out her hand. "I'm glad to know you, Joe. Your wife and I met on our way to Kansas City. I had to travel by myself, and she befriended me. She was a true blessing to me."

Mary helped Susie up, then settled on the next stool. "I see you did well in your interview."

"Yes, I made it."

The other seats in her section had filled up. "What do you want to drink?"

"I'll take an iced tea, and the children will drink milk."

Liz adjusted their cups, then moved on to Joe and the other customers. As she proceeded to take their orders and serve them, a warm glow filled her chest. It was lovely to have someone she knew come and sit at her counter.

A bit later, she picked up their empty plates. "Can I get you some dessert? We have wonderful pies, and today we have strawberry shortcake."

"Oh, yum, strawberry shortcake sounds wonderful." Mary's eyes sparkled. "I'll take that. What about you, Ben, Sally, do you want some?"

"Yes, I do." They both chorused. Joe agreed.

Liz took orders from her other patrons. As she turned to remove the dirty dishes and get their dessert, a loud ruckus erupted from the landing outside the lunchroom door.

"She's my daughter! I didn't give her permission to come here!" Feet stomped up the stairs.

Mr. Stecker's voice was conciliatory. "I'm sorry, sir, but I can't have you barge in here. We're serving dinner."

"Servin' dinner! I don't care what you're doin'. I want my daughter!"

Liz caught sight of Peggy, quickly ducking into the dish room. All the color had drained from her face. What was this all about? Then she remembered the conversation with Peggy at the Kansas City Depot. She had fled her father's abuse and worried he would find her.

Apprehension gripped Liz, she knew she had to remain professional. She didn't want to act like she suspected something amiss or reveal Peggy's hiding place. She walked to the pick-up window to order the desserts and stepped into the dish room to deliver the dishes.

Peggy crouched in a corner behind some shelves. "Liz, don't come in here. They'll know I'm here." She jerked her head towards the door. "That's my pa out there. What if they turn me over to him? I can't go home." Sobs shook her body.

"Shhhh, just stay put." Liz tried to reassure her. "You stay here, out of sight. We'll cover your station. We're almost finished anyway."

Liz walked out, picked up the shortcake plates, and tried to stroll nonchalantly back to the counter.

Mary looked concerned. "What's going on?"

Liz shook her head. "Sounds like that man's out of control. Mr. Stecker will handle it." She glanced at the other girls. Peggy's station was beside Becky's, and Becky had stepped over to take care of Peggy's customers. Liz turned away to avoid more questions.

"What's your daughter's name?" Mr. Stecker still tried to calm the irate man.

"Eusenia Porter! We call her Essie Mae...she may go by that name. The conductor on the train said she'd be here if she came two weeks ago."

"You must be mistaken. We don't have anyone here by that name." Beatrice's voice interceded. "Are you sure you have the right information?"

"She's my daughter. Don't you think I'd know? I was told

she had come to be a Harvey Girl."

"Maybe she changed her plans or didn't get hired. She's not here." Beatrice was firm.

"I want to see your girls, just to make sure!"

"No, sir. We can't allow that. If we had someone by the name you say, we could check into that, but we will not—*Will not*—put our girls at risk!" Mr. Stecker's voice was clear.

Their voices faded as he ushered the angry man down the stairs.

Liz expelled her breath in a rush. She glanced around. It felt as if time had stood still, but most of the patrons were finishing their desserts and had resumed chattering as if nothing had happened. Maggie, Mary Alice, and Ethel all finished serving their customers, while they shared questioning looks, hushed comments, and sighs of relief.

Mary's voice brought Liz back to the present. "Well, I'm glad that's over."

"Yes, I am, too. I'm sorry your meal was interrupted." Liz smiled, broadly. "I'm so glad you came in."

Liz turned to Mary's husband, Joe. "And I am glad to meet you. I'll be here for two more weeks before I get moved to another location. Maybe you can all come in again."

"Yes, we should." Mary smiled as she finished the last of her shortcake and sipped her tea. "We must go now. We have to complete some errands this afternoon."

Liz watched the little family as they strolled from the room. It was so heartwarming to see them again. She gathered the dirty dishes and headed to the dish room. Peggy stood to the side of the doorway.

Liz squinted her eyes at her friend. "Eusenia? Essie Mae Porter? Who's that?"

Peggy looked sheepish. "That's my real name." She pursed her lips. "Hey, wouldn't you change your name if you had one like that? I never did like it. So when I decided to get away, I changed it. Betty, my library friend, helped me. She called me Peggy so I'd get used to it."

Liz smiled as she set down the dishes and grabbed a clean cloth. "Betty helped you a lot, didn't she? I wonder who told where you'd gone."

Peggy frowned. "I think I know. I slipped up and told one of my other friends. At least, I thought she was a friend. I knew I shouldn't have as soon as I told her. She can't keep a secret."

"Well, the name change kept you safe this time."

"I hope I get moved way out west, a long way from Florida." Peggy peeked around the door. "Can you go see if he's gone?" She ducked back in. "Oh, oh, here comes Beatrice. I'll bet I'm in trouble."

Liz stepped out into the lunchroom as Beatrice approached. "Okay, girls, I need to meet with you in the parlor when you get through here. No one's in trouble. We just need to know what's behind this."

Peggy stepped out into view. "Is he gone?" She gazed around. "It's me he wants."

"He's gone. Don't worry. I would just like to talk to you."

"Can Liz come, too?"

Beatrice nodded. "Sure, she can come. Get your area cleaned and straightened then come to the parlor. On second thought, let's go to my office."

Liz hurried to clean her station then walked with her friend through the parlor, to Beatrice's office.

Peggy shook her head, sadly. "I was afraid this was too good to be true. I've never been anywhere as nice as this. If I get fired, I can't go back home."

Liz touched her arm. "I don't think you'll get fired. Don't borrow trouble."

Beatrice waited for them as they entered the office. She stepped forward. "Have a seat. I need to know your story. Why did your father come today? He was irate."

Peggy bowed her head. "I'm sorry for the trouble I caused. I ran away from home. Actually, my ma helped me get away. My pa would get into a drunken rage and beat her, and if I tried to intervene, he'd beat me. It's happened for a long time, more lately." She glanced up. "My friend at the library found the ad for the Harvey Girls and suggested I apply for it. She helped me fill out the application, and we changed my name. I hated to leave Ma, but she insisted I come and gave me some money she'd saved, to buy my ticket."

Tears welled up in her eyes, and her voice quivered. "I can't go back home. No telling what he'd do." Her shoulders slumped. "I'm sorry I left my station, but I was terrified when I heard his voice. All I could think of was to hide."

"It's okay. We're a team, and we work together. The other girls stepped up and covered your station." Beatrice knelt and put her arms around Peggy. "We knew he was out of control. I think he'd been drinking today. Don't worry. You're safe here."

Peggy buried her face in Beatrice's shoulder as her tears flowed and sobs wracked her body.

Liz's heart ached for her roommate, who had quickly become her friend. This sweet girl had already seen too much of the bad side of life. Liz placed her hand on Peggy's back. "You have lots of support here."

Peggy sat back and nodded. "I just want to get transferred as far away from Florida as possible." She gave a nervous laugh. "Thank you, Beatrice, Liz. I better go wash my face and get ready for the evening meal."

Michael looked up as a young errand boy stepped into his office. "Mr. Gilbertson wants you. He said you have a telephone call."

Michael frowned. "Me? I have a telephone call?" He knew there was a telephone in his boss's office, but it was to be used exclusively for railroad business.

"Yes, he told me to come get you."

Michael followed him to Mr. Gilbertson's office.

Daniel motioned for him to enter. "Your mother is on the line. She wants to talk to you."

"Hello?" Michael made a face and voiced a silent "I'm sorry," to his boss as he spoke into the receiver and took a seat.

"Hello, Michael? It's good to talk to you." Margarette McKey's voice was sugary sweet.

"Mother, you're not supposed to call on this line. How'd you get this number?"

"It's the number you used when you applied for the job. I found it in the bureau in your room. Anyway, I wanted to tell you Henry Whitmeyer has a meeting with the Kansas governor.

Miranda is accompanying him. I told Miranda you'd escort her. I know you're not much for the social niceties, but try to be on your best behavior and show her some attention this week, please."

"I don't even want to be around her. She wouldn't let me alone before I left Boston."

"Michael." Her voice hardened. "I'm counting on you. Please don't embarrass your father and me. We deserve your respect and obedience. I gave Miranda your address so she may show up at your boarding house."

He groaned. "I guess if I have to, I will do as you ask, Mother. Goodbye. I'll be in touch." Michael hung the earpiece on the hook. He slumped in his chair beside Daniel's desk.

Daniel gave him a quizzical look. "Are you alright?"

Michael shook his head. "Not, really. The Senator from our home district, Mr. Whitmeyer, is coming to see Governor Stanley. My mother insists that I be his daughter's escort."

"So, you know this young lady?"

"Yes, I know her. Her parents are in my family's social circle. She fancied we were a couple, but we were not." He sighed again. "I've just begun to get settled here." And I've just begun a relationship with Liz, he thought to himself. "I don't need this, right now."

"She won't be here that long, will she? Just honor your parents' wishes while she's here, then it will be over."

"Thank you, sir," Michael nodded. His shoes felt like they were filled with sand, and his heart was heavy as he trudged back to his office. What would happen if Liz found out about Miranda and thought she was his girl?

As he walked toward his boarding house that afternoon, Michael noted with a start an Oldsmobile runabout parked in front. It must be Governor Stanley's automobile. He steeled himself as he headed up the walk. Miranda was sure to be waiting for him.

As soon as he opened the door and entered the parlor, she stood and rushed towards him. "Michael, I've waited ever so long. You must work too hard! It's good to see you. I've missed you terribly since you left." She threw her arms around his neck.

Michael stepped back, disengaged her arms, and pushed her away. "Miranda, please. I've only been gone a month." He glanced around to see if any of the other boarders were near to see her display.

She drew back and raised her chin. "I thought you'd be pleased to see me. After all, we were a two-some before you left."

Michael shook his head. "Uh, no, we weren't. I'm sorry. I've promised to escort you while you're here, but that's all."

Miranda flounced away and sat down in a wing-backed chair. "Well, don't put yourself out on my account." She looked away with disdain, her chin in the air as she pouted.

Michael glared at her. She was attractive, and he had hurt her feelings. Maybe he shouldn't have been so blunt, but he didn't dare encourage her. "I need to go change clothes. I'll be back shortly. Then we can go."

"I may still be here."

Michael climbed the stairs and entered his room. He'd have to be civil, or this would be an extremely miserable few days. He changed into his formal attire.

When he walked back down the stairs, he took a deep

breath and offered Miranda his elbow. "Shall we go? Where are we headed?"

Miranda rose and walked to his side. "Governor Stanley is hosting a reception at the new governor's mansion. He shared with us that he and his family moved in earlier this year. He's the first governor to occupy it." She tucked her hand under his elbow. "He let me come in his runabout. Daddy told him I had driven ours in Boston. You can drive us back."

On the road, Michael relaxed a bit. The new automobile was a thrill to maneuver. Ten minutes later, they arrived at the impressive two-story, red brick Victorian home. Built in the Tudor style it had tall towers and turrets. Michael assisted Miranda down from the vehicle and escorted her inside where he formally met Governor Stanley and was greeted by Miranda's father.

Liz looked around the counter. All was ready for the evening train to arrive, and Maggie and Becky were assigned to wait on local customers during the afternoon lull. Liz walked from the lunchroom toward the parlor door. It was Friday, and she hadn't heard a word from Michael all week. Would he be in this evening, as usual?

"Liz, I received a message for you. It's from the main office, from Michael."

Liz pivoted at the sound of Beatrice's voice. "I wondered if I'd hear from him." She smiled as she reached for the message. "Thank you."

She walked to her room, then tore open the envelope and pulled out the single sheet.

Dear Liz,

I've had to escort Senator Whitmeyer's daughter, Miranda, this week to the state functions at the Governor's mansion. Senator Whitmeyer is from our district in Massachusetts, and my parents insisted I escort her. It's not my choice. I wanted you to know we will be at the Harvey House this evening, but I cannot visit with you. I would much rather be with you.

Michael

Liz stared at the words. Michael had been with this Miranda since when? Wednesday was when she'd first spied the governor's entourage in the Harvey House. And Michael hadn't let her know until right now that they were coming to the Harvey House, tonight? Where she'd be forced to see them? They'd been to the Governor's mansion? *Where else had they been?* Of course, Miranda was suited to him. She was from his social world.

Hurt, anger and frustration flooded through Liz, aimed more at herself than at Michael. She crumpled the note in her hand and dropped it on the floor. Why had she thought she could fit into his social circle? Tears sprang to her eyes. She'd thought Michael was different than Richard! Were men all alike?

And she'd have to see him with *her* this evening!

Liz turned and threw herself on the bed as the tears flowed down her cheeks. She'd let her heart get involved, and she thought Michael had too. When would she learn?

Pulling her handkerchief from her pocket, Liz sat up and wiped her eyes. No matter how much her heart hurt, she'd get through this. She'd do her job as a Harvey Girl. She walked to the dresser, splashed cold water on her face, pinned up the stray curls, and trudged back to the lunchroom. At least the all-important governor's party would be in the dining room, and she wouldn't have to see Michael and that woman sitting side-by-side.

Liz frowned. What would the other Girls say when they saw the two of them together?

Later, after the train passengers had resumed their journey, Liz heard snatches of conversation as she cleaned the counter in her station. "There's Governor Stanley and his family. How exciting! Is that Michael McKey with that pretty woman?" Liz felt their glances directed at her. Warmth flooded up her neck into her cheeks. She caught sight of Michael with Miranda Whitmeyer attached firmly to his arm as they walked by the door. Michael looked in, and Liz quickly lowered her gaze.

"Liz, did you know Michael was coming with the governor's entourage?"

"I wonder if he knew these Boston people back home?"

Liz scrubbed the counter with a vengeance, trying not to hear her friends comments.

"Yes, I knew," She murmured as she hurried back to the dish room. Hopefully, her counter stools would fill quickly, and she could ignore the pitying looks.

She hurried to her room as soon as she finished her evening duties. She'd stay at the Harvey House over the weekend. There was no use risking an encounter with Michael. She picked up the wadded note off the floor and threw it in the trash.

The next morning, Liz walked to breakfast with Peggy. She'd slept fitfully and was in a grumpy mood.

Peggy frowned. "What's up with you? You haven't said five words since yesterday afternoon."

"Don't you know? Michael's with another girl...a rich girl whose father is a friend of the governor...a girl from his old days in Boston? He's been with her all week. How can I hope to compete with that?"

"He sure didn't look like he was having a lark, last night. The word from the dining room was that he looked miserable. He tried to catch your eye while they waited to be seated, but you wouldn't look at him."

"I didn't want to see him with her hanging on his arm."

Peggy raised her eyebrows. "If I were you, I'd find out what the situation really was before I threw him over."

"I can't talk about it right now."

Beatrice met them at the lunchroom entrance. "Good morning, girls. The Whitmeyers left on the morning train so we are finished with the governor's party."

Liz sighed. Michael was probably sad to say goodbye to the beautiful Miranda.

Michael woke with a start. Ahh—it was Saturday. Relief warred with anger and sadness inside him. Relief that the Whitmeyers were to leave this morning. He'd hang his formal clothes in the back of his wardrobe and get back into his boots and jeans. The only bright spot of the week, he thought ruefully, was driving the governor's runabout while he escorted Miranda.

He grimaced. Miranda was an empty-headed social climber, the very reason he'd gladly left Boston. If his mother hadn't threatened him with the family honor, Michael would have steered clear of the whole affair.

The fact that Liz had seen him with Miranda at the Harvey House made his heart contract with pain. He'd tried to ease the situation with his message, but he'd delayed writing it for too long. Liz wouldn't even look at him, last night, after her first cursory glance. He could only imagine the betrayal and hurt she must feel. She'd just recovered from Richard's treachery, and now she must think he was a cad, too! Nothing could be farther from his intentions, but that's not the way it looked. Regret nearly overwhelmed him. Why hadn't he told his mother he had other plans and couldn't accompany them? Somehow he had to make Liz understand.

Liz had probably gone home for the weekend. He'd drive over by her parents' house and see if he could talk to her. Her father knew the truth of the situation. He had heard Michael's mother admonishing him on the phone. Mr. Gilbertson had even encouraged him to do what she asked.

After breakfast, Michael hitched Dolly to his carriage and headed to the Gilbertsons' home. Julien sat on the porch swing with a book. Michael strode toward the porch. "Hey, Julien, is Liz here?"

Julien laid his book down. "Hi, Michael. No, she didn't come home this weekend. She sent a message to Pa that she'd decided to stay at the Harvey House." He stood. "But, you're welcome to come in. I know my parents would be glad to see you."

Michael shook his head. "Thanks, but I think I'll go see if I can talk to Liz."

"Okay." Disappointed, Julien sat back down and picked up his book.

When Michael arrived at the depot, he took the steps two

at a time. No one was on the landing at the top of the stairs, so he walked into the lunchroom. Peggy was polishing salt and pepper shakers at the counter.

Michael scanned the room. "Peggy, is Liz here? Do you think I could talk to her?"

Peggy cocked her head and contemplated him through half-closed eyes. "I don't think she's in any mood to talk to you right now. She was pretty upset when she saw that society gal on your arm last night."

Michael lowered his head and heaved a deep sigh. "I'm sure she was. Peggy, you've got to believe me. I didn't want to be here with Miranda. My parents are friends with the Whitmeyers. My parents insisted that I escort Miss Whitmeyer while she was here. Mother even called me at work—to Mr. Gilbertson's office!—to tell me I better not disgrace the family." Michael ran his hand through his hair. "Liz's father called me to the phone and heard what she told me."

"Why didn't you tell Liz you had to do that? She thought you'd chosen to be with Miranda because she was from your social set in Boston. She thought she didn't measure up."

"Women like Miranda were one of the reasons I wanted to move away from Boston. They can't hold a candle to Liz. I told her in my message that my mother insisted that I do it, and that I'd rather be with her."

Peggy considered him with a quizzical expression. "She didn't say anything about that. Let me find her and see if she wants to talk. I'll tell her what you said. Go wait in the parlor." She turned to Becky. "Can you keep an eye on my section? I'll be back shortly."

Liz was curled up on her bed with a book Peggy had loaned her. She'd mindlessly read the same page three times but still couldn't follow what it said. The scene from last night, of Michael with Miranda on his arm, kept playing in her mind. Why couldn't she get over it? She'd just have to! Obviously, Michael wasn't the man she thought he was.

She looked up as Peggy walked into the room. "Why are you here? Aren't you supposed to be at work?"

Peggy stopped with her hands on her hips. "Liz, where's that note Michael sent you yesterday?"

"I threw it in the trash. Why?"

Peggy leaned down and retrieved the wadded-up paper. She smoothed it out on Liz's dresser and scanned the message. "Did you even read past the first couple of words?" She handed the note to Liz. "Read this. His parents insisted that he escort Miranda. He didn't want to. You can decide if you want to go talk to him. He's in the parlor waiting for you. I have to get back to work." With that, she stalked from the room.

Liz read the message. *"It's not my choice"* and *"I'd rather be with you"* jumped off the page. How had she missed those two statements? She stared at the paper. Maybe she'd misjudged him?

Contrition washed over her. She'd let her fear of rejection rule her actions. Michael had told her several times that he didn't want to be involved in his parents' social life.

Liz laid the book aside and sat up. She needed to talk to him. She washed her face and repinned her hair then tentatively made her way into the parlor.

Michael was sitting on the edge of a chair but jumped up as soon as he saw her. "Liz, I'm so, so sorry for the misunderstanding. I didn't want to be with Miranda."

"Really? You appeared happy to be with her."

"How would you know? You wouldn't even look at me. I was miserable. I knew what you must think, and I couldn't get Miranda to leave me alone. Honestly, Liz, it was one of the most awkward, annoying weeks I've ever spent. The Whitmeyers are in my parents' circle of friends. Miranda was one of the big reasons I wanted to leave Boston. My mother thought I should court her, but I couldn't stand to have her hang all over me like she owned me.

"When Mother found out she and her father planned to come for business with Governor Stanley, she gave Miranda my address. Then she called me on your father's office phone and informed me that I had to escort her while she was here. Your father knew how upset I was, but he told me I needed to honor my mother's wishes. I'm sorry I didn't tell you up front, but I hoped you wouldn't even need to know. I should have known better." Michael lowered his head. "Can you forgive me?"

Liz stared at Michael's unruly, copper colored hair. Love and compassion for him rushed over her. "Yes, I forgive you. I need to ask your forgiveness, as well. I jumped to all the wrong conclusions. I thought you were happy to be back in the high-society lifestyle. I knew I couldn't live up to those standards."

Michael straightened and gazed tenderly into her eyes. "You far exceed any such false standards of the society. Miranda and the other women in my family's social circle don't begin to compare with your beauty or grace."

Liz smiled. "That's not true. Miranda's very beautiful."

"Aah, but not on the inside, and that's what counts."

"Michael, that's the nicest thing you could say." Liz stepped forward, threw her arms around him, and gave him a hug. She stepped back, quickly, wide-eyed and surprised at what she'd done.

He took her arm and pulled her toward him. "That's the nicest thing you could do." He lowered his head and touched her lips in a gentle kiss.

Wonder and awe swept through Liz. Her knees felt unsteady.

Michael pulled back and smiled. "Get your things together. Let's hightail it out of here. I'm ready to spend some time with my real girl."

CHAPTER 18

Liz sat with her mother and Clara over a leisurely breakfast in the dining room. Clara had arrived the day before from Boston, and Elise had offered to let her stay at the Gilbertsons' home until her interview on Monday.

Clara was charming and unaffected with red hair like Michael's but with a dark mahogany hue. She had a porcelain complexion with a sprinkling of freckles across her cheeks and nose.

Liz yawned. "It was nice to sleep in this morning. I'm surprised I didn't wake up at five-thirty."

"I'm glad you could rest." Elise looked at Clara. "Did you sleep well?"

"I did. Thank you."

"How was your trip across the country?"

"It went very well. There's a lot of beautiful scenery between here and Boston. I changed to ATSF railroad in Chicago. The trees are more sparse as you travel farther west."

Elise laughed. "That's true. Well, I'm glad you got here safely. When do you go to Kansas City for your interview?"

"Michael will take me to the train early Monday morning. My interview is at eleven o'clock."

"How's the weather in Boston this time of year? Did you have a severe winter?" Elise pushed her plate back and took a drink of coffee.

"We actually had a fairly mild winter. We had a couple of heavy snows. One in January dropped around a foot of snow. It melted in about a week. Then we had another one in March, right after my grandfather's funeral. The rest of the winter was warmer than usual. As for the weather now, I think it's pretty comparable to what I've experienced here. The flowers were blooming when I left."

"I'm sorry to hear about your grandfather." Elise sat forward and set her cup on the table.

"It's okay. Grandpa had been sick for quite a while." Clara gave a sad smile. "He wasn't an easy person to care for. He about wore my mother and Grandma to a frazzle. It was hard on our family." She looked down and shook her head. "I'm afraid I didn't handle it very well. My mother and I quarrelled more than once. I didn't want to be around him, and she thought I should help with his care."

"Oh, Clara. Let me give you a hug. It's so hard when someone you love is sick and especially if they become cantankerous. Were you able to make it right with your mother before you came?"

"Yes, we talked about it. Mother did understand. She realized I needed to come and have some time away. When Michael told me about the Harvey Girl job, it all fell into place."

"What about your family? Do you have brothers and sisters?"

"I have an older sister, Rebecca, who's married to Henry. I just found out before I left that she's expecting a baby. It's her first." She sat forward and grinned. "So I'll be an aunt. My brother, William, is four years older than me. He works on the shipyards as a bookkeeper. My parents live just a few houses down from my grandma's house. So we've spent a lot of time with my grandparents, especially when my grandfather was so sick."

"You and Michael are cousins, right? Do your families live close together?"

Clara laughed. "We're, actually, like third cousins. My Great-grandmother Mabel and his Great-grandpa Theodore McKey were brother and sister. And, no, we don't live close to one-another so we don't even see each other very often, though we both live in Boston. Our families usually celebrated Christmas with the McKeys. That was mostly so our grandparents could get together.

Michael and I would usually get away from the hubbub and read or play a game. We were the quiet ones in the family."

The urge to find out more about her family flooded through Liz as she heard Clara talk. If only she knew where to start the search. She couldn't afford a trip to Boston and wouldn't know where to look if she could get there."

The lunchroom atmosphere was alive with anticipation. The new Harvey Girls would arrive soon.

Peggy turned from her station at the lunch counter. "Just

think. A month ago at this time, we were on our way here. We didn't know anything about serving the Fred Harvey way. Now we're Harvey Girls about to be sent to our new assignments."

Mary Alice laughed softly. "I was so scared. Our maid did everything for me back home, but I wanted to learn to be on my own. I was afraid I'd make a fool of myself, but thankfully, with everyone's help, I didn't."

"I'm excited to help the next girls get started." Liz arranged the silverware, napkins, and cups in her area in preparation for the evening train rush. "I know at least one of them will be Clara, Michael's cousin. She had her interview at eleven-o'clock this morning."

"*If* she was hired." Maggie leaned against the counter. "I wonder how many girls they turn away?"

"It probably has a lot to do with attitude, and if they agree to obey the rules."

"And, maybe the way they're dressed, or if they wear too much makeup." Becky was next to Liz.

"Well, we'll soon meet them. I just heard the train whistle." Liz smoothed her apron and adjusted the salt and pepper shakers.

They all snapped to attention and stood straight in their sections.

Liz watched the door as the train passengers began to stream into the room. Would Michael come to meet Clara? Liz grinned to herself. She had chatted with him a few minutes that morning when he brought Clara to the train. Did he look forward to their time together as much as she did? It'd be hard to leave him here when she moved to her new Harvey House.

Just then, Clara walked in with two other girls. She spied

Liz and headed straight for her station. "I was hired!" She had a huge grin.

Clara turned to the girls behind her. "This is Ida and Laura. The others will come in tomorrow. They had their interviews this afternoon."

Liz motioned to her stools. "Welcome. Have a seat. What would you like to drink?"

"I'll take iced tea with sugar." Clara turned to the other two. "Watch what she does with the cups. It's a code we have to learn."

Liz tilted Clara's cup against the saucer. "This is the way you place it for iced tea. Then the girl who serves beverages knows what to give the customer." She handed them a menu. "If you have questions, ask us. We were in your shoes four weeks ago."

The next days went by quickly, while the new girls observed and learned the Harvey system. On Thursday afternoon, Beatrice called all of Liz's group into the parlor. She carried a handful of envelopes. "I have your new assignments."

A current of murmurs traveled around the room. Peggy sat on the sofa beside Liz. "I'm so excited. I hope I get New Mexico or Arizona. I want to go where my pa can't find me."

"I'd like to be able to get back home for a visit if I want to," Liz leaned over and whispered. "And it'd be easier for Michael to come to see me if I'm not too far away."

"But, of course! That's a consideration." Peggy grinned.

Beatrice handed out the envelopes. "You can check your destinations, then finish preparations for the six o'clock train if you haven't already."

Liz lifted the flap on the back and slipped out the paper. "Hutchinson, Kansas." Relief rushed through her. "My mama's friend, Tessa, lives there. Her daughter's a Harvey Girl. That's fairly close."

Peggy gave a little squeal. "Winslow, Arizona. That should be far enough away."

Maggie held up her paper. "I'm headed to Dodge City."

Beatrice nodded. "They've built a brand new hotel named El Vaquero there. It was opened last year. I've heard it's quite nice." She scanned the room. "Mary Alice, you'll be in Las Vegas, New Mexico, with Abigail, from our last group. La Castañeda is also one of our newest hotels, and it's impressive. I hear that most of the older Harvey Houses will be rebuilt in the next few years. A new hotel in Hutchinson is in the planning stage."

Becky put her arm around Ethel. "We're both transferred to Newton, Kansas. I'm glad we get to stay together."

"There's a new hotel there in Newton, too, named the Arcade," Beatrice explained. "They've taken over the service that the Harvey House in Florence, Kansas, provided, since it was closed in March of last year. They'll have a huge laundry facility at the Arcade and all our dirty laundry will be sent there by rail to be laundered. Fred Harvey believes in efficiency on a large scale."

Beatrice looked around at the girls. "I'm excited for you, but this is the hardest time for me. I just get acquainted with you all then you leave and go to all these interesting places."

Liz leaned forward. "You could move, couldn't you, if you wanted to?"

"Yes, I'm thinking about it. I've been here for two years. I'd like to have some new scenery." Beatrice straightened. "Now you need to finish your afternoon duties, and I need to get back to the new girls. Have a good evening."

Michael stared at the numbers on the page in front of him. He couldn't concentrate. Too many thoughts crowded into his mind. It was already Thursday, and he hadn't accomplished near what he'd planned.

This had been a busy week. Clara passed her interview and had begun work, and Liz was going to Hutchinson, Kansas, according to her father.

He'd finished the book of John in the Bible and had gone back to reread some of the most compelling verses. He pulled his Bible from the desk drawer where he had placed it that morning and turned to the passage, John 1:11-12: *He came unto His own, and His own received him not, but as many as received Him, to them gave He power to become the sons of God, even to them that believe on His name.* Then he turned to chapter 3 verse 3: *Jesus answered and said unto him, Verily, verily, I say unto thee, Except a man be born again, he cannot see the kingdom of God.* Then verses 15 and 16: *That whosoever believeth in Him should not perish, but have everlasting life. For God so loved the world, that He gave His only begotten Son, that whosoever believeth in Him should not perish, but have everlasting life.*

He believed in Jesus, that He'd died on the cross to pay for his sins. He wanted to be born again, to become a child of God and have eternal life. He wasn't sure how to go about it. He needed to talk to someone, but who?

Then there was his friendship with Liz. He'd known her for less than two months, but he knew she was special. The incident with Miranda made him realize he wanted to formally court Elizabeth Gilbertson. Had it been long enough since she'd been hurt by Richard? Was she ready for a new relationship? He needed to ask Mr. Gilbertson for permission. Liz would leave next week for her new assignment. There wasn't much time.

Michael studied the columns of figures. He needed to get the books reconciled, but his mind wouldn't focus. Sticking his fountain pen in the inkwell, he pushed the ledger back on the desk then stood. He had to get some answers.

He walked down the hall to his boss's office. The door stood open, so he knocked lightly on the doorframe.

Daniel looked up from the papers on his desk. He laid his pen down and stood. "Michael, come in. What can I do for you?"

Michael stepped into the room. "Mr. Gilbertson, if you aren't too busy, I need to talk to you."

"I can do that. I'm just working on some tedious reports. Actually, I welcome a reprieve. Have a seat."

Michael sat down on the chair by his boss's desk. He sighed and shook his head. "I hardly know where to start." He looked up. "The last few weeks, I've been reading the Bible my landlady, Mrs. Bartlett, gave me, at the first boarding house. You see, my family went to church, but I don't recall most of the stories about Jesus. I just finished the Gospel of St. John last night. I believe in Jesus. I want to be His child and have everlasting life. I want to see the Kingdom of God, but how do I accomplish that?"

Daniel leaned forward. "Michael, do you know that you're a sinner? That you've done things that have displeased God? Have you lied or been disobedient to your parents?"

Michael nodded. "Oh, yeah, many times. I definitely know I've sinned."

"Then you are one of those Jesus came to die for. He said, *I came not to call the righteous, but sinners to repentance.* Romans 5:8 says, *But God commendeth his love toward us, in that, while we were yet sinners, Christ died for us.* Jesus knew you way before you were born and He knew you'd be a sinner, but He died for you anyway. Romans 10:9 and 10 say, *That if thou shalt confess with thy mouth the Lord Jesus, and shalt believe in thine heart that God hath raised Him from the dead, thou shalt be saved. For with the heart, man believeth unto righteousness; and with the mouth, confession is made unto salvation.* Verse 13 says, *For whosoever shall call upon the name of the Lord shall be saved.*

Mr. Gilbertson looked at the young man sitting across from him, tenderness in his eyes. "Michael, pray to Jesus. Confess that you're a sinner and that you believe that Jesus died for your sins and rose from the dead. Then ask Him to save you. He will make you His child and give you everlasting life."

"I don't know how to pray," Michael admitted. He wrinkled his brow.

"You just talk to God, like you've talked to me. It's that simple."

Michael bowed his head. "Dear Jesus, I know I'm a sinner, and I believe you died for my sins and rose from the dead like it says in the Bible. Please forgive me and make me your child. I want to have everlasting life and see your kingdom. Thank you, Jesus." He hesitated. "Oh, yeah, Amen." He looked up and smiled. A tremendous burden lifted off of him.

Daniel stood and held out his hand. "Congratulations, Michael. You're now a child of God and my brother in Christ."

Michael stood and shook his hand. "Thank you." He gulped

as a bubble of apprehension balled up in his throat. He took a deep breath. "Uh...I have something else I'd like to ask you."

"Oh, what's that?"

"Uh...would it be okay...is it alright...? Oh...I want to court Liz. May I have your permission?"

Daniel laughed as he sat back in his seat. "Yes, you have my permission, and Mrs. Gilbertson will be agreeable, as well. I think Elizabeth likes you a lot." He paused, then added seriously, "Just take care of her."

Michael let out a sigh of relief. "Thank you. I will!"

"This is quite a momentous afternoon for you."

"Yes, yes, it is. Now I have to get my books done. I couldn't concentrate before." Michael hurried from the room.

The next afternoon, Michael closed the ledger in front of him. Thankfully, he'd gotten the accounts caught up and balanced, at least the ones he could reconcile. He was sure the Harvey Houses brought business to the ATSF. The new hotels which were being built along the line drew more passengers, so the fact that they operated at a deficit was not a concern to anyone else but him. He set the books on their shelves and pushed his chair back.

Excitement and trepidation mingled in his gut. He wanted to ask Liz to court him, but what if she said, no? Was she ready for a new relationship? She'd signed an agreement not to marry for at least six months. That was okay with him. They needed time to get better acquainted.

There was a quickness to his step as he turned off the light and left his office. He'd experienced fantastic peace and joy since he'd prayed to receive Jesus as his Savior. He was anxious to share his good news. He strode out into the afternoon sunlight and drove his rig to the Harvey House. Mrs. Gilbertson had invited Clara to spend the weekend with Liz and he was to escort them there after they finished work. The heat of the afternoon sun wrapped around him as he traveled along Kansas Avenue. This was the first day of summer, and it definitely felt like it.

He'd known Liz would leave for another assignment, but it had come sooner than he wanted. He was glad she wouldn't be too far away. At least she wouldn't be in New Mexico like Abigail!

Ten minutes later, he turned into the depot parking lot. The train would arrive soon. As he secured Dolly and ambled into the lobby, he heard the train whistle. There wasn't any hurry. He'd wait until the train passengers were served to visit with Liz.

His heart rate quickened as he saw the train passengers begin to descend the stairs. He'd see Liz in a few minutes. Would she want to commit to court him before she left for her new assignment?

As he reached the top of the stairs, Beatrice waved him into the lunchroom. "Liz will be glad to see you." She pointed toward the dining room. "Clara's still observing tonight."

Michael chuckled. "Two months ago I hadn't even heard of the Harvey Houses. Now I personally know two young women who are Harvey Girls and quite a few others as well." He stepped through the door and hesitated as he watched Liz. She wiped the counter and arranged clean napkins, silverware, cups, and saucers. Her natural beauty and grace touched him. He smiled. An errant golden curl had escaped her chignon and hung beside her face.

Just then, she glanced up. Michael was warmed by the sparkle of welcome he saw in her eyes. She gestured for him to come to her section and he moved quickly toward her, across the floor and straddled a stool.

Liz tidied her counter space. One more group of diners and she'd be off for the weekend. Next week at this time she'd be in Hutchinson. What would she experience in the new Harvey House?

She stepped back and looked up. Her pulse increased, and happiness filled her. Michael stood inside the door and watched her. He was so handsome. His coppery hair and hazel eyes set him apart from any other man she'd seen. She couldn't stop the smile that spread across her face. She motioned for him to come and sit down.

Oblivious to the other customers who filled her section, she watched as he made his way and took his seat. "Hello, Michael. Did you have a good week?"

"Yes, as a matter of fact, I did. I have something exciting to tell you. What about you?"

"Really, what's your news?"

"You'll have to wait to find out."

"That's not fair." She tightened her mouth. "But, yes, it was a good week. It's been fun to have the new girls here. I can't believe I've only been training here a month." She leaned forward. "Did you hear, I'll transfer to Hutchinson, Kansas? That's not very far away."

"I did hear. Your father told me you had sent a message." He wrinkled his nose. "I guess that's better than New Mexico or Arizona."

"That's what I thought. We can talk later. Now, I have to get busy. Do you want iced tea?" She handed him a menu.

Michael grinned. "That sounds great. You know what I like."

"I'm learning." Liz continued to take drink preferences. Soon she was back to take his supper order.

"I'll take the beef stroganoff with egg noodles, the fresh green peas, and sliced tomatoes. Then I'll have the fresh peach shortcake for dessert."

"That sounds good." Liz took his order, and the rest of the meal went smoothly.

Michael ate the last bite of his shortcake and pushed his plate back. "That was delightful, once again." He picked up his glass, took a drink, and sat back."You look like you've done this all your life. I knew you'd do well."

"Thanks, Michael."

Michael set down his glass and stood. "I'll wait for you in the parlor."

"Okay, I shouldn't be too long. Clara will be in soon, too." Liz watched him with mixed emotions as he left the lunchroom. She was excited about the move to Hutchinson, but she'd miss him terribly when she left.

Michael was vitally aware of Liz's presence beside him on the carriage seat as they traveled toward her house. He slipped his hand into his pocket and felt the package that contained the pearl brooch he'd bought for her. His gift needed to be something small. She couldn't wear jewelry when she worked, but maybe it would be a reminder of his feelings.

As Liz and Clara chattered about their experiences in the Harvey House, he mentally rehearsed his words for later in the evening. He swallowed to moisten his mouth. He couldn't remember ever feeling this nervous, even when he started his new job or talked to her father.

The evening sun was still up quite a ways in the western sky as they pulled up in front of the Gilbertson home. Michael jumped down, then assisted Liz and Clara down before he grabbed their bags.

Liz tucked her hand under his elbow. "Now you can tell me your exciting news."

"I'll tell you when we get inside. I want your mother to hear." He reached to open the front door.

Liz stepped inside. "We're home. Anyone here?" They walked toward the library.

Julien's head appeared around the library door. "Hi, I'm here. Daddy had a church meeting, and Mama's upstairs, I think." He stepped out into the hall. "Hey, Michael, my teacher goes to our church. She said you could come to tell us about Boston and the revolution when school starts again in the fall. I'll be in the seventh grade. Will you do that?."

"Sounds good. We'll figure it out, champ."

"Right now, we need to go up and find Mother." Liz tousled Julien's hair.

He ducked away from her with a frown. "You never let me talk to Michael."

Michael touched his shoulder. "Next week your sister will move to another city. Then we'll have plenty of time to visit."

Julien perked up, then frowned at Liz. "Where you goin'?"

241

"I'll work at the Harvey House in Hutchinson, Kansas. It's not too far away. We'll be able to visit."

"I didn't know you were gonna move." He pulled his face into a pout.

"I know. I just found out yesterday. Why don't you go see what you can find out about Hutchinson?"

Julien gave her another long look then disappeared back into the library.

Clara laughed. "I wish I had a little brother. My brother's four years older than me, and he's busy with his own life. My sister is even older than him."

The three of them headed up the stairs. The evening sunlight cast shadows across the bed in Liz's bedroom, where Michael set the bags. Down the hall, Liz knocked on the door frame of Elise's room. "Mama, we're home. Is it okay if we come in?"

Elise appeared in the door of her sunroom. "Oh, my goodness! Is it that time already? I was engrossed in my church committee work, and the time got away from me. Yes, yes, come on in." She acknowledged the others. "Hello, Clara and Michael. Glad to have you here." She gestured with her hand. "Come out into the sun porch. It's so much cooler here with the evening breeze blowing through."

She stepped back as they filed in and found seats. Michael sat beside Liz on a wicker loveseat.

Liz sat forward. "Mama, did you hear I'll be moved to Hutchinson? I hope I'll see your friend, Tessa, and her family."

Elise sat in her easy chair and tucked her legs under her. "I did hear. Your father got your message yesterday. I'm sure you'll meet Tessa. Her daughter, Anna, is a Harvey Girl there. I think she may be the head waitress. I'll write Tessa and let her know you're moving there. I'd love to come to see her, too, once you get settled in. I already sent a letter to Grandpa Gilbertson to let him know you'd come through Emporia next Thursday. I'm sure he, Thomas, Rebecca, and their children will all be at the depot to greet you. Maybe you can eat lunch there."

"I hope so. It will be lovely to see the family. Let's see, Jacob, their baby, must be two already. That doesn't seem possible."

Elise smiled. "I know." She turned to Clara. "And how did your first week go?"

"It went very well. I had the same trainer that Liz had. Her name is Alice, and she does a great job. I'm excited to be in the lunchroom next week."

"So you think you'll like it?"

"Oh, yes. The Harvey House is so organized and runs so smoothly. Interesting people come in every day. It's also a relief to be on my own."

Liz turned. "Michael has something exciting to tell us. He wouldn't tell me until you could hear, too."

Interest sparked in Elise's eyes. "Tell us your news."

Michael shifted on the seat. "I've been reading the Bible that Mrs. Bartlett gave me. On Thursday, I couldn't wait any longer. I knew I believed in Jesus. I asked Mr. Gilbertson for further clarification. He guided me to pray for forgiveness, and to accept Jesus as my Savior."

Liz whirled toward him. "That's wonderful, Michael. I'm so glad." She threw her arms around him and gave him a hug.

His eyes danced as he returned her hug. He hadn't expected such a reaction.

Liz sat back. Her face was pink, and her eyes glowed. "I'm sorry. I'm just so happy for you."

Elise beamed and reached out to pat his knee. "That's wonderful news. That's the best decision you could ever make in your life."

"I want to pray for my family. We attended church, but we never heard that we needed to believe or accept Jesus as Savior. I wrote my brother, and he said he's found a Bible and has started to read it, so I pray he'll find the truth."

"We'll pray with you for them." Elise agreed. "I know Daniel was ecstatic to be able to pray with you. He didn't say anything, though. I'm sure he wanted you to be able to share it yourself." She stood. "We better get you girls settled in. Clara, you'll be in the extra bedroom again." She stood, and they walked from the room.

Michael touched Liz's hand. "I'll go down and visit with Julien. Would you please come down after you get done? I want to talk to you."

Liz's eyes flitted around the room that had been hers for the last fourteen years. Her mama had moved her in here from the nursery when Adam was born. It was a beautiful, comfortable room. This was the last weekend she'd be here for a long time. It was time for Rachel to have a place of her own.

Clara was still settling in so Liz walked downstairs. Michael glanced up as she stepped into the library. "Come and look. Julien found Hutchinson, Kansas, in the encyclopedia. It was founded by C.C. Hutchinson in 1872. There are salt mines there. It looks like an up and coming city."

"I guess I'll find out soon enough." Liz looked at the few pictures in the book.

Michael stood. "Let's go out on the porch swing."

"Oh, yes! It's a beautiful evening." She turned toward her brother. "Julien, will you please entertain Clara when she comes down?"

Settled on the porch swing, Liz sighed contentedly. "It's nice to just relax. It's been a busy week."

Michael hesitated then moved closer. "Yes, it has. We've been extra busy in the office. Travel on the railroad has picked up since the Fred Harvey Company started to build the fancy, modern hotels along the line. The new rooms encourage stopover visits in these towns as well as meals for train passengers. I hear there's one planned for Hutchinson in honor of Fred Harvey. Louis Curtiss, a well-known Kansas architect, is designing it."

Liz touched Michael's hand and leaned her head against the back of the swing. "I just want to relax and talk about other things. When do you think you'll be able to come visit me?"

Michael chuckled nervously. "I'm sorry, here I am nattering on like a magpie. We will have to write with our schedules to plan a visit."

"It's okay. I like to hear you talk...and yes, I will write, often."

"Uh...Liz, "Michael stammered. "Could I court you? I know we've only been acquainted for a short time, but it seems like I've known you forever."

Liz raised her head and stared at him, wide-eyed. Had she heard right? "What did you say?"

"I asked, may I court you? I've wanted to ask for a while. I talked to your father. He agreed it was fine. He even said your mother would think so, too."

Liz scooted back in the swing and sat straight. "I'd like very much for you to court me. But what would your parents say? I don't fit into their social realm."

"They will love you when they meet you. I've never fit in that lifestyle. I was afraid it was too soon since you were hurt by Richard."

Liz turned toward him. "Actually, Richard did me a favor. I wouldn't have been happy with him."

Michael sighed, and Liz felt him relax. He shifted and pulled an object from his pocket. "I want you to have a small token to take with you so you'll know I'm thinking about you when I can't be with you." He held out a small brown package.

"You don't have to give me a gift."

"I know, but I want you to have it."

Liz took it and broke open the seal on the wrapping. Inside was a beautiful miniature pearl brooch set in gold. She drew in her breath. "It's gorgeous! I love it!"

"I know you can't wear jewelry when you work, but I thought you could wear it for special occasions."

"I will wear it and enjoy it. Thank you." She pinned it on her blouse.

Michael took her hands. "May I give you a kiss?"

Liz let her eyes give her assent as she leaned toward him. Then their lips met. Ecstasy and joy rushed through Liz. Michael was all she'd ever wanted in a man.

CHAPTER 19

Liz awoke the next morning with an old hymn on her mind. She sang it softly as she got dressed. *"Praise God from Whom all blessings flow, Praise Him all creatures here below, Praise Him above all Heavenly hosts, Praise Father, Son, and Holy Ghost."*

Happiness flooded through her. Michael had prayed to accept Jesus as his Savior, and then he'd asked to court her. She walked to the dresser and picked up the pearl brooch he'd given her. She ran her thumb over the pearls. It would be hard to leave on Thursday for her new Harvey House, with the knowledge that she wouldn't be able to see him as often. But, she knew he'd think of her. They would make it through this time of separation.

She smiled. Elise had told her about Daniel's time away, as a surveyor, when she was a Harvey Girl. He hadn't asked her to wait, but she did, in spite of another man who tried to get her attention. God had worked it all out.

"You sound happy in here."

Liz spun toward the door. Clara stood there in her robe and

slippers, her auburn hair fell in waves around her shoulders.

"I am happy." Liz laid the brooch on the dresser. "I like Michael a lot. I'm delighted that he asked to court me."

Clara shuffled into the room and sat on the end of Liz's bed. "You're probably the first girl Michael's ever even been interested in. We didn't see a lot of each other back in Boston, but I think I'd have heard if he'd been sweet on any of the highfalutin gals his parents approved of. Everyone knew about Miranda Whitmeyer. She's out to get a rich husband any way she can." She turned to face Liz. "I'm glad Michael likes you. I hope it works out for you both."

"Thank you, Clara. That means a lot." Liz walked to the window seat and scooted back on the cushions, and Clara took a seat on the vanity stool. "You've said you didn't see a lot of each other. Did you live far apart?"

"We grew up with two different lifestyles, even though I lived just a few miles from him. Michael's great-grandfather inherited the bank and became bank president. My great-grandmother married a businessman who owned a large mercantile, Hughes Department Store. They did quite well. My Grandma Grace, their daughter, inherited it and she operated it until she sold it five years ago. My mother worked there as a clerk. I loved to go in and wander around. There were always new and fascinating things to see. Grandma hated to sell it, but it was more than she could handle, and neither my parents or my Aunt Amelia and her husband were willing to take it over. I would have tried to run it, but I was too young.

"My Grandpa Tilman first worked in the bank with Michael's dad and grandfather, but he enjoyed his spirits too much and would go into angry rages. He eventually lost his job. Our cousins didn't want to be associated with him so we kind of lost touch these last few years. It was hard on Grandma. But, we still got together for Christmas, and I looked forward to the time spent with Michael. He's my favorite cousin."

"Well, I'm glad you're here now. I already feel like we're good friends. Liz glanced at her clock. "Oh, goodness, we better get dressed and go down for breakfast. Catherine probably wonders where we are."

Clara stood and headed for the door. "I'll be ready in a jiffy. It's nice to have a leisurely morning."

"Yes, it is." Liz rose as Clara left the room and walked to the dresser. She ran the brush through her hair, braided it and arranged it into a chignon then put on her socks and shoes.

Rachel ran up the stairs. "Liz, you awake? Breakfast is ready."

"We'll be down in a little bit."

Minutes later, they descended the stairs, arm-in-arm. Elise sat at the table, sipping coffee and looking at the previous evening's newspaper. "Well, did you girls decide to get up?" She smiled. "Liz, you better take advantage of the opportunity to sleep in. Your schedule will pick up once you get to your new house. You'll be one of the regular staff. You should be ready to serve in the dining room, soon."

Liz filled her plate from the sideboard and sat down at the table. "I know. I have to serve a full-course meal to the manager and head waitress, right?"

"Yes. It's a bit intimidating, but you'll do fine." She turned to Clara. "And, you'll be moving, too, before you know it. Our home will feel emptier without you girls."

Liz turned to Clara. Would you like to go with me to visit my friend, Anna Lisa? She lives down the street."

"Yes, I would." Clara pushed her chair out. They placed their plates and cups on the dish cart. "I need to get some fresh air." She followed Liz from the room.

As they headed off the front porch, Liz looked up at the clouds that had built up in the west. The air was warm and balmy, with the threat of rain. "Maybe I better get an umbrella. We may get wet before we get back."

Clara waited on the porch as Liz hurried back inside.

A few minutes later, she returned with a large umbrella, and they started down the street toward Anna Lisa's house. "Mother said she'd come to get us in the carriage if it starts to rain hard."

"I'm not too concerned. I enjoy the summer rains in Boston."

"We get real downpours here, with wind and lightning sometimes. They can come up pretty fast."

"Well, let's hurry. Hopefully, we'll get there before it starts."

The first large drops of rain had begun to fall as they scampered up the steps to the door of the Stoops home. Liz turned the doorbell knob. When the door swung open, Anna Lisa's mother pushed the screen door open and scolded, "Get in here, you two. You'll get soaked. This looks like it may be a frog strangler." She waved them inside.

Liz and Clara stepped through the door and into the entry hall. "That's what we figured out when we were half-way here."

"How've you been, Liz? And who's your friend?" Mrs. Stoops moved back as they entered.

"I'm fine. This is Michael McKey's cousin from Boston. She's started her training to be a Harvey Girl."

"From Boston, huh? Why did you come out here to be a Harvey Girl?"

"I wanted to get away from the big city, and Michael enjoys it here. He told me all about it and invited me. I appreciate the opportunity to work at the Harvey House."

"Humph, I guess it's alright if your parents approve. I'm glad Anna Lisa didn't get caught up in that foolishness."

Liz frowned. "It's not foolishness, Mrs. Stoops. It's an honorable job."

"We'll see." She raised her eyebrows, disdainfully. "I suppose you've come to see Anna Lisa. She's dusting in the parlor. I'll tell her you're here." She wheeled around and left the hall.

"Thank you, ma'am," Liz spoke to her retreating back.

Within seconds, Anna Lisa appeared from a side door. She rushed to Liz and threw her arms around her in a hug. "Liz, it's good to see you. I miss our visits." She stepped back and turned to Clara. "Hi, I'm Anna Lisa, as you probably already know." She grinned.

"I'm Clara Bryan. Michael McKey's my cousin."

"Oh, yes, I remember Liz said he'd informed you about the Harvey Girl job." She faced Liz. "Come on up to my room. We can talk there." She gestured for them to follow her up the stairs. "I'll get a chair from the sitting room."

"No, this is fine. We can both sit on the bed. " Liz sat down near the head of the bed.

Anna Lisa pulled the small seat out from under her vanity. "Here, Clara. You can sit on here." She settled next to Liz. "Now, tell me. What's it like to be a Harvey Girl?"

"It's interesting. You have to learn all the details of the Fred

Harvey system, but you meet the most fascinating people. You definitely don't get bored. I wish you could have come." Liz pulled her legs up under her. "Next Thursday, I'm being transferred to Hutchinson, Kansas. You and Billy are invited to a going-away reception at the Harvey House Wednesday evening."

"We'll plan to come. Billy's never eaten at the Harvey House." Anna Lisa pursed her lips. "I wish I could have gone with you, but..." She shrugged her shoulders. "It wouldn't have worked out. My mother would've had a fit if I'd gotten sent somewhere far away."

Liz nodded. "What's the story with you and Billy?"

Anna Lisa sighed happily. "It's better than I could have imagined. He asked me to marry him." She scrunched her face "Mother doesn't approve. She says it's too soon. She wants me to finish my music in college...but we've known each other forever, since we were in grade school." She brightened. "I know now, I've loved him for a long time. I was just too stubborn to admit it."

Liz nodded. "I thought you liked him more than you let on. I hope it all works out for you."

"It will. "Anna Lisa chuckled. "My father will be relieved to have me married off. And Mother will come around. She always does."

"When do you plan to get married? I, for sure, want to come for that."

"We haven't set a date yet. I'll let you know. Hutchinson's not that far away, is it?"

"No. We should be able to visit on weekends."

"What about you and Michael?"

Liz's eyes sparkled, and she gave a little bounce. "He asked to court me, and Daddy gave his consent." She leaned forward to show Anna Lisa the brooch she wore on her blouse. "Michael gave me this."

"That's beautiful." Anna Lisa touched the pearls. "I'm excited for you. He seems like a humdinger of a young man."

"He is."

Anna Lisa turned to Clara. "When did you start? You weren't in Liz's group, were you?"

"I had my interview on Monday and started training on Wednesday. I'm a month behind Liz."

Anna Lisa wrinkled her nose. "I wanted to be a Harvey Girl, but my parents didn't approve." She studied Clara. "What made you want to be a Harvey Girl?"

Clara squinted her eyes and cocked her head. "I wanted to be on my own...get out of the big city and earn some money."

Just then, a loud thunderclap and low, extended rumble sounded outside the window. Liz jumped as rain and hail lashed the window. "Whew! That sounded close! We may be here a while. Mama did say she'd come to get us in the carriage if it began to rain hard." She shifted to look out the window. "It's really dark outside."

Lightning flashed, and another clap of thunder reverberated through the room.

"What...what is that?" Clara's shaky voice caught Liz's attention. She turned from the window. The color had drained from Clara's face, and her eyes were huge. Liz scrambled off the bed. "I'm sorry, Clara. I guess you're not used to Kansas thunderstorms." She knelt down in front of Clara and grabbed her hands. "The wind and thunder usually move through pretty fast. It shouldn't last much longer."

Just then, another crackling bolt of lightning, and loud rumble rolled across the sky. The window pane rattled as the wind whipped around the house.

"Why don't you girls come on downstairs." Mrs. Stoop's voice came from the foot of the stairs.

"Yes, let's go." Clara's voice quivered.

Liz grabbed her arm as she stood. "You're shaking like a leaf. I guess I don't think that much about it. I've grown up around these storms." They followed Anna Lisa from the room.

Mrs. Stoops waited at the bottom of the stairs. "Come into the library. It only has one small window." She turned to Clara. "You may wish you'd stayed in Boston."

Clara solemnly nodded.

Liz stopped and listened. "I think the worst has blown through. The wind and hail have stopped. Now there's mostly rain." The thunder still rumbled, but it sounded farther away.

Anna Lisa led the way toward the library. She lit the lantern. "We need to settle down. Let's play a table game until the storm clears out or your mother comes to get you."

Clara began to relax as the thunder grew softer. The rain pattered on the window. "I've never experienced anything like that. Does it do that often?"

"Fairly often. It's an awesome display of God's power and strength. Occasionally, there will be hard winds or hail with it that can do damage, but usually, there's just the lightning and thunder." Liz paused.

Clara's hands still shook as she helped distribute the tokens for the game.

They had just finished the game when the doorbell rang. A few minutes later, Elise and Mrs. Stoops walked into the room. Elise brushed water droplets from her skirt. "That was some storm. Wasn't it?"

Liz gestured toward Clara. "It nearly scared Clara to death."

Clara nodded. "We don't have storms like that in Boston."

"Oh, I bet that was scary. I'm glad it didn't last any longer than it did." Elise placed her hand on Clara's arm. "The Harvey Houses all have emergency plans in place for severe weather."

"I'm glad of that." Clara gathered up the game playing pieces.

Elise visited with Anna Lisa's mother as the girls put the game away. "I'm glad you girls got here for your visit before that storm blew in. But, now, we better get on back home."

Clara shuddered. "Me, too! It would have been terrible if we'd been out in it."

Liz gave Anna Lisa a hug. "I'll see you on Wednesday evening. I'm happy for you. God's working things out for us."

"Yes, He is."

Wednesday afternoon, Liz and Peggy packed their belongings. Peggy took her new dress from the wardrobe and held it up. "Maggie did a fantastic job. I haven't had a new dress like this in a very long time. Betty gave me the outfit I wore for my interview."

"It's beautiful. I'm glad Maggie got it done in time." Liz opened her dresser drawer and took out the white silk rose she'd bought at the mercantile. "Here, Peggy, I want you to have this.

It will look charming with your dress."

"Oh, Liz, you bought that for yourself."

"I know, but you've been a wonderful friend and roommate. I want you to have it."

Tears welled-up in Peggy's eyes as she gave Liz a hug. "Thank you. I don't deserve such friends." She folded the dress carefully and placed it in her trunk along with her well-worn clothes then placed the rose beside it. "Are we supposed to take the uniforms we got here?"

"Yes, they were issued to each of us. These uniforms are the ones we'll wear when we work in our new Harvey Houses."

Liz removed the box that contained her mother's jewelry from her dresser drawer and placed it on top. She lifted the lid, took out the diamond brooch, and ran her finger across the intricate pattern. She studied the picture next to it. If only she could have shared these experiences with her mother.

"That's exquisite. Where did you get such a beautiful brooch?" Peggy had walked up behind her.

Liz turned. "It belonged to my mother. My father gave it to her for their wedding." She pointed. "See, she wore it in the picture. My real mother and father died in a carriage accident when I was four years old." She put her hand on the trunk. "This was theirs, too."

"Oh, Liz, I'm sorry to hear that. I knew there was a story behind that picture, but I didn't want to pry."

"It's okay. I've learned to live with the fact. I have a wonderful family, now. In fact Daniel is my mother's brother, so he's my uncle. Sometimes, though, I wonder what it would be like to share experiences with my real parents." She reached into the drawer and took out the small dagger. "This was in the trunk, too. It belonged to my father. I found a letter from his grandmother...she gave it to him." She rubbed the pattern on the side of the scabbard and on the handle. "I don't know what I'll do with it. There has to be a story behind it."

Peggy reached to touch it. "That looks like a family crest on the handle. Maybe, you're royalty, and it's a family heirloom you can use to claim a treasure!" She giggled.

"It could be," Liz laughed. "I'll probably never know. I don't have any information about my father's family."

"That's crazy. I want to get as far away from my Pa as possible, and you'd give almost anything to know your father."

"That's true." Liz laid the dagger beside the picture on the dresser and opened the next drawer. She lifted out a pile of underclothes and put them in the trunk.

Liz changed the subject. "It seems like a dream that we'll be in a new town by tomorrow evening. I'm glad we plan to stop at the Harvey House in Emporia. My grandpa and my uncle and his family—on my real mother's side—live on a large ranch there. Mama sent a letter to tell them I'll be there. I hope they got the message to meet us. I haven't seen them since Thanksgiving." She noticed the clock. "Oh, the time got away. We better get to the lunchroom." She slipped her apron on. "It's our last night to serve here."

Clara stepped through the doorway. "You girls about ready? The parlor's set up for the reception. It looks nice." She glanced around their room. "Are you almost packed?" Clara's voice trailed off and her eyes widened as she stared at Liz's dresser. She took a step toward it. "Where'd you get that dagger?"

Liz frowned, "It belonged to my real father. It was with his things."

"It was your father's?" Clara picked it up and touched the crest on the handle.

"Yes, I have a letter from his grandmother Mabel. She gave it to him when he moved out here to Kansas. He was from Boston like you and Michael."

Clara laid the dagger back on the dresser and picked up the photo. "And these people are your parents?" She turned it over.

"Yes, they died when I was four years old." Liz opened the drawer and took out another picture. "Here's one of me with them when I was a baby."

Clara studied it then turned and stared at Liz with wide-eyes. "Liz…"

"You girls ready?" Mary Alice stuck her head in. "Our last night of training."

"Yes, we're on our way." Liz took the pictures from Clara and laid them back on the dresser. She shooed Clara and Peggy out of the room and followed them down the hall.

Michael stood in the lunchroom doorway as Daniel Gilbertson talked to Beatrice. Elise and the younger children waited close by. Michael watched Clara as she placed the napkins and silverware at her station. Liz stood behind her. After tonight, Clara would be on her own. It was amazing how quickly these women learned the Harvey House routine. And, tomorrow Liz would leave to go to another House. The Fourth of July was next week, but it fell in the middle of the week, and he would only have one day off. There wouldn't be another holiday anytime soon.

Mr. Gilbertson stepped up beside him. "Let's go on in to eat. Beatrice said they should be ready."

Michael kept his eyes focused on Liz as he walked toward the counter and caught her eye. Her broad smile and the sparkle in her eyes made heat radiate through his entire being. His Liz was beautiful both inside and out. He knew he would miss her terribly when he couldn't see her regularly. As he sat on the stool next to Julien, he gave her a wink and was gratified to see a pink flush creep up her cheeks.

"Good evening, everyone." Clara's voice captured his attention. "It's good to see you. We are happy you've joined us here at our Harvey House." She grinned. "I'm glad I get to serve you." She glanced over her shoulder. "Liz has been my trainer this week. I'll miss her. We've already become good friends."

Michael watched as Clara took drink orders. Liz followed to fill their cups and glasses. After she poured his tea, she placed a small dish beside his glass and ladled out two sugar cubes.

She looked up with a coy expression. "Just the way you like it, kind sir."

He reached over and touched her hand. "Thank you."

When Clara reached him to take his order, she pointed to the menu, excited. "Did you see? We have grilled Boston Cod this evening. I had some, and it was delicious."

Michael looked up. "Is it really from Boston?"

"Yes. Fred Harvey brings it in ice cars to keep it fresh. That's the advantage of having the Santa Fe to transport food. We can serve it fresh from both coasts."

"I'll take the cod, the new potatoes in cream and the Astoria salad," Michael ordered as he dropped his sugar cubes into his tea. "And I'd like some of that fresh peach shortcake."

Clara paused. "We'll have cake and punch at the reception."

Michael grinned. "That's okay. I'll eat that, too. I can't pass up the shortcake."

Liz smiled at him. "That's a wise choice. The shortcake's delicious."

Julien wrinkled his nose. "I don't want no fish. I just want a pork loin sandwich and french fried potatoes."

"That sounds fine Julien, but it's I don't want any fish," his mother corrected.

After the others made their choices, Clara hurried to the serving window to place their orders.

Liz stepped over in front of Michael. "How's your week been?"

He pursed his lips and nodded. "It's been good. Just wish we could have spent more time together. What about you? Are you all packed?"

"I have a few more things to put in. We leave at seven-thirty in the morning." Liz turned as sadness filled her. "I better go help Clara serve the meals."

Fifteen minutes later, Michael pushed his dessert plate away. "Mmm. That was a first-class meal. The cod was heavenly. Tasted like it was freshly caught in Boston Harbor just today. And, the shortcake was out of this world. Couldn't ask for better."

"I agree." Daniel placed his hand on his stomach. "I don't know if I can hold a piece of cake after that meal. The prime rib of beef cut like butter. It was so tender. I need to come back and order that again." He watched Liz and Clara as they gathered plates and prepared to clean their station. "I guess we better move on into the parlor and see if we can find a place to sit."

As Elise stepped down from the stool, she caught Liz's attention. "We'll go on. You girls come when you're through here."

Liz nodded. "See you in a bit."

The parlor was already full of people when Michael and the rest of the Gilbertson's stepped through the door. A table with the cake and punch sat along the wall. Michael pointed. "Look there are a couple of seats on the sofa back in the corner. Let's head that way. Even if we have to stand, it won't be that long." He led the way across the room, around and between the men and women gathered in clusters.

Elise claimed the final seat, and Rachel sat on her lap. "Where'd all these folks come from? Liz is the only Harvey Girl from here in Topeka."

"Most of them either work here at the Harvey House or for the railroad." Daniel stepped behind the sofa. "They all get to know each other. I recognize several from our office."

"Look, there's Anna Lisa. Why is she here?" Julien pointed at the door.

"I suppose she came to say goodbye to Liz, the same as we did." Adam elbowed him.

Liz, Clara, Anna Lisa, and Billy finally strolled in with the other Harvey Girls. Liz scanned the room, then started in their direction. The others followed her through the knots of people.

Michael stepped forward as she approached, took her hand, and drew her over to stand beside him. "This is your night to be honored." He relished the warmth of her body beside him.

"Hello, Mr. and Mrs. Gilbertson," Peggy greeted them. "It's

good to see you. We made it through the training. We're off to our new Houses. I'm moving to Winslow, Arizona."

"That is a long way away."

"Yes, I'm glad. I want to be as far west as possible."

Elise looked at Becky and Ethel. "Where are you girls headed?"

"We'll both be in Newton, Kansas." Becky smiled at Ethel. "We're excited to be together."

Mr. Stecker's voice interrupted, "May we please have your attention?" He and Beatrice stood beside the refreshment table and as the room quieted, Beatrice stepped forward. "We're here to honor our Harvey Girls who have finished their training. They will leave us tomorrow and move on to their new Houses. I'd like to have Hank, our baker, and Fred, our head cook, come and serve the cake and punch. As you know, Hank made this wonderful cake." With a light applause, the men took their places and she called the girls to come forward.

Michael leaned down. "I want to talk to you after this is over."

"Of course. I'll come back over here." Liz and the others walked toward the center of the crowded room, while everyone applauded.

"These are the six new Harvey Girls who have trained here for the last month, Peggy Baxter, Ethel Walters, Maggie Bates, Becky Reynolds, Mary Alice Ringwald, and Liz Gilbertson. Congratulations to you girls. We wish you all well." She indicated for them to go through the line first. "Our kitchen staff, John, William, David, and George will bring cake and punch around if you'd rather not stand in line."

Elise settled back on the sofa. "That sounds like the best idea.

It would take forever for all these people to go through the line."

Soon, they received their cake and punch as Liz made her way back across the room. She stopped several times to visit with well-wishers. She was obviously well-liked.

As she grew closer, Michael's chest ached at the thought of telling her goodbye. She was beautiful and intelligent, yet kind and thoughtful—everything he'd ever wanted in a mate. He briefly considered his new-found faith. Would God work out the details for them to be together?

Daniel stepped from behind the sofa. "Liz, I want you to know I'm very proud of you. We'll miss you, but I know you'll do well as a Harvey Girl." He gave her a long hug.

"Yes." Elise moved Rachel from her lap and stood. "We will keep you in our daily prayers." She pulled Liz into an embrace. "Greet Tessa and her family, and tell them I will come for a visit, soon. And, you be sure to write. Let us know you get there safely. Oh, and, I received a letter from your Aunt Rebecca. She said they would meet you at the Harvey House in Emporia tomorrow. Grandpa has a gift he wants to give you.

Rachel threw her arms around Liz. "I'll miss you. I don't want you to go."

Liz tousled her hair. "I'll miss you, too, little one. I tell you what. Why don't you move into my room and keep it company for me? That way we'll feel closer together."

Rachel stepped back and gazed up at her sister. "Really? You want me to take care of your room?"

"Yes, I do. I'm sure Mama will help you move your things there."

"But, what about when you come home?"

"Well, sweetheart, I'll have to work a lot, so I won't be home very often, But, when I come home, we can sleep together. How about that?"

"We could do that?"

"Yep. Remember, I love you, and I'll depend on you."

Rachel nodded.

"It's time for us to go, children." Daniel put his arm around Rachel, and the family began their goodbyes. Liz gave the boys each a light hug. Michael caught Adam surreptitiously wiping tears from his eyes as they walked from the parlor.

Anna Lisa moved to give Liz a hug. "I guess we better go, too. Be sure to write and let us know how you are. I'll miss our visits."

"And, you need to keep me informed of your big plans." Liz took Anna Lisa's hand. "I'll miss my visits with you, too. We'll always be special friends."

Billy shook hands with Michael and nodded to Liz. "I know Anna Lisa hates to see you leave, but I'll take care of her."

"You better." Liz playfully shook her finger at him.

Billy grinned. "I'm glad we came and ate here. That was some good eatin'. We'll have to come back again."

Anna Lisa tucked her hand under his elbow. "See, I told you so."

CHAPTER 20

Liz scanned the parlor. Anna Lisa and most of the visitors had left, and the Harvey Girls and staff sat around and visited. Clara and one of her new friends talked to a couple of the railroad men.

She turned to Michael. "Well, we finally have some time to ourselves."

He took her hand and gazed at her. "You're so beautiful tonight. I'm proud of you."

"Thank you." Liz put her hand in her apron pocket and pulled it inside out. The pearl brooch pinned inside, glistened in the glow from the wall light. "See, I did wear it. Even though no one could see it. I knew it was there."

Michael's eyes grew dark with emotion. "I'm glad." He glanced around. "Is there somewhere we can go to talk?"

"You want to go outside? Maybe it will be cooler, and it's still light out."

Michael looked at his pocket watch. "It's only eight-thirty.

We'd have time." He took her hand, and they strolled out of the room and down the stairs.

The lobby was quiet with only a few people conversing quietly in groups of two or three. Liz led Michael to the door. "Mama told me about a small park near here where she and Daddy used to go when she was a Harvey Girl. I wonder if it's still there." They stepped out onto the platform. "I think it's beside the street down that way."

"Well, let's go see if we can find it." Michael took her hand and assisted her off the platform and across the tracks toward the street beyond.

The warmth of the summer evening enveloped them as they set off. The pungent aroma of the nearby livestock barn mingled with the scent of coal smoke and warm soil made her wrinkle her nose. She chuckled. "I bet Boston never smelled like this."

Michael squeezed her hand. "I'm sure it does in some places. Down by the wharves, it smells a lot worse than this. I don't mind these smells. It means you're close to the earth."

Liz turned her head and gazed at him—a big-city fellow who really liked small town Kansas. Joyful contentment flooded through her. "I'm glad you like it here."

"I'm glad I met you. I know, now, that God brought me here. I needed to learn about Him, too. I'm grateful you invited me to church."

"I should have been more of an encouragement to you."

"You have. Your whole family has encouraged me."

Liz pointed to the left. "Look, there's the little park. Mama said there was a fountain and a bench. Let's see if we can find them." They strolled off the street onto the grassy plot. Someone had recently mowed it. Irises and daisies bloomed around the edge, and a large flowering bush grew in the far corner. Beside it was an old stone bench.

"There it is." Liz pulled Michael across the grass. In front of the bench was a small structure that had obviously once been a working fountain, now crumbled and corroded. "And, there's the fountain." She frowned. "Kind of makes you sad to see it neglected and broken, doesn't it?"

Michael walked to the bench and brushed it off. "This looks sturdy enough. Let's sit here. It's shaded from the sun."

Liz sat beside him. "It seems surreal to sit here where my daddy and mama got to know each other."

Michael took her hand. "I hope our story turns out as good as theirs."

"Me, too." She looked down at their intertwined fingers. "My daddy had to leave and go lead a survey team in Oklahoma. Now, it's me who's about to leave."

"I'm very proud of you. I wish we didn't have to be apart, but it won't be that long, and I can come to see you. That's the best part about a job with the ATSF...free train travel."

"I'll look forward to your visits." Liz leaned against his shoulder.

"Just don't forget, you're my girl."

"How could I forget that? It's what I've wanted ever since I met you."

"Even after your recent break-up with Richard?"

"I feel different about you than I did him. I don't know how I ever thought I could marry him. I see, now, he was very selfish and controlling. You're kind and caring."

"Aww. Thank you. That's the way I want to be." Michael released her hand and put his arm around her back. "Can I give you a kiss?"

Liz nodded and leaned toward him. He cupped her chin with his hand. The touch of his lips was feathery soft but firm. Warmth spread through her as she responded to his kiss. She wrapped her arms around his neck. If only it could go on and on.

Michael drew back and gazed at her, his hazel eyes were dark with emotion. Then he pulled her close again. Liz was sure her heart, thumping wildly, would burst with happiness. Finally, he sat back and lowered his hands with a sigh. "Thank you. That'll take me through the days ahead."

Liz felt dazed. Richard's kisses had never affected her this way. A sudden thought flitted through her mind...if she had married Richard, she'd never have known what she'd missed!

The sun was about to drop below the horizon in brilliant shades of red, pink, and orange. Dusk had begun to overtake the sky. Michael stood and offered his hand. "We better get back. It'll be dark before long."

Liz allowed him to assist her. "I'm glad we found this park. There are good memories here, and now we have new ones."

They slowly strolled back up the street, both reluctant for the evening to end. Tomorrow, Liz would board the train for the next phase of her life.

Michael escorted her up the stairs to the parlor door. He lifted her hand and kissed her fingers. "I'd like to come back in, but it's almost ten. It would just be harder to leave. I'll look forward to your letters. Let me know about your new Harvey House."

"Okay. You write to me, too."

"I will. I promise."

Liz watched Michael descend the stairs. At the bottom, he turned and threw her a kiss, then strode resolutely out of her sight without looking back. Suddenly, she was assailed by two conflicting emotions. Her heart was heavy with the loss of leaving Michael. But, at the same time, she felt buoyed, excited at the thought of the move to a new House.

Beatrice had shown the last of the young men out as Liz walked back through the parlor. Peggy had changed into her night clothes and was sitting on her bed reading a book by the light of the gas lantern when Liz entered their room. She looked up. "I wondered if you'd make it in by curfew? Did you and Michael have a good time?"

"It was good and sad at the same time. You know what I mean? I love our time together, and it's hard to say goodbye."

Peggy nodded. "Yeah, I know." She frowned. "Clara came in and studied the dagger and that picture of you as a baby with your parents. I told her she shouldn't mess with your things."

Liz walked over to the dresser. It appeared to be as she'd left it. "She did seem to be extremely interested in them. This dagger's pretty intriguing. I wish I knew more about it." She wrapped it in the cloth and placed it along with the box of jewelry and pictures in the tray of her trunk. "I have a few more items to pack when I get up in the morning."

"Me too." Peggy laid her book down. "Arizona's a long way from here. I hope I have some good girls to work with."

"I'm sure you will. Fred Harvey only hires *exceptional* girls." Liz grinned. "Like us."

"Oh, yeah, sure." Peggy's eyes misted. "We will stay in touch and see each other again, right? I never had a family like you. All the Harvey Girls have stepped up to befriend and shelter me. I can't tell you how much I appreciate it."

Liz gave her a hug. "You have been a wonderful friend to me. We will stay in touch!"

Liz prepared for bed. Tomorrow would undoubtedly be a long day.

～✕

The next morning, Liz stood on the platform with the other girls. She pointed. "Our seats are on the third car. We might as well go ahead and board. We can get settled before the other train passengers return from the Harvey House."

"Sounds like a good idea to me." Maggie grabbed her carpet bag and started in that direction as the others followed.

The porter stood beside the step at the back of the passenger car. "Good-mornin', young ladies. Are you the new Harvey Girls travelin' with us today?" He extended his hand to assist them. "I was told I'd have some on board."

Mary Alice took his hand and ascended the steps. "We're on our way to our new locations today."

"So I heard." He smiled broadly. "You have a good trip. If you need anything, you let me know."

"Thank you," the girls chorused.

Liz stepped up and surveyed the interior of the coach. Leather-covered bench seats lined each side of the car. Her number was 5D, on the right side. She made her way up the aisle and kept an eye on the numbers above the seats. "Here's our seat." She scooted in to sit beside the window.

Peggy plopped down beside her. "Whew! It's good to sit down. I didn't sleep well last night. I woke up almost every hour, afraid I'd oversleep."

"I imagine the stress of our move had a lot to do with it." Liz placed her bag on the floor beside her feet. "We're headed into the unknown."

"I am a bit anxious about the trip west. Beatrice told me this morning that one of the Harvey Girls from Albuquerque, New Mexico, has chosen to transfer to Winslow, Arizona. So, I'll have a companion. I'm happy about that."

"I'm glad you won't have to travel, so far, alone."

"It's hard to believe this month has passed so quickly. Except for the scare when Pa came, it's been good. I was terrified he'd find me, or that I'd lose my job."

"Have you let your mother know where you're transferring to? I'll bet she's worried."

"I wrote to Betty. She'll tell Ma."

Liz rested her head on the back of the seat and looked at Peggy. "I hope she's safe."

"Betty sent me a letter and said Ma moved out when my Pa came to search for me. She's with some of Betty's friends in another town. When I get enough money, I'll have her come to live in Winslow or wherever I end up."

"That sounds like a good plan. It will be wonderful for you to be together. Then you can make sure she's taken care of."

Liz ran her hand down the front of her navy skirt. The new walking dress had been a timely purchase. Satisfaction flooded through her at the smooth feel of the fabric. She felt confident and grown-up when she wore it.

Afraid she'd break the Harvey House rule, not to wear jewelry, Liz had pinned the pearl brooch under the lapel of her jacket. She sighed as she fingered the pearls. She already missed Michael and her family, but she needed to spread her wings. There'd be time to settle down after she finished her time as a Harvey Girl.

As the other passengers began to board, Liz glanced around. Most of the seats were filled. The whistle blew, and the car creaked as it started to move slowly forward, then picked up speed. She watched out the window as Topeka's depot slid out of sight. They rolled through the edge of town and out into the countryside.

"Well, we're on our way." Liz settled back in her seat. "I'm excited to see my family at Emporia. I hope they make it into town. They live outside of town on a ranch called the Lazy G. I wish I had time to go see it. I haven't seen them since Thanksgiving. They always have a huge meal for all their ranch hands and their families. It's quite an occasion."

"I'd love to see a ranch. Maybe I will in Arizona." Peggy pulled a book from her bag. "I guess I'll use this time to read."

"How many books did you bring?"

"I've got four. I hope that's enough to last me throughout the trip. Betty sent me some new ones this last week." Peggy opened the book and began to read.

Liz turned to the window and watched as the train moved past scattered farmhouses and the rolling flint hills. Cattle dotted the pastures. What would she find at the Hutchinson Harvey House in the Santa Fe Hotel? It'd be fun to meet Tessa,

Mama's longtime friend. Her mother had said that Anna, Tessa's daughter, was one of the Harvey Girls.

Liz's mind drifted back to her early memories. Her Grandpa and Grandma Gilbertson had taken her in with open arms when her parents died. Liz's memory of Grandma Esther was hazy, but it was accompanied by the warmth of love. As a child, the sadness was intense when her new-found Grandma died, but then Uncle Daniel and Aunt Elise had brought her into their home and treated her as their daughter.

Elise had led her to receive Jesus as her Savior when she was nine. She'd had a full, happy life, but recently there was an empty place in her heart. Who did she really belong to? Was there more family out there somewhere? Was there a story behind the dagger she'd found? Would she ever find out? Her thoughts meandered as she stared out the window at the grass-covered hills and valleys.

Peggy nudged her with her elbow. "Here comes the conductor."

Liz straightened in the seat as he approached.

He stopped at their aisle. "Do you plan to eat at the Emporia Harvey House?"

Peggy shook her head. "We plan to eat lunch at Newton."

"We will have a twenty minute stop in Emporia. You're welcome to stay on the train or get off for a brief break." He turned to the other girls, then proceeded on up the aisle.

Peggy stretched her legs. "I need to get out and walk."

"Twenty minutes isn't very long, but it's better than nothing."

Before long, ranch houses began to dot the vast prairie.

Excitement welled up in Liz, and it was hard to sit still. If Grandpa Gilbertson didn't make it into town, she'd be very disappointed. It had been six months since she'd seen him, and he was getting older.

A few minutes later, the first houses on the outskirts of Emporia appeared. Liz grabbed her bag and scooted forward on her seat. She needed to be ready since there wasn't much time. As soon as the train screeched to a stop, she was on her feet. "I need to get out, please."

"Yes, you go first." Peggy stood and moved out of the way.

Liz made her way out into the aisle, impatient with the other travelers who headed slowly toward the door. *Hurry, hurry.* Finally, she reached the door at the rear of the car. The porter assisted her down onto the platform. Passengers streamed toward the depot entrance as the bellboy pounded on the gong and yelled, "This way to the Harvey House." Liz scanned the area. Her family must be inside.

She followed the crowd into the depot and searched the lobby. Ahh, there they were! Grandpa and Uncle Thomas stood near some chairs across the room. Relief made Liz's knees weak. Grandpa looked so good! He was tall and stalwart in his blue jeans, cowboy shirt, boots, and Stetson. His silver hair gave him a distinguished look. She hurried toward her family, dodging through the line of people who were waiting to ascend the stairs to the Harvey House.

Grandpa Gilbertson spread his arms, and she ran into his embrace. She basked in the strength of his arms around her. "I love you, Grandpa. I've looked forward to this." She gave him an extra squeeze then stepped back and turned toward Uncle

Thomas and Aunt Rebecca, who waited to the side. Louise, their eight-year-old daughter, stood beside them with five-year-old Paul peeking out around Rebecca's skirts. Liz gave her aunt a hug, and Louise wiggled her way between them. Then, Liz stepped back and faced Uncle Thomas. "It's so good to see you all." She gave him a hug then leaned down to greet Paul. He scooted behind his mama's skirts again. Liz laughed as Rebecca tried to pull him out. "That's okay. We'll get acquainted. It's been too long since we were together."

She led the way to a nearby sofa. Rebecca and the children settled beside her.

Liz looked at Grandpa. "You need to tell me all the news about the ranch. I wish I had time to go out there. Maybe I can come over, if I can get a weekend off."

Grandpa moved to a chair across from her. "There's not much to tell. We just keep busy with the ranch duties—calving, working the cattle, building fences. Always things to do. We've had a good year. We're about ready to sell some of the bull calves. Oh, and Slim's gettin' ready to retire."

Aunt Rebecca turned toward Liz. "So, fill us in. I thought you planned to get married."

Liz sighed. "Long story, but Richard found another woman at college. We aren't together anymore."

"Oh, I'm sorry to hear that."

"Actually, it's good." Liz smiled. "I wasn't ready for marriage, and now I realize Richard wasn't the man I thought he was. I've met someone named Michael. He's from Boston and works in Daddy's office. Daddy likes Michael a lot."

"That's good. When did you decide to become a Harvey

Girl?"

"After Richard and I parted ways, I wasn't sure what to do with myself. I decided to become a Harvey Girl to give me some time to get my thoughts sorted out and consider my future. I like the work so far. I'll be in Hutchinson until December."

"Hutchinson's not that far away. I don't know why we don't get together more often to visit and not just on holidays. We just get too busy in our own lives, I guess."

Peggy approached, stood beside the couch, and smiled at the Gilbertson's "I'm sorry to interrupt, but we need to reboard the train. People have begun to leave the Harvey House."

Liz made a pouty face as she stood. "I knew it wouldn't be long enough, but I'm so happy I got to visit with all of you even for such a short time."

Grandpa reached to the table beside him and picked up a paper-wrapped parcel, then rose from his chair. "I have something for you. I went through your grandma's desk, and I found this at the bottom of one of the drawers. I don't know why I hadn't seen it before, but I think you will appreciate it. It's your mama Mary's Bible. Somehow, we didn't get it in the trunk with the other items that belonged to them." He handed it to her. "I want you to have it."

Liz put her fingers to her open lips as she stared at the gift. Mama Mary's Bible. What secrets would it hold?

Her hands trembled as she took the package and grasped it to her chest. She was breathless, and her eyes widened with anticipation. "Thank you, Grandpa. You don't know what this means to me." She threw her arms around him and kissed his cheek. Then she turned to the others. "Thank you all for meeting me here. This has been so special."

Peggy touched her arm. "We need to go."

"I know." Liz grimaced as she glanced at the nearly empty lobby. "I have to go, but I plan to come back and see you soon. I want to go out to the ranch. I love you, all." She grabbed her bag, gave them a brief wave, then followed Peggy rapidly across the room. They stepped out the door and ran to the train car steps.

The porter gave them a hand up as the conductor called, "All aboard!"

They quickly made their way up the aisle to their seat. "We cut that pretty close." Liz giggled.

"I was afraid we wouldn't make it." Peggy scooted in beside her and let out her breath in a rush. "It looked like you had a good visit."

"Oh, yes. My grandpa has always been special to me. Uncle Thomas was sixteen when I went to live with them. I thought the sun rose and set with him so it's nice to be with his family."

"Must be nice to have a big family. I just have my mother now." Peggy laid her head back on the seat.

"I do have a wonderful family." Liz said quietly. She gazed at her friend. So, why was she so restless inside?

She stared at the Bible, wrapped in brown paper. Would it hold more information about her father's side of the family? Liz was glad it hadn't been in the trunk. This was extra special, somehow. She lifted the package and held it close. She'd wait until she got to her new room in Hutchinson and open it in private.

They were soon on their way again rolling through the flint hill prairie. As Liz watched the hills and valleys go by the window, it was hard to keep her eyes open. Peggy had started on her book again. Liz might as well rest while she had a chance. She let the drowsiness overtake her.

Chapter 21

The next she knew, Peggy was shaking her arm. "The conductor wants to know what you want to eat for lunch." She handed Liz a menu. "I told him we would eat in the lunchroom."

Liz frowned and sat up straight. She tried to shake the sleep from her brain. She'd been dreaming about Michael. The parcel with her mother's Bible had wedged between her lap and the side of the train car. She righted it then reached for the menu. "I'll take the chicken salad sandwich with hash browned potatoes and peas in cream. That sounds good."

Becky and Ethel talked and giggled in the seat across the aisle. The next House would be their destination, their new home for a while.

Soon the train pulled up to the Newton depot. Liz stared wide-eyed at the long three-story brick building. It was much larger than either the Topeka or Emporia Harvey House's and had arched windows all across the front. "Wow, look how big that is!"

"It's called the Arcade." Becky stood and waved her arm

toward its expansive grandeur. "All the dirty uniforms and linen from the Kansas Harvey Houses are sent here to be laundered so it has to be big." She started toward the back of the train car. "Come on, girls, let's go. I'm really hungry."

Peggy turned toward Liz. "Surely, we can leave our bags on the train. The porter will watch them."

"I guess you're right." Liz pushed the Bible into her bag, then set it on her seat. "It'll be easier to eat and get back to our seats if we don't have to carry our bags."

They followed the other passengers off the train and across the platform to the door marked "Harvey House." The bellboy was striking the gong with a mallet and directing the passengers inside. The Harvey House lobby was cool and refreshing, in contrast to the summer heat outside.

Becky and Ethel stepped back and waited as the head waitress greeted the other patrons, then approached her. She smiled. "You must be our new Harvey Girls, Becky Reynolds and Ethel Walters, right? We're happy to have you." She looked at Liz and the others. "And these girls must be your friends. Where are you headed?"

Peggy spoke up and shared all their destinations.

"I'm happy for you. Now, let's get you fed in the lunchroom. You don't have a lot of time." She turned to Becky and Ethel. "I'll meet with you after dinner to show you to your rooms and get your trunks delivered."

A short while later, the other four Harvey Girls bade farewell to Becky and Ethel then reboarded the train. "It's sad to say goodbye. We've become friends over this month." Maggie plopped down in her seat.

"We can write letters and stay in touch. Delivery is fast along the rail line." Liz gathered her bag and seated herself. "Now it's on to Hutchinson. My turn."

"It's interesting to see all the different styles of Harvey Houses." Mary Alice slid in beside Maggie. "We just found out that Peggy, and I will stay the night with Maggie at the El Vaquero in Dodge City before we travel on to New Mexico and Arizona tomorrow."

"That should be fun. I'm glad you get to stopover. This has been a tiring day." Liz clutched her bag in her arms. She'd soon be to her destination. Her stomach clenched, and her chest became tight. What would the new House be like?

Before long, she saw a row of houses along the railroad. The buildings were closer together, and the train rolled past streets busy with horses and buggies.

A few minutes later, a large, red brick depot came into sight with "Hutchinson" displayed on the side. The porter stood at the front of their train car as it came to a stop. "We will have a twenty minute stop. If this is your destination the depot is to the left. If, however, you'd like to walk a bit and get a sandwich, dessert or coffee the Santa Fe Hotel and Harvey House are in a separate building to your right across the tracks and up the street. We will arrive in Dodge City by supper time."

Liz tried to take it all in as she stood. She stooped to peek out the window, at the beautiful three-story, Queen Anne style structure which stood majestically along the north side of the tracks. A wide porch surrounded the south and east sides. "That's the most beautiful Harvey House I've seen."

Peggy grabbed her arm. "Come on. Are you gonna admire

it all afternoon? We need to go in. There isn't much time."

Liz scrambled across the seat and followed her friends from the train car.

They walked the half-block to the Harvey House along with the other passengers. The large porch, with it's white double columns and lounge chairs scattered around seemed to embrace her in a welcoming hug.

She stepped aside to let a young family with a small child and a baby go in, then followed them into the coolness of the lobby. It took a few seconds for her eyes to adjust from the bright sunlight. She scanned the spacious room. As in the other Harvey House lobbies, arrangements of chairs and couches were scattered about the room with plants placed at strategic positions for privacy. The entrances to the dining room and lunchroom were on the far side, at the back of the lobby. The dining room was on the left and the lunchroom on the right. A man in a black jacket stood near a registration desk beside an imposing staircase on the far left of the room.

"Come on. I need to go see where the manager wants me to go." Liz led the way across the lobby.

The man looked up as they approached. "May I help you? Oh, are you our new Harvey Girl?"

Liz nodded. "I'm Liz Gilbertson. I'm assigned to work here." She gestured toward the others. "My friends are headed to other Harvey Houses, Maggie, Mary Alice, and Peggy."

"I'm glad to meet you all. I'm Mr. Schmidt, the manager of this House." He waved toward the lunchroom. "Come on over here. I'll introduce you to our head waitress. You can leave your bag here at the desk."

Liz appraised the young woman who stood beside the lunchroom door as she welcomed a well-dressed couple. She was tall with lively, brown eyes, and light brown hair. She turned to them as they approached. "Hello, are you our new Harvey Girl?"

"Yes. This is Liz Gilbertson. She will work here with us. These are her friends, also new Harvey Girls, but they are traveling on." He gestured. "Anna McNance is our head waitress and house mother. She'll help you get settled in."

Anna smiled. "Why don't you girls come on in? Would you like something to drink and a piece of pie or cake, with ice cream or maybe a cool bowl of fruit?" She indicated some vacant seats at the counter.

"Thank you, that sounds refreshing. I want a piece of the pie." Peggy strode into the lunchroom. The others followed her in, and found seats as the Harvey Girl approached.

Mary Alice grinned. "I'd like a bowl of ice cream. That's my favorite."

Liz sat between Mary Alice and Maggie. "Oh, yum. Look they have coconut cream pie. I want a piece of that."

After they ate, Liz walked them back to the front door of the Harvey House. On the porch, she gave them each a hug. "It's been fun to work with you. I'll miss you. Don't forget to write." She watched them as they ambled back down the track. Peggy turned and waved before she disappeared into the passenger car. A few minutes later, the train rolled past her and out of sight.

Liz heaved a sigh then returned to the Harvey House. Anna waited beside the desk. "Goodbyes are always hard. But, I think you'll enjoy it here. We have a good team of Harvey Girls and staff."

Liz smiled. "I've looked forward to the move here." She gazed at Anna. "Did you say your name's McNance? Is your mother Tessa?"

Anna looked puzzled. "Yes, how did you know?"

My mama, Elise Dumond, roomed with your mother when they trained as Harvey Girls. Mom has talked a lot about her friend Tessa. She was elated that this was my new Harvey House."

"Oh, yes, my mother has spoken about Elise many times. And she'll be excited to meet you." Anna stepped from behind the desk. "Is this your bag? I'll show you to your room and introduce you to some of the other girls." She headed toward the elaborately embellished staircase, with walnut banisters polished to a high sheen. They climbed to the landing, turned left and up to the second floor. "The hotel guest rooms are on this floor. The staff rooms are on the third floor." They continued up to the next level. The Harvey House parlor, at the top of the stairs, was furnished similar to the Topeka Harvey House.

Anna turned to the right and opened a door which led into a hallway. "Our rooms are on this wing. The male staff members are on the other end." She walked down the hall and stopped about halfway down. "Your room's on the south side. I like the view from here. You can see up Main Street." She motioned for Liz to enter her new room, then stepped in behind her. "Your roommate is Hazel Murphy. She's been here for about six months. Her former roommate moved to Dodge City to be closer to family."

She glanced around. "It looks like she's still at work in the dining room. Your trunk's here. You might as well get unpacked and settle in this evening before you begin work tomorrow. You'll be in the lunchroom until we can find time for you to serve a meal to Mr. Schmidt and me. Then we have a rotation, so no one is stuck in one place."

Liz nodded. At that moment, one of the other girls leaned in through the door. "Hello. You must be the new girl. I'm Jessie Baker. I live next door."

"I'm glad to meet you, Jessie. My name's Liz Gilbertson."

"Come over after work this evening. I'll introduce you to the other girls."

"Thank you, I appreciate that."

Anna grinned. "You'll be in good hands. We have a fun group of girls. Now I better go get prepared for the next train. Come on down for supper when you're ready."

After she left, Liz sat on the unmade bed. Her trunk sat at the foot. The room was furnished similar to the one in Topeka. Hazel's side was neat and clean. Liz set her small bag on the bed beside her. She could feel the Bible inside, but she needed to get her bed made and clothes put away before she took a look at it, or her room might not get finished before suppertime. Examining her mother's Bible would be her reward for getting unpacked.

Liz retrieved her trunk key from her handbag and knelt to open the trunk. The latch popped open, and she lifted the lid. Her eyes immediately fell on the dagger and jewelry box. She picked them up, along with her pictures, then stood and placed them on the dresser. She needed to change into her day dress before she straightened the room. As she hung her traveling suit in the wardrobe, she unpinned the brooch from under the lapel. Its soft sheen reminded her of the glow in Michael's eyes when he asked her to court him. She was so blessed to have him in her life, and to know that he had decided to follow Jesus as his Savior made her heart sing. God was so good!

She laid the brooch on the dresser then removed the sheets and blankets and made her bed. The room felt more home-like with the wedding ring quilt spread across the top. Next, she hung up her other clothes and arranged her belongings in the dresser drawers. She laid the dagger and jewelry in the top drawer. Her uniforms would have to be ironed before she could wear them, so she laid them aside on top of the chest. As she finished, a tall, dark-haired young woman walked in.

"Hi. You're Liz, right? I heard you were here. My name's Hazel Murphy. It was my turn to polish the coffee pots this afternoon, so that took longer than usual." She glanced around. "I see you've unpacked and settled in. You're speedy."

Liz stepped forward and nodded. "I'm Liz Gilbertson. It feels good to get everything put away."

"I agree. I like things in their place. Did you have a good trip?"

"Yes, I did. I got to see my grandpa and my aunt and uncle and little cousins in Emporia. They live on a ranch near there, and they met me at the depot."

"Where are you from?" Hazel sat on her bed, and Liz sat across from her.

"My family lives in Topeka, Kansas. My father works for the ATSF at the main office. "

So they aren't far away. My family lives in Tennessee. I haven't seen them since the end of December. I hope to take a week soon and go visit them. I've fulfilled my first six-month contract."

286

"Do you plan to continue?"

"Oh, yes. I love this job. Plus, I make money to send home to my family. I like that. I have two little brothers." Hazel scooted back on her bed. She ran her hand across her lap. "Oh, dear, I have a stain on my apron. Must have had some of the silver polish on my fingers." She reached behind her back to untie it. "I'll have to change before I go back to work."

"Where can I iron my uniforms? They wrinkled in my trunk."

"The laundry's on the second floor at the end of the west hall. Flat irons are kept hot in there all day. You can use them to iron your uniforms. The soiled uniforms and bedding are sent from there to Newton to be laundered.

"I better go do that. I can't wear them the way they are."

Hazel nodded. "I'll probably leave before you get back. I'm in the dining room this week, so I have to go set up. I'll see you later."

Liz gathered her uniforms and left the room and turned in the direction Hazel had indicated.

All finished, Liz returned to an empty room. She changed into her freshly ironed uniform and apron, then sat on her bed and gingerly removed the parcel from her bag. Her hands trembled as she untied the string and folded back the paper. Inside was a black book with the words, *Holy Bible,* stamped in faded gold across the front. Grandpa had said it was her mother, Mary's Bible. Liz thumbed through the first few pages to the "Presented to" page. Sure enough the words, Mary Gilbertson Tilman, was written below. Liz stared at the handwriting—her mama's writing. It was a carefully crafted script.

Liz lifted the Bible and lightly kissed the name. The next line declared that it had been given to Mary by her parents for her sixteenth birthday.

She turned to the next page: "Births and Deaths." Liz recognized the first names—her mother's family. Then a thrill shot through her. The names of her father's family were there, too—in the same neat script—with their birthdays. She studied the dates. Grace HughesTilman was born in 1835, about the same time as Grandpa Gilbertson. William Tilman was older, but he must be her grandpa—then Grace Tilman was her grandma. To see their names on the page was an extraordinary revelation.

She examined the other names and dates. George Tilman, her father, was born in 1856. He must have had two sisters. The older one, Martha was married to Andrew Bryan and had two small children—well, they wouldn't be children now. The oldest daughter, Rebecca, was born in 1876, so she'd be twenty-five now. The son William would be twenty-three.

Hmm, Liz thought, Bryan was Clara's last name.

George Tilman's other sister, Amelia, was born in 1865. She'd now be thirty-six. Her marriage wasn't noted.

Liz got up and danced around the room at her discoveries, but then stopped short as she saw her clock. Oh, no! She didn't have much time before she needed to go down to supper. She quickly scanned through the marriages, then down to the deaths. She stared at the names written there—Grandfather Alden Tilman, Great-Grandfather Patrick McKey, and Great-Grandmother Sarah Brady McKey. She frowned. Patrick and Sarah McKey would be her great-great grandpa and grandma. They had the same last name as Michael. That was strange.

She glanced at the clock again. She had to hurry, or she'd miss her supper. She closed the Bible and laid it on the bed beside her. She was excited to find the names of her family members, but would that information help her find them.

The hallway and parlor were empty as she hurried through and down the stairs. The other Harvey Girls would all be busy. As she reached the second floor, Liz joined men, women, and children—hotel patrons, who leisurely strolled down the stairs and toward the dining room and lunchroom. "Excuse me." She bustled her way around them to the lunchroom door.

Anna paused as she greeted the customers and glanced Liz's direction with a smile. "Go on in. I think there's a seat on the far end, by the coffee pots. Ida's at that station. Introduce yourself and enjoy your supper."

"Thank you." Liz nodded then slipped through the door into the lunchroom. The circular counter took up a large share of the room. High backed swivel stools were situated at regular intervals around the perimeter. Sunlight and a slight breeze flowed in through the open windows on the east side of the room. The door to the kitchen and the serving window were on the left, along with a large pie safe. Liz made her way around the counter to a vacant stool at the end. She watched the girls clear their spaces to prepare for the second wave of diners.

One of the Harvey Girls wiped the counter beside her. "Hi. You must be Liz. My name's Ida. I wondered when you'd come to eat. Hazel said you had to iron your uniform."

Liz smirked sheepishly. "I'm sorry. I sat down to read for a few minutes, and the time got away from me."

"It's okay. You still have plenty of time. We haven't served the hotel customers and locals yet. Here's a menu if you want to check out the options."

Liz looked around. "I feel like I need to be back there help-ing instead of being waited on."

Ida chuckled. "Take advantage of it. You'll get your share of work starting tomorrow."

Liz grinned. "I guess you're right." She scanned the menu as she waited for the lunchroom to fill. She watched as the Girls went through the routine. Already, it had become almost second nature to her. She was reassured to know it was the same in all the Harvey Houses. What an efficient training process Fred Harvey had developed!

Ida turned Liz's cup up for coffee, and she enjoyed the Virginia ham, candied sweet potatoes, and cauliflower that she'd ordered.

At the end of the meal, Liz waited until the other Harvey Girls had cleaned their stations. Several of them introduced themselves: Alice, Bertha, Sarah, and Frances. There were others, but Liz couldn't recall all their names. The girls from the dining room joined them. They joked and laughed as they climbed the stairs.

At the top, Liz paused and scanned the parlor. The cozy arrangement reminded her of the parlor in the Topeka Harvey House. A grand piano sat in the corner of the room, and railroad-related pictures hung on the walls.

Jessie stopped beside her. "Do you all want to sit here in the parlor and visit? Or we can go to Sarah's and my room and visit. Paul sent some cookies for us." She turned toward Liz. "He's our baker. He makes extra so we can have a treat now and then."

"Let's go to your room." Bertha headed down the hall.

"I want to change out of this uniform into more comfortable clothes. My feet are killing me."

"Okay, come on in when you're ready. Bring a pillow if you don't want to sit on the rug."

The girls all scattered to their rooms. Liz gently bit her lip as she followed Hazel into their room. She felt light-hearted like she already fit in. These girls seemed to have a camaraderie she hadn't felt at Topeka. Maybe because the Harvey Girls there were expected to move to other houses, they didn't have time to establish strong bonds.

Hazel removed her uniform and slipped into a dress of lightweight fabric. "You might as well change into something cooler." She sat on her bed, took off her shoes and wiggled her toes. "Whew, that feels better. I'm a barefoot girl when I get a chance."

Liz glanced at the Bible on her bed as she changed into the dress she'd worn earlier. The old book seemed to draw her. Hopefully, she'd have time to read some more before she went to sleep. She took off her shoes and put on her slippers.

"Come on, we might as well go." Hazel grabbed her pillow and started toward the door.

The other girls streamed into Jessie and Sarah's room. Hazel touched Liz's arm. "Let's grab a seat on the bed. I'd rather not sit on the floor if I don't have to." She hurried across the room, and Liz followed. The other girls found seats wherever they could. Liz counted fourteen girls.

Anna was the last to enter. Hazel scooted over. "Here, Anna, you can sit here on the bed. You gotta be tired. You never stop all day."

"Thanks." Anna sat between Hazel and Liz. She looked

around. "This is Liz Gilbertson. She just joined us today. I don't know if you've had a chance to meet her, but let's give her a warm welcome." The other girls smiled and offered greetings. "It'll take a few days for her to get your names straight, I'm sure." She turned to Liz. "We alternate between the dining room and lunchroom. I try to change up who you work with, so that should give you a chance to get acquainted."

Jessie held up a tray. "Here are the cookies Paul made for us. They're made from that peanut butter spread. They smell heavenly. Take one and hand them around. Don't forget to thank him when you see him."

The girls began to chat among themselves. Several spoke directly to Liz, repeating their names. A few told of funny incidents they had witnessed.

Anna spoke up with a chuckle. "But, you have to remember, the customer is always right no matter what they say or do."

Before long, the group began to disperse. As the weary girls scattered to their own rooms, Jessie faced Liz. "It's good to have you here, Liz. If you need anything, don't hesitate to ask. We'll all be glad to help you. We have a close-knit group. We get along well with the male staff, too, and they treat us nicely."

"Thank you, I appreciate that." Liz smiled, then walked with Hazel back to their room.

Hazel opened the window then took some clean clothes from her dresser. "I'm so hot and sweaty, I need to take a bath. I'll be back in a bit."

Liz nodded. "I think I'll read my Bible." She sat on the bed and held her gift from Grandpa Gilbertson to her chest for a couple of minutes, then opened it again to the "Births and

Deaths" page. Her gaze fell to the deaths recorded at the bottom. *Patrick McKey* and *Sarah Brady McKey.* She stared at the names. They would have been her great-great-grandparents. Michael's name was McKey. *Could these people also be Michael's great-great grandparents?* If so, he was her cousin. And Clara would be her cousin, too.

Warmth radiated throughout her body, and her racing heartbeat drummed in her chest. *Could it possibly be true? Could she actually have been among her family and didn't know it?* She looked back at the top of the page. George Tilman's mother's name was Grace and Clara had talked about her Grandma Grace. *Could she and Clara have the same Grandma? Was Clara Martha's daughter?* She checked the Bible—no Clara mentioned, but then she wouldn't have been born when George left home to come West.

Liz turned to the next page. A folded sheet of paper was tucked between the pages. *BIRTHDAYS YOU NEED TO REMEMBER* was written neatly across the top. But, the handwriting was different, it was in a broader, firmer script. The same birthdays were recorded, with some additional ones: *Father – William Tilman, June 20, 1828; Mother – Grace Hughes Tilman, Sept 5,1835; Grandpa Alden Tilman - B. January 29, 1797 D. 1877; Grandma Marie Baxter Tilman - Oct. 12, 1806; Grandpa Richard Hughes - March 12, 1805; Grandma Mabel McKey Hughes - Jan. 20, 1810.*

Under the dates was written in the same firm handwriting. *Dear George,*

I know you are headed out to seek your own life and future, but don't forget your family. Never forget that you are a McKey. Your great-grandfather Patrick immigrated to this country from Scotland in 1790. You have a proud heritage.

Keep in touch. I love you very much.

Grandma Mabel

Liz stared at the words, then laid the Bible down beside her and hurried to her dresser. She rifled through the pictures and letters, took out the one that told about the dagger, and carried it back to the bed. Trembling, she removed it from the envelope. The handwriting was the same! She danced a couple of steps then fell to her knees, threw her head back, and looked up. "Yes, yes. Thank you, Jesus!! You've answered my prayer to find my family."

The next instant, she grew quiet. She caught her breath and covered her face with her hands. *Michael.* If this was all true, Michael *was* her cousin. A cold wave of disappointment washed over her and settled in her stomach. She'd fallen in love with her cousin!

Granted, he'd be a distant cousin. Would that count? *Could she marry her cousin?* She stood up and sat on the bed. How could a person be so happy and so devastated at the same time? How would she ever tell him? Tears gathered in her eyes. What could she do? What should she do? She wanted to know her family, but what if it meant she shouldn't marry Michael.

She picked up the Bible and closed her eyes. *"God, what do you want me to do? I've grown to love Michael, but how can I marry him?"* A calm stillness suffused her body. *"Trust me."* The words formed in her mind. Liz opened her eyes and looked around. Then she opened the Bible. She noticed the ribbon protruded from the pages and tugged on it. It fell open to Proverbs. Some verses were underlined on the page. Chapter 3, verses 5 and 6: *"Trust in the Lord with all thine heart, and lean not unto thine own understanding. In all thy ways acknowledge Him, and He shall direct thy paths."*

Lean not on thine own understanding. Did that mean not to try to figure it out on her own? This was the same verse she'd heard at Uncle Jule's church before her interview. She stared in amazement at the page. *God had just spoken to her!* She knew in her spirit that God had reached down and touched her. Somehow, He would work it out. She grew still and content.

She laid the Bible aside, stood, and walked to the dresser. She picked up Michael's brooch and ran her finger over the smooth surface of the pearls, then held it to her heart. She whispered, *"Thank you, Jesus, I know you love me. You've given me my family and Michael. I don't know how it can work out, but I trust You."*

Chapter 22

"Hey, Mr. McKey, you got a communique', just came in."

Michael scooted his chair back with a jerk and turned toward William at his office door. "Who's it from?"

His hand trembled, and his heart beat in his throat as he reached for the envelope. He'd had Liz on his mind all day. She was on her way to the new Harvey House in Hutchinson. His mouth went dry. What if something had happened to her?

William shook his head. "It's from someone named Clara. It came from the Harvey House, here."

Michael's breath rushed out in a swoosh as relief poured over him. He felt for a moment like he might pass out, and he rubbed his hand over his eyes. "Okay, thank you." His voice sounded shaky.

"Are you alright?" William looked concerned.

Michael swallowed. "Yeah, I'm fine. I just had a scare. My girl is on her way to Hutchinson to work in the Harvey House there. I just had a vision of her in an accident."

"Surely that's not what this is about."

"No, no, this is from my cousin. She's a Harvey Girl, too, training here." He grinned. "Thanks, I'm fine."

William raised his eyebrows and backed out of the office.

Michael swiveled back around, propped his elbows on his desk, and put his face to his hands. The ache in his heart crawled up his throat. How would he make it until he could see Liz again?

He sat back, tore open the letter, and pulled out a sheet of paper.

Michael,

I need to talk to you. Can you come out to the Harvey House on Saturday? Also, I'd like to go to church with you on Sunday if you don't mind.

Clara

Of course, he could go out and visit with her, and he'd be more than glad to take her to church. He had a suspicion that her family had been more involved in church than his family as they grew up. He wondered if she'd prayed to receive Jesus as her Savior? He intended to find out.

Late Saturday morning, Michael headed toward the Topeka's Santa Fe depot and Harvey House. He'd eat lunch, and afterwards, he and Clara could talk. She was probably homesick and wanted to share family stories. He drove into the parking lot as the train passengers boarded the train. He'd timed it about right for the second "local crowd" serving time.

He made his way up the stairs along with the other local

folks. Beatrice greeted him as he approached the lunchroom door. "Hello, Michael. Are you here to see Clara?"

"Yes, she wanted to talk. Have you heard anything from Liz?"

"I did hear that she arrived at her destination. All the girls did, in fact. I think she'll like it there. I've heard it's a good team."

"I'm glad she made it safely. I already miss her."

"Well, she's not too far away. You can go see her one of these weekends once she gets settled."

"I plan to do that." Michael walked into the lunchroom.

After he ate his meal, he sat and watched the girls as they scurried around to clean and put things in order. Clara wiped off the counter and picked up his empty coffee cup. "I'll meet you in the parlor when I'm through here."

Michael nodded and stepped down from the stool. In the parlor, he settled in a chair by the open window. A warm breeze ruffled the drapes and brushed his neck as he picked up a *National Geographic* magazine from the table beside him.

Ten minutes later, Clara walked in with two other girls. She scanned the room. "I'll see you girls later. My cousin's here."

Michael laid down the magazine as she approached. "How'd the last two days go without Liz and the other girls?"

Clara sat across from him and smoothed her skirt. "It was fine. There's a lot to remember, but I did okay."

"Good. I'm glad you've got it down, What did you want to talk to me about?"

Clara leaned forward. "Michael, I think Liz is my Uncle George's daughter."

Michael frowned and wrinkled his forehead. "What? Why

would you think that? Her last name is Gilbertson."

"That's her adopted name. Her real parents were killed in a carriage accident. She showed me their picture. I looked on the back. It said "George Tilman and Mary Gilbertson, married April 20, 1880. That's right after Uncle George left home."

Michael stared at her. He shook his head and pressed his lips together as tightness constricted his chest. "So? I'm sure he's not the only George Tilman in the world."

"There's something else. You know, the Scottish *dirk* that hangs over the mantle in your grandparents' great room? Liz has the matching *sgian*—the small dagger. You know the story. Great-great-grandpa McKey gave your family the *dirk* and gave Great-grandma Mabel the *sgian*. She said she gave it to George before he left. Liz has it. I saw it. It has the same family crest. I've admired the *dirk* at your home so many times, I'd recognize it anywhere."

Michael slumped back against the sofa and groaned. He closed his eyes, then opened them and sat forward. "Don't you know what this means? If Liz is your Uncle George's daughter, then she's your cousin. And that makes her *my* cousin." He rubbed his forehead. "Clara, I can't marry my cousin. I know your grandma will be ecstatic to find that Liz is her granddaughter, but…" His voice trailed off with a note of misery.

Clara peered at him. "No one would have to know. Well, I guess our families would know. I can't keep it from Grandma Grace. But what would be the difference? You fell in love with her when you didn't know she was related."

Michael shook his head with a deep sigh. "That's just it. The family would know. It's against the law to marry your cousin."

"Even your third cousin?"

"Oh, I don't know. It wouldn't be right. I couldn't marry you. You're my third cousin."

"Well, of course, you wouldn't marry me, silly. We've known each other since we were babies, almost. You didn't even know Liz was related." Clara drew a frown. "You wouldn't know now if I hadn't found this stuff. I'm sorry I saw the picture and dagger."

"No, no. It's incredible for your family to rediscover your Uncle George's story and finally find your cousin. Somehow, it'll all work out. I just don't know how I'll tell Liz."

"I know." Clara scrunched her face. "Grandma will want to meet her...that is if I tell her." She hesitated. "She knew Uncle George was married and had a baby girl. He'd written to Great-Grandma Mabel, but as far as Grandma knew, he never contacted them. After Grandpa William died, she found the letters he'd hidden, and she was devastated. No one knew what happened to Uncle George. He just quit writing, and Grandma Mabel's letters were returned by the postal service. She thought Uncle George had abandoned them."

Michael sighed. His stomach clenched in pain. "You have to tell your grandma. You couldn't keep that news from her. One thing for sure. Liz will be a wonderful addition to our family. I thought she would come into the family as my *wife.*"

Clara frowned. "I'm gonna pray you can still get married."

"Thanks, Clara." Michael smiled weakly. "I guess I need to pray about it, too. I'm pretty new at that. I don't always think to pray when I should."

"I asked Jesus to be my Savior when I was ten, but I don't remember to pray, either." She held out her hand. "Let's agree together to pray that God will work out the details."

Michael grasped her hands and bowed his head as Clara prayed.

Liz smiled as she gathered the soiled breakfast dishes. She'd received forty cents in tips. The girls were so friendly and helpful. She knew she'd enjoy the work here. She carried the dishes to the washroom and grabbed the cleaning cloth. She wanted to have her area straightened as soon as possible. Anna had asked to talk with her when she was finished. Liz wiped the counter, rubbed a fingerprint off of the salt shaker and replaced it and the pepper shaker in their rack. When she was satisfied everything was in its proper place, she hurried to the front lobby where Anna waited beside the reception desk.

"There you are, Liz. How did your first morning-train-rush go?"

"It was a bit challenging to find where all the supplies were stored in this Harvey House. But, the other girls were super helpful. I picked it up pretty quickly."

"Would you feel confident to serve Mr. Schmidt and me our four-course meal on Monday? We'd probably do it after the noon meal. I'd like for you rotate in to work in the dining room as soon as possible."

Butterfly flutters took up residence in Liz's stomach, but she nodded. "Yes, I can do that."

"Good. We'll plan on that. Also, would you like to go home with me this evening? I know you wanted to see my mother. She's always ready to welcome guests."

"Oh, yes! I'd love to go with you if she wouldn't mind. You live on a ranch, right?"

"Well, actually around here it's called a farm instead of a ranch. We have stock as well as farm ground. We grow wheat, corn, and maize."

"Is it okay for me to be off so soon after I arrived here?"

Anna turned toward one of the Harvey Girls, who stood beside her. "Lucy will take my place as the hostess this evening, and since I haven't worked you into the rotation yet, it'll be a good time for you to go. Be sure and take a dress for church tomorrow. My pa will pick us up about three this afternoon."

"Thank you, I'm excited to visit your farm and meet your family."

"It's quite a brood when we all get there."

That afternoon, Liz hurried to the reception desk, where Anna was writing in a ledger. She glanced up as Liz approached. "I have to fill out the lunch report before we go. The entire week's report has to be sent to the home office this afternoon. I'm almost through."

Liz set her bag on the floor. "I was afraid I was late. It was hard to fit my dress in my bag. I'll probably need to iron it tomorrow before church."

"That's fine. I'll need to iron mine, too. There's no easy way to keep them from wrinkling."

Liz walked to a nearby chair and watched the Harvey House patrons. Through the front windows, she could see people on the porch visiting. Others were in the lobby. Ceiling fans whirled throughout the room, attempting to dispel the afternoon warmth. Drowsiness nearly overtook her as she relaxed against the back of a comfortable chair. She thought about her mother's Bible. Before turning in last night, she'd read several other verses that were underlined. It had been well used. She had put the Bible in her bag to bring along.

Just then, Anna stood. "There, that's done, ready to send in. We have to put supper on next week's account." She grabbed her bag and indicated Liz's bag. "Pa should be here soon, if he isn't already." She walked onto the porch and down the steps to the parking lot. "There he is, coming this way, and he brought my sisters, Sophia and Caroline." She hurried to greet them with a hug.

As Liz caught up, Anna turned toward her. "Pa, this is Liz Gilbertson. Do you remember Mama talking about her friend, Elise, her roommate when she was a Harvey Girl?"

"Yes, I remember. That's where our little Elise got her name, from your mama's friend."

"Well, Pa, Liz is her daughter. She arrived yesterday to work as a Harvey Girl here. She is excited to meet our family."

Liz appraised Mr. McNance. He appeared to be a few years older than her own father, dark-haired, tall and muscular. He was obviously a hard worker. Michael would approve of his attire from the boots to his well-worn cowboy hat. The younger girls were dressed in colorful calico dresses.

"Mrs. McNance is excited to meet you, too. She received a letter from your mother saying you would be here." He turned and led the way to a rig hitched in the side lot. Liz accepted his hand and settled in the back between Sophia and Caroline. He swung up and seated himself beside Anna in the front. "We need to stop by the creamery to drop off the eggs and cream.

We already went to the general store. The girls helped me get the groceries.

He drove out of the lot, turned left past the depot, and pulled up in front of a small building. "It won't take me long to deliver the cream and eggs, and I need to get a block of ice for the icebox."

Caroline turned toward Liz. "How do you know Anna?"

"We work together, now, as Harvey Girls. And our mothers were best friends and roommates when they were Harvey Girls back before they got married."

A few minutes later, Mr. McNance returned with the ice, and they set out for home. At Main Street he turned north. Soon there were fewer and fewer houses, although the streets were laid out in expectation of future growth. Off to the right, Liz saw what looked like a sizeable oblong racetrack and some new buildings. "What is that over there?"

Anna shifted on her seat. "That's the new Kansas state fairgrounds. We've had the state fair here in Hutchinson since the 1870s, but they recently moved the location here from the other side of town. There'll be fireworks and a concert there on the Fourth of July, which is next Thursday. Mr. Schmidt usually extends the curfew for that night so we can come to see them."

"Can we come too, Pa?" Caroline bounced on the seat.

"We'll see. I'll have to talk to your mother." Mr. McNance turned right onto 17th Street and drove along the north side of the track, then out into the country. Grass covered, rolling hills extended on both sides of the road. Lazy, white clouds formed majestic sculptures against the broad expanse of cerulean blue sky. Liz pointed out the vague caricature of a small dog racing through the clouds to Caroline and Sophia. She took a deep breath and leaned back in the seat. The scene gave her a sense of calm and serenity.

She touched the pearl brooch at her neck, then closed her eyes. The day would be perfect if Michael were here with her. The thought of him—as her cousin—made her stomach clench. How could the discovery of her much-desired family connections produce such jumbled emotions? How would she ever tell him?

She jumped as Sophia touched her arm. "Look, there's our farm. Elise is waiting for us at the end of the driveway."

A neat farmstead sat on the right side of the road. A large white two-storied farmhouse with a picket fence around the front yard welcomed them. Beside the house was a neatly tilled garden patch with row after row of healthy vegetables. On the other side of the farmyard stood a huge red barn, a cattle shed, a chicken house and various other farm buildings. Several horses browsed the paddock beside the road and cows grazed in the pasture behind the barn. On down the road and to the left Liz spied another similar farmstead.

Anna pointed to the other house. "My oldest sister, Esther, and her family live there."

Elise jumped up and down and clapped her hands as they approached the driveway and turned in. She ran along beside the carriage as they drove up to the front of the house. "I didn't think you'd ever get here." She waited as Anna stepped down, then gave her a hug.

Anna laughed. "You'd think I'd been gone a year. I was with you last Sunday." She stepped back as Sophia, Liz, and Caroline climbed out of the carriage. "Elise, this is Liz Gilbertson. Her mother worked with our mama as a Harvey Girl. You are named after her mother, Elise."

Just then a woman about Elise Gilbertson's age hurried out the door, wiping her hands on her colorful apron. Her blonde hair was pulled up into a neat bun, and her face was wreathed in a huge smile.

"Liz, this has to be you! Elise sent me a letter and said you were transferred here to Hutchinson." Tessa folded Liz into a warm hug then stepped back with her hands still on Liz's arms. "Let me look at you. I'm so glad you're here. I hope your mama can come soon. She's the best friend I've ever had."

Liz looked into Tessa's friendly brown eyes. "She counts you as a wonderful friend, too. I've heard about you ever since I can remember. Mother was so excited when she heard I was transferred to Hutchinson."

Tessa turned. "Well, come on in. Let's get you settled. Girls, help your father carry in the groceries."

Elise grabbed Anna's hand. "I get to sleep with you."

Liz smiled at Elise, remembering Rachel's similar reaction, then followed Tessa into the house. As they stepped inside, the aroma of homemade bread and apple pie permeated the air. "Oh, yum, it smells heavenly in here."

"Thank you. I'm sorry, it's so warm in here. I usually try not to fire up the oven when it's this hot, but I just had to today for our special guest." Tessa fanned her face with a cardboard fan. "I think we'll set up a table in the backyard and eat outside under the trees. At least there'll be a breeze."

A teenage boy walked into the kitchen with the block of

ice. "Can somebody open the back of the icebox for me? This is heavy."

Caroline quickly moved to help him unwrap the ice and slide it into the insulated compartment then latch the door. His mother stopped him as he strode back through the kitchen. "Walter, this is our guest, Liz. Will you find Charles and have him help you set up the tables in the backyard? It's too warm to eat in here. Anthony and Esther and their families will be here for supper."

"Charles is in the barn. I saw him go in when we got home." Caroline followed Walter out. "I'll help you set up the tables."

Tessa led Liz through the kitchen and dining room to the stairs. "Your room will be up here. The girls will switch around."

"I'm sorry to make them move. I could sleep on the sofa."

"It's okay. Elise wants to sleep with Anna, anyway. They'll be fine for one night."

Downstairs, Liz and Anna helped Tessa prepare the meal. Homegrown green beans simmered on the back of the stove and a huge ham was in the warmer over the stove. "I think we'll boil the new potatoes and put butter on them. They're already peeled and ready to cook." Tessa looked at Anna. "Will you please go out to the root cellar and get a jar of pickles and a jar of pickled beets?"

As they finished the preparations, a carriage came in the driveway. Tessa wiped her hands on her apron. "There's Esther and her husband, Joseph Miller. Come on out, and I'll introduce you." Liz followed her out the door.

A young couple climbed from the carriage then reached up to lift out two small children. Their young son ran to Tessa.

"Nana, we came to eat supper with you."

"I know, Bert." She turned to Liz. "This is our four-year-old grandson, Bertram."

His little sister ran after him and threw her arms around Tessa's legs. "Nana, we gonna eat supper."

Tessa picked her up. "Yes, you are, sweet Rose. I want you to meet Liz. She's here to visit for a couple of days." Rose hid her face in her grandma's shoulder. Tessa turned to Esther. "Liz, this is Esther, our oldest daughter, and her husband, Joseph." Tessa put her hand on Liz's arm. "And this is Liz Gilbertson. She's the daughter of one of my very best friends from my Harvey Girl days."

Esther smiled and acknowledged the introduction.

Anna stepped up. "Liz is a new Harvey Girl. She just moved here to work in our Harvey House."

Tessa set Rose down and headed back to the house. "Let's get the food dished up. It's blazing hot in the kitchen, so we're eating outside. Anthony and Mariam will be along a little later. He has to finish feeding. Hopefully, they will be here by the time we get the food out there and ready." The girls all trooped into the kitchen after her and soon had the food ready to carry out to the impromptu tables.

The sight of the beautifully browned hot rolls and home-made butter and jam made Liz's mouth water. And the smells! The fresh apple and cherry pies were nearly irresistible. As they carried the last dish out, another carriage entered the farmyard.

Soon Liz was introduced to Anthony, his wife, Mariam, nine-year-old Joanna, seven-year-old Robert, and five-year-old Louisa.

After a prayer of thanks from their father, they all filled their plates and sat on blankets that had been spread on the grass. Rose and Louisa squeezed in between Anna and Liz. A short time later, the older kids ran off to play.

Liz enjoyed the conversations about the garden and the various farming operations. She studied the members of this incredible extended family. They were obviously drawn together by love. If she were to find more about her Boston family, would they love her like this? She sighed as she remembered that she'd have to share her discovery with Michael and Clara. She fingered the pearl brooch. What was God's plan? If only she could see into the future.

As the sun began to descend into the western sky, the young families packed up in preparation to return to their homes. Anthony and Joseph lifted the children into their carriages. "We'll see you all at church tomorrow."

The rest of the hours on the farm went by quickly. The next morning, Liz accompanied the McNance family to their little Mennonite country church. Then they enjoyed another fabulous country meal with crispy fried chicken, mashed potatoes and cream gravy, corn-on-the-cob, and fresh tomatoes from the garden. In the middle of the afternoon, Anna's father hitched up the carriage and returned them to the Harvey House in Hutchinson.

Liz awoke before dawn the next day. Anxiety settled around her shoulders and tied knots in her stomach. Today she would serve a meal to Anna and Mr. Schmidt. Her performance would determine if she was ready to work in the dining room. She'd rehearsed the serving sequence in her mind most of the night, but would she remember it when she had to put it all into practice? It only she could do it this morning instead of after the noon meal. That would get it over with!

She gazed out the window and watched the sky begin to grow lighter. Then she crawled out of bed and knelt on the rug. *Dear Jesus, I need your help today. Please help me remember everything I've learned. Calm my mind and heart, and give me peace. Also, Lord, please take care of the strange situation with Michael and me. Thank you, Lord. In Jesus' name, Amen.*

Liz sat on the side of the bed and reached for her mother's Bible. She moved close to the window. Was there enough light to read? She didn't want to turn on the lamp and awaken Hazel. She thumbed through the New Testament and looked for verses that had been underlined. One caught her eye in the fourth chapter of Philippians. It was verses six and seven. *Be careful for nothing; but in everything by prayer and supplication with thanksgiving, let your requests be made known unto God. And the peace of God, which passeth all understanding, will keep your hearts and minds through Christ Jesus.* She shook her head in wonder. Once again, the Lord had given her precisely the verse she needed. The weight of anxiety slipped away, and peace flowed through her.

CHAPTER 23

Michael headed his carriage down Kansas Avenue toward the Harvey House in Topeka. It was Sunday morning, so there was very little traffic. Clara had attended church with him for the past two weeks. He was gratified to know that she, too, had accepted Jesus as her Savior. She'd attended church regularly with her grandmother and her parents.

Michael had a jumble of mixed feelings. He was glad he'd contacted Clara about the Harvey Girl job. But, her evidence that Liz was her long-lost cousin and, by extension, his cousin, caused a sadness to surround him like a cloud. He was happy to know she was part of his family, but he'd wanted her to be his *wife,* not his cousin. It was so strange.

If this new information hadn't surfaced, they could have been married, and no one would have known or cared about their family connection. How would he ever tell Liz? Or, her parents, for that matter?

Clara waited in front of the depot when he drove up. "Hi,

Michael. it's a beautiful day."

Michael jumped down and strode to the other side of the carriage to assist her, then made his way slowly to his side. He picked up the reins and guided Dolly out of the lot. He'd been so wrapped up in his own feelings, he hadn't noticed the warm sunshine and slight south breeze.

Clara turned toward him. "I found out yesterday that I'll stay here in Topeka instead of being transferred. Beatrice and one of the other more experienced Harvey Girls want to move to other Houses, so Mr. Stecker asked Deborah and me if we'd stay here. I was more than glad to. I like this Harvey House, and I like Topeka."

Michael smiled and nodded. "That's good. I like being able to see you." He felt ashamed at his less than enthusiastic response. If only Liz could have stayed here! But then, what difference would it have made? She probably wouldn't want to marry him when she found out he was her cousin. A dark shroud of gloom settled around his shoulders. It didn't seem fair. Wasn't His life supposed to be better after he chose to follow Jesus? Liz had left. Then Clara made her discovery!

Michael had written to Liz, though he didn't tell her about the family relationship. He'd received two letters from her. She shared about the new Harvey House and her visit at the farm of her mother's friend. She'd also described the Fourth of July fireworks display she attended with the other Harvey Girls. She seemed to enjoy her new assignment in Hutchinson. That was more than he could say about his present situation.

"I hope we'll have time to talk today, Michael. You act like you're in another world." Clara scooted away from him with a flounce. "I received a letter from my grandma. She's really excited to know about Liz and wants to come out to visit."

Michael swiveled toward her. "We need to tell Liz before your grandma comes out here."

"I know that, silly. Maybe we can go out to see Liz weekend after next. That'll be the weekend before I actually start on the staff here. We could go out on Saturday and come back on Sunday. My grandma and my mother can't come until September, anyway."

Michael's gut knotted at the thought of telling Liz she was his cousin. He'd rehearsed it over in his mind, but there didn't seem to be a right way to say it. "I don't know. I'll have to think about it."

"Well, you can't put it off forever."

"I know." Michael guided his horse into the church parking lot. "We can talk about it later. I guess we need to tell Liz's parents before we go to tell her." He pulled up to the hitching post.

"I think that would be wise." Clara gave him an exasperated look, then stepped down from the carriage, not waiting for his help.

Michael jumped down and secured Dolly to the post. He gave her a pat. "We won't be gone long." Dolly shook her head with a snort. "Now, don't you get mouthy with me. We have to hang together." He ran his hand down her neck, then walked dejectedly toward the church.

"Hey, Michael." Julien appeared out of nowhere and fell into step with him. "I haven't seen you in like forever! Where've you been? Just 'cause Liz left doesn't mean you shouldn't come over. Are you gonna sit with our family? I want to sit by you."

Michael smiled and ruffled his hair. "It's good to see you, Julien. Sure, I'll sit with you." He turned to greet the rest of the family walking behind him. "I'm sorry, I didn't even see you arrive."

Elise patted his arm. "We've missed you. You'll have to bring Clara and come over for supper some evening. How about next Saturday?"

Michael bit his lip and nodded slowly. "As far as I know, that would work for me. I'll talk to Clara."

"I'll invite her, too." Elise waited to let Daniel open the door for her. "Won't you please sit with our family?"

"Thank you." Michael followed them into the church lobby. What would they think when they heard Clara's news? He sighed as he walked with them to their pew toward the front of the church.

Julien scooted in and patted the seat beside him. "Here, sit beside me."

Michael sat on the pew. He felt like the weight of the world rested on his shoulders. Why was he so depressed? He wasn't sure he could sing as the song leader announced the first song, "It Is Well With My Soul." Was it well with his soul? The words flowed over him. *"When peace like a river, attendeth my way, When sorrows like sea billows roll; Whatever my lot, thou hast taught me to say, it is well, it is well with my soul."* Mr. and Mrs. Gilbertson sang strongly beside him. It was obvious they knew all the verses.

Michael bowed his head. *Jesus, please let it be well with my soul. I know You're my Savior. You know what is best for me. I need You to speak to me.*

After the song service, the pastor stood and announced his

text. Philippians 1:6 *Being confident of this very thing, that he which hath begun a good work in you will perform it until the day of Jesus Christ.* "My friend, if you have received Jesus as your Savior, he will bring His will about in your life. He loves you. He wants only the best for you." As the sermon continued, peace slowly filtered into Michael's heart. *God, you know I want Liz to be my wife, but You do know best. Help me to accept your will. Amen.*

After the service, Clara fell into step with Michael on the way out of the sanctuary. "John McDonald has offered to take me to the Harvey House so you won't have to go back out there."

"If he wants to, that's fine. But, I don't mind the drive." Michael glanced at her. "Did Mrs. Gilbertson talk to you about supper at their house on Saturday?"

Clara nodded. "Yes, she did. We can talk to them then."

Michael grimaced then grinned. "Alright. I'll pick you up at three o'clock."

─────

Saturday afternoon, Michael drove into the parking lot of the depot, secured Dolly, and strode inside.

Clara was waiting in the lobby and stood when he entered. "Hello, Michael. It's good to see you. Did you have a good week?"

"Yes. We were busy at the office, but that's okay. I didn't have a lot of time to think and that was good. How about you?" They walked together from the building.

"My week was interesting. I'm more confident about the Harvey Girl routine. The next group of new girls arrived this week."

"How'd it go with John McDonald Sunday?"

Clara smiled, and her cheeks took on a rosy hue. "It was enjoyable. I'd visited with him at church a few times, but I was surprised when he offered to bring me home. He came and ate supper here last night. I hope we can get better acquainted. His parents own the mercantile the same as my grandma."

Michael nodded and grinned at her. "He's a capital guy! I hope it works out for you." He gave her a hand up into the carriage then walked around to his side. "I received another letter from Liz. It seems the job has gone well in Hutchinson. She likes the girls there."

"So, have you decided if you want to go next weekend? I'm not sure I can get away after that."

"Yes, we need to go. Liz probably wonders why I haven't headed her way before now." Michael drove from the depot lot.

Clara turned toward him. "Michael, I know this is very hard for you. Remember that song we sang at church on Sunday? "It is Well With My Soul?" The man who wrote it lost all his children in a shipwreck. They were drowned at sea. Only his wife was spared. He wrote the song as he crossed the ocean to join his wife. If he could survive that, we can surely survive this situation, don't you think?"

Michael nodded. "I've had more peace about it since Sunday. I know God will work it out. I just need to be willing to let Him have His way."

Clara paused. "I received a letter from my mother. She and Grandma found another box. There was a letter from Mrs. Esther Gilbertson. She wrote that George and Mary were killed in a carriage accident, and their daughter, Elizabeth, was living with them—her grandparents—on the Lazy G Ranch. She wanted to let my grandparents know." She shook her head. "I don't understand why Grandpa didn't tell Grandma he'd received that. He was such a stubborn, prideful man. I'm sure he didn't want to admit he'd been wrong."

Michael wasn't too surprised at that assessment of William Tilman. It was well-known in Michael's family that Clara's grandpa had a volatile temper and was a fiercely, prideful man. Michael stared straight ahead as he drove toward the Gilbertson home. He'd prayed all week for strength and wisdom to face Liz's family with their news about her past.

When they approached the house, Adam rode toward them on his high-wheeler. As he reached the carriage, he jumped down off the back and stopped. "You can go on in. Mother expects you." He waited until they climbed from the carriage then walked with them to the house, pushing his bicycle along.

Julien jumped up from the swing and ran down the steps. "What took you so long? I've waited all afternoon."

"Oh, Julien, you haven't either." Adam cuffed his brother on the shoulder. "The afternoon isn't even half over."

"I've waited since dinner." Julien pouted.

"Well, you don't have to wait any longer, because we're here." Michael patted Julien's disheveled hair.

Elise greeted them as they entered the house. "Hello, you two, it's good to have you here. It feels like you're part of the family."

Michael glanced at Clara and smiled, wryly. "Well, we have something to tell you."

"Oh?" Elise cocked her head and frowned slightly. "What's that?" She gestured toward the hallway. "Why don't you come into the sitting room? We can talk in there." She waved Adam and Julien back outside. "I'll call you two in pretty soon."

"Aww. Why can't we go talk, too?" Julien scowled.

"Not now." Elise shooed them out the door, then turned to follow Michael and Clara.

Clara spoke in a soft voice. "What's that all about? I didn't think you wanted to tell them."

"We have to and I just want to get it over." Michael motioned Clara into the room and followed. They each found a chair as Elise joined them.

"What are you young people up to?" Elise sat across from them.

Michael leaned forward. "Clara made a discovery about Liz's family. We want...no actually, we need, to tell you." He turned to Clara. "Tell her what you found out."

Clara frowned at him. "Why can't you tell her?"

"Because it's your news about your family."

She took a deep breath. "Years ago, before I was born, my Grandpa William and Uncle George, my mother's brother, had a huge fight. My uncle had been offered a position as a lawyer in the family bank. Uncle George didn't want to stay in Boston so he left home to become a lawyer out west. Grandpa Tilman vowed not to speak his name or have any contact with him, and my grandpa was a very stubborn man."

Elise sat forward, her eyes intent.

Clara continued. "I've heard the story of my Uncle George for as long as I can remember. My mother, Martha, was 23 when he left home, and she and Grandma Grace were devastated. For a while, George kept in contact with my great-grandma Mabel. They knew he'd married and had a daughter, but then the communication stopped and her letters were returned unopened. Grandma thought George had cut off contact. After Grandpa died, earlier this year, she found a box full of letters that Grandpa had hidden. Some were opened, and some left sealed. Uncle George had tried and tried to make amends. Grandma Grace was heartbroken."

Elise sucked in a quick breath and placed her hand over her heart.

Clara leaned forward. "When Liz packed to move to Hutchinson, she showed me a dagger she'd found in her parents' trunk. It looked familiar to me. My great-great-grandfather, and Michael's, too, was from a Scottish family. He came to America during the clan wars in Scotland but was very loyal to his family. He gave his son, Michael's Great-Grandfather Theodore McKey, his *dirk*—that's a large dagger—and my Great-Grandmother Mabel his *sgian*—or a small dagger, often carried in the boot— that matched. Great-grandma Mabel gave hers to Uncle George when he left home. Michael's Grandpa Philip McKey has the *dirk* mounted above the mantel in their parlor in Boston, and I've admired it many times. When I saw Liz's dagger, I recognized the crest and the design."

Elise had listened intently, her eyes wide and her mouth slightly open. Now she slowly shook her head. "That's incredible. So, Clara, you believe you're Liz's cousin?"

Clara nodded. "I looked on the back of her parents' picture, and their names were on the back, George Tilman and Mary Gilbertson."

Elise raised her eyebrows. "Yes, that was their names. Mary was Daniel's sister. They were killed in a carriage accident in May of 1885. I never got to meet them. They lived in Columbia, Missouri. George had a law practice there. After the accident, Daniel went to get Elizabeth from the pastor's family who'd taken care of her and brought her to live with his parents on their ranch near Emporia, Kansas. His mother tried to contact George's family, but with no success."

Clara's shoulders slumped. "Grandma found the letter from Esther Gilbertson. It was in a hidden box."

Elise nodded. "So, it did get there. She thought she had the wrong address." She relaxed a bit and sighed. "Grandma Esther died the next spring. Daniel and I brought Elizabeth here to raise when we got married. When our son Adam was born, he couldn't say Elizabeth so he called her Liz."

Elise paused. A slight smile on her face. "Liz will be beyond excited to know you are her cousin, and that she has a grandma who desires to meet her. She's wanted to find out about her father's family for quite a while now."

Clara looked at Michael. "I love Liz. I'm excited to find out she's my cousin, and Grandma Grace wants to come to meet her. But, Michael is upset. He thinks that he can't court her if she's his cousin."

"It's all well and good that Clara found her cousin, and that her grandma will know her granddaughter, but why did she have to be the girl I fell in love with?" Michael looked down at his clasped hands. "I'm glad she's part of our family, but I wanted her to be my wife." He shook his head and groaned. "I feel so selfish."

Elise studied him, her brows knit. "So you don't think you can court her? What would she be, your third cousin? That's actually quite a distant relative."

Michael's shoulders slumped. "My family would never give approval for me to court and possibly marry my cousin. If she'd been back home, we'd have grown up together, like Clara and me."

"Do you feel the same toward Liz as you do Clara?"

Michael looked up. "No, not at all! I didn't know she was my cousin until Clara made her discoveries."

"Do you love her enough to fight for her?"

Michael stared at her as a spark of hope flared in his heart. He straightened and lifted his chin. "Yes. Yes, I do."

"I think you've given up too easily, Michael. Have you written to your parents about it? Do you even know what they think?"

"No."

"Don't you think that would be a good place to start? I'm sure they want what's best for you."

"Yes. I'll do that. I just took it for granted that my parents wouldn't approve."

Rachel peeked in through the door. "What're you talkin' about in here? Oh, hi, Michael, and Clara. I didn't know you were here." She skipped into the room. "I'm glad to see you. I miss Liz."

Clara patted the seat beside her. "Come sit down and give me a hug. We miss Liz, too. We'll see her next weekend. What would you like us to tell her?" She put her arm around Rachel. "I have a good idea. Why don't you write her a letter and we'll take it to her."

"Yeah." Rachel ran to the desk in the corner of the room and pulled out a sheet of paper.

Elise stood. "I should go check on our meal. You, two, relax in here. I'll tell the boys they can come in and visit with you until suppertime."

Michael relaxed against the back of his chair. The weight on his shoulders had lightened. Maybe there was hope for him and Liz.

Chapter 24

Liz watched as the last of the noon customers moved out of the dining room. She gathered her station's dirty dishes and carried them to the dish room. Butterflies and bullfrogs had taken up residence in her stomach.

Michael and Clara would come that afternoon. What would it be like to see Michael, since she knew he was related to her? What should she say? What could she say?

Liz was excited to know Clara was her cousin and that she had family on her father's side; a grandma, and aunts, and cousins. It was almost more than she could grasp. How would she tell them what she'd discovered?

She grabbed the clean linen and dishes and hurried back to her tables. She needed to clean and re-set them so she'd be free when Michael and Clara arrived. She'd worked in the dining room since serving Mr. Schmidt and Anna their four-course meal two weeks ago.

Liz arranged the silverware, crystal, and napkins then

checked to make sure everything was in order. She turned to Jessie, who worked at the table next to hers, polishing the silver water pitchers. "My tables are ready for supper. I need to go. My friends will be on the afternoon train."

"Okay, go ahead. Have a good time."

Liz walked across the dining room and into the lobby, where Anna sat at the reception desk writing in the ledger. Liz was glad she didn't have to keep track of all the numbers.

A family with three children met her as she ascended the stairs. She had an hour before Michael and Clara's train would arrive. Liz wanted to freshen up and get her mother's Bible to show them. She still wasn't sure how she'd tell them about the family connections.

As she climbed to the third floor, she remembered that there was to be a social and a dance that evening. The chairs had been moved out of the center of the parlor. Would Michael even want to dance with her after he found out she was his cousin? Her stomach gave a lurch. She put her hand into her pocket and felt the smooth pearls on the brooch. She'd pinned it inside her apron pocket almost every day. The knowledge of their new family relationship didn't change her feelings toward that sweet copper-haired man.

When she reached her room, Liz picked up the Bible and sat on the bed. *Please, God, don't let this change our courtship. Please show us the way. Help me to know what to say to Michael and Clara.* She held the Bible to her chest. Then, she opened it and took out the paper with the list of names and birthdays. She'd read and studied it so many times she almost knew it by heart. What would Clara think? And more to the point, what would Michael think?

She stood and checked her hair in the mirror over her dresser. A few unruly curls had escaped the pins. She wiped the perspiration from her forehead. This summer heat made it nearly impossible to keep her hair in place. She strolled from the room back to the parlor and placed her Bible on a table by a group of chairs. She'd bring Michael and Clara up here to talk. It would be quieter.

Liz heard the train whistle as it approached the depot. Her heart jumped up into her throat, and her stomach knotted. They were here, and she would have to tell them about her discovery. She hurried down the stairs and out onto the porch as the train screeched to a stop next to the depot.

A few long minutes later, she saw Michael and Clara step down from the train car and walk her way. Michael was so handsome in his boots and jeans. His coppery red hair set off his cowboy hat. She could see his infectious smile as he approached beside Clara, whose mahogany red hair set off her classic features and porcelain skin. Was it really possible she was related to them?

Before she could collect her thoughts, they were beside her on the porch, exchanging quick hugs.

Michael caught her eye. "You are a beautiful sight for a fellow to see as he gets off the train. The sun made your hair look like a halo."

Liz laughed. "There must be something wrong with your vision. I don't have a halo. That's for sure." She stepped forward and gave him another hug then turned and grasped Clara's hands. "It's so good to see you, both. This has been a long month." She led them to the wooden chairs on the porch.

After they were seated, Liz hesitated, uncertain how to begin the conversation. She turned to Clara. "Beatrice came through with the other girls on Thursday. She said you're assigned to stay in Topeka. Are you happy about that?"

"Yes, I like the Harvey House and the city, and, of course, Michael's there. Mr. Stecker asked Deborah Jackson and me if we'd stay on and we both agreed since Beatrice and one of the other girls were ready to move on. I start a full schedule on Monday. Do you work in the dining room, yet?"

Liz nodded. "I served my test meal two weeks ago. We rotate between the lunchroom and the dining room. It's nice to have a change, and the tips are sometimes bigger in the dining room," She added with a chuckle.

Liz turned to Michael. "How have you been?"

"Not nearly as well with you gone. My weekends are too long. Clara and I did go over and have supper with your parents last Saturday. It was delicious as usual."

"I'm glad you got to see them. I miss them all so much. I imagine Julien talked your ear off."

"Julien's a good buddy. He loves to learn." Michael paused and stared at Liz, then glanced at Clara.

Clara lowered her eyebrow at him then took a deep breath. "Liz, in sort of an odd way, I figured out, just before you left, that we're related."

Liz straightened in her chair and her eyes widened. Her mouth dropped open. "You know?"

Clara frowned. "Know?" She cocked her head. "You know that we're cousins?"

"I wasn't sure how to tell you." Liz let out her breath in a rush.

"How did you know? When did you find out?" Clara sat forward.

Liz relaxed her shoulders. "My Grandpa Gilbertson gave me my mother's Bible when I stopped by to see him on my way here. Inside was a paper that Great-Grandmother Mabel had given to my father, with a list of birthdays. I recognized the names of people you had talked about. It wasn't hard to put two and two together." She looked at Michael. " Great-Great-Grandfather and Great-Great-Grandmother McKey's names were in the Bible under deaths. I knew that had to be the same ones you talked about." Liz shook her head. "But how did you know? I thought I'd have to tell you."

Clara shifted on the seat. "When you packed to come here, I saw the dagger you'd found in your parents' trunk. The family crest and design on the scabbard matched the Scottish *dirk*, or larger dagger, that Michael's family has. It's been displayed over their mantel for years. Our great-great-grandpa Patrick McKey gave his son, Theodore, the *dirk* and our great-grandma Mabel the smaller dagger or *sgian*. She gave it to Uncle George, my mother's brother and your father, when he left home and came west.

"I could hardly believe my eyes when I saw the *sgian* with your things as you packed. Then I saw the names on the back of your parents' photo. I was so surprised, I couldn't think of a way to tell you."

Tears sprang to Liz's eyes as she leaned forward and gave Clara a hug. "It's hard to believe you're my family. I've wanted to find my father's family, and now, here you are. I can't wait to meet my Grandma Grace."

"She plans to come to see you in September when the weather cools off. I think my mother will come, too. I'll let you know when."

Liz saw Michael's shoulders slump on her other side. "Oh, Michael. I know. I've been so conflicted. What can we do? How can a person be so happy and sad at the same time?"

"I don't know. But I won't give up. I sent a letter to my parents that explained the situation. I'm waiting for an answer. Your father thinks we're such distant cousins, it shouldn't matter." He grabbed her hand. "We could run off and get married, then no one could do anything about it."

Liz's breath caught in her throat, and her heart pounded. *Michael had asked her to marry him.* She shook her head. "That's sweet, but you know we can't do that. This family has had one too many run-away members. I've just found my family. I don't want to be separated from them again. Besides, I signed a contract that I wouldn't get married for six months."

"I know." He scowled. "It was just a thought."

Clara leaned forward. "Let's pray about it. God brought you two together and let you grow to care for each other. He already knew you were related, and that we would all find out. Don't you think He can work out the details for the future?"

Liz nodded. "Of course, He can. Even if it seems impossible to us. In fact, He gave me a verse when I first figured out about our family. It's in Proverbs and says we need to trust in the Lord with all our hearts and not try to figure things out on our own." She stood and smoothed her skirt. "Let's go up to the parlor. I'll show you my mother's Bible."

As they walked toward the reception desk, Anna closed the

ledger she'd written in. "Are these your friends?"

"Yes, Clara is my cousin and Michael's my beau."

"Oh, I'm glad to meet you both. I'm Anna McNance, the head waitress here. I hope you have a good weekend visiting Hutchinson." She turned to Liz. "Have you invited your visitors to the social this evening?" She focused her attention back to Michael and Clara. "Our baker and chef have prepared refreshments for us, and we'll have an impromptu dance."

"That sounds like fun." Clara smiled and nodded. "We know all about those Harvey House refreshments."

"By the way, do either of you play the piano? Our piano player moved to another House. We have a new Victrola, but we don't have very many records and I like live piano music better."

"Liz plays. I've heard her." Michael's eyes sparkled.

"Michael." Reluctance filled Liz. "I'm not that good."

Anna turned to Liz. "Would you play for us? I have sheet music. You wouldn't have to play a lot. We do have the Victrola."

"I guess I could."

"Thank you, I appreciate it."

The three of them headed up the two flights of stairs. "You didn't have to tell Anna that I played."

"She wanted to know." Michael took her hand as they made the last few steps and walked into the residential parlor. "And I wanted to hear you play again."

Liz motioned for them to sit in the parlor. "There's my mother's Bible. I'll go to my room and get the dagger." She returned a few minutes later and handed the *sgian* to Michael.

He took it and turned it over in his hands. "It does have the McKey family crest. Clara, you were very observant."

For the next hour, they discussed their family. Finally, Liz looked up at the clock on the wall. "Oh, dear. I have to go get ready for the evening train. Clara, Anna said there's an empty bed down our hall in room eight. Ida is the other Harvey Girl in there. Michael, you will be down the other hall with the male staff in room fourteen. There are hotel linens on the beds, but you'll have to make them up. Come on down to the dining room when you're ready, maybe after the train rush."

After the meal was over and Liz had cleaned her station, she hurried upstairs to change clothes. It was a lovely evening. The social went well. When she didn't play the piano, Michael and Liz danced together. Some of the hotel guests ventured up to share the fun, but most were Harvey Girls and staff including railroad workers and a few other friends.

When Anna announced the dance was ending and placed the last record on the Victrola, Michael held Liz and guided her across the floor. "You are so beautiful tonight. I like that pearl brooch you have on your dress."

Liz leaned back and gazed into his eyes. "I wear it in my pocket every day. A special man gave it to me."

"He must love you very much."

Liz felt a warm flush diffuse her face. She smiled shyly. "I hope so. I love him." Michael gave her a light hug, and they walked hand in hand from the dance floor.

The next morning after breakfast, Michael and Clara boarded the train to head back to Topeka. Liz was sorry to see them go, but her heart was light, and she hummed "Oh How I Love Jesus" as she prepared to walk to the small church down the street.

Morning sunlight streamed through the dining room windows as Liz cleared the tables. She'd just served breakfast to the second crowd of diners and received fifty cents in tips. Happiness filled her and the song, "It is Well With My Soul," ran through her thoughts. She occasionally hummed a snatch as she worked.

Two weeks had passed since her visit from Michael and Clara. Yesterday, she'd received a letter from Clara which confirmed that her Grandma Grace and Aunt Martha, Clara's mother, would come on September eleventh. She'd finally get to meet them. It had to be God who'd worked it all out. The only cloud on her horizon was the cousin thing with Michael, but they both believed God would work that out, too, somehow. They all continued to pray about it.

Liz worked quickly to clean and reset her tables. This was her day to polish the large coffee pots and she wanted to get it done this morning. She walked to the dish room and grabbed the silver polish and cloth. There wasn't to be even one fingerprint on the shiny silver. She hummed the lovely tune of the "It Is Well" chorus as she scrubbed and polished, standing on a stool to reach the top. When she was sure there weren't any streaks or blemishes left, she headed to her tables and polished her salt and pepper shakers, too.

Jessie turned from the next table. "May I use that cloth after you're done? I need to do that, too. There are a couple of fingerprints on mine."

With a final swipe Liz handed the cloth over. The dining room appeared ready for the next surge of train passengers.

Just then, Anna rushed into the room. "Liz, did you get the coffee pots done? Are the windows dusted?" She looked around.

"Yes, I just polished the coffee pots. I think Ruth Ann dusted yesterday afternoon. Why?"

Anna grimaced. "Fred Harvey's sons, Byron and Ford are here with the architect Louis Curtiss to discuss the new Harvey House they plan to build here in Hutchinson. They will meet with the mayor and the city council after dinner, but they'll all be here to eat.

"Jessie, I'll seat them at your tables. The Harveys may do an inspection before they leave, so make sure everything is spotless."

"We'll spread the word. Do you want Liz to warn the kitchen crew?"

"Yes, let's do that, although they're usually prepared for anything."

As Anna hurried from the dining room Liz headed to the kitchen. She was eager to see Mr. Ford Harvey again.

The word soon spread, and all the girls, even the ones on split shifts, double-checked to make sure everything was in order.

As they stood by their tables and waited for the local patrons and hotel guests, Jessie put her hands behind her back. "I'm shaking so hard. I hope I don't drop a plate of food. I could hardly serve the train passengers."

"You'll do great. Just treat them like you would anyone else. I'll say a pray for you."

"Thanks."

Just then, Anna headed across the dining room followed by a group of men, all in suits ties and polished shoes. Liz recognized Ford Harvey, so the man beside him must be his brother. He looked older. The mayor and several of the other men had been in before. Anna seated them at Jessie's table, and she sprang into action, greeted them, and began to ask their drink preferences.

Liz pulled her attention away to greet the patrons who were escorted to her table. It wouldn't help Jessie—or anyone else—if she stared. Liz began her practiced routine. She took the drink orders, then served the lettuce wedges with Thousand Island dressing or fruit salads.

As she placed the last fruit salad on the table, she heard a booming voice behind her. "So, Mr. Curtiss, this new Harvey House you plan to build, how many guest rooms will it have?"

"It will have eighty guest rooms with a bathroom between every two rooms. The Harvey Girls will be able to serve over one hundred sixty meals at one time, one hundred-twenty in the dining room and forty around the lunchroom counter."

"Why do we need all that?" Liz recognized the Mayor's voice. "This here Santa Fe Hotel is doin' just fine."

Ford Harvey spoke up. "Yes, it is, but it's at capacity most of the time. We want even more people to come and stay in your fair city. As the number of easterners who travel by train increases, we need to be able to welcome them. If they have comfortable accommodations, they will stay longer and spend money in Hutchinson."

Liz focused her attention back on her patrons and began to take their meal orders. She was excited to hear about the new Harvey House, but she'd have to get the details from Jessie later. It was hard to concentrate with the drone of voices behind her, and she was relieved when she'd served all the meals without mishap.

As she stepped back to let her customers eat, she heard Ford Harvey's voice. "We'll build this Harvey House in honor of our late father, Fred Harvey, who, as you know, passed last March. It will be designed in the English Tudor style to celebrate his English ancestry. There will be red-tiled, peaked roofs, dark wood-beamed ceilings, wide, lofty stairways, and large, shaded porches. We will build on the large vacant lot south of the Santa Fe tracks at Third and Walnut. Jim Hurley, the Santa Fe general manager, has suggested we name it 'Bisonte,' which means buffalo in Spanish, as a tribute to the vast buffalo herds that once roamed this area." The voices mingled as the conversation ensued.

Liz stepped forward to remove the soiled dishes and take the dessert orders. Her mind swirled with the details of the grand Harvey House that would soon be built nearby.

In early September, the Kansas heat was still sweltering. Liz hung up her cleaning cloth in the dish room and pulled a handkerchief from her pocket to wipe her forehead. The windows were open, but there wasn't any breeze to stir the air. She'd been working in the lunchroom for the last two weeks.

Ida stepped in behind her. "Whew! It's like an oven in here. I need a drink of water." She grabbed a glass from the dish rack and filled it at the water tank.

"I need one, too. You wouldn't think it would be so hot on the sixth of September."

"It must be an Indian summer. It'll get cold before you know it."

Liz took a swallow of the cool spring water. It was one of the perks of the Harvey Girl job. Fred Harvey transported water by rail to all the Harvey Houses so the coffee would taste the same all along the line.

She brushed at her apron. "I have to go up and change. I bumped my elbow on the counter and sloshed coffee on my apron. It was so busy, I couldn't get away during the lunch rush."

"It has been crazy busy the last few days." Ida set her empty glass on the dishwashing table. "One of my train customers said people were headed to New York for the Pan-American Exposition. President McKinley is there. He was supposed to give a speech yesterday. He seems to be pretty popular."

Liz wrinkled her nose. "I suppose that explains the large train loads."

"Go on up. We'll cover for you. It'd be just our luck that one of the Harvey superintendents would come in for an inspection if you didn't get it changed. We're due for one since the Harvey brothers were too busy to do it when they were here a couple of weeks ago."

"I'll get back as quickly as I can." Liz downed the rest of her water.

Anna stood at the registration desk. "Liz, you had two letters in the mail today." She held them out.

"Thank you." Liz scanned the return addresses: Michael and her Grandmother Tilman. Excitement spiraled through her. She always loved to hear from Michael and had hoped to receive a letter from her grandmother to confirm the upcoming visit. Liz hurried up the stairs to her room.

She sat on the bed and tore open the letter from her grandma.

Dear Liz,

My sweet granddaughter, I am so excited to meet you. I can't tell you how happy I was when Clara wrote and said she'd found you. We had no idea where to even start an investigation. I believe God led us together.

I want to let you know that my daughter, Martha, Clara's mother, and I will travel to Kansas to see you. I'm not sure, but I think Michael's parents may come with us. We will leave Monday, September ninth and plan to be in Hutchinson on the twelfth. We will stop in Topeka to see Clara and Michael first. We hope they can get off to come with us to visit you. I received a sweet letter from Mrs. Daniel Gilbertson. She invited us to stay the night at their home.

We look forward, with anticipation, to our visit.

Love,

Grandma Grace Tilman

Liz stared at the name, written in her grandma's handwriting. Anticipation mingled with anxiety, coursed through her. What if she didn't live up to her grandma's expectations?

Liz had written a long letter to her mama and daddy to share her discovery with them, and Elise had responded with encouragement and love. Daniel, Elise, Adam, Julien, and Rachel would always be her family.

She picked up Michael's letter. She needed to get back to work, but she couldn't wait to read it. She quickly ran her finger under the flap and pulled it out.

Dear Liz,

I wanted to let you know, I received a letter from my father. He was interested to know that Clara and I had met you, and that you are his cousin, George's, daughter. I told him we are courting.

He and my mother want to meet you. They will come with your grandma and aunt next week on the train.

I don't know what he'll say about our relationship, but I know we're supposed to be together. We'll work it out somehow. You are the best person who has ever come into my life. Keep praying.

I know, I should tell you in person, but I can't wait.

I love you,

Michael

Liz stared at the letter. Warmth radiated through her at his words. Maybe she should have waited to read it. She ran her fingers into her hair. How would she ever concentrate on her work with the impending visits? She'd never met these people, and yet they were her family.

Her stomach knotted. *Dear God, please calm my spirit. I pray You will work out all the details.* The words, *Trust in the Lord with all thine heart and lean not on your own understanding,* ran through her mind. *Thank you, Jesus. I'll trust you.*

Liz quickly took off the soiled apron, laid it on the bed and grabbed a clean one from the wardrobe. She glanced in the mirror then walked out the door, tying the apron strings as she hurried through the parlor.

She had just taken her place behind the counter when the train whistle sounded. In the seconds before the rush, she turned to Ida. "I'm so excited. Today, I received a letter from my grandma, whom I've never met. She and my aunt will be here next week from Boston. I found out they were my family when I moved here at the end of July."

"Oh, my goodness, that's fascinating." Ida wrinkled her forehead. "Why didn't you know about them?"

"It's a long story. My father lost contact with his family, in Boston, when he moved west to be a lawyer."

The train passengers began to filter into the lunchroom, and the girls focused their attention on the patrons. Liz liked the afternoon train. Most of the customers wanted a refreshing drink and a sandwich or dessert. As Liz dished up two pieces of pie, Mr. Schmidt hurried into the room. "May I have your attention, please. We have just received the word, via telegraph, that President McKinley, the President of the United States, has been shot while at the Pan-American Exposition. He's in surgery. They ask that the citizens of the country be in prayer for him. Shall we bow our heads for a moment?" After the prayer ended, there was a brief lull in the conversation. Then the room was abuzz with exclamations of shock and disbelief.

Liz stared at the door as Mr. Schmidt quietly left the room. Her heart had skipped a beat at his announcement, and now it pounded in her ears. How could someone shoot the President? She felt disconnected from her surroundings. Would life go on as usual?

Ida touched her arm. "Are you through with the apple pie? I need a piece."

Liz focused on her idle hands. "Oh, yes." She picked up the plates and went to serve her customers. But, no one seemed to be hungry any longer.

Chapter 25

Liz awoke and raised up on her elbow to see the alarm clock on the dresser. Four-thirty. It was still half an hour until time to get up. She'd been awake nearly every hour through the night. Her Grandma Grace and Aunt Martha would be here this afternoon. She settled back, pulled the blanket up under her chin and relived the last nine months, in her mind.

Until last Christmas, she hadn't given her extended family much thought. Her future had been planned out. She would marry Richard, settle down, have children, and live near their parents. Her energy was centered on wedding plans and a new home.

But, when Richard came home from college for the Christmas holiday, he'd changed. She noticed a definite difference in his attitude. He was distant and didn't want to spend time with her. She began to question her future with him as his correspondence waned. She wasn't entirely surprised when Richard announced, in April, that he'd met someone else. At first, she was devastated, but as time went by she realized she wasn't ready for marriage.

In retrospect, she realized God's hand was in all of that. God had brought Michael into her life to help her move on from Richard. How could any of them know Michael was the connection with her father's family? She smiled in the dark. Or that they would fall in love? Her heart warmed at Michael's declarations of love, and his insistence that their relationship would work out.

Hazel rolled over then threw back her cover and sat up. She squinted at Liz. "You awake?"

Liz pushed back her blanket. "Yes, I've been awake off and on all night. I keep thinking about my grandma. What will she be like?"

"I'm excited for you, but I know you must be uncertain about meeting her for the first time. Just be yourself. She can't help but love you."

"Thank you, Hazel. I appreciate that."

Hazel thrust her feet into her slippers and padded across the floor to turn off the alarm clock. "B-r-r-r. It got chilly during the night. Fall must be on the way." She picked up the pitcher and headed down the hall.

The days were indeed growing shorter. Liz got up and lit the lantern. She picked up her mother's Bible and sat on her bed. It had become her practice to read at least a few verses each day before she prepared for work. She'd read almost all the book of Philippians. Today she was at the last few verses. Philippians 4:19 caught her eye. *But my God shall supply all your need according to his riches in glory by Christ Jesus.* She also looked back up in the chapter to verse 13. *I can do all things through Christ, which strengtheneth me.* She smiled. God had brought her to this day and this verse. He would work out all the details.

That afternoon, Liz stepped out onto the front porch of the hotel and pulled her cloak around her. Fall was definitely in the air. A chilly breeze blew through the enclosure. She sat on the edge of one of the deck chairs and idly picked up a newspaper from the table beside her chair. The headlines read, "President expected to make a full recovery." She settled back and read the article. President McKinley was awake, alert, and had even read the newspaper. The vice-president, Theodore Roosevelt, had been so confident of his recovery that he'd gone on a camping trip in the Adirondack Mountains.

Liz sighed with relief. It was horrible that someone had tried to kill the President. Many people around her were unnerved and panicky when they heard he'd been shot. And, of course, she would never forget her shock and fear when she heard the news.

Liz quickly laid the newspaper aside when she heard the train whistle. She stood and paced in front of the chairs. Her stomach fluttered, and she clasped her hands together to keep them from trembling. She was excited and happy, but nervous, too. Would she know what to say? She tried to calm herself as she watched the train pull into the depot. Then she had a thought. Would they know to come here to the Harvey House? Maybe she should have gone to the depot to meet them.

She hurried down the steps then slowed to watch the passengers disembark. How would she even know it was them? Somehow, she thought she'd know.

Just then, Liz saw a middle-aged woman exit the train. She

turned and held out her hand to an older, white-haired woman who stepped down beside her. Liz's insides lurched, and she stared with wide eyes. That had to be them. She wanted to run to meet them, but her feet were anchored to the ground.

As they approached, Liz noticed that the younger woman had brown hair, but other than that, she was the image of Clara, just a few years older. Her grandma's eyes danced with excitement as she hurried up the walk.

She smiled broadly at Liz, who was tongue-tied. "Are you, by any chance, Elizabeth Gilbertson?"

Liz nodded as she stared into the loving eyes before her. Instead of answering, she moved forward into the waiting arms of her grandmother. Tears sprang to her eyes as she felt the kisses and heard the words, "I love you so much." She clung to this woman she'd been afraid she'd never find, never meet.

Finally, Liz stepped back. "You're beautiful, like Clara said you were." She laughed shakily. "I didn't think I'd ever find you." She turned to her Aunt Martha and gave her a hug. "Thankfully, Clara recognized the dagger that had belonged to my father."

"That's what she told us."

Suddenly, Liz felt the cold wind whip around them. "Come on in where it's warm. We had a cold snap come in last night." She turned and led the way into the warm lobby. They walked to the registration desk where Mr. Schmidt and Anna checked in hotel patrons. When it was their turn, Liz gestured toward them. "Anna, this is my Grandma Grace and my Aunt Martha. They live in Boston."

Anna smiled. "I'm glad to know you. We're happy to have you here, but not nearly as happy as Liz. She's been so excited to see you, she nearly burst." She picked up a room key. "I've reserved room 112 for you. It's up the stairs and to the right. Your luggage will be brought over from the depot and should be here soon." She glanced at the ledger. "I see you'll be here through the weekend. Just make yourselves at home."

Grandma Grace took the key. "We'll have more family arrive on Saturday afternoon."

"Yes, I have three more rooms reserved. I also have the upstairs parlor reserved for Saturday night." She glanced at Liz, adding, "Clara and Michael can sleep up on the staff floor."

Grandma nodded. "That's wonderful. Thank you for your hospitality."

They headed up the stairs and Liz showed them to their room. She took in the elegant furnishings. The richly hued walnut bedstead matched the dresser and wardrobe. A beautifully patterned china vanity set, of pitcher and bowl, sat on a small table, and a cushioned chair was in the corner. The bedspread and curtains were a lovely floral pattern.

Liz turned toward her grandmother. "I have to work in the dining room tonight and tomorrow for breakfast and noon, but then I have tomorrow evening and Saturday off. Come down about six-thirty. That will be after the train passengers are served. Anna will seat you at my table. We can visit after I get off duty."

"We'll be fine. You do what you need to." Grandma Grace placed her handbag on the dresser.

Liz gave them both another hug then hurried from the room. Her footsteps were light, and a song resonated in her heart. She couldn't keep the smile away. Her grandma loved her!

After supper, Liz took Grandma and Aunt Martha up to

the residential parlor. "We can visit here. It's more private and quieter than the lobby."

Grandma Grace sat down and scanned the room. "This hotel is elegant, and the service from the Harvey Girls is exceptional. I can see why you enjoy working here."

"The Harveys are great to work for." Liz smiled as she chose the sofa.

Aunt Martha moved to one of the wingback chairs. "Clara's father and I were skeptical when she wanted to come work as a waitress. She was insistent she needed to move out on her own. Since Michael recommended the Harvey Girl job, we finally reluctantly gave our permission. After I observed her work and learned of the conditions required by Fred Harvey, I was glad we did. She seems to enjoy it tremendously."

"It's a great job. My mother, Elise, worked as a Harvey Girl before she married my father. She encouraged me to apply for the job, after I expressed an interest."

"How old were you when your parents died in the carriage accident?"

"I was four years old. I barely remember any of it. I lived with Grandpa and Grandma Gilbertson until Grandma died the next spring, then Uncle Daniel and Aunt Elise got married and took me to live with them and be their daughter. Did you stay with them in Topeka?"

"Yes, we did. You have a wonderful family."

"I think so." Liz leaned forward. "Would you like to see some pictures of my parents before they died? I also have some of my baby pictures and the dagger that belonged to my father." She wrinkled her nose. "Clara calls it *sgian*."

"That's the Scottish name for it." Aunt Martha laughed. "We'd like that very much."

"I'll go back to my room and get them." Liz rose and hurried down the hall and returned a few minutes later. She handed the pictures to her grandmother.

Grandma Grace stared at the picture of George and Mary. Tears gathered in her eyes. "That's definitely my George. I have never seen this photograph. Oh, how I wish I'd been more insistent on learning their whereabouts. William could be so difficult, and I didn't want to stir up more trouble."

Aunt Martha put her arm around her mother. "You did what you thought was right."

"But it wasn't right. Liz, can you forgive me?"

"Oh, yes. Just knowing I have you now means more to me than anything. I've had a great life with Daddy and Mama."

Her grandma smiled as she looked at the baby pictures. "I missed out on so much."

"Let's just move forward from here." Aunt Martha studied the pictures Grandma handed her.

A tremendous burden had lifted from Liz's shoulders. Her grandma loved her and wanted to be part of her life.

Saturday afternoon, Liz could hardly contain her excitement as the train whistle sounded. Her head was spinning! So much had happened in the last few weeks and now, the past few days. She wasn't sure she could handle it. Today, she'd meet more of her extended family. Michael and his parents would be here, along with Clara, who had received time off. Daddy and Mama were coming, too, but the younger Gilbertsons were staying home with Lucia, Liz's former nanny.

Liz sat on the Harvey House porch with her grandma and aunt. Thankfully, the weather had moderated, and a southerly breeze wafted around them.

"I like your little city." Grandma Grace looked up Main Street, which was visible from where they sat. "I'm glad we were able to walk up town this morning and explore the shops."

"Me, too." Liz hugged her. "Thank you for my new dress. I'm sure Clara will like hers too."

"Hutchinson is a surprising oasis on the prairie. You can get everything you need here, as far as I can tell."

Liz nodded as she eagerly watched the train pull into the depot. It was so hard to sit still. She'd love to fly down the steps and run to greet her family, but she needed to maintain some decorum around her grandma. She didn't want to appear to be a hoyden! She grinned at the picture in her mind.

"Look, there's Clara...and Michael...and my parents."

"Michael's parents are behind them," Aunt Martha pointed.

Liz couldn't sit still. She stood and walked to the top of the steps. She smiled broadly as they drew closer, and she saw the welcoming light in Michael's eyes. He was so handsome. Today, he was dressed in his more formal clothes, black trousers, white shirt, a well-cut black day jacket, and a dark tie. With a spring in his step, Michael bounded up the walk and reached the porch first. He held out his hand to her. "Come, I want you to meet my parents."

Her hand in his, he guided her down the steps. "Father, Mother, this is my dear friend, Elizabeth Tilman Gilbertson. We call her Liz."

Then he turned to her. "My father, David McKey, and my mother, Margarette McKey."

Liz smiled. "I'm so glad to meet you." She extended her hand.

Michael's mother gave a slight gasp as she accepted the gesture. "You look like George." She gazed up at Grandma Grace, who stood at the top of the steps. "Don't you think so?"

"Yes, of course, she does."

Michael gave Liz's hand a reassuring squeeze then released it as Liz turned to her parents. She nearly fell into Elise's arms and gave her a huge hug. She didn't want to let go. She needed to draw strength from her mama, the one who'd been her rock for so many years. "I love you." The whispered words were shaky.

"I know. I love you, too, so much, sweetheart. This is what you've prayed for."

Liz closed her eyes against the sudden tears that gathered. She gave Elise another hug, then turned to Daniel and embraced him.

He leaned down close to her ear. "We're here for you, little chick. We're not going anywhere." Liz almost lost her composure at the use of his childhood endearment. Then, strength and resolve flowed through her. They'd always be there for her, but she now had an amazing, complete family.

She stepped back, gazed at the new family members around her, and let out a sigh. "This is rather overwhelming." She gave a quavery laugh. "I didn't think I'd ever know my father's family, and now you're all here."

Michael's mother put her arm around Liz's shoulder. "It is a bit overwhelming, for all of us. But just know that we all love you and are happy to know you."

Liz looked at Michael. It was hard to read his expression,

but he looked a bit worried. She wanted to feel his arms around her, experience his wonderful kisses. Would his parents approve of their relationship, or did they just want her to be part of the extended family?

Then Michael's expression softened, and she saw the desire that lurked in his eyes. He moved forward and took her hand. "Here, we're blocking the way. These other people can't get in." He led the way onto the porch, where Grandma Grace, Aunt Martha, and Clara waited.

"Fred Mason, is that you?" Grandma Grace greeted the white-haired man who'd followed them. "I haven't seen you in years, but I'd recognize you anywhere."

He nodded. "Yes, that's me, and you must be Grace Tilman—used to be Hughes."

Grandma turned to the others. "Fred and I went all through grammar school and high school together in Boston. His first wife and I were best of friends."

He nodded. "That's right."

"I knew you lived out here somewhere, so I contacted your sister, Evangeline. She told me your wife, Florence, had died. She gave me your address in Newton, Kansas."

She included the others. "I've invited Fred to have supper with us and meet with us afterward. It's not often you can reconnect with old friends." She smiled slightly at the surprised expressions around her.

David McKey extended his hand. "Glad to meet you, Fred. It appears we have a lot of people to get acquainted with."

Liz straightened and assumed her Harvey Girl manner. "Let's go on into the lobby. You will need to get registered for your rooms. Michael and Clara, you'll be up on the third floor with the staff, the same as last time. I think Anna even has you in the same rooms." She led the way inside, with Michael right behind her. They strolled through the lobby to the registration desk.

Anna met them with a smile. "So, Liz, this is the rest of your family."

Liz nodded. "Yes, they've finally arrived and we've been getting acquainted." She turned to her family, then grinned at Elise. "This is Anna McNance. She is our head waitress. Her mother and my mama, Elise, were roommates when they were both Harvey Girls."

Elise stepped forward and held out her hand. "Anna, I'm glad to meet you! I'm anxious to see Tessa. Will your family be in town this weekend?"

Anna grasped her hand. "I'm happy to meet you, too. They plan to come in for dinner tomorrow. Mama is excited to see you."

"I'll look forward to that." Elise chuckled as she stepped aside. "But, here I better get out of the way so we can get checked in."

Anna turned to the others. "I have your rooms ready." She marked in the ledger. "That will be a dollar-fifty a night."

Mr. McKey pulled out his wallet. "I'll cover two rooms for McKey and Gilbertson."

Daniel stepped up. "No, no. You don't have to do that."

"Please let me. I want to get it."

Anna took the money and handed the keys across the desk. "Your rooms are ready so you may go on up if you'd like. They are all in the east hall. Your luggage will be delivered from the depot within the next ten minutes."

A commotion at the door disrupted Anna's welcome. A

young man raced in, his eyes wide with anguish. He rushed to the desk where they stood. "We just got a message by telegraph. The President has died. Vice President Theodore Roosevelt's been sworn in as President."

Michael's father touched the messenger's arm. "What're you saying, man? The word was that he would recover."

"I know, but here's the telegram." He laid the paper on the registration desk.

David McKey snatched it up and read it. "Blast it! McKinley wasn't perfect, but he was the best we had. I hope Roosevelt can quit galavanting around the country and settle down. We need a steady hand in the government right now."

His wife took his arm. "Come on, David, let's go find our room. You don't need to worry about that right now."

"And when do you think I should worry about it?" He followed her to the staircase.

Liz stared at the telegram. The President was dead! The carpet seemed to be swept from her feet. What would happen next? Michael put his hand on her back. "It'll be okay. I heard Theodore Roosevelt speak at Harvard several times. I think he'll be a good president." Liz leaned toward him. His calm presence soothed her racing heart.

Grandma Grace hesitated then moved up to the registration desk. "Here, I'll pay for the other room."

"No, I'll pay for that." Fred insisted, stepping up beside her.

"But I invited you." She turned toward him.

"I know, but you're not gonna pay for my room." He whipped out his wallet. "It's worth it just to see you again and meet your family."

Grandma turned toward the Gilbertsons. "Why don't you all go on up and get settled in your rooms? Martha and I will stay down here with the young people." She turned toward Liz. "Then we can all eat about six thirty, right?"

At Liz's nod, the others started upstairs and Grandma herded Michael, Liz, and Clara toward the chairs in the middle of the room. "So tell me, how is life in Topeka? You were both so busy, we didn't get to talk much while we were there."

Clara leaned forward. "I know it was hard for you to understand why I came to work as a Harvey Girl, and I didn't know what I would get into, but it's the best decision I ever made. I work with a great group of people, both the Harvey Girls and the other staff. Fred Harvey is strict, and there are a lot of rules." She scrunched her nose. "But, it wasn't hard to learn the routine. Then when the previous head waitress and another girl decided to move on to other houses, they asked me to stay on in Topeka to help fill the vacancy. I'm glad. I like it there."

Her mother chuckled. "I'm happy you like it. You sure didn't like to follow the rules at home."

Clara smiled. "That was different."

"And you, Michael? How's your job? Are you glad you moved." Grandma Grace addressed him.

Michael took Liz's hand. "If I hadn't moved to Topeka, I'd never have met Liz. I work for her father at the Atchison, Topeka and Santa Fe office, and I get to do what I enjoy, ciphering. The only thing that would make it better is if Liz was still there."

Grandma smiled at Liz and nodded. "You make a handsome couple."

Michael frowned. "I'm not sure Dad will give his blessing to us since we found out we're cousins." He looked at the stairs as his parents and the others descended to the lobby. Mr. McKey and Mr. Gilbertson were conversing like old friends.

After a tasty supper in the dining room, they all climbed the stairs to the third floor parlor and found seats on the comfortable sofas and chairs.

Grace stood in front of the group and took charge. "We are gathered here to welcome Liz into our family." Her smile warmed Liz's heart. "I am so thankful that Clara was observant and realized that Liz was George's daughter. I understand that Liz discovered it, too, from a list of birthdays in her mother's Bible. God is good to us.

"As you know, when George was twenty-two, he left home to pursue a law career. He had graduated from Harvard's law school and was eager to be on his own, so he moved west to set up his practice. Grandfather William refused to give his blessing. He wanted George to stay in Boston and work with the family bank to set up a prominent law practice. An awful argument ensued. William called George—his own son—horrible names and told him to get out. He told him never to come back and vowed he would never say George's name.

"To my shame, I didn't interfere. I was afraid of arousing William's anger even further. For awhile, my mother, Mabel, kept in contact with George. We knew he'd married and had a daughter, but then we lost contact. I was misled to believe George hadn't tried to make contact with his father or me, but after William's death, I discovered that George had written many letters, which William hid in a locked box. I was devastated to know George had tried to make amends, and he never heard back from us! He and his wife, Mary, Liz's parents were both killed in a carriage accident—not knowing how much I loved them. Elizabeth was cared for and loved by these wonderful people, Daniel and Elise Gilbertson. Daniel is Mary's brother."

Grace paused and gazed around the room. Her eyes rested on Fred Mason. "Now, I need to tell you a part of the story that only a few people know. When our daughter, Martha, was a year old, a young man came to our door with a tiny baby boy in his arms. His wife had just died in childbirth. He wanted to move west but knew he couldn't care for the baby. He asked us if we would take his baby as our own and care for him. William wanted a son, so we agreed." She focused on Michael's father, David McKey. "Your father, Philip McKey, helped us draw up the necessary papers for adoption. He agreed to secrecy as William was adamant that no one knew he wasn't our biological son."

Her eyes softened. "That young man with the baby was Fred Mason. And that baby boy was George."

A collective gasp sounded around the room, and all eyes turned to Fred, as everyone attempted to absorb Grace's revelation. Tears wet his cheeks.

"Fred moved west, remarried and had another family. He is now a widower again." Grace glanced at him. "As far as I know he never heard an update on his son again, until today." She handed him the pictures that Liz had found in her parents' trunk. He gazed at them, then held them to his heart as his shoulders shook with sobs. When they subsided, Grandma continued. "Liz, honey, I know you're already overwhelmed, but I wanted you to know the whole story. You now know about your grandpa and your grandma on your father's side of the family."

Liz rose, hurried to Fred's side and put her arms around him. They laughed as he gave her an awkward hug and wiped his eyes again.

Liz peered around the room at all the people who were her family. Family she thought she'd never meet. Gratitude to God filled her heart. She'd asked Him to help her find her family, and He'd given her more than she'd ever imagined.

Her eyes found Michael's. He beamed with love. Suddenly, it dawned on her. He wasn't her cousin!

Amazement rushed through Michael as Mrs. Tilman related the story. Liz's father had been adopted! Liz wasn't his cousin!

Michael watched her as she hugged her new-found grandpa, then caught her eye when she turned toward him. Love for her nearly overcame him.

He focused on his parents seated across from him. His father had a slight smile on his face. Michael held his breath and studied his father's expression. What was he thinking? Would he give his approval?

David McKey took his wife's hand, cleared his throat, and stood with her beside him. "There's something I need to say. Michael shared with us his desire to court Miss Gilbertson. We were reluctant to grant our approval since we hadn't met her, but now we are happy to give our blessing to this young couple."

Michael let his breath out in a rush. He wanted to shout with happiness as he jumped up and walked to Liz. He knelt and took her hand. "Elizabeth Tilman Gilbertson, will you marry me?"

"Yes, oh, yes!"

He gathered her into his arms, and was lost in her sweet kisses as their family cheered and clapped around them. They had received more love than they could have imagined, and Liz had found a home for her heart.

Epilogue

June 7, 1907
Hutchinson, Kansas

Liz McKey watched as Michael grasped four-year-old Teddy's hand and stepped down from the train onto the platform at the Santa Fe Depot in Hutchinson, Kansas. He turned to assist her and two-year-old Alida. They had returned to Hutchinson to celebrate their fifth wedding anniversary with their friends and family.

John and Clara McDonald followed them. John carried two-year-old Sarah. Next, Billy and Anna Lisa Walker and their three-year-old daughter, Evangeline, exited the train.

They stepped to one side and waited as Daniel and Elise Gilbertson disembarked. Then came nineteen-year-old Adam. Liz was so proud of him. He'd finished his first year at Kansas State Agricultural College, studying to be an accountant like Michael. Next was seventeen-year-old Julien, who had just finished high school. No one was surprised when he announced he wanted to teach history. Rachel, quite a young lady at twelve, loved to babysit all the little ones.

Michael walked back to the passenger car step and reached up to give Grandma Grace and Grandpa Fred Mason a hand as they stepped down. Grandpa Fred had sold his farm, moved back to Boston, and he and Grace had gotten married, to the family's delight. Liz felt honored that they had traveled out to Kansas to help them celebrate.

Liz gazed at the Bisonte, the magnificent new Santa Fe Harvey House. Built in the English Tudor style, it occupied nearly a full city block. Three-story, brick with red tiled peaked roofs, dormers and porches all around, it almost took her breath away. It was a masterpiece on the prairie. The older Santa Fe Hotel in Hutchinson, where she had worked as a Harvey Girl, had seemed impressive, but it didn't compare to the Bisonte.

"Come on, let's go inside." Elise took Teddy's hand. "Tessa said she and her family would meet us in the lobby. I'm so excited to see her. It's been almost six years since we were here with the Boston family."

They walked into the spacious, high-ceilinged lobby. Liz stopped short. It was impressive! A massive fireplace dominated one side of the room, and grand pillars delineated the seating areas. Colorful rugs and decorator tile covered the floor. To one side, a sweeping staircase led to the upper floors.

Cliff and Tessa NcNance and their family had chosen seats near some large windows. Tessa stood as they approached and rushed forward to hug Elise, then Liz. "It's so good to see you. I've looked forward to this ever since I received your letter."

She moved back. "And this is your family. I don't think I've met your three youngest. They must be about the same age as ours. Walter is nineteen. Sophia is seventeen, Caroline is fifteen, and Elise is thirteen. Can you believe they're all teenagers? Our others are all married and away from home. But here are two of our granddaughters. Rebekah is ten, Anthony's youngest, and Rose is Esther and Joseph's baby. She's seven." She put her arms around her two granddaughters then turned toward Liz. "Anna married a Santa Fe engineer, Howard Jackson, and moved to New Mexico. We miss her."

Elise nodded. "I know, they grow up so fast. Our children are about same age. I love meeting your granddaughters." Elise took little Alida from Liz's arms. "This is our granddaughter, Alida. She and Teddy belong to Liz and Michael, and we also claim John and Clara's Sarah."

Daniel Gilbertson walked over to where the young men stood behind the women. "We better go get checked in. Then can we eat? I'm hungry."

When the men returned, Liz grasped Michael's arm with one hand and Teddy's hand with the other and walked toward the dining room. They waited for the head waitress to seat them.

Liz could barely believe her eyes as they walked across the expansive room. The Harvey girls were standing beside the tables. "It's so large. Look, Clara, it's newer, but the routine is still the same." She leaned close to Michael. "Thank you for bringing us back here for our anniversary. I couldn't have asked for anything better.

ABOUT THE AUTHOR

JOYCE VALDOIS SMITH is wife to Bob, mother to four married children and grandmother to twelve beautiful grandchildren. She is a retired public health and school nurse. Writing has been her long time passion. Joyce is an author of Christian historical and contemporary fiction as well as children's books. She lives with her husband and Cavalier King Charles Spaniel, Lady Catherine (Katie), in southwest Missouri.

Visit her online at: www.joycevaldoissmith.com

Made in the USA
Lexington, KY
12 November 2019